Four-time RITA® Award nominee **Joanne Rock** has penned over seventy stories for Mills & Boon. An optimist by nature and a perpetual seeker of silver linings, Joanne finds romance fits her life outlook perfectly—love is worth fighting for. A former Golden Heart® Award recipient, she has won numerous awards for her stories. Learn more about Joanne's imaginative Muse by visiting her website, www.joannerock.com, or following @joannerock6 on Twitter.

Andrea Laurence is an award-winning author of contemporary romances filled with seduction and sass. She has been a lover of reading and writing stories since she was young. A dedicated West Coast girl transplanted into the Deep South, she is thrilled to share her special blend of sensuality and dry, sarcastic humor with readers.

FOR THE SAKE OF HIS HEIR

JOANNE ROCK

RAGS TO RICHES BABY

ANDREA LAURENCE

MILLS & BOON

First Published in Great Britain 2018
by Mills & Boon, an imprint of HarperCollinsPublishers,
1 London Bridge Street, London, SE1 9GF

For the Sake of His Heir © 2018 Joanne Rock
Rags to Riches Baby © 2018 Andrea Laurence

ISBN: 978-0-263-93589-9

51-0218

MIX
Paper from
responsible sources
FSC C007454

This book is produced from independently certified FSC™ paper to ensure responsible forest management.

For more information visit: www.harpercollins.co.uk/green

Printed and bound in Spain
by CPI, Barcelona

FOR THE SAKE
OF HIS HEIR

JOANNE ROCK

For my Writerspace family, Cissy Hartley, Celeste Faurie, Susan Simpson and Degan Outridge. Working with you all has been a bright spot in my career. You're awesome all the time, but especially on the days when I'm tearing my hair out and feeling overwhelmed. Thank you for the help, the support and making me feel like I always have a team behind me.

One

Brianne Hanson's crush on her boss had died a swift and brutal death when he'd walked down the aisle with another woman. And she hadn't even dreamed of resurrecting it after his extremely unhappy divorce. She would never want to be that rebound fling a man lived to regret.

But every now and then, the old spark came back to burn her. Like today.

She'd just taken a break from her work in the gardens of Gabe's resort, the Birdsong Hotel, in Martinique. As a landscape designer, Brianne had worked on dozens of island properties before Gabe convinced her to take on the Birdsong as a full-time gig a year ago. It was a job she loved since she had carte blanche to design whatever she wanted on Gabe's considerable budget. He was committed to the project and shared her basic aesthetic vision, so they got along just fine. All business, boundaries in place.

Today, however, was different. She'd stopped by his workshop in a converted shed to ask him about his plans for upgrading the entrance to one of the bungalows. The resort grounds were a never-ending labor of love for Gabe, a talented woodworker who spent his free time handcrafting ceiling panels and restoring custom cabinets.

And damn if she wasn't caught by the pull of that old crush as she stood on the threshold of the workshop. The dust extractor hummed in the background, cleaning the air of particles kicked up by the table saw he'd just been using. Gabe was currently laboring over a curved piece of wood clamped down to another table, running a hand planer over the surface. This segment of wood— a molding destined for a curved archway in the lobby, she knew—was at least five feet long. Gabe shaved the length of it with the shallow blade, drawing the scraper toward him again and again while wood bits went flying.

Intent on his work, Brianne's six-foot-plus boss stared down at the mahogany piece through his safety goggles, giving her time to enjoy the view of male muscle in motion. He was handsome enough any day of the week, as his dark hair and ocean-blue eyes were traits he shared with his equally attractive older brothers. The McNeill men had caused plenty of female heads to turn throughout Martinique and beyond, since their wealth and business interests extended to New York and Silicon Valley. But Gabe was unique among his brothers for his down-to-earth, easygoing ways, and his affinity for manual labor.

With the door to his workshop open, a sea breeze swirled through the sawdust-scented air. Gabe's white T-shirt clung to his upper back, highlighting bands of muscle that ran along his shoulder blades. His forearms were lightly coated with a sheen of sweat and wood dust, which shouldn't have been sexy, or so she told herself. But the strength there was testament to the physical labor he did every day. His jeans rode low on narrow hips, thanks in part to the weight of a tool belt.

And just like that, her temperature went from garden-variety warm to scorching. So much for kicking the crush.

"Hey, Brianne." He turned a sudden, easy smile her way as he put aside the blade, leaving the plank tilted in the brace he'd made to support it. "What can I do for you?"

He shoved the safety glasses up into his dark hair, revealing those azure-blue eyes. Then he leaned over to the abandoned table saw and switched off the dust extractor. As he strode closer, she sternly reminded herself ogling time was over. She needed to keep her paychecks coming now that the last of her dysfunctional family had deserted her grandmother back in Brooklyn. Brianne owed everything—her work ethic, her life in Martinique, her very sanity—to the woman who'd given her a chance at a better life away from the painful dramas at home. As her grandmother became more frail, Brianne hoped to relocate Nana to the Caribbean to care for her.

Besides, complicating matters more? Gabe McNeill had become her closest friend.

"Hey." Forcing a smile to mask any leftover traces of feminine yearning, Brianne tried to remember why she'd come to the workshop in the first place. "Sorry to interrupt. I thought you might be ready to break for lunch and I wanted to see if you had a minute to walk me through your plans for bungalow two."

He unfastened his tool belt and hung it on a hook near the workbench.

"You mean the Butterfly Bungalow?" he teased, winking at her and nudging her shoulder with his as he walked past.

She'd been resistant to using the names Gabe's new promotions company had assigned to all the suites and villas on the property since they made the hotel sound more like a touristy amusement park.

"Right. Butterfly Boudoir. Whatever." She had to hurry to catch up with him as he headed there now, his long-legged stride carrying him far even though he wasn't moving fast.

Gabe never moved fast.

It was one of the qualities that made him an excellent woodworker. He had a deliberate way of doing things, slow and thoughtful, because he gave each task his undivided attention. Tourists who stayed at the resort chalked it up to Gabe being on "island time." But Brianne knew him better than that. He was actually very dialed in. Intense. He just put a charming face on it.

"Let's stop at the main house." Gabe shifted direction on the planked walkways that connected disparate parts of the property and provided the framework for her garden designs. "I've got a drawing you can take with you to see what I have in mind for the bungalow."

He passed two empty cabins in need of upgrades as he approached the back door of the Birdsong Hotel's central building, which housed ten units with terraces overlooking the Atlantic. The dark-tiled mansard roof with dormers was a nod to the historic French architecture of the island. The rest of the building was white clapboard with heavy gray shutters and louvers over the windows—the shutters were decorative unless a hurricane came, and then they could be employed for safety measures. The louvers, another historic feature of many of the houses in downtown Fort-de-France, the island's capital, could be used for extra shade.

"I don't want to plant anything in the front garden that will be in the way of the redesign." Brianne knew better than to think that an upgrade for Gabe only meant a couple of new windows or a better door. She loved seeing the way the buildings took shape with him guiding the redesign, the thoughtful details he included that made each building unique. Special.

She liked to think they made a great team. Her gardens were like the decorative frames for his work, drawing attention to the best features.

"This project is going to be more streamlined." He brushed away some of the dust on his shirt, then pulled open the screen door on a private entrance in back that led to his office and downstairs suite. "I was planning on talking to you today about some changes in my plans. I'm going to hand off some of the remodel to a contractor."

He held the screen door open for her, waiting for her to step inside. She could see his eleven-month-old son, Jason, seated in a high chair. The boy's caregiver, Ms. Camille, bustled around the small kitchen reserved for Gabe's use. The expansive one-bedroom unit was larger than most. Gabe kept a villa of his own at the farthest edge of the resort and only needed this space for a centrally located office and day care, so it provided plenty of space.

"A contractor?" She must have misunderstood. "You've been personally handling every detail of this remodel for two years because it's your hotel and you're the best on the island. I don't understand."

"Come in." He gently propelled her forward, one hand on the middle of her back while he waved a greeting to the caregiver with the other. "Ms. Camille, I've got Jason if you want some lunch."

The older woman nodded. "Be *en garde*, Monsieur Gabriel," she said, her native French thick in her accent as she passed Gabe a stack of mail. "Our sweet Jason is in a mischievous mood."

Brianne's gaze went to the dark-haired boy strapped in his high chair, his bare toes curling and butt bouncing at the sight of his father. Two little teeth gleamed in an otherwise gummy grin. Dressed in striped blue shorts and a bright blue T-shirt, the boy banged a fat spoon against his tray.

"I'm on it," Gabe assured her, bending to kiss the baby's forehead, a gesture that clutched at Brianne's heart, making her wonder how Jason's mother could ever abandon him—the child or the father, for that matter.

Theresa Bauder had lived among them for all of six months. She was a beautiful, gifted songstress Gabe met when she'd given up on her dreams to Martinique after a frustrating three years of trying to make it in the music business. Brianne had been envious of everything about the woman, from her eye-popping beauty and natural elegance, to her clear, sweet singing voice on nights when she performed with her acoustic guitar out on the beach.

The fact that Theresa had also landed—in Brianne's opinion—the most eligible of the McNeill men was also enviable. But then, when the woman was expecting Jason, she'd gotten a call from her former manager back in Nashville. A top country artist wanted to perform one of Theresa's songs. Even more exciting, the artist was in talks to do a movie about her life, and wanted Theresa to come out to Los Angeles to play a younger version of her in the film. Theresa left. Her home, her husband, her marriage. To hear the local gossips, Gabe had only gone to LA with her to wait for his son to be born since Theresa had also decided she didn't want to be a mother with a career heating up. Gabe had said little about it, but he'd returned to Martinique with his son when Jason was just four weeks old.

Brianne took a turn kissing the boy's head, too, as she'd become good buddies with the little one over the last ten months. "How are you today, cutie?" she asked him, her heart melting when Jason gave her a drooly grin. She spotted one of his toys on the counter—a fat green dinosaur—and perched it on the edge of his lunch tray, hopping it closer to him.

"There's something for you, Brianne." Gabe plucked a small envelope off the stack of letters Camille had handed him before setting the rest of the resort's mail in a wooden tray near the door. "Looks like it's from home."

"Thanks." She saw the return address in Nana's familiar handwriting and hoped everything was okay with her grandmother. Distracted, she forgot about her dinosaur game with Jason until the boy poked at the toy.

Dutifully, she made the figure hop around his lunch tray while she considered the letter from her grandmother.

"And sorry to spring it on you like this that I'm leaving." Gabe reached into the kitchen's stainless-steel refrigerator and withdrew two bottles of water, passing one to her. "That's why I'm handing off some of the projects to a local contractor. I need to finish up a few more of the bungalows to accommodate the increase in visitors, but I'm taking Jason to New York and I'm not sure when we'll return."

"You're leaving?" She squeezed the water bottle without opening it, the cold condensation chilling her palms while a wave of disappointment washed over her.

Old crush on Gabe aside, she liked him. Considered him her best friend. He'd given her an amazing opportunity when he'd hired her to design the gardens at the Birdsong, a long-term project that gave her stability and allowed her to be creative. It was a far better job than the temporary gigs she'd been hired for prior to this. She'd met him while helping another landscaper revamp the historic gardens at McNeill Meadows plantation home. Gabe had been building an arbor for his family's expansive compound in Le François. He'd been planning his wedding back then, so she'd ignored the attraction and concentrated on impressing him professionally.

"Yes. I'm going to New York to spend some time with my grandfather." Gabe rifled through a kitchen drawer and pulled out a small sheet of paper, then he ambled over to the round table in the breakfast nook with a view of the ocean. "Have a seat, Brianne."

He pulled out a curved wicker chair for her near the open French doors that led to a side patio shaded by a tall acacia tree. The temperature in Martinique didn't vary much, but on a February day like this, it was less humid and there was a breeze off the water. Brianne never tired of the beautiful weather here after the cold, desperate winters of her childhood in Brooklyn.

"Your grandfather. You mean Malcolm McNeill?" She'd followed news about his wealthy family online, from the disappearance of his sister-in-law, heiress Caroline Degraff, to the revelation that he had a connection to McNeill Resorts' wealthy owner, Malcolm McNeill. Gabe's mother had been Liam McNeill's mistress. Liam had fathered three children by her but then abandoned them when Gabe was just eleven years old. Liam had been married to someone else at that time, and had three legitimate sons based in Manhattan.

"That's right." Gabe drew Jason's high chair closer to the table, earning more gummy grins from his son and another round of spoon banging. "I have a good life here and I'm happiest working on the Birdsong, but I keep thinking it's not fair to limit Jason's future to this place when he's an heir to the McNeill legacy."

The thought of her world without Gabe in it unsettled her. She liked working with him. For him. She didn't want to think about how empty the Birdsong would be without him. And Jason. Her gaze went to the boy, as she thought about all the impromptu lunches they'd had together.

"Are you moving there permanently?" She tried not to let the unexpected swell of emotions show in her voice.

Gabe gave his son a sectioned tray with some sliced-up toast pieces and carrots. Withdrawing the toy dinosaur so as not to distract the baby from his lunch, Brianne clutched it tighter.

"No." He swung into the chair next to her, keeping Jason between them. "Just until I can learn more about the McNeill holdings and convince my grandfather that the terms of his will are prehistoric."

"What do you mean?"

"He's stipulated that all his heirs need to be married for at least a year in order to inherit their share of the fortune." He set down the sheet of paper he'd retrieved from the kitchen drawer; she could see it was a sketch of the bungalow that she'd inquired about earlier, a project that couldn't be further from her mind now. "I don't know if the guy is going senile or what, but my personal experience makes me an excellent case study for why marriage is a bad idea."

His expression darkened, the way it always did when

he referred to his ex-wife. It upset Brianne to think Theresa had skewed Gabe's view of love forever.

"You wouldn't be eligible to inherit because you
weren't married long enough." She couldn't envision
Gabe living in Manhattan or moving in that high-pow-
ered business world, but that was probably naive of her.
He was a major owner of Transparent, the new social-
media software-integration giant run by his brother
Damon that seemed to be in the news daily.

"Right." Gabe took a long swig from his water bottle. "I'll never marry again, but does that mean Jason
shouldn't inherit? It's not fair to an innocent kid. So
I'm going to visit the family in New York and convince
Gramps to tweak the will to ensure his great grandson
has a fair share of the legacy." He ruffled his son's dark
wispy baby curls. "Who could resist this little guy?"

Jason kicked the tray with his bare toes, sending carrots jumping on his plate. The movement preoccupied
him, and the baby became fixated with studying the
bright orange bits.

"You have a point." Smiling, Brianne reached over to
give the baby's feet a fond squeeze, her heart warming
at the sight of the two McNeills, one so adorable and the
other so...off-limits.

Damn it.

No matter how appealing Gabe might be, he wasn't
in any position to start a relationship in the wake of his
unhappy marriage. Brianne knew it was too soon to
get involved with a man nursing a broken heart. And
now? She might never have the chance to be more than
a friend.

"So Jason and I are going to spend some time in Manhattan. A few months at least." He tipped back in his chair
and reached behind him to drag the baby's sippy cup off

the granite kitchen counter. "I've been making drawings of the next few units for you so you can see the changes I'm going to ask the contractor to implement." As he passed her the sketch, his hand stalled on the envelope from Nana. "Should you read this?" he asked, handing it to her a second time. "Your grandmother doesn't write you very often."

As her gaze returned to the shaky scrawl on the outside of the note, a pang of worry pierced through the knot of unhappy emotions she felt over Gabe's departure. How disloyal of her it was to put her life in Martinique—her complicated feelings for Gabe—in front of her own family.

"You're right." Brianne slid a finger under the envelope flap and raked it open. "I know she doesn't write as much lately because her arthritis has gotten worse."

"All the more reason it might be important if she took the time and effort to write to you now," Gabe added, standing up to grab a damp dishrag from the sink.

He used the cloth to clean up some stray carrots on the tray while Brianne read the brief letter. The scrawl was shaky. Nana took a couple of paragraphs to talk about the failed effort to get a rooftop communal garden in her building, something she'd been excited about. Brianne scanned the rest quickly, thinking she'd take her time to read more closely later. The last paragraph jumped out at her.

> I had a little run-in with a mugger yesterday—your standard local junkie, nothing personal. I'm fine. Just a bit sore. It's not a problem really, but makes getting to the market harder. If the offer is still open to have some groceries delivered, your Nana might just take you up on it. I've got plenty

to get me through this week, though, so don't you worry.

Love you, child.

"Oh, my God." Brianne's heart was in total free fall.

Her grandmother, the most important person in her whole world, was hurt and alone this week while Brianne had been planting beautiful flowers, living in a Caribbean paradise and mooning over an impossible man. The knowledge sliced right through her.

"What's wrong?" Gabe was by her side instantly, a hand on her shoulder.

"I need to go home." Shakily, she tried to stand, her knees feeling unsteady. "Now."

"Whoa. Wait." Gabe half caught Brianne in his arms, something that at any other time would have brought with it a forbidden pleasure he'd enjoy even though he didn't deserve to.

Today, however, she was clearly distressed. Pale and shaking. What the hell was in that letter?

"I need to go home, Gabe. She's hurt." The broken sound of Brianne's voice stunned him.

He'd seen this woman heft twenty-five-pound bags of dirt under one slender arm and collar snakes with lightning-fast reflexes so she could "relocate" them. He would have never imagined her in tears, but her dark brown eyes were unnaturally bright with them.

"Who's hurt? Your grandmother?" Reluctantly, he pulled his hand from her back, where his fingers briefly tangled in her thick, dark ponytail. He made sure she was steady before he let go of her. Her black T-shirt with an American rock-band logo was wrinkled, the fabric hitching up on one side away from the lightweight cargo pants that were her everyday work uniform.

Her breath came in fast pants as one tear rolled down her cheek. Her normally olive skin had gone as white as the envelope she still clutched. Just a moment ago, she'd been teasing smiles from his son, her beauty naturally captivating even when she wasn't making silly faces to entertain the boy.

"Read it." She thrust the note at Gabe and his eyes scanned the short message from Rose Hanson while Brianne fumbled in the leg pocket of her cargo pants and pulled out her cell phone. "I've been saving money to move her down here with me. I was going to talk to her this weekend when we're supposed to have a video call. I should have been connecting with her every day, but I'm calling her now."

Brianne held the phone to her ear. Gabe could hear someone speaking on the other end, but the call must have gone straight to voice mail message because Brianne punched a button and tried again.

"It's okay." He moved around the high chair so he could be closer to her, and yes, put his arm around her again. He gave her a gentle, one-armed hug, hoping to comfort her somehow as he steeled himself for the shock of pleasure that touching her created. "We'll send someone to check on her. A home health nurse."

Brianne left a message for her grandmother, asking her to call her back right away. Shoving her phone back in her pants pocket, she slumped over the table.

He regretted that he didn't know more about Brianne's family background. All he knew was that her upbringing had been rough enough to make her grandmother cash in the last of her savings to send her off to Martinique with a friend who was retiring to the island. Brianne had been just twelve years old at the time. Her guardian had been little more than a stranger, but she helped Brianne finish her schooling and find an apprenticeship with a local botanist.

Gabe had been caught up in his own drama for so damn long he'd never really gotten to know Brianne as well as he would have liked to. Of course, there was always a hint—just a hint—of a spark with her. He'd ignored it easily enough when he'd been with Theresa, telling himself that the feelings for Brianne were of the creative-professional variety, that he admired her design skills and commitment to her projects.

But there was more to it than that, and it roared to life when he tucked her head under his chin. The scent of her hair was as vibrantly floral as the gardens she tended every day. He couldn't ignore the feel of her against him, the lush feminine curves at odds with her utilitarian work clothes.

"There's no one." She shook her head, her soft, dark hair brushing his jaw. "My stepmother was living with Nana Rose, but then Wendy got a new boyfriend and moved out last month. I've been so worried—"

"I'll find a home health-care service and make a call right now." He pulled his phone from the back pocket of his jeans, hoping Jason's caregiver returned from lunch soon so Gabe could give Brianne his undivided attention.

The protective instinct was too strong to ignore. Brianne had been a positive force in his life during his worst days. And her daily, sunny presence in his son's world soothed a small portion of Gabe's guilt and resentment over not being able to provide a mother for his own child.

"No." Brianne straightened suddenly, tensing as she withdrew from his touch. "It's my job, not yours, Gabe. But thank you." She took out her phone again and keyed in a code with trembling fingers. "That's a good idea to have someone check on her until I can get there."

"Gah!" his son shouted behind him and Gabe turned to see the boy tossing a carrot in the air.

Even though she was upset and distracted, Brianne managed a shaky smile for Jason. She was so different from the baby's mother, who seemed content to leave the parenting to Gabe no matter how often he'd offered to fly to the States so she could see their son. She had no plans to see her baby until Valentine's Day, when she'd arranged a photo shoot in New York with a country-music magazine. As if a child was a prop to show off when needed.

Nevertheless, Gabe would be there to facilitate in the small window of time available for his son to see his mother.

"Maybe you won't have to travel all the way to New York once you have a report on how she's doing from an outside source." Gabe hated to see Brianne return to a life that made her unhappy. No matter how much she loved her grandmother, he knew Brianne had bad memories of the home she'd left behind. "You can have a health-care aide for her as often as you want until you're ready to move her down here."

He wanted to fix this. To keep her happy and comfortable in a life she seemed to thrive in. Something about the gardens and Brianne was forever connected in his mind. She had a healthy vibrancy that was reflected in her work and he knew somehow the hotel wouldn't be the same—nothing would be the same here—if she left.

"I'm taking the next available flight." Her fingers stilled on the phone as she scrolled through screens, her dark eyes meeting his. "That is, I hope you understand I'll need some emergency time away from work."

"Of course, that's a given." He didn't want her to worry about her job. Although selfishly, he hoped her family wouldn't somehow convince her to relocate to New York. He wanted her to return to Martinique eventually since this was his permanent home. He hadn't realized how much he looked forward to working with her every day until he considered the proposition of not seeing her cutting fresh blooms for the lobby desk each morning. "Your position here is secure."

"Thank you." She nodded, long bangs catching on the thick fringe of her eyelashes. "I need to pack in case I can catch something on stand-by tonight." Backing toward the door, she shoved the letter in her pocket. Her cargo pants momentarily pulled tight across her hips.

What was the matter with him that he noticed all the wrong things on a day she needed his friendship? She'd been a rock in his world. He wouldn't allow her to deal with this family emergency on her own when she was clearly upset.

"Don't fly stand-by." He wanted to help her. She never asked for anything and worked hard every day to make the hotel a more beautiful place. She'd been a source of laughter and escape during the hellish weeks after his separation from Theresa.

And he couldn't let her go this way.

"Gabe, I have to." The passion—the vehemence—in her voice surprised him; he'd never heard her use that tone. "She's *hurt*. Someone hurt her. She's eighty years old and she gave me everything I have."

Just like that, he knew he wasn't going to let her go alone. Not when it was this important to her and she was so upset.

"And you shouldn't figure all of this out on your own when you're so distracted and worried." He didn't want her driving when she was still shaking. Or hiring a car from the airport that would take her the long way to Brooklyn because she was too rattled to notice. "I was planning to go to New York anyhow." It made far more sense for them to go together. "I'll take you there myself on my family's jet. Tonight."

"You can't do that." She lifted her arms in the air, exasperated. A long section of dark hair escaped the ponytail to tease against her cheek and she blew it aside impatiently. "You have a son to think about. You can't disrupt Jason's schedule to fly at the last minute."

Brianne gave the boy a tender look, her expression visibly softening as she stroked the back of her knuckle along the baby's arm.

Through the window Gabe spotted Camille, Jason's caregiver, walking up the planked path. He was glad she was back so he could focus on convincing Brianne to travel with him.

"My grandfather has been trying to entice my brothers and me to spend time in Manhattan for months," he explained, pulling Jason out of his high chair and giving the boy a kiss on his head. "I can move up my departure date. My half brother Cam gave me the number of a local pilot who can have a flight plan filed with an hour's notice. If you want to go to New York tonight, I'll call him to take us. It will be faster than navigating the airport crush."

As Camille entered, he passed her the boy and asked her to pack the child's clothes for a two-week trip. He planned to stay longer than that, but would buy more things once they were settled. Camille cooed at Jason and gave Gabe a nod to indicate she'd heard him while he ushered Brianne out of the kitchen and into the afternoon sun outside.

"Gabe, I could never begin to repay you—"

"Why would you have to?" he interrupted, unwilling to let her think in those terms. "I told you, I need to be in New York anyhow so it makes sense for us to travel together. I owe you more than I've paid you, Brianne, if it comes right down to it. But you never hear me complain when you work long hours and contribute more to this place than anyone else. Now it's your turn to accept something extra from me."

She seemed to weigh this, her lips pursing as she visibly wrestled with the idea of arguing. But in the end, she put up both her hands in surrender.

"You know what? For Nana Rose, I'm just going to say thank you and go pack."

"Good." He nodded, already making a mental to-do list, starting with booking the plane and contacting the nanny who would be making the trip with them. "I'll let you know when I've got our flight time confirmed. After we land, we can share a car from the airport, so count on me to bring you straight to your grandmother's doorstep."

"Fine." Her jaw tightened. "That is, thank you."

As she retreated, he wanted to offer more. To suggest additional ways he could help out since she might be facing more medical bills and travel arrangements where her grandmother was concerned. But he didn't want to push his luck with his proud and prickly landscape designer. He had a whole plane ride to talk to her and convince her to let him give her a hand moving her beloved relative back to Martinique. He and Brianne made such a good team at work. Why couldn't they carry that into their personal lives, especially when they were both going through some tough transitions?

The idea held a whole lot of appeal. Maybe that should

have troubled him given that he'd just emerged from a disastrous marriage and divorce. Instead, he felt an undeniable pull of awareness that had been absent from his life ever since his wife was two months pregnant and had announced she was leaving him.

Two

Brianne paced outside her cabin in front of the huge strangler fig that listed to one side after years of leaning with the prevailing winds. Suitcase haphazardly packed and ready to go on her tiny wooden porch, she forced herself to take a deep breath while she waited for Gabe to pick her up. Dusk was just settling over the island, casting the resort in shades of pink and peach. Her cabin was already dark from the shadows cast by the wide branches of the tree.

Kneeling down, she scraped a few leaves off the plaque she'd placed there last fall, a final gift bequeathed to her from Nana's friend Carol, who had brought Brianne to this place fourteen years ago as a smart-mouthed preteen. Carol had run out of her retirement funds by the end, her final years in a nursing home having depleted her account. But she'd left the plaque for Brianne, a wrought-iron piece with a Chinese proverb in raised letters reading, "When the root is deep, there is no reason to fear the wind."

Brianne had understood the message—that she needed to rely on the roots Carol had helped her to set down in Martinique, and the values that Nana had tried to impart before Brianne's world imploded with family drama. It didn't matter that Brianne's mom had been a junkie who deserted the family when her dealer moved to Miami, leaving eight-year-old Brianne with a father who was allergic to work but not women. Even then, Brianne had felt like the adult in the house, forging her father's signature on papers from school, instinctively guessing her troubles would multiply if anyone found out how often she went unsupervised.

At the time, she couldn't have known how much worse off she'd be once her dad's girlfriend moved in with them, bringing kids from previous relationships and a surprise half sibling, whose combined support cost far more than the toxic couple could afford. If not for free school lunches, Brianne didn't know how she would have survived those lonely years, where no one remembered to feed her let alone buy her new shoes or check her homework. But when puberty hit, delivering feminine assets no eleven-year-old should have to contend with, she suddenly had all the wrong kinds of attention.

She shuddered at the memories, grateful to hear Gabe's SUV tires crunch the gravel on the far side of the cabin. He'd texted her two hours ago that they could leave at 7:00 p.m., and now here he was—as promised—fifteen minutes before their scheduled departure. Because apparently on a private jet they could take off almost as soon as they buckled into the seats.

Somehow, that kind of favor seemed far more generous than the extra hours she occasionally put in at the Birdsong carefully training a vine over an arbor or watering a temperamental new planting. But for Nana's sake, she sure wasn't going to argue with Gabe about a lift to New York on such short notice. With her bank account, she'd be hard-pressed to afford the rest of the trip and relocating her grandmother, let alone a plane ticket. Still, although she understood the McNeill family could easily afford this kind of travel, she was touched that he wanted to bring her. That was a dangerous feeling to have about her boss, who already appealed to her on far too many levels.

Wheeling her battered duffel bag around to the driveway behind the cabin, she got there in time to see Gabe open the liftgate on the back of the dark gray Mercedes SUV. In a nod to traveling with her employer, she'd dressed in her best dark jeans and a flowy, floral blouse in bright tangerine and yellow that slid off her shoulders and made her feel pretty. Gabe, on the other hand, looked ready to escort an A-list actress to an Oscars after-party, his jacket and slim-fitting navy pants the sort of clothes that came from a tailor and not the department-store racks. Even his shirt, open at the neck, was beautiful—it was snowy white and embroidered with extra white stitching around the placket. The dark tasseled loafers were, she supposed, his effort to keep things less formal.

"Any news about your grandmother?" he asked.

"She hasn't picked up any of my calls or returned my messages." Brianne didn't know if the phone was dead or the ringer was shut off, but each time she tried Nana's number and got no answer only made her worry more.

"Did you get someone to go over to see her?"

"No." Guilt nipped at her, and she wondered if Gabe could have managed the feat if she'd allowed him to take the task as he'd wanted. "The agency I called said it was too late in the afternoon to schedule a same-day visit.

They suggested I call the police if I was worried about her safety."

"Did you?" His blue eyes skimmed over her, making her too aware of his nearness.

Nodding, she tried not to notice how good he smelled. "I did. I wanted to find out if Nana had reported the mugging, first of all, but there's nothing on file with the police. Then, when I asked about someone checking on her, they promised they would send a car out in the morning."

"We'll be there sooner than that," he assured her. "Is this all your luggage?" He reached for the soft-sided bag and retracted the handle into the bottom before he set it in the trunk of the SUV, muscles flexing in a way that pulled the fabric of his jacket taut across his shoulders.

"That's it." She peered into the vehicle and saw Ms. Camille's daughter, Nadine, sitting beside Jason's car seat and called out a greeting before returning her attention to Gabe. "I'm not even sure what I packed. I think I just grabbed something out of each drawer and tossed it in there."

She kept picturing the nightmarish scene of a mugger stealing from her grandmother. She hated that anyone would target someone elderly and frail.

Gabe frowned as he walked with her to the passenger side of the vehicle and opened the door for her. "You should stay with me when we get to New York. My half brother Ian invited me to use his place for the next month while he and his wife are abroad. They have a spacious five-bedroom apartment in a hotel in midtown. There's concierge service, so if you've forgotten anything—"

"No, thank you." She buckled her seat belt and leaned into the soft leather chair, hoping he would drop it. She didn't want to be rude, but she couldn't accept more gifts from him. Her pride wouldn't allow it. She'd been a charity case once and knew how demoralizing it felt to need a handout. "You're already doing enough for me."

Turning to Nadine and Jason, she gave the baby's chubby knee a pat to say hello. Jason tipped his head sideways against the car seat, as if he couldn't keep it upright any longer, but smiled at her sweetly. "Gah!"

The boy was so adorable, his dark curls and blue eyes already like his father's. She wondered if it made it easier or more difficult for Gabe that Jason didn't favor his mother more. How could Theresa have signed away her rights to raise this precious child?

Gabe took his place behind the wheel and they began the drive inland, leaving the hotel and everything she'd worked hard for in her life.

"Do you know I haven't been on a plane since I arrived here fourteen years ago?" She made the observation as a peace offering, hoping he'd forget about her refusal to take up residence with him in a fancy Manhattan hotel.

It was tough enough to be around him as an employee today. She wouldn't push her luck by getting closer to him personally.

"Are you a nervous flyer?" he asked, steering around a tourist caravan pulled off to one side of the road to snap photos.

She was only nervous about sitting too close to him. His kindness and attention were quickly wearing away the boundaries she'd put up, defenses she thought were solid.

"I don't think so." She didn't recall much about the long-ago journey. She'd cried most of the way, convinced her life was over. "It was a stressful trip, but only because I was being uprooted. I should have returned home long before this."

She had plenty of reasons, none of them good enough to fully explain her complicated feelings about her family.

"I'm glad you're going with me." He glanced her way as he rolled to a stop at a quiet intersection.

The remark was a garden-variety, friendly thing to say. But ever since he'd held her earlier—even though it had been strictly for comfort—she'd been hyperaware of Gabe McNeill. Her throat went dry.

"That's kind of you to say, but I can't imagine it was easy wrapping up your business at the hotel in just a few hours." She smiled over her shoulder at Nadine, needing a distraction from the warmth in Gabe's blue eyes. "Nadine, you must have been surprised to get a call with so little notice."

"I have been asking my mother daily when Monsieur McNeill would be ready to take this trip. I am anxious to see New York City." She grinned widely, her smile so warm and open, like her mother's. "I started packing two weeks ago when I first learned this might happen."

"You see, Brianne?" Gabe downshifted as he turned into the private airfield, a little-used amenity for the island's most privileged. "The trip was meant to be, and it was just as well you lit a fire to get us underway. I might have spent another week tweaking that archway molding."

Grateful to speak about something besides the family problems waiting for her on the other end of their flight, Brianne seized on the topic with both hands.

"You do beautiful work."

"It's an indulgence. A hobby I invest too much time in." His expression darkened as he parked the SUV beside an exotic black sports car in the small lot. "Now that I'm a father, I need to spend less time on personal pursuits and more time developing my business to provide for Jason's future."

In the back seat, Nadine unbuckled the baby, prattling to him about the great adventure they were going to have.

Brianne followed him to the back of the SUV to help with the bags. She'd never seen anyone restore historic woodwork with as much precision and commitment to craft as Gabe. "What you do is a gift few people have. It's a dying art."

She pulled out her bag and started to reach for a smaller suitcase when a uniformed attendant greeted them, a cart at the ready to wheel their luggage to the plane. A warm breeze blew strands of her ponytail around her neck to stick briefly on her lip balm. She peeled her hair aside, tossing it back behind her shoulder.

"And it's dying for a reason," Gabe replied as they followed the airfield staffer to a gleaming white Cessna with the stairs lowered and ready. "Not enough people care about those kinds of details when you can purchase a prefabricated piece for a fraction of the cost."

He greeted the pilot while the ground attendant loaded their bags for them, leaving Brianne to consider his words. She would have never guessed he'd be so dismissive of the craft he'd spent years honing.

While the attendant ushered them on board the private plane, Brianne weighed what he'd said. Maybe she didn't know him nearly as well as she thought she did. As if the sleek jet at his disposal didn't already highlight that they came from different worlds, now she questioned how much value he placed on her chosen career field if he viewed his own as simply a "hobby."

Bristling, she told herself not to let it bother her. She was worried about her grandmother and on edge to begin with. She buckled into the deluxe white leather seat as the attendant who saw them on to the plane briefly reviewed some of the amenities. There was a fully stocked bar, Wi-Fi access throughout the journey, global channels available and a simplified cold menu since there would be no server on board with them.

Gabe thanked her, then settled Nadine and Jason in a private compartment in the back. He returned to take the spot beside Brianne, his arm brushing hers briefly as he fastened his seat belt. The pilot pulled up the stairs and locked the exterior door before closing himself in the cockpit for the flight. Not long after, the engine rumbled as the aircraft taxied forward.

Now that they were settled, Brianne picked up the thread of their conversation. "I still can't believe you'd put woodworking down like that. What about landscape design? Is that a dying art best left to wither?"

"Of course not—" he said.

But she wasn't finished. Some of the agitation of the day came out now, her argument picking up momentum as the plane picked up speed.

"Because you can surely purchase a random tree or bush at your local nursery and throw it in the ground. Who needs beauty and refinement when there's a buck to be made?"

As the plane left the ground and gained altitude, the view from the windows shifted from the scattered lights of buildings to a deeper darkness. The cabin lights dimmed automatically, casting them in deep shadow until Gabe switched on the reading lamp over the vacant seating across from them. Only then could she see the level look in those blue eyes as he studied her.

"You think I'm suggesting it's all about money?" His voice gave nothing away.

"That's how it sounds to me. Like your craftsmanship

is less important than learning the art of moneymaking at the elbow of a business titan like Malcolm McNeill." But some of the steam went out of her argument at his cool words, and she wondered if she'd misunderstood him.

He leaned forward in his seat and turned toward her, giving her his full attention.

"I have a son to think about. His future is more important to me than any job, passion or hobby." The intensity in his expression was unmistakable. She used to see it, to some degree, when he worked on a restoration project. But this was different.

Powerful.

"I understand that." Truly, she did. "I admire it tremendously given the careless way other people parent their children." Drawing a breath, she ventured closer to her point. "But what if you teach your son that success can be found in things that make you happy?"

Air blew on her from the vents overhead, giving her a sudden chill. Or maybe it was caused by the look on Gabe's face.

"Do I want to teach Jason that it's okay to walk away from responsibilities to pursue any self-centered shot at happiness just because it's shiny and different?" He smoothed the sleeve of his jacket, his forearm resting on the white leather chair between them. "His mother already turned her back on family for a chance at fame. I'll be damned if I make the same selfish choices, too."

Three

Talk about a conversation fail.

Two hours into the flight to New York, Gabe cursed himself for allowing emotions he normally kept in check to bubble to the surface with Brianne. But her words had reopened a wound he'd been determined to ignore. He refused to let thoughts of his ex-wife ruin his relationships—not with Brianne, and most especially not with his son.

Brianne had slipped past his defenses in other ways, too, stirring to life an attraction he'd had on lockdown since they met. And that had given rise to an outrageous idea. Instead of arguing with her, he needed to use this flight to talk to her about working together to help further one another's interests.

There was still time to reevaluate his strategy, of course. He could keep the scheme brewing in his head to himself and simply escort her to Brooklyn as they'd agreed. In light of the disconnect they had after boarding the plane, maybe that would be the best solution. Except his plan wasn't just about helping himself. It would offer her a face-saving solution to aid her grandmother. It was a way around Brianne's prickly pride to deliver assistance she would otherwise never accept.

He felt Brianne's fingers brush the sleeve of his jacket—the barest of touches to capture his attention. Turning, he found her curled sideways in her seat, facing him. Shoes off, she had her feet tucked under her in the wide leather armchair. At some point during the flight, she had taken her hair down from its ponytail, and the silky dark waves spilled over the lightweight gray wrap she'd pulled around herself like a blanket. In the lamplight, he could see the spatter of golden freckles over the bridge of her nose.

"I'm sorry." She let her fingers linger on his sleeve for just a moment, lightly rubbing back and forth across his wrist, before the touch fell away. "I have no business telling you what's right or wrong to teach your son. I'm so wound up and worried about Nana, I'm not thinking straight."

He set aside his phone, where he'd been scrolling through messages, including a text from Theresa's personal assistant scheduling an "appointment" to have Jason at the photographer's studio in Nashville for the Valentine's Day photo shoot. As much as he wanted Jason to have time with his mother, a magazine spread wasn't what he had in mind. And he worried about Jason's future if Theresa decided to pop in and out of his life. Their son needed stability.

Shoving the troubling thoughts aside, he turned briefly to check the private compartment behind them. No sounds had come from Nadine or Jason in the last hour. Confirming that Jason was all settled, he turned back to Brianne to give her his undivided attention.

"You have nothing to apologize for." He tipped his head against the seat rest and stared up at the jet's contoured ceiling. "You had no way of knowing my concerns for Jason's future." He debated how much more to say about it. But if he was going to propose his new plan to Brianne, he would need to share more with her about his personal life. "You couldn't have possibly known how much time I spent trying to convince Jason's mother to make room in her career so that she could be there for her family."

The old resentment was still fresh.

Brianne tilted her head to one side. "So you want Jason to have more opportunities because Theresa saw only one for herself, and it cost her her family?"

"I don't want my son to ever feel so locked in to one life choice that he can't compromise for the sake of love. Family. Personal relationships." Gabe had offered Theresa so many possible ways to make a family work while she pursued her dream, but she hadn't seriously considered any of them. Stardom and family didn't mix, apparently. She wanted to be "free" to travel as much as she chose without worrying about returning home to the needs of an infant.

He'd told Theresa he would always be there for her, no matter how far she traveled. But she seemed to check out on their marriage the moment something more interesting came along. He could have dealt with that. What killed him was that she'd checked out on motherhood before even giving birth, spending less than a week with Jason before pleading with Gabe to take him back to Martinique so she could concentrate.

Beside him, Brianne pulled the wrap more tightly around her. "I understand. I just hope you find time one day to do what makes *you* happiest, as well."

"For now, I'm content to focus on Jason. There's nothing more important to me than giving him stability. A sense of family."

He had a lot to make up to the boy after being unable to keep his mother around.

"Tell me more about the McNeills who live in New York." Brianne tilted forward to rest her chin on one knee. "Is your extended family large?"

"Besides my grandfather, Malcolm, I've got three half brothers—Cameron, Quinn and Ian. They all married in the last year."

"Because of the terms of Malcolm's will?" Idly, she spun one of her gold rings around her finger with her thumb. The topaz stone appeared and disappeared as she rotated it. Did he make her nervous?

She didn't normally wear jewelry while working. Taking this trip together gave Gabe a different view of her; this was a softer, more vulnerable side of the woman he'd only known through their work. Or maybe he'd never allowed himself to see this aspect of her, knowing he would be drawn to her even more. There was something compelling about Brianne. And something very, very sexy.

He forced his thoughts back to her question. "I'm not close enough with that branch of the family to know their reasons, but it seems highly coincidental they all happened to find true love within months of discovering they wouldn't inherit the family business if they weren't married for at least a calendar year." Then he considered his own brothers and their new marriages. "But both Damon and Jager are over the moon about their wives, so who knows?"

Brianne bit her lip as she considered what he said. Gabe's gaze lingered on her mouth, on the straight, white teeth pressing into her full lower lip. A bolt of hunger pierced right through him.

"And your dad?" she asked tentatively.

He hissed out a heated breath even as he wondered how she would taste if he took a sip of that lush mouth.

"My biological father is out of the picture." He knew that in no uncertain terms. "Apparently Malcolm put Liam at the helm of the company a few years ago and McNeill Resorts started to falter, which is some of what prompted all the new emphasis on the next generation and inspired the unorthodox terms of the will. Liam never placed any importance on family."

"So Jason will be introduced to his great-grandfather, three new uncles, plus their wives." Brianne ticked them off on her fingers, putting the size of the family into perspective. "Are there any cousins in the mix yet?"

Gabe noticed the rose-colored stone on her pinkie ring was facing the wrong way and couldn't resist reaching over to rotate it a quarter turn, letting his fingers brush hers for a second longer than necessary. He wanted to touch her more.

And often.

The awareness between them wasn't going away. If anything, it increased every hour they spent together.

"Cameron's wife, Maresa, had a daughter coming into their marriage. And you heard that Damon and Caroline now have a son, Lucas?" He looked at her for confirmation. Damon lived in Silicon Valley these days, but he'd made an appearance at the family compound in Martinique a few weeks ago. Caroline hadn't even known she was pregnant when she was kidnapped a year ago, so Damon had been shocked to discover they had a son when she returned from her captivity after a bout of amnesia. "Plus Jager and Delia are expecting their first child this summer."

"Jason will be surrounded by cousins." Smiling, Brianne reached up to adjust the vent near her seat. The cool air wafted a soft hint of her fragrance his way, a single fragrant note. "No wonder you'd like closer ties to the family."

She understood. Family was important to her, and now she recognized how deeply significant it was for him. The knowledge eased the last of his worries about his plan even as the traces of her scent heightened the urge to get closer.

"I want to strengthen that bond." He knew Brianne would appreciate directness. But he'd definitely never envisioned himself making this kind of appeal. "That's why I'm second-guessing myself about my approach with Malcolm." Sensing the time was drawing near to make his pitch, he retrieved the carafe from the small table in front of them. "More water?"

"Sure." She lifted her cut crystal glass and held it out to him. "What do you mean? I thought you were going to try and convince him to remove the marriage stipulation from his will?"

Gabe's hand touched hers briefly as she passed him the glass. He couldn't deny that touching her more often was a definite benefit of his plan. Brianne fascinated him, from her down-to-earth beauty to her easy way around his son. She had values he shared. And yes, she was a sensual, appealing woman.

Just thinking about her made him remember the need to top off his own glass. A cool drink would be a wise idea right about now.

"It occurs to me I'm the odd man out when all of my brothers and half brothers have already fallen in line with Malcolm's wishes." But Gabe knew even that could change, since there was a whole other branch of the family that Malcolm had only revealed to them a few weeks ago. Liam's older brother, Donovan, had disavowed his father long ago, and refused to acknowledge McNeill Resorts or any of the McNeill legacy. No doubt Donovan had started over again in Wyoming, making his own fortune, and no doubt there were potential heirs out there whom Malcolm would try to draw back into the fold. But considering the way Donovan had shunned the rest of the family, Gabe wasn't sure any of those cousins would be interested.

"I thought that was one of your biggest reasons for going to New York?" Brianne's dark eyebrows furrowed as she accepted the glass from him, the gray cashmere wrap sliding off her shoulder when she moved.

"No. My main focus is learning more about their business and strengthening ties with the McNeills for Jason's sake."

"Because you can't allow Jason to be left out of the will. It's not fair that he can't inherit because Theresa chose to walk away." She sipped her water, the ice cubes clinking against the glass. "No one could have foreseen that."

He couldn't help but smile. "Thank you for being defensive on my son's behalf."

"He is your son," she said simply. "He deserves all the privileges that come with the McNeill name."

"I couldn't agree more. But there may be a better way to secure those rights. One that won't put me at odds with my grandfather as soon as I set foot in New York." He set aside the water pitcher and his untouched glass. The jet would be initiating descent soon and he wanted to secure an answer from Brianne before they reached their destination.

"How?" She set her drink aside, too, curious. Unsuspecting.

"I could do what the rest of my brothers have done." He watched her carefully. "I could marry."

Her eyes went wide, jaw dropping. "Seriously?" Then she shook her head, as if none of what he'd said made any sense. "I thought you said you would never marry again?"

That had been before he acknowledged the danger of Theresa deciding she wanted to revisit the custody terms they'd already settled upon legally. Yes, she'd been glad to give him full custody at the time of their divorce. Grateful, even. But if she suddenly decided it would be a marketing hook for her career to have a baby in tow, might she try to convince a judge to overturn the agreement? As much as Gabe wanted Jason to know his birth mother, he wouldn't allow it to happen at the expense of a stable home. Being married could give Gabe an extra edge legally.

Not that he would complicate matters with Brianne by dragging all that up.

"This marriage would be very different," he said instead. "A practical arrangement to serve a particular need." He meant that. But damn. As soon as he'd spoken the words, his brain conjured very different practical needs that might be served if he wed in name only.

And had Brianne in his bed.

"A marriage of convenience?" The words came out on a horrified half whisper almost drowned out by the drone of the plane's engines.

He'd managed to scandalize her. Not quite what he was going for. So he concentrated on laying out the terms the same way he'd sketch out a plan for a building, help-

ing her to see the final product before she dressed it up with landscaping.

"A legal union for twelve months and a day. Just long enough to ensure Jason can inherit his share of the Mc-Neill legacy." He studied her, surprised she hadn't made the connection yet about where this was headed. About her role in it. But he knew she felt the spark of attraction that he did, even if she ignored it as studiously as he had.

He needed to get past that careful facade now. Acknowledge the heat for what it was—a sensual connection that could make the next twelve months incredibly rewarding for both of them. Reaching across the leather armrest between them, Gabe took her hands in his. Her skin was cool to the touch. The pale pink paint on her short nails shone under the dome light.

"Brianne." He slid his thumbs over the insides of her palms, stroking light circles there before he met her dark gaze again. "I want you to marry me."

Breathless, Brianne felt mesmerized by the man and the moment. The proposal was so ludicrous, so impossible, it was like one of those delicious dreams where she knew she was dreaming but didn't want to wake up. Because in a dream, a woman could explore forbidden things like a sexy attraction to her wealthy, gorgeous boss. In that moment between waking and sleeping, there was no harm in feeling that tingle of hot awareness down both thighs. Along the lower spine.

In her breasts.

The simple stroke of Gabe's hands had that same effect on her. But unfortunately, Brianne was not dreaming. She needed to wake up and put a stop to all this right now before things ventured into even more forbidden territory.

She needed her job, now more than ever. Too much

to risk a misstep with Gabe, no matter how much she wanted to run her lips along his whisker-rough jaw and inhale the woodsy cedar scent of him.

"Very funny." She tugged her hands out from between his, tucking them between her knees. That way, she wouldn't be tempted to touch him back. "I can see where marrying your gardener would be a nice, in-your-face gesture to your megarich grandfather, but I'm sure you'll come up with something better than that."

"I'm not joking." Gabe's voice was even, his expression grave. "My back's against a wall with Malcolm's will, and a marriage is the simplest way to ensure my son's future."

In that moment, she realized he hadn't been joking. Which made the proposition all the more unsettling.

"So marry. Fine. I get it." She knew how much value he placed on giving his son every advantage in life. She admired that about him, but she couldn't possibly help him. "But you have to know I can't take part in a scheme like that. There's far too much for me to lose."

His gaze narrowed slightly. "You haven't let me outline the full extent of the plan or what you stand to gain." He seemed to shift gears, appealing to her on a business level. "Half the reason I want to do this would be for your benefit. If you help me with the marriage, I will extend to you every advantage that comes from being a McNeill in return. That means no more worrying about your grandmother or where she'll live. As my wife, you'll have access to the best doctors and round-the-clock nurse aides, if you need help caring for her."

The possibilities spun in front of her eyes, as she contemplated the way Gabe could wave the wand of his wealth and power over her life and fix things—just like that. It brought into sharp focus what he was offering.

Not just to her. To Nana.

"I couldn't marry someone for the sake of money." What kind of person did that make her? She shook her head. "It's too...bloodless. Not that I have any great romantic plans for my future, but I also never pictured myself heading to the altar for the sake of a hospital bill."

Shifting positions, she straightened in her seat and placed her feet back on the floor. No more cozy intimacies with this man. It was too risky. Too tempting.

"There are worse reasons to marry, I promise you." The dark resentment in his voice reminded Brianne of how devastating marrying for love could be. "And the reason I thought of you, Brianne, is not just because this marriage would benefit you. But also because I trust you."

Her gaze snapped up to meet his.

"Yes," he said, answering her wordless question. "It's true. This marriage would place a tremendous amount of power in a woman's hands for the next year. It also gives my wife access to my family, which means more to me than anything. I can't think of anyone else I would trust the way I trust you."

"Why?" She shook her head, not understanding. "We only just work together. I mean, we share a few laughs and things, but—"

"Two reasons. One, you're good with Jason. I see how gentle you are with him. How your eyes smile when you look at him. You can't fake that kind of warmth or enjoyment of kids."

She opened her mouth, but snapped it shut again; she wasn't sure what to say. "Everyone loves babies."

"That's not true. Not even close," he said with unmistakable bitterness. "But the second reason I trust you is this." He took her hand again and held it. Firmly. "There was a spark between us from the moment we met."

"No."

"Don't deny it. We both ignored it and that was good. That was the right thing to do." He squeezed her fingers gently and that warmth trickled through her veins again, like an injection of adrenaline. "Not many women would have ignored that spark. At the risk of being immodest, Brianne, the McNeill wealth attracts way too much feminine attention, and I haven't always done a good job of appreciating the women who wanted me for my own sake versus the ones who wanted to get close to the lifestyle our world affords."

She'd never thought about that before, but knowing what she did of human nature, she wasn't surprised, either. Had Theresa been one of those women? She didn't dare to ask; she was too overwhelmed by this shocking outpouring from Gabe.

"You, on the other hand—" he tipped up her chin to see into her eyes, and the warmth of his touch there made her mouth go dry "—you respected my marriage and my family, right through the day it all went up in flames and long afterward. That's how I know I can trust you."

"Gabe." She couldn't find the right words, was still stunned by his admission. He'd known about the attraction all along and hadn't said a word. Hadn't acted on it. "If what you're saying is true, that there is a…spark—"

"Do you doubt it?" He loomed closer.

Her heart beat faster.

"Just, let's say that there is an attraction." The word scraped her throat. "It would be playing with fire to get married and play house. I can't throw away my job—my future—for the sake of one year. I wouldn't be able to work for you anymore."

The fact that she'd tossed out an excuse rather than outright saying "hell, no" made her realize she was ac-

tually considering it in some corner of her mind. She guessed that he sensed as much since he leaned forward, a glint in his eyes that she recognized from when she'd seen him close a deal. He spotted an advantage.

"We'll have a prenuptial agreement. You can name your terms for a settlement so you don't need to concern yourself with work."

"I like my job." It was more than just a paycheck. She lived at the Birdsong. The gardens were a work in progress she hoped to develop for years to come. "I had plans to make the grounds an attraction people would visit there just to see."

"So we'll add in job security as part of the settlement." He shrugged like it was such a small concern.

The plane dipped on a patch of turbulence and her belly pitched along with it. Gabe's arm went around her shoulders automatically, steadying her.

She didn't even realize that she'd grabbed him—his thigh, to be exact—until the plane was sailing smoothly again. Releasing him, she peered up into his eyes and tried to regain her equilibrium.

The heat glittering in his gaze didn't come close to helping.

"We'd have to keep ignoring it." The words slipped from her lips before she had time to think them over, making her realize she was already mulling over how this crazy idea might work.

"What?" He tensed, his arm tightening a fraction around her shoulders where he still held on to her.

"The attraction." She plowed forward, knowing she might regret it but unable to turn down the offer of help for Nana. The level of help that Gabe could give her— the comfort his wealth could provide for her—was the kind of thing her selfless grandmother deserved in her late years. There was nothing Brianne wouldn't do to repay Nana Rose. "We would have to keep a lock on any attraction, the same way we've always done." That was nonnegotiable. "I don't want to feel like I sold my soul for the sake of Nana's care."

His eyes dipped to her lips. Lingered for a moment, then came back to hers. "I would respect your wishes, of course."

Did he know how much his heated glance sent her pulse racing?

"And I would need to trust you. You'd have to promise not to use that attraction to…" She'd never been a woman who minced words, but this was new territory. "What I mean is, you can't try persuading me to go outside my comfort zone, even if you see I might be caving. *Especially* if you see I might be caving."

Instantly, he removed his arm from around her shoulders.

Already, she mourned the loss.

"Done." He nodded. All business.

And shouldn't that be a lesson to her? Gabe McNeill was well versed in sensuality. If he could shut it down that fast, no doubt he could apply it when necessary, as well. She needed to be wary around him.

"Then, if you're really serious about going through with this—"

"I can have our agreement drawn up by noon. We can apply for a marriage license tomorrow before the offices close for the day. Assuming you retained your U.S. citizenship?"

He was serious all right. She nodded.

"So did I. And New York only requires a twenty-four hour waiting period after we apply, so that makes it simple."

So for Nana's sake, she would find a way to make it work.

Before she could second-guess herself, she blurted, "In that case, you have yourself a deal."

And with one look at his heat-filled eyes, Brianne had the feeling she was in over her head even before she said "I do."

Four

She'd said yes.

An hour later, Gabe had to remind himself of the fact as he peered over at Brianne beside him in the limousine. Her expression was tense. She didn't look like a woman who had any reason to celebrate as the lights from the bridge flashed on her face while they crossed the East River and headed into Brooklyn. The drive from the airport had been quick thanks to light traffic, and Gabe had sent Nadine and Jason ahead to the apartment in midtown Manhattan in a separate vehicle so the baby could have some rest after the long trip.

Which left Gabe and Brianne alone for this next leg of the journey. Their first trip as an engaged couple.

The drive into Brooklyn's Bushwick neighborhood was a far cry from how he'd celebrated his first wedding proposal. He'd taken Theresa to Paris to propose over dinner—a romantic night he'd wanted for a woman who adored being romanced. In the long run, what had it meant to her? While he regretted that he hadn't even given Brianne a ring with his proposal, he still felt relieved that this marriage agreement was nothing like the first one. They both knew what they were getting into. There would be a prenuptial agreement. Clear terms for the future. He'd messaged his attorney's office from the plane after Brianne agreed to his plan and she'd seemed content to let him make the arrangements.

No one needed to be disappointed. On the contrary, they could both enjoy the peace of mind that came with knowing their interests were well protected. That they were helping one another.

So why did Brianne's dark expression make her look like she'd just made a deal with the devil?

"Are you okay?" he asked, laying a hand on her arm hidden inside the cashmere wrap she'd worn in place of a jacket.

The clothes were plenty warm for Martinique in February. Not so much for New York. He'd have to see about having a winter wardrobe delivered for her. He wished he could put her at ease, but maybe she was just keyed up about her grandmother. No doubt she was worried.

"I didn't realize how strange it would feel to come home." She stared out the limousine window into a dark and silent park as they sped deeper into Brooklyn. "I was so sure I didn't miss this place, and yet now..." She shook her head. "I have so many memories here. Not all of them bad, though."

"You've never really said why your grandmother sent you away." He hoped maybe talking would help her relax. Or at least distract her from worrying about her grandmother. He'd called a private health-care service to meet them at the Brooklyn address in case Brianne needed help moving her grandmother. She hadn't protested when he made the call now that they'd agreed to the marriage deal.

For his part, Gabe was glad to focus on helping her. Maybe that would alleviate the twinge of guilt over how he hadn't mentioned that a marriage might help him with custody if Theresa decided to revisit the terms they'd agreed to previously.

"My family life was complicated even before my father remarried." She turned to stare at an all-night diner lit up in bright pink lights. "Then, once he brought Wendy home, I was the odd one out."

Something her father should have never allowed to happen. Gabe wouldn't let anyone near his son who didn't care about the boy. Jason had already been abandoned by his mother.

"You two didn't get along?" Gabe asked, trying to envision her life as a kid.

Brianne had told him once that her mother had a long-term problem with prescription painkillers and had run off with her dealer when Brianne was only eight, leaving her in the care of a disinterested father. Even then, the grandmother had been Brianne's role model, the woman who kept her family together.

"Something like that." She glanced up at the high, neon vacancy sign flashing on a nearby hotel. "My stepmother had a jealous streak. She didn't see me as a threat when I was nine, and gladly ignored me. But once I hit puberty, she turned vicious if anyone noticed me."

Defensiveness for the girl she'd been had him straightening in his seat. He was angry on her behalf.

"Vicious how?" he asked, keeping his voice even. "Did she hit you?"

"No. Not quite." She pivoted her shoulders toward him, dragging her attention from the window. "Some shoving once or twice. Mostly, she raged at me to keep my, um, breasts to myself while trying to wrench my too-small clothes around me to cover more." She shook her head, dragging weary fingers through her thick waves. "A real class act."

And Brianne had been just a kid. Damn.

His hand found her wrist, and he squeezed gently.

"No wonder your grandmother wanted you out of there." He hated to think about an adult manhandling her like that when she was a child. "I'm so sorry you went through that."

"I've heard Wendy is on medication now for some of her issues." She crossed her legs, her foot swinging with the motion of the limousine as it made a sudden stop for a red light. "She was taking reasonable care of Nana and helping out with the rent up until a couple of months ago."

He sincerely hoped he didn't run into the woman who'd treated Brianne that way.

"Where's your father these days? He doesn't participate in caring for his family?" Gabe would trade almost anything to have his mom back. Losing her to cancer while he was a teen had devastated him far more than when his father quit showing up.

He couldn't imagine a son not stepping up to take care of a mother. Although, now that he thought about it, how would Jason feel about Theresa one day if he ever discovered how easily she'd walked away from them both? Resentment simmered.

"One of his sons with Wendy has had some success as a singer on YouTube, believe it or not." She lifted an eyebrow, showing some skepticism. "My dad followed their oldest, Tyler, to Los Angeles to help 'manage' him."

"You have some half siblings, too, then," he observed

as the limo rolled to a stop in front of a string of old brownstones on Bushwick Avenue.

"A few." She nodded distractedly, her attention focused on the brownstone. "Tyler was born while my mother was still in the picture, so he's only a few years younger than me. This is it." She pointed to the building with no lights on, sandwiched between two others that were still lit and humming with activity—a loud television blaring from the first floor of one, a couple kissing feverishly on the front step of the other.

The five brownstones looked just alike—same wrought-iron fire escapes, same sets of garbage cans at even intervals. A bright Laundromat sat on the corner of the block, machines still spinning and door open to the street even though it was almost midnight.

He wanted to ask her more, find out why none of the half siblings were checking on their grandmother, but Brianne was already launching herself toward the limo door. Gabe opened it for her before the driver had gotten around the car. He didn't blame her for the hurry.

"Do you have a key?" He helped her from the vehicle, sliding an arm around her waist as she stepped onto the curb under a blinking fluorescent streetlamp.

"I do—unless the locks have been changed." She held up a cloth change purse embroidered with roses. "Nana gave me this as a going-away present." She opened the metal fastening and showed him the interior lined with pink satin. Inside, there were two keys and a coin. "A quarter so I could always call home and keys for the doors."

Her voice wobbled with emotion.

Noticing the limo was drawing attention, Gabe reached to take the keys, then guided her up the stairs of the brownstone. The kissing couple had quit breathing down each other's throats to stare. Normal curiosity, maybe. But he'd feel better when he got Brianne safely inside.

"Good." He worked the bigger key in the outdoor lock, feeling the mechanism give way. "The home health-care workers should be here any minute. I told our driver to circle the block until we text him so there's room for the transport vehicle."

"I hope we don't need it." He could sense the tension tightening her shoulders and he didn't even try to resist the urge to rub away the knots as they stepped into the darkened hallway. A night-light from a floor above shined dully on the warped staircase.

Brianne turned to the left, her feet gravitating toward what must be her grandmother's first-floor apartment. A withered clump of evergreen boughs tied with a red ribbon still hung on the door—a holiday leftover too long neglected.

"She's going to be in good hands," Gabe assured her, checking his phone when he felt it vibrate, his hand falling away from her shoulder. "That'll be the health-care workers now."

Headlights flashed on the road outside, where a bigger vehicle double-parked while Brianne knocked on the apartment door.

Waited.

Rang the bell.

He glanced over at her, trying to gauge what she was feeling. How he could help. He remembered those brief awful months of his mother's illness and how it had devastated him. Sure, he'd been a kid. But he knew even now dealing with that—seeing a loved one deteriorate in front of your eyes—would level him.

"Okay." Brianne drew in a deep breath. "I just need a minute with her first. Just to see her with my own eyes."

"I'd like to go in with you." He didn't trust the rest of her family from the little bit he'd learned about them. What if the stepmother was helping herself to the apartment while the grandmother recovered? Or someone else?

Just because no one answered the door didn't mean no one else was inside. A surge of protectiveness had him itching to tuck her under his arm again.

"That's fine." She nodded, withdrawing the second key from her purse. "Just not anyone else. Not yet."

"Of course." He planned to make this reunion as easy as possible for Brianne. That had been his part of the wedding bargain—the main reason she'd agreed to his terms. "I'll tell them to wait until you're ready."

Nodding, she turned the key in the door of apartment 1A and stepped inside.

"Nana?" Brianne's legs were shaking even more than her voice. She cleared her throat and tried again. "Nana, it's me. Brianne."

She didn't want to frighten her grandmother, but then again, she wanted to lay eyes on her fast. What if she was more hurt than her letter had suggested? Heading toward the apartment's only bedroom, she felt for a light switch on the wall near the tiny stove in the galley kitchen. A weak bulb over the table buzzed to life in the cold apartment. It couldn't be more than sixty degrees. The kitchen was clean enough, though. No smells of spoiled food. One clean cup and plate sat in the sink drainer.

With her hand on the bedroom doorknob, she leaped back at a sudden, rough voice shouting on the other side.

"I've got a gun this time, you son of a—"

Gabe was between Brianne and the door instantly, shoving her behind him.

"Nana?" Brianne's heart beat triple-time. She recognized that scary voice meant to put the fear of God into misbehaving children. "It's Brianne," she blurted, relief making her legs weak. She clutched Gabe without thought, gripping his upper arm and taking strength from his shoulder as she tipped her head to it for just a moment. "I flew home when I got your letter."

The bedroom door swung wide.

Gabe scuttled sideways with Brianne, still keeping himself between her and her grandmother. Around his shoulder, Brianne could see Rose Hanson, dressed in a pink floral nightgown and matching housecoat, her matted gray braid threaded with a bedraggled ribbon.

"Do you have a weapon, ma'am?" Gabe asked, even as Brianne stepped out from behind him and rushed toward Nana Rose.

"Just this." She held up an old smartphone that had seen better days, the case cracked away on one side. "My son showed me an app that sounds like an automatic rifle, but I'll be damned if I could find it." Her hazel eyes turned toward Brianne then, her expression softening as she lifted a stiff hand to skim over Brianne's cheek. "You scared the pants off me, girlie."

"I was so worried you were hurt and I didn't know how to reach you." She closed her eyes and two tears leaked free as she hugged her grandmother carefully. She didn't think anyone would notice she was crying in the dim shadows from the lamp over the kitchen table. "Are you okay?" Leaning back, she tried to see Nana's face while surreptitiously scrubbing away the tears. "It's so cold in here."

"Who's he?" Nana asked, stepping more fully into the kitchen. She was favoring her right side. She looked the same, but smaller, as if time had eroded away a few inches from her height and the plumpness that used to animate her features. A Latina beauty—her mother's family had come to New York from Puerto Rico—Rose Hanson had miles of thick, wavy hair, deep golden skin and an expressive smile. Her hair had gone fully steel-gray, but it was as long as ever judging by the braid. "You never told me you had a beau."

"This is Gabriel McNeill, Nana." Brianne's eyes went briefly to Gabe's. He still stood close to her grandmother, looking ready to steady her at a moment's notice. "I told you about him. He owns the Birdsong, where I work."

Nana eyeballed him thoroughly, the same way she'd done to any friends Brianne had brought over to her house to play after school. Brianne had lived with her father two blocks away in a building that she'd heard had been ripped down years ago.

"You're a long way from home, Gabriel McNeill," Nana observed, swaying slightly on her feet as if a wave of tiredness had just hit her. She looked pale, but Brianne couldn't tell if that was just simply because she'd aged, or if she had hidden injuries and wasn't feeling well.

"We're newly engaged, Mrs. Hanson," Gabe announced, reaching to pull out a chair from the kitchen table for her. "I wanted to be with Brianne for this trip." He gestured to the seat. "We're worried about you."

Nana eyed the chair warily. "No need to cosset the old lady." Her chin lifted. "I'm fine. I just wanted a little help getting some groceries until I get better."

Something in the older woman's expression made Brianne doubt she was telling the truth. Stubborn and proud, Rose Hanson had been a performer in her youth, a torch singer at a New York jazz club with a backup band of her own. There were posters of her around the apartment—or there had been long ago—advertising performance dates. Now the walls looked barren in the living area.

The whole apartment looked like someone had come in and stolen most of her things.

Had she pawned extra furnishings for cash?

"Get better how?" Brianne gave Gabe a private nod, hoping he'd understand she was ready for the home health-care workers to come inside. "Where are you hurt?"

"Nowhere." Rose shook her head while Gabe moved quietly toward the front door, his phone already in hand. "I don't need the cavalry, honey, just some bread and eggs." She ambled awkwardly over to a cupboard near the sink and tugged it open. "I'm down to some cracker crumbs."

Brianne glanced in the cabinet to find nothing but some cracker packs pilfered from a restaurant—the kind they give you with an order of soup.

"Ow." With a wince of pain, her grandmother lowered her right arm slowly, then cradled it.

Brianne ached for her. She wished she could have arrived sooner.

"You're not fine." Brianne could hear Gabe admitting the health-care aides out in the hallway of the building. "Nana, we brought a nurse to check you out. We want you to come with us tonight and stay with me until you're fully recovered."

The older woman's gaze darted to the door, where Gabe was entering with two younger men dressed in dark cargo pants and T-shirts, ID badges around their necks. One carried a medical kit and had a stethoscope around his neck. Armed with friendly smiles, the health-care workers introduced themselves to Nana and were able to help her into the kitchen chair.

One of the guys brought out a small spotlight, flooding the kitchen with a brightness that brought into stark relief how dingy and dilapidated things looked. Another pang of guilt hit Brianne. She should have come to New York sooner.

"I haven't had so many people in my kitchen since the nineteen-sixties," Nana grumbled at the men before launching into tales of her heyday and the wild after-parties she used to host on Bushwick Avenue following her performances.

"Gabe and I will just be right here," Brianne called to her, backing away to afford her some privacy while they asked questions and checked over her arm.

"How does she look to you?" Gabe asked, one shoulder against the pantry door in the cramped space, a look of concern in his blue eyes.

No matter what else became of this contract marriage in the coming year, Brianne felt intensely grateful to have him there with her. To have the help of professional nursing aides to look after her grandmother.

"Exhausted, wary and hurt," she blurted, unable to hold back her worries from him. "She has no food in the cabinets and most of her possessions are gone. I don't know if she's been pawning things over the years or—"

Rapid-fire pounding on the front door interrupted her.

"Excuse me!" A shrill feminine shout accompanied the knocking. "Open up!"

Brianne froze, recognizing the caustic tone. For a second, she was eleven years old again, scared speechless.

Gabe glanced through the peephole, not seeing her distress. "A five-foot-two tornado with red hair and a considerable amount of cosmetics for one in the morning," he announced before turning around. "Anyone you know?"

"Better open up before she shrieks down the whole house," Nana called from her seat on the chair, her head popping up over the shoulders of the two men who were taking her vitals and assessing her bruises.

"I thought she moved out," Brianne replied woodenly, reminding herself she wasn't a kid anymore. She'd known that coming to New York would mean facing family members, not just her grandmother.

The pounding continued along with the shouting. Expletives peppered the demands to open the door.

"She sure did," her grandmother replied. "And I made her return her keys, too."

"Would you like me to call the police?" Gabe seemed undisturbed by the racket, his attention fully focused on Brianne. "She's causing a disturbance."

Unwilling to appear weak in front of a man who knew a completely different person from the scared kid she used to be, Brianne shook her head.

"I'll have to speak to my stepmother sooner or later. Might as well get it over with now."

Five

Gabe pulled open the door during the next round of pounding. He couldn't help but feel a bit gratified when the obnoxious guest stumbled forward a step at the sudden admittance and tripped on the thin braid rug. He steadied the woman enough to keep her upright, like a gentleman should. And that was going to be the extent of the chivalry he extended to the stepmother responsible for making Brianne's early adolescence a traumatic time.

The wiry woman with hair dyed bright crimson glared up at him as she shook off his hand. She wore a loose men's T-shirt and a shrink-wrapped miniskirt, her hair sticking out at odd angles like she'd just woken up despite the massive amount of eye makeup. Her narrowed gaze swept the scene, dismissing him and skipping over Rose until she spotted Brianne.

"Look who decided to grace us with her presence."

The woman straightened to her full height—which wasn't saying much—and curled her lower lip in a sneer. "Should I be impressed you finally decided to show some loyalty to the family?" Brianne's stepmother marched toward the medics still working on Brianne's grandmother. "Just what the hell is going on here?"

Brianne tracked her progress, but didn't move to intervene. Gabe half expected her to collar the intruder and relocate her out the door the same way she would have done with a reptilian visitor to her garden. But she looked rattled. Gabe made a half step toward her grandmother before Rose spoke up.

"Pipe down, Wendy," Rose told her easily, swatting in her direction like the woman was little more than a pesky fly. "If you cared what was going on in here, you could have shown up last week when I could barely move," Rose chided her. "Heaven forbid that spoiled brat of yours who lives next door come over here personally to check on me. Does she have a deal with you where she only calls when there might be some drama?"

Brianne seemed to find her voice, stepping forward. "Who lives next door, Nana?"

"None of your business," her stepmother retorted, glaring at her as she wavered precariously on her spiky heels. Had she been drinking?

Gabe wanted to get Brianne away from her ASAP. The woman certainly made no secret of her dislike.

"Vanessa lives over there now," Rose answered while the health-care workers wrapped her right arm in a splint. "Wendy's oldest girl. I'll bet she was outside on the stoop canoodling with that big lug she calls her boyfriend when you arrived, Brianne. Scrawny baggage couldn't run to the phone fast enough is my guess."

Gabe liked Nana. He'd been prepared to respect and

admire her even before they met, just knowing that she was responsible for sending Brianne to Martinique, for giving her a better life than she'd had in New York. But now, meeting her in person, he couldn't help but smile. He heard some of Brianne's toughness in this woman's voice. Understood now where that came from.

Wendy put her hands on her hips, angling between the health-care aides to fume at Rose. "You should be happy she's keeping an eye on your apartment. She called me because she thought a gangster was after you when she saw a limo pull up." She eased back a step when one of the medics put out a hand to keep her at bay. Wendy looked at Brianne again. "I never guessed Ms. Big Time would pay us a visit, and in a limousine, no less."

"I'm not here to see you," Brianne retorted, arms folded. "I'm taking Nana home with me."

"You're doing what now?" Rose asked, leaning forward to let one of the health-care workers put a coat around her thin shoulders.

It was freezing in the apartment, making Gabe wonder if the lower temperature was for cost savings or if there was a problem with the heater. Either way, it was obvious that an injured elderly woman shouldn't be staying here alone. Brianne had been wise to fly to New York as fast as possible.

"Rose isn't going anywhere," Wendy informed her, chest thrust out like she was about to start a fistfight. "You can't just waltz in here after all this and start making decisions that don't concern you."

Gabe wondered why the woman cared one way or another if she wasn't involved with her mother-in-law's life. Or was it her former mother-in-law? He wasn't even sure Wendy was still married to Brianne's father. It brought Gabe no joy to learn that Brianne's family life had been even more convoluted than his own. At least he'd had the stability of one parent, who'd tried her best to raise him, Jager and Damon the best she could.

One of the health-care workers stood from where he'd been wrapping bandages around Rose's arm. "It appears Miss Rose has a broken ulna bone, and possibly a couple of broken ribs. I'd like to get some X-rays as soon as possible."

Wendy sucked her teeth and made a skeptical sound but the announcement seemed to give Brianne new resolve. She darted past her stepmother to kneel beside Rose's chair.

"Nana, there is a medical van outside," she explained softly. "We can go to the hospital tonight."

Gabe watched them, hoping Brianne would convince her. He knew his future bride wouldn't rest until she'd made sure her grandmother was properly cared for. And because that meant everything to her, it meant a whole lot to him, too. Before he could hear Rose's response, however, Brianne's stepmother sidled in front of him.

"So who are you if you're not a thug?" she asked, eyeing him with open curiosity.

"Brianne's fiancé. Gabe McNeill." He didn't offer his hand.

"McNeill?" The woman's lips pursed tight. "Rose told me you were Brianne's boss."

"Not anymore." He tried to sidestep her, to rejoin Brianne.

But Wendy proved shifty. She stayed right with him, her gaze narrowing. "I don't see a ring on her finger."

"It's being sized." The truth was not her concern, for one thing. And for another, he didn't trust the gleam of interest in her eyes. He wasn't going to allow her to make any hassle for Brianne.

Behind her, the medical workers helped Rose to her feet while Brianne found her some shoes.

Wendy pointed a finger at him. "You're the one who was married to the uppity wife." She nodded, satisfied with herself. "I read about you in one of Brianne's letters."

Brianne glanced up, shooting an apologetic look his way.

"Those letters were to me, you snoop," Rose called over. Her hearing had to be very good to key in on that. "And leave that man alone," she scolded while she slid into a pair of scuffed boots.

Gabe said nothing; he was finished with the conversation. He knew Brianne well enough to know she hadn't spilled intimate details of his life to anyone. There was no positive spin to put on his divorce, after all. Then again, he wondered how much Brianne had shared if she thought her letters were only being read by her grandmother. Could her stepmother know anything about him or his family that could prove awkward down the road?

He wasn't worried for himself. But if Wendy tried to stir trouble for Brianne, or for his son, there would be hell to pay.

Brianne scooped up her grandmother's purse from a chair in the living room before she made her way closer to Gabe.

"I'm going to the hospital with Nana. I need to ride in the van with her."

"Of course." He heard the worry in her voice. "I'm going with you."

"You don't need to do that." She shook her head, her gaze tracking Rose's slow progress across the kitchen as the older woman shuffled along with the help of an arm from one of the health-care workers. "You'll want to be with Jason if he has any trouble adjusting to a new environment."

"Nadine is completely in her element with any child-care crisis, and she has my number if she needs anything at all. Jason is in good hands. I'm going with you."

He wanted to help her. To spend more time with her. And yes, put that ring on her finger as soon as possible. He had enough problems of his own dealing with the aftermath of his divorce and being a good father to Jason. He didn't need a bitter stepmother suspicious about the validity of his upcoming union.

The sooner he married Brianne, the better.

"Shhh. We don't want to wake her." A man's soft voice outside Brianne's door drifted through her dreams the next morning.

Blinking and disoriented, she stared at the moldings on the tall door of the unfamiliar room. Dull winter daylight filtered over her. Her new home for the foreseeable future, she remembered groggily. She'd arrived here at Gabe's half brother's vacant apartment after four in the morning. She'd been just awake enough to help Rose, who now had a cast on her arm, into a bedroom on the second floor before falling into the king-size bed that Gabe had directed her toward on the main level.

"Gah!" A baby shout-squealed just outside of the door to her suite, making her smile. There was a soft scuffling noise and then a trailing echo of "Gah, gah, gah!" as the sound moved farther away.

Clearly, father and son were up and about this morning. Envisioning the two of them playing together kept her smile in place.

Her soon-to-be husband and temporary son.

The smile faded.

What on earth had she agreed to yesterday? Sitting up in the most exquisite sheets she'd ever felt, Brianne shoved her tangled hair behind her shoulder and glanced at the old-fashioned bedside clock, only to discover it was almost noon. Muted views of falling snow were visible through the half-drawn shades, and the sounds of the city on the street below were so different from the birds she normally heard in the morning. Here there was the dull rumble of traffic: brakes and horns punctuated with the occasional shrill whistle or shout. A siren in the distance.

Slowly, reality sank into her foggy brain. She'd agreed to marry her boss in exchange for help with her grandmother. In the clear light of day, without the mesmerizing power of Gabe's seductive blue eyes on her, Brianne realized how much was at stake now. Her pride? Too late to salvage that. Her heart? She'd have to watch it like a hawk to keep herself from getting too swoony over her sexy fiancé.

But those costs were nothing compared to that precious baby boy of Gabe's. Jason had already been semiabandoned by his mother. Gabe had been devastated when Theresa insisted he return to Martinique with the baby while she pursued her career alone. How was it any better for Brianne to form an attachment to the child and then walk away a year later? Jason wasn't going to understand how important the temporary marriage was for his "legacy." What would a toddler care about that?

Throwing aside the covers, she hurried into the shower and rinsed off fast. She towel-dried her hair, brushed her teeth and threw on some wrinkled clothes from her suitcase before padding out into a library full of books about architecture and design. Beautiful prints of the New York skyline covered the walls in the few spots there were no books or windows.

She followed the sounds of baby giggles and found Nadine with Jason in the kitchen. The boy whacked a wooden spoon against a silver mixing bowl on the floor.

"Morning." Nadine offered a cheery smile from her spot at the kitchen counter, where she sat with a map of the city and a highlighter. "I hope we weren't too noisy."

Jason stared up at Brianne from his spot on the marble tiles, his shoulders bobbing as if he had a song in his heart. He shook the spoon at her. She bent to smooth his dark curls and helped him to tap his makeshift drum.

"Goodness no. I should have gotten out of bed ages ago." Straightening, she tried to glance into the next room, down the hall, but couldn't see past a set of partially closed French doors. "Do you know if my grandmother is awake?"

"It's been quiet upstairs. Mr. McNeill said you got home really late." Nadine folded the map, then slid her papers and phone to the far side of the stainless-steel countertop. "A nurse's aide arrived about ten this morning, though, and she's upstairs in the study outside of your grandmother's bedroom in case she needs anything."

"Great." That was a thoughtful gesture from Gabe, who'd arranged for rotating nursing staff the night before while they'd been waiting for Nana to get her X-rays. "I'll go introduce myself in a minute. Is Gabe here?"

She needed to see him. Speak to him. Explain that they must put Jason first and foremost before they went through with this marriage.

"In the office." Nadine pointed through the French doors. "It's on the right through there."

"Thanks." Brianne wouldn't have thought twice about joining him in his workshop back in Martinique, but this place was a whole different world from the Birdsong Hotel.

Views of Central Park blanketed in frosty white glittered through the windowpanes, with more flurries swirling in the air. She hadn't seen snow since she was a kid and part of her still longed to run outside and play in it. But seeing her grandmother's injuries and living conditions had made her more committed than ever to take more responsibility.

But the snow wasn't the only difference in the scenery. Here, there was no escaping the vast divide between the world she came from and the one Gabe moved in. She remembered the icy chill of a cheap studio apartment in winter like her grandmother's. Gabe McNeill, on the other hand, was no stranger to homes like this one, a full-amenity hotel with a prestigious Fifth Avenue address. He'd introduced her to the wonders of concierge service and twenty-four-hour in-room dining the night before, explaining how she could order food from the hotel's restaurants anytime.

He traveled with a nanny for his son. Produced home health care for her grandmother at the snap of his fingers. Brianne owed him so much. And she was so out of her league with this man.

"Gabe?" She tapped the back of her knuckles on the half-open office door. Brianne peeked inside to see him wave her forward.

Cell phone tucked between his ear and his shoulder, he pointed toward a silver tea cart with a coffee carafe and two small warming trays with domes. It was a breakfast invitation that her grumbling stomach answered before she'd made up her mind to stay. He was already wheeling the tea cart closer to the window, next to a couple of gray wingback chairs.

"I came here to spend time with Malcolm and the rest of the family," Gabe said into the phone, juggling it from one hand to the other. "I hope to spend time with him. So if he's not going to be in New York, maybe I should head out to Wyoming see him." He paused, listening. "Sure. Let me know either way, Ian. And thanks for the apartment."

He disconnected the call while Brianne stood in the middle of the office, watching him. She wouldn't have guessed he'd been up until four in the morning with her and then out of bed before her to play with his son. He was dressed more casually today in a pair of jeans worn in all the right places. The black button-down he wore was another one of those custom-made pieces that fit him perfectly, his nipped-in waist and broad shoulders accentuated just enough to make a woman's pulse leap a bit.

"Morning." He greeted her with a warm smile that made her remember how easy it had been to strike up a friendship with him. "Come join me for breakfast. I ordered the darkest roast coffee in the whole hotel, just the way you like."

She realized she'd been staring. Gawking, really. Apparently having a marriage proposal on the table was counterproductive to keeping her thoughts platonic. But damn it, they'd started as friends. Surely she could still have a reasonable conversation with him.

"Thank you." The fragrant scent had her moving toward the wingbacks. "I didn't mean to interrupt, but I need to talk to you."

"You're not interrupting anything." He waited for her to sit and then pulled the domes off the breakfast trays. "I've been anxious to speak to you, too." He poured her a cup of coffee and passed her the mug. "Did you sleep well?"

"Like a rock, thank you." Memories of waking up to his voice skated over her skin. "I was shocked at how long I was out."

"You needed it after yesterday." He filled a white china plate with eggs and toast, then passed that to her, too. "You must be hungry."

Taking a second dish, he arranged more food on it for himself before sitting in the chair beside her. Brianne fixed her coffee, adding the cream, while she thought about how to raise the issue of their temporary marriage.

"I feel like I dreamed half of what happened yesterday," she admitted, taking a careful sip of her drink.

He stilled for a moment, then set his breakfast on the end table nearby. "If you're referring to the proposal, I hope it was a good dream." He reached for a flat box under the tea cart and set the heavy wooden case on the ottoman in front of her. "Although this might make our arrangement feel more real."

Flicking open the metal clasp on the box, he lifted the lid to reveal an expanse of blue satin filled with diamonds.

Wedding rings glittered and winked in the light. Her breath caught at the dazzling display, millions of dollars' worth of jewels casually there for the taking. Perhaps he heard her small gasp because Gabe rose and came around to stand behind her chair, his hands suddenly on her shoulders. She felt a solid, steadying warmth. More than that, even.

Affection. And yes, desire. Her heartbeat stuttered.

Leaning closer, he kissed her temple and stared into the box with her.

"I'd like you to choose a ring for our wedding, Brianne."

Six

Anticipation firing through him, Gabe angled back to see her reaction.

The tense worry pulling her eyebrows tight wasn't exactly what he'd been going for.

"What's wrong?" Shoving over the display case, he shifted to sit on the ottoman across from her so he could see her better. "You're not having second thoughts, I hope."

Unease dimmed his excitement. He'd already filed for the marriage license. He needed her to go through with this for the sake of his grandfather's will and to bolster his position with regard to custody of his son. But more than that, he wanted Brianne in his life. The attraction they'd been ignoring wasn't going away this time. Spending the last twenty-four hours together had only strengthened their connection, something she must recognize, too.

"Not exactly." She shook her head, the dark, damp

strands of her hair swishing against her white sweater. With no makeup and fresh from the shower, she looked the way she did at the start of so many work mornings, except she hadn't tied back her hair.

Natural. Unaffected. Beautiful.

He laid a hand on her knee, a privilege he wouldn't have allowed himself just last week.

"Is it your family? Are you worried about anything?" He had tried to make things as easy as possible for her the night before, but she wouldn't hear of leaving her grandmother at the ER alone and he didn't blame her.

"We agreed to the marriage for our own personal reasons, and they still stand." She set aside her plate. "Already, you're helping me so much with my grandmother, and I couldn't be more grateful. But I woke up this morning thinking about Jason. How's this going to affect him? We're going to get attached to each other..." She blinked fast. Shook her head. "That is, Jason and I—we'll spend a lot of time together this year. And where does that leave him twelve months from now?"

The concern in her voice, the worry in her eyes, should have touched Gabe. He knew that—and somewhere inside, he was moved by her thoughtfulness. Her ability to put Jason first. But more than anything, her words lit a new fire under the old resentment at Theresa for never voicing any such concern about her own defection.

With an effort, he swallowed back that bitterness in order to reassure Brianne.

"The fact that you care how he'll feel means you're going to handle it the right way." He let his thumb stroke the top of her knee. "Every parenting book I read says that as long as you're caring and trying, you're ahead of the curve. And I know you'll do both those things, Brianne. You care, and you'll try to make any separation easier for Jason."

Her gaze slid from his down to where he touched her, but he couldn't pull away. Not until he knew she understood.

Slowly, she lowered her hand to his and held it, effectively stilling his movement. Or taking comfort from him? He couldn't tell with Brianne. She'd asked him not to press the attraction, but they were still friends. Still capable of offering one another comfort.

"I had a lot of people walk away from me when I was a kid, and I know how much it hurts," she confided, her dark eyes bright with emotion.

"I would never stop you from seeing Jason afterward." He wanted more relationships for his son. "I want love in his life, Brianne."

"Thank you." She blinked away the tears in her eyes, seeming to tighten the reins on her composure. "That helps."

How often did she do that? he wondered. Hold a piece of her heart back for safekeeping?

"And don't forget, not everyone walked away from you when you were a kid. Yes, your grandmother sent you away," he reminded her gently, "but did you ever doubt her love for a minute?" He didn't need an answer from her since the truth was obvious. "Kids feel it when the grown-ups around them are trying to do the right thing. They sense that care and connection."

She nodded. "I know what you mean." She smiled slightly. "Nana's pretty great, isn't she?"

"Yes. Just like you." He gave her fingers one more squeeze and then let go, turning to pick up the ring box again. "So let's not worry about the future anymore and focus on important things like diamonds and breakfast."

He handed her back the white china plate while he slid free the ring closest to her, holding it up to the daylight through the window. "What do you think of this? A round diamond is supposed to be the most stable in a setting. I thought you'd like that since you work with your hands a lot."

"Gabe." She pointed her fork at him between bites. "Those diamonds are all outrageous. You have to know they are too over-the-top for a down-to-earth girl like me."

"Carat size is nonnegotiable." He liked that teasing light in her dark eyes. But he set down the ring with the round diamond. "How about this one? The jeweler told me it's technically called a rose cut, which is an old-fashioned way to polish a diamond, apparently." He held up another ring for her to see the facets. "I thought you might like it as a nod to your grandmother. Another Rose."

He had her attention now. She set down her plate again and leaned closer.

"I've never heard of a rose cut." Taking the platinum set piece from him, she tilted it this way and that.

"I hadn't, either, until this morning, when the jeweler dropped these off." He popped another ring from its satin slot. "This one is a pink diamond that's rose cut. Double the roses."

"It's stunning." She ran one fingertip along the band, her hand brushing his.

She studied the ring and he watched her. He could tell this one was the winner, and liked that she'd chosen something so overtly feminine.

"Would you like to try it on?" He took the first ring from her hand and set it on top of the case, keeping her fingers captive all the while.

"Are we really doing this?" Her breathless voice skipped along his senses like a tentative touch.

"Yes." He rolled the platinum band back and forth between two fingers, the pink diamond glinting. "We absolutely are."

He needed this marriage.

And even more? He wanted this woman.

"Then I guess it can't hurt to try it on." The grin spreading over her face made him smile, too.

Damn, but he wanted to make her happy.

The urge to kiss her was strong. Any other time, with any other woman, he wouldn't have thought twice about giving in to that urge. But Brianne had asked him to hold back.

So he would. At least for a little longer.

Turning his attention to her hand, he lifted her ring finger and slid the pink stone into place. Outside the office, he could hear Jason banging on pots in the kitchen while Nadine tried to sing accompaniment.

"A perfect fit," he announced, admiring the way the jewel looked against her deeper skin tone. "Like it was made for you."

"How did you know what size?" She peered up at him, her dark waves taking shape as her hair dried.

"Last night in the emergency room, I held your hand for a minute and got a feel of that topaz ring you were wearing yesterday." The move hadn't been calculated, but feeling the band around her finger had reminded him he needed to seal their bargain with an engagement ring. "When I let go, I drew what I thought the size was on a piece of paper from the nurses' station. The jeweler matched up the drawing with a real size after I sent it over this morning."

"I guess that shouldn't surprise me. You're always

superdexterous when you're working with wood." She flexed her fingers back and forth, as if getting used to the feel of it. Her gaze darted self-consciously toward him for a moment before she lifted a miniature sweet roll from her plate and took a bite, chewing thoughtfully. "You're very good with your hands."

Because he was staring at her, he could see the moment the comment took on a sensual dimension in her thoughts. Her eyes widened. Two fingers covered her lips as if she could still catch the words she'd just uttered.

"I'm glad you've noticed." He imagined applying that skill set to his bride's luscious curves. Envisioned the slow stroke of his hand up her thigh. Over her hip. "I hope you'll consider putting my hands to work for the common good in the months ahead."

"The common good?" Skepticism dripped from her words. "I'll keep that in mind if I need any historic woodwork restored."

"Surely you can be more imaginative than that," he replied, enjoying the way the heat spiked between them. Wanting her to consider the possibilities this marriage offered. "You work in a creative field, after all."

"Wicked man." She straightened in her seat and faced him head-on even though her cheeks were flushed pink. "I'm not sure my job is all that creative, but landscaping definitely has taught me how to wade through... BS."

He had to laugh at that one. "It's not BS if I mean every word." He stood, not wanting to pressure her when he hadn't yet completed the primary objective: marriage. "But how's your schedule look for tomorrow afternoon? I spoke to the same court clerk who married Jager and Delia, and he said he could make a trip out here if we're ready for the wedding ceremony by noon tomorrow."

"Really? So soon?" Blinking, she shoved to her feet

and seemed to take a few calming breaths. She tugged her phone from the side pocket of her cargo pants. Pressing the button to light up the screen, she glanced back up at him. "That would make us husband and wife in twenty-four hours."

"Why delay?" He couldn't afford to lose the advantage now that she'd said yes. "I had a few gowns brought in this morning along with some flower options. Would you like to see?" He'd had the household staff hopping from the moment he'd rolled out of bed this morning, but it turned out his half brother employed extremely competent help.

Then again, Ian's personal assistant had seemed glad for the work after managing a quiet apartment for the past week. Which was a good thing, since Gabe wasn't letting anything stand between him and Brianne, or their wedding.

"You're serious." Brianne shook her head. "I don't need to see the gowns now. I'm just surprised how fast everything is coming together.

"As promised." He'd made additional arrangements to leak the news of the wedding so that Theresa would hear.

Not that she would care one way or the other, but Gabe wanted his ex—and her lawyers—to know that Jason was living in a secure, two-parent home. Sooner rather than later.

"I'd hoped my grandmother could be one of our witnesses, but I'm not sure she'll feel up to it." Brianne worried her lower lip.

Fixated on the movement, he wished he could swoop in and capture her mouth with his, saving her lower lip from the torment. But he didn't want to push her more off-kilter when he needed to nail down plans for a wedding.

"We can see how she feels in the morning. But it might

be easier to get a couple of staffers to be our witnesses so Rose can rest. The nurse was going to ask her doctor about increasing the pain medications for a couple of days so your grandmother can get some extra sleep and recover." His phone buzzed with an incoming message and he picked it up to check it.

"I'll go upstairs and speak to the nurse right now." Brianne didn't move, though. She put a hand on his arm. "Is everything okay?"

Inwardly cursing the frustrating news he'd just received on the phone, Gabe mentally reworked his plans to accommodate the sudden turn of events. He turned off the screen.

"Just a note from Ian, the half brother I was speaking to when you first came in." He huffed out a breath of irritation as he pocketed the phone. "Apparently my grandfather won't be returning to New York until he can convince his estranged older son to see him."

"Even though you traveled all this way to meet with him?" She tilted her head, the same way she did when she stared at a new landscaping space, as if she couldn't quite take its measure.

He was having a tough time figuring it out himself. But he'd come this far to solidify his son's legacy. He wasn't going to turn around and go home or let Malcolm McNeill off the hook. He planned to meet the man face-to-face. Become an irrefutable part of this family to protect Jason's interests.

"He's an old man in failing health. He wants to conserve his resources and minimize his own time in the air." Gabe only hoped Brianne would be on board with the plan B taking shape in his mind.

He'd simply have to go to Malcolm.

Brianne frowned. "I don't understand. How long will

we stay in New York to wait for him?" Her dark eyes searched his.

"We could avoid waiting around if we went to him. Your grandmother has around-the-clock nursing care, and Jason is in excellent hands, so we're not needed here for a few days." He couldn't deny there was a whole lot of appeal to having Brianne all to himself. "What do you say to a honeymoon in Wyoming?"

Twenty-four hours later, Brianne was so nervous that the delphinium petals in her wedding bouquet were jiggling in her hand as she waited beside her grandmother's bed. She'd spoken to the nurse about increasing Nana's dose of pain medication for the next few days so she could heal and sleep. Brianne approved of the plan wholeheartedly, except she sure wished she could get Nana Rose's blessing before she said her vows in Gabe's half brother's living room.

What a crazy few days it had been.

"Nana?" Brianne sank to the edge of the bed. Her grandmother's face was peaceful, her bandaged arm resting on the cream-colored linens.

Was it wishful thinking, or did her color look a little better today? Nana had been so weary by the time they returned from the emergency room, her skin pale and breathing shallow.

"Try again, honey," the gray-haired nurse, Adella, urged from the doorway, her starched white uniform bearing little resemblance to the colorful scrubs the ER staff had sported. "I've been holding off her next dose so she has a chance of hearing you."

"Nana?" Brianne said again, louder, lowering a hand to her grandmother's thin shoulder.

Already, she could hear Nadine calling for her from

downstairs. No doubt they were waiting for her to start the wedding ceremony.

"Brianne," Nana replied in a scratchy voice from the bed. "What's wrong?"

Her grandmother hadn't even opened her eyes. Brianne squeezed her hand, careful to touch only the uninjured arm. Behind her, she heard Adella intercede with Nadine to wait another minute before interrupting them.

"Nothing's wrong, Nana. Can you open your eyes?" She really wanted her grandmother to see her in the outrageously beautiful gown made of imported Italian lace and satin. "I'm getting married to Gabe today, and I wanted you to see me. You're the closest family I have."

With a slow flutter of lashes, Nana's eyelids lifted.

"Oh, child. Look at you." Rose's eyes roamed Brianne from head to toe. "Stand up so I can take a peek at that dress."

Brianne couldn't help a twinge of self-consciousness even as she got to her feet. She was romanticizing this when the ceremony was a formality for a marriage that would end one year from now. But what if she never married again? A wistful piece of her heart wanted to savor the joy of twirling in this beautiful lace minidress and matching jacket. She'd left her dark hair down to fall over one shoulder. Her pale blue sling-backs echoed the deep indigo of the delphiniums she carried. She had never placed much importance on appearance, often dressing to deflect attention after her stepmother's criticism during her preteen years. But today, she felt beautiful.

Gabe had given her that.

"I'm getting married downstairs." And then she was hopping on a plane again, to share a honeymoon in Wyoming with her outrageously sexy former boss. "The city clerk is already here, Nana, but I wanted you to know."

Nana's smile was fleeting as her eyes closed again. For a moment, Brianne thought she'd fallen back asleep, but then came a whispered rasp from the bed.

"Be true to yourself, Brianne." Nana Rose mumbled the words, her lips barely moving. "You can't make anyone else happy until you're happy."

Brianne's throat burned a little at the advice that didn't quite apply since she and Gabe were marrying for very particular reasons. She wished she wasn't deceiving the person she loved most in the world. But she'd done what she'd come here to do.

Now it was time to get married.

"Thank you, Nana. I love you." She kissed her grandmother's forehead. "I'm going to take a honeymoon for a few days, but I'll be back before you know it, and Adella is going to stay with you."

"Love you, too, Bri. And don't you dare rush home to sit with your granny when you have a hot-looking husband to enjoy." Her eyes opened long enough to give Brianne a sly wink. "Go on and have fun, honey."

"I'll…um. Okay." She didn't have a response to that one when she had no idea what a honeymoon for a contract marriage would be like. Platonic, right? Her heart beat too fast; she was fairly certain she was lying to herself. She might have used up all her restraint where Gabe was concerned while he'd been married to someone else.

Especially now that it was clear she had his full attention. The attraction was undeniable.

"Bri?" Nana stirred again. "Wendy is breaking in to the apartment when I go out. If you want anything out of there, better lock the windows before she takes what little I have left."

A moment's horror made Brianne almost trip. No wonder Nana's apartment had been so bare. Anger burned through her that someone who'd married in to their dysfunctional family could be so cruel. The strains of a violin drifted into the room, the lilting classical composition at odds with the dark implication of Nana's revelation.

"I'll make sure she doesn't take anything else." Brianne would ask Gabe if they could have the apartment contents cleared and moved to a storage facility until it was time to move her grandmother to Martinique. "Should we ask the police to get involved? I'm sure we can recover—"

"No need." Nana held up a weak hand and waved off the idea. "I hid all the best stuff where she'd never think to look."

"Where?" she pressed, fearful her grandmother would fall back into a drug-induced sleep before revealing her secret hiding place.

Nana's satisfied chuckle assured Brianne she wasn't sleeping yet. "In the broom closet there's a false wall behind the cleaning supplies. Ms. Wendy would never bother to pick up the ammonia, and that's the truth." She pointed an arthritic finger in Brianne's direction. "Go get married, girlie, and have extra fun for your Nana who doesn't have a man in her life right now."

"Okay." Brianne hurried back toward the bed and gave her grandmother's cheek a second kiss. "Feel better soon, Nana."

Backing away, she almost ran in to the nurse, who was hustling closer.

"Don't you worry about a thing, miss," Adella said, drawing up a fresh needle to attach to the port in Nana's arm. "Her vitals are strong and I'm going to take good care of her with the help of two respite workers. She'll be much improved by the time you return."

"Thank you." Brianne wanted to hug the woman for the tender way she nursed Nana. "I'm so grateful."

"Call me anytime you're worried or want an update," Adella urged before gesturing toward the door. "Now don't make that handsome groom of yours wait any longer. Many blessings to you both on your wedding day."

Brianne's chest tightened again at the reminder of all the people she was deceiving, and would continue to deceive all year long.

"Thank you." She tried to smile like any other bride, but the truth was, her delphinium petals were quivering even harder as she walked out of her grandmother's room and headed toward the stairs.

Now she was nervous not just about the wedding, but about her stepmother's underhanded schemes to get her hands on Nana's few belongings. As soon as the ceremony was over, Brianne would solicit Gabe's help to secure that Brooklyn apartment and clear out the contents.

Strains of classical music rose from the living room. A lone violinist played something festive. Not a traditional wedding song, but the sound was rich and beautiful.

Would Gabe have gone to the trouble and expense of a violinist for their justice-of-the-peace vows? Her sling-back heel caught on the last step and she steadied herself on the banister.

Of course he would. Just look at how much he'd spent on the selection of dresses—seven to choose from—and shoes. Then there was the pink rose-cut diamond and matching wedding band he would slide on her finger any moment. He was a good, thoughtful man, and he'd made it very clear he wanted her to be happy.

If only he knew that's what she was afraid of. What if he made her so happy she couldn't walk away?

Reaching the formal living room, Brianne spotted

Nadine and Jason playing off to one side while two household staffers—a maid and Ian McNeill's personal assistant—signed a book on the antique secretary. Gabe had hoped one of his half brothers might be able to attend—especially since one of them lived in the same building. But Ian, Quinn and Cameron were all out of town this week, leaving Gabe and Brianne to celebrate the wedding with the few people on staff.

A female violinist wearing a long, velvet skirt sat in a straight-backed chair in the farthest corner of the room, her head bowed over her instrument as she glided over the strings to produce the exquisite Mozart melody filling the room.

The most commanding presence, however, was Gabe himself. His dark jacket and silver-colored tie suited him, lending a formality to their day wedding. The clothes were perfectly pressed, and his hair, still damp from a shower, was sleeker than normal. It made her realize how starkly handsome his features were without any hair falling over his forehead in appealing disarray. Today, he looked every bit the billionaire, from his thin timepiece to his polished loafers.

She was so busy gawking, Brianne almost forgot she was the bride until the whole room grew quiet.

Every head turned to her as she hovered uncertainly at the archway leading into the gray, modern living area. She felt all the eyes upon her in a vague way since the only gaze that really mattered was Gabe's. His blue eyes seemed to speak to her across the room, the slow simmer of appreciative heat giving her courage to lift her chin.

Uphold her end of their hasty bargain.

Almost as soon as she had the thought, the violinist began the recognizable strains of the "Wedding March." It didn't feel like a marriage in name only with that music playing, with the delphiniums wavering in her bouquet, the ivory-colored lace skimming her thighs as she stepped deeper into the room. Her pulse quickened and her gaze locked with Gabe's.

How many times had she sneaked hungry glances at him over the last year? How often had she reminded herself he was off-limits?

Now he was all hers.

For an entire year.

As she drew even with him near the window overlooking Central Park, Brianne handed off her bouquet to Nadine and thought about her grandmother's words.

Make yourself happy first.

It didn't apply. Shouldn't matter since she wasn't marrying Gabe for real. But how could she *not* imagine making herself happy with this sexy and endlessly capable man looking at her like he might kiss her at any moment?

She faced him when the violin music halted and the city clerk launched into the celebrant's speech. They hadn't written vows so they were using the simplest ceremony possible.

Too nervous to hear any of it, Brianne tried to tell herself Gabriel McNeill was the same guy she'd worked for at Birdsong. The one she'd teased and shoulder-bumped. The one who could raise an old building from the dead with his woodworking prowess and—yes—talented hands. She trusted him to protect her grandmother's things—and Nana herself—while they were on their honeymoon.

"I do," she blurted at what seemed to be the right time, although she had a moment's horror that the clerk had asked Gabe to repeat the words and not her.

But no, he was asking Gabe the same questions now.

The rings slid onto her finger. She placed a platinum band on Gabe's hand.

Their fingers interlaced afterward. She didn't know if she'd initiated that or Gabe had, but she didn't want to let go. His nearness bolstered her when she was feeling nervous. Weird, because he was half the reason she felt nervous in the first place. But she couldn't shake the comfort she took in his presence after the working relationship they'd developed. She hoped she didn't mess up that friendship by marrying him.

"You may kiss the bride." The words intruded on her frenzy of worries. It was the first truly clear message that had gotten through to her brain in the past fifteen minutes.

Kiss. The. Bride.

Each word echoed in slow motion in Brianne's mind. She watched Gabe's response to them, seeing the way he smiled at the representative from the clerk's office and then turned his full attention back to her.

The heat in his midnight blue eyes burned away everything else: the quiet of the room as a handful of people watched them, Jason with his distinctive baby sounds squealing over something. All of it seemed to happen elsewhere as Gabe wrapped his strong hands around her waist.

His touch warmed her right through two layers of lace and silk. Her senses swirled as he lowered his head toward hers, just the same way it had happened in countless forbidden fantasies. Her eyelids fluttered. She might have swayed on her feet.

The man had her spellbound.

Suspense killing her, she couldn't wait another moment or she risked swooning in his arms like a starry-eyed teenager. She clutched the lapels of his dark gray suit, anchoring herself upright. Tilting her face, she brushed her mouth to his in the barest imitation of a kiss. But before she could ease away, Gabe's fingers splayed wider on her back, spanning more of her spine as he drew her fully against him.

Heat scorched through her. His lips claimed hers, and he kissed her like he had all the time in the world to show her how rewarding being Mrs. Gabe McNeill could be.

Seven

The kiss was meant to seal the deal. As a bonus, Gabe thought the contact might awaken his bride to the idea that physical intimacy could be a source of tremendous pleasure for them both.

What he hadn't bargained on was how much the feel of her lips would sear straight through his carefully laid plans to set his own body on fire. Brianne's fingers flexed against his chest, her nails lightly scoring his jacket before she pulled him tighter against her.

For a moment, he ignored everything else. While the witnesses held their collective breaths, Gabe deepened the kiss, taking the full taste of Brianne that he'd secretly craved from the first time they'd met. He sipped and savored her, letting the minty hesitation of her tongue melt away beneath his. The flavor of her raced through his bloodstream like a direct injection.

Off to Gabe's side, he heard a discreet cough followed

by the clearing of a throat. The celebrant, he realized dimly, giving him a cue.

Reluctantly, Gabe pulled away from his new wife. His one consolation was watching her eyelids flutter open slowly, and her lips part in surprise.

As Nadine and the rest of their witnesses applauded, Gabe wanted to whisk away his bride with a fierceness that surprised him. The attraction felt like a fire suddenly exposed to oxygen. It whooshed around him so fast he wondered if it had singed his eyebrows.

"Congratulations, Mr. McNeill," the official from the clerk's office said as he packed up his book and paperwork. "I'll leave a copy of the marriage certificate with you."

Gabe took another moment to pull away his eyes from Brianne's dazed brown gaze.

"Of course." He passed the man a check and tried to run through his mental checklist of things to do before he and Brianne boarded their private flight to Cheyenne.

"May I take a photo, Mr. McNeill?" one of the maids asked as she shook Brianne's hand.

The woman was already holding up her phone. In fact, Gabe had asked her to quietly submit a story to the tabloid of her choice to make a little extra money on the side. She'd only accepted once he convinced her she could give the fee to a charity of her choice. Apparently, Ian's wife worked closely with a single mothers' charity and the maid had agreed it would be a worthy place to contribute the funds.

Beside him, Brianne reached for her bouquet for their photo, her eyes a little glazed and shell-shocked. He understood the feeling. Because even though they'd wed for practical purposes, they had still changed their lives forever. Nadine brought over Jason and handed the baby to him for the picture. His son wore a baby version of a tux, although the bow tie was simply sewn onto the cotton shirt.

"I would be glad to have a copy of the photo," Gabe told the maid, drawing Brianne closer for a picture he knew would be circulating online before they landed in Wyoming tonight.

Automatically, Brianne kissed Jason's head as she tipped her temple closer to the boy, reminding Gabe how connected the two of them had become these last ten months. Jason adored her. Was it so wrong of Gabe to want that strong feminine presence in the boy's life? There was no denying Brianne had an ease with the child and she seemed as smitten with Jason as he was with her.

"I need to speak to you privately," Brianne whispered while the woman snapped a few photos of the three of them. "It's urgent."

"Of course. I've already paid the clerk and we have the license. The violinist is packing up. We're all finished here." Gabe handed Jason back to Nadine so the boy could have his nap. Gabe was only too happy to have an excuse to disband the small group assembled to witness the wedding so he could speak to her alone. But her tone concerned him. "Is everything all right?" he asked as they strode out of the living room and into a small butler's pantry nearby.

"No." She shook her head, her beautiful dark hair shimmering in the overhead lights as they stood in the tight space full of floor-to-ceiling gray cabinets. "I spoke to Nana just before the ceremony and she said Wendy has been stealing from her and that we need to take precautions before my stepmother empties the whole house."

Gabe resisted the urge to swear. Barely.

"I'll call the police." He withdrew his phone from the pocket of his jacket.

"No. Nana asked me not to." Brianne put her hand over his to stop him, her touch reminding him how good she'd felt in his arms. "I wondered if we could have the place cleaned out and Nana's things put into storage until we move to Martinique."

He took a moment to absorb Brianne's words since the rest of him was all about the feel of her touch. Her gaze held his for a moment before she went to pull away her hand. He prevented her from moving too far, linking their fingers instead while that crackle of awareness fired through him.

"If that's really what you prefer." He nodded, remembering a conversation he'd had with Damon earlier in the day. "When Damon was staying in New York, he had a couple of bodyguards from a security firm that specializes in privacy and protection." They were based in Silicon Valley, close to where Damon lived these days, but Gabe was familiar with the group from his time out there working on their software start-up. And they had a branch in New York. "I can get a couple of guys over there today, I'm sure."

"Would you?" Her fingers brushed the back of his hand, her pink diamond wedding ring glinting. She swayed ever so slightly toward him.

"I'll make it my top priority and call now." He was glad to do this for her, considering the way he was leaking the marriage news without telling her.

"Thank you." She squeezed his wrist. "So much."

"Of course. Brianne, we're married now. I'll do whatever I can to make your life easier and happier." It wasn't a declaration of love, but after the hellish experience he'd had with marriage, this was a vow that he meant. One he would keep. He already cared about Brianne deeply, so it was a pleasure to repay her for all the ways she'd been a good friend to him and to his son. "Do you think you can be ready to leave in another hour?"

"Easily. I've got a bag packed. I just need to get out of this dress." Letting go of him, she stared down at the close fitting minidress and the matching long jacket. "It's only got a million buttons up the back."

He couldn't imagine a better reason to delay their flight. Visions of helping Brianne out of her lace dress turned the air sultry in the narrow butler's pantry.

He lowered his voice, speaking close to her ear. "Once again, my services are at your disposal."

She glanced up fast. "That wasn't what I meant."

There was a hint of wariness in her tone. But there was something else, too. Awareness? Curiosity? Perhaps the kiss had sparked a new hunger in her, too. There'd always been the possibility of more simmering under the surface of their friendship.

"And yet think how much time it will save you if I get the top few buttons started." He reached around her and pushed some of her hair from the center of her back, feeling the warmth of her skin through the layers of lace. "I can unfasten a few, and then you can put the jacket back on so no one will know they're undone when you walk to your room. You can go through the kitchen, if you want, but I think the living room will be empty in another minute."

Lips pursed, she seemed to think it over.

Then, slowly, she turned around, presenting him with her back. Shrugging the lace jacket partially off her shoulders, she let the fabric catch at her elbows so that the top of her dress was exposed.

His heart rate accelerated.

He could lock the doors on either end of the narrow pantry and have guaranteed privacy. Instead, he simply slid a finger beneath the collar of the white lace dress and lifted it away from her warm skin. He used a thumb to push the first button back through the loop, freeing it. Then he repeated the action with another and another, revealing a narrow patch of bronzed skin between her shoulder blades.

He leaned closer, breathing in the scent of her soap and floral shampoo while she couldn't see him. Tucking his fingers deeper in the dress, he let his knuckles brush her skin for a moment. Then they grazed the silk of her undergarments—the stiff strap of the bra that kept her lush curves in place.

"That's good," she said hastily, stepping forward so fast he nearly pulled off a button accidentally. "Thank you."

She kept her back turned for another moment as she shrugged into the matching lace jacket again.

Gabe's heart pounded so hard he was about to get light-headed in another minute. Touching her at all had been a bonus, he reminded himself.

"The car will be here at three o'clock to take us to the airport," he told her, his voice rough with unfulfilled want.

"I'll be ready." She glanced over her shoulder, her cheeks flushed and her eyes bright.

He'd bet her heart was hammering, too. Knowing that made him all the more ready to start the honeymoon.

Four hours and sixteen hundred miles later, Brianne still couldn't get Gabe's touch off her mind.

They disembarked in a private airfield north of Cheyenne, Wyoming, to a bitter wind that left her breathless.

When they were in New York, she'd accepted a wool coat left behind by a guest of the McNeills, and now she clutched the long, dark cape tighter as Gabe guided her toward the hulking black SUV waiting nearby with its lights on. Because of the time difference, it was still daylight here. The airstrip was so deserted it looked like an open field except for the two lit runways and one small metal hangar. Snow swirled around her feet like a fluffy tornado, the white crystalline flakes glinting like the facets of her pink diamond as they swirled.

And even in that shock of cold whipping off the nearby mountains, Brianne's skin still warmed automatically when her husband touched her through heavy wool, the sensory memory of what had happened in the butler's pantry heating a shivery path down her spine.

The driver from the Range Rover sprinted past them to take a rolling cart of bags off the plane. The man wore a parka so big his head looked unnaturally small even with a knit hat pulled low on his head. She seriously envied the coat, even with the warmth of Gabe's leather glove splayed between her shoulder blades.

"Are you warm enough?" he asked in her right ear, his voice triggering another sensual flashback to their time in the butler's pantry.

She was getting used to the tone he used only for her. His wife.

His *second* wife, now that she thought about it. Had he even bothered to warn Theresa that he was getting remarried? The thought threatened to take Brianne's legs out from under her faster than the slippery ice as they crossed the tarmac.

"I think it's the wind more than the cold." She half shouted to be heard, the gusts blowing past her ear hard enough to make a high-pitched howl.

Without slowing his step, he raised the shawl-like hood on the cape and twined the ends around her neck to secure it. The movement sent a quick smattering of snowflakes into her hair, but the fabric quickly blocked the wind around her ears.

If only he could solve her other worry as easily. Would Jason's mother resent her fiercely for marrying Gabe? Or might Gabe be honest with her about their reasons for the wedding? She needed to ask him about it.

A moment later, they were in the back of the Range Rover and the driver had the bags loaded. Once they were underway and she'd thawed out a little, she lowered the hood and peered out the window into the swirl of white snow.

"I feel like we're in the middle of nowhere." There weren't many vehicles on the road. "It's like driving in a white vacuum."

More than that, being at Gabe's side in the lonesome emptiness only enhanced the urge to wrap herself around him. She felt like they could be the last two people on earth out here.

"I spent a lot of time on the plane looking into places for us to stay, but in the end, I think it will be easiest to take a cabin on a hobby ranch my grandfather has rented for his stay out here." Gabe pressed a button on his phone and showed her a map. "This pin is the ranch."

"Wait a second." She straightened and edged back to get a better look. "Did you say he rented a *whole ranch*? For himself?"

"He's had one of his grandsons here with him on and off as he waits for his estranged son to see him." Gabe leaned deeper into the leather seat beside her, his arm stretched along the back of her headrest. "So he hasn't been totally alone. He travels with a personal assistant and a medical caretaker, too, so he needs room for a few staffers."

Just when she thought she had a handle on this family's wealth and lifestyle, something else made her jaw drop.

"And now we'll stay with him, too?" She told herself that was a good thing since being alone with Gabe for a honeymoon—no matter how much of a pretense their marriage was—could only lead to temptation.

"Not in the same building, just on the same property." He pointed toward the phone again. "The red pin is the main ranch house. This blue dot is the guest cottage." He skimmed his finger west on the map a bit, a distance the scale showed to be a mile or two. "I thought we'd be more comfortable there. It's got maid service and I messaged the caretaker to stock the fridge, so they're expecting us. But it's not too late to book a hotel, or a house of our own, if you prefer."

Of course it wasn't too late. The man had arranged a wedding with a day's notice.

"The cottage sounds great." She tried to smile to show this was all fine by her. But the reality of this being her honeymoon night was sinking in fast. Even now, Gabe's gloved fingers toyed with a lock of her hair, igniting fresh shivers.

And still she hadn't asked him what his ex-wife thought about their marriage. Or if he'd told her at all. Brianne had never formed much of a relationship with the woman other than saying hello in passing and having one conversation about what flowers hummingbirds liked best. Unlike Gabe, Theresa had always viewed Brianne as a domestic—a staff member whose sole function was to keep her employer happy.

"Are you worried about anything?" Gabe returned the

phone to the pocket of his camel-colored overcoat. "Have you been getting regular updates on your grandmother?"

"She's fine, thank you. And yes, Adella has been great about sending me messages." Brianne appreciated his thoughtfulness.

Still, it was difficult to think about anything else beyond the fact that she was heading to a remote Wyoming retreat to spend her wedding night with Gabe. No matter that he'd agreed not to press the attraction between them, the possibility of something happening loomed large in her thoughts.

"And the security team I hired to clean out your grandmother's apartment is still uploading the photos of the contents."

"No hurry. I'm just glad to know Wendy won't be able to take anything else." She'd been researching touristy things to do near Cheyenne, Wyoming, about an hour before their flight landed, when Gabe had let her know Nana's apartment had been secured and her things successfully moved out. "I'm most curious about what she's been hiding in the broom closet."

She'd shared the secret of Nana's hiding place with Gabe, of course, so he could relay the information to the team he'd sent into the Brooklyn apartment. Not that she believed her grandmother owned anything very valuable in the financial sense. But there was a nostalgic value to anything that was important to Rose, and Brianne wanted to be sure nothing was left behind when she relocated her to Martinique.

"When we're settled in the cottage, I'll check the link again and see what new photos are up so you can go through them." His arm shifted from the headrest to slide around her shoulders. "Something else is bothering you, though. I can tell."

Two things, actually.

It seemed easier to admit her worries about his ex than to confess her other fear: that she wouldn't be able to keep her hands off him once they were settled into some romantic honeymoon suite in the middle of nowhere. The fact that she kept replaying the feel of his hands on her back when he'd unbuttoned her wedding dress sure didn't inspire confidence in her ability to keep things platonic.

"There is something." She knew his ex was a sore subject, so she took a deep breath before she blurted, "Did you warn Theresa we were getting married?"

He tensed beside her. The reaction was immediate and reminded Brianne how much emotion he still had invested in that broken relationship.

"No," he admitted stiffly, straightening in his seat as the Range Rover pulled off the main road onto a rough rural lane. "Our relationship is not her concern. And especially not on our wedding day."

Right. Except that he'd married Theresa because he'd loved her.

As for Brianne?

She was his means to an end.

And if that didn't put a damper on the hot, sensual desire she'd been feeling for Gabe, she didn't know what would. Before she could argue the point, however, the big SUV lurched to a stop in front of a big, Craftsman-style home with well-lit windows looking into cozy rooms with pine-log walls and rafters.

Her only consolation in seeing the snow-swept winter retreat was that maybe resisting Gabe tonight would be easier with the subject of his ex a newly raw ache between them.

Eight

He simply needed to regroup.

After his misstep with Brianne in the Range Rover, he'd sensed her retreat. When they'd entered the cabin, she'd slipped away to unpack at the earliest opportunity. In theory, he understood why she would have preferred that he warn his ex-wife about their new marriage. That would have been kinder, perhaps. But it hadn't occurred to him since his parting with Theresa had been acrimonious at every turn, despite his best efforts to make it easy for her to see Jason and maintain a relationship with their son.

Yes, he'd taken steps to ensure his ex-wife found out about the marriage to Brianne. But no doubt the pictures leaked to the tabloids weren't the method Brianne would have chosen. So now, he was regrouping to salvage his honeymoon and make amends with his new bride, a woman he did not wish to hurt. Brianne was different from his ex in every way, and she deserved his best efforts in this marriage, even if their reasons for the union had been practical and not romantic.

Gabe set the timer on the oven to remind himself to flip the steaks and mentally ran through his dinner preparations. He had the candles lit in the dining room, but he'd laid a fire in the huge stone hearth in the living room if she preferred to eat there. The wine had been chilled before they arrived, but he'd opened it to breathe. He'd put a loaf of fresh bread in the warming drawer, and tossed some salads. In a moment of optimism, he'd even switched on the heat for the outdoor hot tub on the master bedroom balcony in case he could convince Brianne to join him after dinner.

Now he needed to make amends to her. Steer the talk away from conversational powder kegs and focus on all the positive things that this marriage meant for both of them. Health care and stability for her aging grandparent. Securing Jason's place in Malcolm McNeill's powerful family. And, if he could convince her to follow the attraction that had long been simmering between them, a tremendous amount of pleasure.

Turning off the broiler, he left the oven door slightly open and went upstairs to call Brianne down for the meal. He passed wall after wall of darkened glass, since the sun had set here even though they'd gained a couple of hours on the day by flying west. The house would feel like a fishbowl anywhere else but not in this remote corner of the world, where there was nothing else around them for miles. Although the place was part of the larger ranch his grandfather had rented for the month, they couldn't see any other outbuildings from here.

"Dinner is ready," he announced outside her bedroom door. He'd tried to talk her into taking the master suite, but she'd been quietly adamant when they first arrived, making herself at home in the second bedroom on the upper floor.

He rapped on the solid pine door now, and it swung open at his touch. Light spilled from the room.

"Brianne?" He didn't want to intrude, but maybe she'd decided to nap.

Or shower.

A surge of awareness crackled across his skin as he was overcome with memories of kissing her during their wedding. Unbuttoning her afterward. As sensual encounters went, they were tame. Outwardly, they looked pretty innocent.

The effect on him, however, was anything but.

Striding inside the bedroom, he found no clues to her whereabouts. The white quilt on the huge bed was untouched except for the few clothes left scattered there. There were shopping bags on the floor from local stores that must have contained some of the winter items he'd ordered for her. The rental agency had said it would be no problem to rush-deliver hats, gloves and more outerwear along with some warm sweaters and slippers. Maybe not the height of fashion, but he knew Brianne wouldn't care.

Still, she deserved beautiful things. Seeing the unisex insulated gloves in different sizes made him all the more determined to indulge her. Hearing the stories about her stepmother had shed some light on the clothing choices Brianne made. Gabe had thought she dressed in cargo pants and T-shirts for work because they were functional for gardening. After meeting Wendy and learning about the way she'd made Brianne uncomfortable in her own skin as a child, he'd been angry. It explained a lot about the way his wife downplayed her beauty.

He was about to go back downstairs to search for her when something pelted the French door near him.

What the hell?

Turning, he thought maybe an icy branch had fallen from a tree to knock against the glass. But while he stared out the window, a blob of heavy snow hit the pane and slid down. This time, the sound was accompanied by muted feminine laughter.

A shadow moved outside the window on the second-floor balcony that wrapped around the whole back of the house. He reached back toward the bed long enough to jam a navy hat on his head and stuff his fingers into a pair of black Gore-Tex gloves. Charging outside, he faced the culprit head-on.

Brianne was busy scooping up another snowball, scraping red gloves through the foot of accumulation on the wooden deck. She'd traded her wool cape for a red down parka and boots. A gray knit cap was pulled low over her eyes, her ponytail covered with snow and hanging bedraggled over one shoulder.

His loafers would be ruined, but he had no intention of leaving the aggression unanswered, especially after he'd heard that laughter of hers. Had she moved on from their earlier disagreement? Or simply found an outlet for her frustration with him? He'd thought dinner would smooth things over between them, but if she preferred a snowy standoff, he was ready.

"I'd think carefully about your next move," he warned her, taking in her pink cheeks and bright eyes as she stalked closer to him, the wind lifting her hair off her shoulder and whipping it across the front of her parka. "I can't very well lob snow missiles at my new bride, but I can get even other ways."

"You can't play that card." She wagged one gloved finger at him, her voice raised so he could hear her over the howl of the wind. "No veiled threats allowed, Mr.

McNeill. I give you my permission to get into an old-fashioned snowball fight with me."

He'd missed this part of their relationship. The teasing and one-upping. Only now, there was a new dimension to it thanks to their wedding vows. The possibility of things getting much more interesting.

"I'd hardly call it a veiled threat." He kept one eye on the snowball in her hand as they squared off a few feet apart in the middle of the balcony. "You make it sound ominous."

"Okay. No *mystery* threats, then. No suggestive innuendo allowed."

"I draw the line there, Mrs. McNeill." He liked her expression as he tested out the new name. Even in the reflected light from the house, he could see a flare of something that looked like pleasure in her eyes. "Half the reason I married you was for the suggestive innuendo."

Her gaze narrowed as her fingers closed harder around the snowball. "Maybe I should have read that contract more carefully."

They both knew she'd read it exhaustively, working on a tentative draft while her grandmother was in the emergency room. She'd changed wording in a handful of places and argued against several points of the settlement to try and decrease the amount she would receive after they'd been married for a year. He'd tweaked the wording as she wished, but he'd left the settlement terms as generous as originally written.

"You didn't see the suggestive-language addendum?" He moved fractionally closer, ready to disarm her if the opportunity presented itself.

A light snow fell, or else the wind kicked up enough to make it feel like it was actively snowing. There was a swirl of white between them. Behind her, he could see the outline of the railing. Down on the far end of the balcony, he could see the shape of the hot tub he'd warmed up earlier. He shifted closer still.

"I know perfectly well there's no such thing. We're married for a handful of hours and we're already at odds about the agreement." She tsked and sighed dramatically.

"I'm the one who has come under attack, though." He nodded meaningfully toward the hand that still held the snowball. "Maybe I'd be more amenable if you put down your arms."

"And risk retribution?" She shook her head. "I'll go on firing, thank you very much."

"At such close range?" He put a hand to his chest. He only wore a sweater and a shirt in the chilly winter air, but the thought of touching Brianne heated him inside and out. "I don't think you can pull the trigger on your new groom, Brianne. Not when you know how much I'm dying for payback."

He closed the distance between them even more; they were so close his body blocked the snowflakes from landing on her. So close he could see her sway on her feet for a moment, as if she wanted to fall into his arms as much as he wanted her to.

Her eyelashes fluttered. She dragged in a slow breath.

And socked him square in the chest with the snowball.

Leaping back with a squeal of delight, she grinned at him, delighted with herself.

He was nothing less than delighted with her, too. He didn't think twice about going after her, wrapping his arms around her from behind and plunging them both into the snowdrift built up against one side of the balcony.

Rolling himself in a way that he fell first, he cushioned her fall with his body. The shock of cold against his back was a minor inconvenience for the reward of having her curves pressed snug to the front of him, her wiggling weight a delectable and unexpected treat.

She laughed herself breathless, her breasts brushing his hands where he held her around her ribs. He battled the desire to slide his palms under the parka, since that would only make her cold.

It wasn't that bad out, he decided. Midforties, maybe. And although he was lying in the snow, at least the drift blocked the wind coming off the mountains. He could lie there a little longer. Especially if he got her turned around.

Gently, he rocked her sideways, putting enough space between them to spin her in his arms as he moved her so they ended up nose-to-nose.

"You're insane," she accused softly, her breath a warm huff on his cheek. "You don't even have a coat on."

He kept his lower arm pillowing his head and hers. "I've never met a nicer way to stay warm." He used his free hand to pluck a few icy strands of her hair from her cheek and set them behind her.

"We should go inside," she insisted, her expression turning more serious. "It's cold out here."

"I'm taking my payback." He watched her while the words sank in.

He heard the hitch in her breathing. Saw the wordless movement of her lips as she thought through whatever argument that wasn't going to fly.

Then her teeth sank into her lower lip and he would swear she was biting back a smile.

"Is it too late for me to give in gracefully?" she asked, edging closer to him in the mound of snow, her hips seal-ing tighter to his.

Adrenaline surged through him so fast he knew he

could consummate the whole wedding night right here if she wanted him to.

"It's definitely not too late." He cupped her shoulder to pull her against him. "Tell me, wife." He let the word hang between them, tasting it on his tongue the way he wanted to taste her again. "How are you going to make it up to me?"

Brianne had been deluding herself to think anything would keep her away from Gabe tonight.

She'd instigated the snowball fight in a misguided attempt to return to the playfulness of their relationship from years past. Thinking about Gabe's ex had made her doubt herself and her hasty decision to wed. She'd been longing to return to more comfortable terrain with him, where they could tease one another and have fun.

But of course that had been naive. Or maybe subconsciously she'd just been trying to push past the discomfort of his ex-wife's shadow over this day. Either way, Brianne gulped in breaths of the thin mountain air, hoping to cool the fire in her belly. A fire that leaped higher the more Gabe touched her.

"I can make it up to you by cooking dinner," she offered, out of her element when it came to flirting.

"I already prepared the meal." He shrugged a shoulder like he had all the time in the world to wade through this dilemma, when here he was lying in a snowbank with just a shirt and a sweater between his skin and the frosty white powder. "That's not going to work."

Her cheek rested on his arm, its muscle warm and strong beneath the cashmere and wool. Her breasts were pressed to his chest, causing a pleasurable ache as his gloved hand stroked up her spine through her parka.

"I could dry your clothes for you since it's my fault you

got plastered with a well-aimed snowball." She strived to keep things light, knowing she was swimming against the current with all the sparks streaking between them. But it was better than being over her head.

"Now we're getting somewhere." He nodded his satisfaction at the plan. "I can't wait for you to start undressing me."

She opened her mouth to argue and realized she had no comeback. Not while her brain got busy supplying mental pictures of her tunneling her hands under his sweater. Unbuttoning the fastenings on his shirt. Splaying her fingers over the sculpted torso she'd ogled on more than one occasion.

"I'm going to let you in on a secret that may surprise you." She tipped her head to his chest for a moment, feeling awkward, then telling herself to get over it. Lifting her face to his again, she blurted, "I'm not all that experienced with men."

He didn't appear terribly surprised. He peered down at her, his blue eyes intent. Thoughtful.

"Does it make you uncomfortable when I talk about you undressing me?" he asked.

A shiver went through her.

"Um. Not exactly." She tried to identify what it made her feel. "I would say I'm intrigued, but possibly ill-prepared."

"Intrigued is good." The smile he gave her inspired another shiver. "But you're starting to get cold. I think we should move this discussion to the hot tub." He pointed to the other end of the snow-covered balcony.

"There's a hot tub?" Sure enough, she could make out the shape of it, a chunky rectangle with blue lights around the rim barely visible under a cover of some kind.

"I turned the heat on in the sauna next to it, and put

robes and towels inside." He sat up, bringing her with him. "You can change in there and meet me in the tub."

"Where are you going?" She stood with his help.

"I'd like to see what I can salvage of dinner so we have something to eat afterward." Giving her a gentle push in one direction, he moved in the other. "Go warm up and I'll be there in a minute."

Brianne headed to the wooden hut at the end of the house, ducked through the cedar door into the fragrant heat of the sauna and closed the insulated entrance behind her. She ignored the light switch, able to see well enough in the glow of coals in the fire box. She peeled off her coat, hat and gloves, then piled them on a built-in bench. After spotting the thick white spa robes, she tugged off her sweater and jeans, but left her underwear on since she had no bathing suit. She gave herself another minute to warm up in the dry heat before throwing on a robe and darting back out into the snow.

Squealing at the feel of snow on her bare feet, she padded through it fast and climbed two steps to the hot tub. After lifting off the heavy leather cover and folding it in half, she unfastened her robe at warp speed, tossing it on the cover and sinking down into the bubbling spa.

She had just closed her eyes and settled into one of the molded seats covered in jets when she heard Gabe's footsteps on the balcony.

Was he naked? She wondered, but she didn't cheat and open her eyes. Well, not until it was too late to tell for sure. By the time she peeked at him sidelong, all she saw was a glimpse of his bare chest disappearing down into the water. A tantalizing hint of corded muscle as steam rose all around him.

"That feels amazing." He tipped his head back on the headrest beside hers, and their shoulders brushed.

Awareness crackled to life.

"I've never moved so fast as I did between the sauna and the tub." She stared at his profile illuminated in the ambient light from the house.

She still couldn't believe she'd married him today. The ceremony had been a blur, with her mind on her grandmother's health and the news about her stepmother pilfering things from Rose's few possessions. But the marriage felt real enough now, as she sat mostly naked at Gabe's side in the middle of nowhere. Snow swirled just above her nose, most of it melting before it landed.

"I brought some wine." He pried open an eyelid and reached behind him to retrieve an open bottle on the step. "It might warm you up on the inside."

Also, it might help with the nervous butterflies she had about her wedding night.

"Sure." She reached behind him to retrieve the bottle and a glass. "I'll pour while you warm up, though. I'm still feeling a little guilty for luring you out into the frigid temperatures without your jacket."

"It's not really that cold out." He watched her pour the first glass and handed her the second. "And you have no reason to feel guilty when we already agreed that payback is forthcoming."

Setting the wine on the step outside the tub, Brianne sat sideways in her seat to face him, the hot bubbles bursting all around her shoulders as air injectors worked their magic.

"Since it's our honeymoon and all, maybe you'll feel compelled to grant clemency." She sipped the wine and appreciated the subtle heat it put in her veins.

"I do owe you a wedding gift." He tipped his glass to hers even though she'd already stolen a sip. After the gentle clink, he raised the cut crystal. "Here's to marrying my best friend."

A ripple of unexpected pleasure that he would call her that went through her.

"Cheers." She lifted her glass and drank to the toast, feeling the weight of his gaze on her the whole time.

The nerve endings all along her arms and shoulders went haywire, making goose bumps appear.

"I didn't think about a wedding gift for you," she admitted, setting aside the glass on one of the drink platforms along the outside edge of the tub.

The curtain of hazy snow and steam around them gave the sense that they were all alone in the world, a veil of cold mist separating them from everything but one another.

Or maybe the wine was going to her head. She felt a sweet happiness all over to be with Gabe. It was dangerous, perhaps, to feel that way. But she'd never been with a man like him, someone strong and noble, kind and warmhearted.

And so very sexy.

Her eyes dipped to the top of his chest above the water as he drained his glass and set it aside, his triceps flexing in a way that made her want to take a bite.

"I certainly didn't expect a wedding gift." He shook his head, a wry smile kicking up one side of his mouth. "We'll have to make our own rules for this marriage since the regular conventions aren't going to apply."

"Like tonight, for example." She hadn't meant to say it out loud, but there it was, floating on the cold breeze before she could take it back. Drawing a steadying breath, she explained herself. "I don't need to worry about your expectations because—"

"Because there are none." He cupped her shoulders with his hands, a warm weight that anchored her in the swirling water. "I thought we deserved this time together to get to know each other as more than friends, but I will be glad just to talk to you tonight. To learn how to make you happy."

"I know that." She wanted to close her eyes and concentrate on how his hands felt on her. To soak up all the sensations of being with him. "You never made me feel like you brought me here for more than that, but still… it's a wedding night. I can't deny I've been thinking about the possibilities of what that means."

His thumbs skated a slow circle over the tops of her shoulders, a subtle touch that set the rest of her on fire.

"I've been doing plenty of thinking of my own," he admitted. "But that doesn't mean we have to act on it."

If he kept touching her, though, the possibility of her launching across the hot tub to kiss him was very real.

"When I said I wasn't all that experienced, I didn't mean to suggest I've never been with a guy. Of course I have." Though she had kept her virginity longer than any of her friends, haunted by her stepmother's taunts long after they should have lost their power to hurt her. "I just don't feel like I ever got high marks. You know?"

"Sex shouldn't be a graded assignment." He said it with one-hundred-percent seriousness.

But she laughed anyway, because it was a strange conversation for a wedding night. "Right. I get that." She flipped a damp piece of hair out of her eyes as she warmed to the discussion. "But when I decided to lose my virginity, I think I was probably…too determined. I did some research and felt well-prepared, but in the end—epic fail." She shook her head, remembering the expression on her boyfriend's face afterward. It hadn't been blissful pleasure.

More like being shell-shocked, maybe.

"The thought of you researching to the point of being overprepared is going to animate some very good dreams for me." He never stopped touching her. His thumbs trailed down the satin straps of her bra in the back. Then in the front. Over and over. "It's my turn to be intrigued."

"I think I was studying techniques that were too advanced for a beginner." She shrugged, the water around her splashing with the movement. "But I don't like looking foolish, and I'd waited so long to give sex a try that I put a lot of pressure on myself not to make it obvious that I was a first-timer."

"What about afterward?" Gabe's knee grazed hers under the water and she didn't skitter away because it felt too good. "Didn't things get better once the first time was out of the way?"

"I wasn't keen to repeat the experiment at the time." She retrieved her wineglass and took another small sip. "But now, I think maybe I'd like to."

Nine

Go slow.

Gabe repeated the mantra to himself, waiting to move—waiting to breathe—until he was certain his revved-up body got the message. He bit the inside of his cheek and focused on the sting because he sure as hell wasn't going to ruin Brianne's *second* time. The pressure was on to make sure the night was perfect after the first experience had underwhelmed her so thoroughly she hadn't cared to try again.

Until now.

It was the "until now" that made him hunger to bury himself inside her. Show her how pleased it made him that she'd chosen him even after whatever had happened that first time. He breathed deep, more turned on than he'd ever been and knowing he couldn't act on it. Yet. Or at least not the way he wanted to.

Go slow.

"How about we start with a kiss?" His gaze lowered to her delectable mouth.

With his fingers curved around her shoulders, he could feel her quick intake of breath. The trip of her pulse under the heel of his hand.

She shifted closer to him in the swirling water, her knee pressing higher on his thigh as she repositioned herself. Then she raised her hands to his face, her damp fingers sliding along his jaw.

Gazes locked, he watched her until the last moment, when the feel of her lips sent a bolt of heat up his spine. She tasted like cabernet and snowflakes, sexy and innocent at the same time. Unbidden visions of her researching "advanced" sex techniques flickered across his mind's eye.

Go slow.

Shoving the wild imaginings out of his head, he tipped her chin up to kiss his way down her delicate throat. Her skin was hot despite the cold night air and the flurries that were gaining momentum. She smelled like exotic flowers, like the gardens she coaxed out of the earth. He inhaled the fragrance, stronger behind one ear, and combed his fingers through the damp hair falling out of the haphazard clasp.

Brianne gripped his forearms and pulled herself so close she was half-sprawled across his lap. Having her hip nudge his erection was not helping the go-slow approach. Her breasts pressing against his chest fulfilled several of his fantasies, and he did everything he could do not to peel off the satin cups of her bra to feel all of her. Instead, he gently nipped her neck. Her ear. Her fingers splayed wider on his chest, her touches more urgent as she arched to give him better access.

He took his time kissing places along her collarbone

and shoulder, licking a path under the bra strap until she raked both satin strips down herself.

"I want more than kisses," she demanded suddenly, her dark eyes blazing with a new fire he could see even out here, under the stars. "I am ready."

He reminded himself that her idea of being ready for more probably wasn't the same as his. But he gladly took the opportunity to flick open the clasp of the satin bra and let it float away on a tide of bubbles. She filled his hands and then some, her softness making him impossibly harder. When she arched her back, her breasts lifted out of the water, rivulets streaking down her skin as he bent to kiss first one taut peak and then the other. She rocked against his lap, her throaty moan a plea for more that he damn well wanted to give her.

"We should go inside." He gauged the distance from the tub to the bed in the master suite, just on the other side of the sliding glass door nearby.

"I'm having fun, though," she whispered in his ear, her lips lingering to kiss him there. "I hate to stop."

"It'll only be for a minute." He wanted her in bed, where she would be most comfortable. If Brianne's second time was going to happen, he wasn't going to risk a hot-tub encounter. "If you stand up, I'll wrap that robe around you and have you inside before you can blink."

She glanced over her shoulder and nodded, grinning with a playful sexiness. "Okay. If you insist."

Springing out of the water, she wrapped her arms around herself while he lunged for the robe to cover her. He moved the wine bottle off the steps and then bounded out of the tub himself before plucking her off her feet and carrying her inside. Her light laughter revved him higher, assuring him she was fully on board with his haste. What an incredible surprise this woman was turning out to be.

He toed the French door closed with one foot while he carried her into the master bathroom, setting her on the tiled surround of the raised garden tub. Still in his cotton boxers, he was dripping water everywhere. He took two towels off the warmer near the shower and handed her one, keeping the other to dry himself off. He dug another towel out of the closet to throw on the floor so she didn't slip.

"How was that?" He watched her wring out her long hair and then dab it dry.

"Getting out of the water wasn't nearly as bad as when I went in. I'm warmer now." She set aside the towel and turned dark eyes toward him. "And less nervous. Thank you for that."

He wrapped his towel around his waist and pulled her to her feet. "I'm glad you relaxed."

"It helped to feel like I warned you." Her wry smile, he now knew, hid an old hurt.

He planned to do whatever he could to heal that. Now, and every other night they were together. Tipping her chin up, he grazed her lips with his and breathed her in.

"I should warn you, too." He tunneled his fingers through her thick, damp hair. "You're going to forget everything that came before tonight."

Folding her in his arms, he kissed her, and it was better than all the times he'd secretly thought about it. He could taste her passion, and she met his hunger with a new need of her own.

She wrapped her arms around his neck, arching against him, and it wasn't enough. He carried her to the bed, making sure she stayed in the moment with him, very ready to make good on his promise to her. He could tell from the kisses that this was going to be better than anything he'd ever imagined. Anything he'd ever dreamed.

He laid her in the center of the bed. Her dark eyes were bright with passion, her hair spilling in every direction on the starched white pillowcase. He stripped off his towel and boxers and she surprised him by shrugging out of her robe and wriggling out of her panties. She lay before him, gloriously naked, and for a moment, he could only stare. His mouth went dry, and his body ached for her with a desperation he'd never felt for another woman.

"Please." Her voice was ragged as she lifted a hand to reach for him. "Don't stop."

Her touch, just a sweep of her knuckles along his chest, propelled him forward. He joined her on the bed, rolling her to her side, her skin like silk against him. A sigh of satisfaction hissed from between his lips, and he thought he heard a soft moan of pleasure from her at the same moment.

Finally.

He sketched a caress down her spine, waiting for his heartbeat to steady. Brianne was having none of it, though. She wriggled closer, raining kisses along his chest. Curving a hand around her hip, he cupped the heat between her thighs. She made a hungry sound, her head falling back on the pillow, her beautiful breasts drawing even with his mouth.

Unable to resist, he licked his way along the tight peaks and sank his finger deep inside her. She wrapped herself around him, legs and arms, giving herself to him. He took his time, loving the feel of her. Learning the touches she liked best until her hips arched and her breath caught.

She came apart in his arms in a rush of heat, her whole body shuddering with her completion. He held her, stroking her while her body quaked, then kissed her neck when she quieted.

* * *

Brianne waited for her breathing to return to normal. The orgasm was an amazing—and generous—surprise. She hadn't been expecting it and now she felt a heady pleasure streaking through her veins, making her feel boneless with sensual bliss.

A bliss Gabe had delivered with ease and—judging by the erection nudging her thighs—considerable pleasure. Seized with the need to give him every bit as much fulfillment in return, she remembered the research she'd done before her first time.

She felt compelled to apply the teachings now.

Except he was already palming a condom.

"Gabe?" She wrapped her hand around his, halting his movement. "I'd love to repay the favor in kind." She meant it. Her pulse quickened. "I want you to feel as good as I do right now and, as I mentioned, I did study how to—"

He kissed her until she all but forgot what she'd been about to say.

"I will enjoy that even more when I have some restraint left." His words were a warm vibration against her ear. "I can't hold back much longer, Brianne."

A thrill shot through her and she let go of his wrist, ready for whatever he wanted next. She sensed that when he pleased himself he was going to please her, too.

Still, the thought didn't prepare her for the feel of him between her thighs. Pressing. Filling. She wrapped her arms around his neck and hung on, her hips meeting his as he moved inside her. She'd dreamed about him often enough in the years she'd worked for him, but she'd never imagined being with him would be like this. Transporting. So good, her toes curled when she wrapped her legs around his waist to hold him tighter.

This time, there was no thinking. No research had been needed. Her body knew what it wanted.

Gabe.

Everywhere. Skin to skin. Flesh to flesh. Savoring the bristle of his chin, the calluses of his fingers, every nuance of this man.

She arched up to kiss him and found him staring down at her. His gaze locked on hers. They drew out the moment. Even as they moved together, driving each other higher, he leaned down to take her lips. Kiss her deeply.

That was when another wave of release hit her. Sweet spasms rocked her, again and again. She clung to Gabe, helpless while the sensations gripped her fiercely. She felt him go rigid moments later, heard his hoarse shout as he found that same completion.

Sometime afterward, when her heart had finally steadied, Gabe rolled her to his side, tucking her against him. A languid warmth persisted everywhere, her body tender with the newness of so much pleasure. She peeked at him through her lashes and saw him stretched beside her, his hand still curled possessively around her hip.

A swell of emotion rose in her chest and she tried not to notice it. Maybe she'd been wise to avoid sex since that first time. Maybe, deep down inside, she'd known that she was the kind of woman given to romantic longings and…whatever it was she was feeling for Gabe.

She couldn't afford to venture down that road with him, and she knew it. Gabe McNeill married her because they were friends. Because he trusted her not to fall in love with him or take advantage of his generous nature.

The latter part of that equation was simple, of course. She'd never want to hurt this man. But the sudden crushing weight on her chest told her how difficult it was going to be to keep her feelings on lockdown. Especially when the physical intimacy had the power to lay bare her emotions.

"Brianne." He spoke her name against her hair, making her realize he'd been watching her, too.

Turning her gaze up to meet his, she found a seriousness in his expression. Had he felt the same cataclysmic shift in their relationship that she had?

"Mmm?" She couldn't speak past the burn in her throat, afraid she would blurt out something unwise and far too revealing.

"Are you hungry? I can bring us dinner anytime." He stroked her hair, following the line of the waves that resulted from air-drying.

"I'm good for now." She didn't want to move. And, heaven help her, she wasn't ready for him to get up, either.

Maybe, if they waited long enough, the feelings would subside. All that churned-up emotion would simply settle back down into her being and sink beneath the surface, where she could manage it again. But then he tipped up her face to his, holding her steady while he looked into her eyes.

She felt herself falling in that blue gaze. Weightless, and with nothing to anchor her.

When he kissed her this time, the charge between them was still electric, but it was stronger. Deeper. She reached for him hungrily, as if they hadn't just worn each other out with passion. He skimmed a touch up her hip, over her belly and breasts, and set her on fire again.

She couldn't get enough of him. Kissing, licking, tasting, touching. She needed him everywhere and he fulfilled her slightest desire as if they'd been made for one another. He slid into her once more. Slowly. Deliberately.

Breathless from the sensual heat, she gave herself to

him completely. No defenses. It all happened so fast, there was no time to resurrect a single barrier between them.

When he drove them both over the edge this time, Brianne felt a piece of her heart give way, too.

Ten

When Brianne awoke the second time, the savory scent of dinner made her stomach growl. The bed beside her was empty, the sheets tangled around her legs. She checked her phone and it was only ten o'clock Wyoming time. That meant midnight for her body.

No wonder her stomach was rumbling.

Slipping on the fluffy white spa robe, she could hear Gabe moving around the kitchen downstairs. Cabinet doors closing. The clink of silverware and dishes. That he'd left her side to prepare them both a meal didn't surprise her. He'd always been warmhearted. Thoughtful. So she wasn't foolish enough to think that dinner came as the result of any new tenderness toward her. Running her fingers through her tousled hair, she told herself to keep things light between them.

And guard the rest of her heart with a whole lot more vigilance.

She stopped by her bedroom for a pair of socks, then followed her nose through the airy Craftsman home. The walls were natural pine log in every room, but the modern furnishings kept the place contemporary. High ceilings and exposed rafters mingled with stainless-steel fixtures and gray twill seating brightened with punches of red or yellow, depending on the room.

There were paintings of Wyoming landscapes in all the rooms. She recognized the Devils Tower and Grand Tetons. As she reached the kitchen and the source of all the appealing scents, the paintings gave way to natural wood cabinets and a rounded island set for two, white tapers already burning. Gabe was pulling a broiler pan with two steaks out of the oven.

"Perfect timing." He grinned as he put the pan between the place settings on the island. Dressed in a pair of low-slung sweatpants and no shirt, he made her mouth water even more than the dinner. "The meat looks pretty good considering I had to warm it up a second time."

Tossing aside a pot holder, he leaned over to kiss her cheek and pull out one of the padded leather bar stools in front of the gray granite countertop. She closed her eyes for a moment, savoring the contact, even as she guessed that he was straining to keep things light between them, too.

"Thank you. I'm so hungry, I might not notice if I was chewing on a rawhide bone." She lifted her glass to toast the chef. "Cheers to you."

He clinked his chilled water to hers. "I'd rather drink to a night I'll never forget."

Surprise nearly made her slosh her beverage over the side. She wasn't prepared to talk about what had just happened between them when she hadn't had enough time to pick through the events in her mind. To resurrect those defenses she needed so desperately.

"Cheers," she said gamely, not wanting to draw even more attention to her post-wedding-night awkwardness. She gulped the water too fast and then dug in to her meal.

Gabe didn't call her on her gracelessness, letting the moment slip past without comment. When she'd sated the worst of her hunger, she searched for a topic to move them back to safer conversational ground, and distract her from how good he looked shirtless.

"Did you let your grandfather know that you've arrived?" As she buttered a slice of crusty warm bread, she realized she'd never complimented him on the meal. "The food is delicious, by the way. I'm so busy scarfing it down I didn't say as much, but thank you."

"My pleasure." Gabe ate more slowly than her, leaning back in the padded leather bar stool to watch her. "I sent a message to my grandfather when our plane landed. I notified my half brother Quinn, who is staying with him, as well."

She frowned. "Wasn't it Ian who was staying with Malcolm? Ian was the one who called you and let you know your grandfather was staying on in Cheyenne."

"True." Gabe picked up the bottle of red wine that they'd shared in the hot tub. He must have gone outside to retrieve it. He poured them each a glass. "But Ian and his wife were expected in Singapore this week, where the family is involved in a remodel of a flagship McNeill property. Lydia, Ian's wife, is an interior decorator."

The apartment where her grandmother was ensconced belonged to Ian and Lydia, Brianne recalled. It made sense Lydia was a decorator, given how beautiful that space was.

"Ian and Quinn tag-teamed staying with Malcolm?"

Spearing a little more salad, she wished she'd had better relationships with her half siblings. It would have been nice to know someone she trusted was watching over Nana when Brianne wasn't with her.

A gust of wind beat against the windowpanes.

"Correct. Cameron helps out as well. From what I can see, Liam's other sons are all very close to Malcolm. Much closer to the old man than to our father, Liam." Frowning, Gabe took a sip of wine as if to wash away the taste of his father's name. "But that's something I've come to admire about them. Even though Quinn, Ian and Cameron are legally recognized as Liam's sons, they don't show Liam any more allegiance than Damon, Jager and I do."

Liam wasn't all that different from her own father. She wondered if Liam's older brother was a higher quality character. Plus, talking about Gabe's family meant delaying discussion of where things were headed for them in this new marriage, which was a conversation she still wasn't ready to have.

"What about Donovan, Malcolm's estranged son?" She pushed her plate aside and leaned back in her chair. "Do you know much about him or what kind of person he is?"

"My grandfather never mentioned him when I met Malcolm briefly last fall." Gabe finished his wine and started to clear their plates. "I'm hoping to learn more about Donovan when we visit my grandfather tomorrow for dinner."

"We?" Brianne hopped up to help even though he tried to wave her off. She rinsed the dishes while he cleaned the countertops. They'd always made a good team when it came to working together.

"Malcolm is anxious, of course, to meet my wife. He told me as much on the phone." He moved around her as she stood at the sink, his body brushing hers in a way that made her nerve endings sing.

He dropped a kiss on her shoulder when he added a plate to her pile of dishes.

"Of course." With an effort, she focused on her words and not the contact that made her want to sway toward him. "Securing Malcolm's favor is the main reason we married."

She said it more as a reminder to herself, a piece of reality she couldn't ignore in her growing romantic feelings for Gabe.

But the effect on Gabe was tangible. He went still. For a moment, the only sounds in the kitchen were the ticking of a heavy wall clock and the howl of the wind.

"Gabe?" Turning toward him, she shook the water from her hands and dried them. "What's wrong?"

He stared down at his phone screen as he stood motionless at the island.

"There's something I didn't tell you about the wedding." His jaw flexed as he met her gaze. "About my other reason for needing a wife."

She didn't miss his word choice.

A wife. Not necessarily Brianne. Just a woman filling the role of legal spouse. A chill came over her, but she resisted the urge to wrap her arms around herself. She wouldn't show weakness now when she was already so vulnerable.

"What reason?" She willed strength into her voice even as it leaked out of her limbs.

He passed her the phone. She glanced down at the screen to see one of the wedding photos. Gabe was holding Jason in his arms and Brianne was clutching her delphiniums and wearing that gorgeous lace dress. At first, she didn't understand what the photo had to do with anything. But then, she spied the caption.

Country music queen Theresa Bauder's ex-husband, Gabe McNeill, takes his revenge on the singer with a quickie marriage to the former couple's gardener.

The photo was part of a tabloid story on some online gossip site. It was the private photo taken by a trusted employee of Ian McNeill.

Passing back the phone without reading the rest of the article, Brianne shook her head.

"I don't understand." She battled the sick feeling in her stomach from being made to look like an afterthought in Gabe's life. A woman not worthy of being named. "What does this have to do with your other reason for marrying me?"

When he drew in a breath, giving her a second to shift the puzzle pieces around in her mind, she suddenly understood perfectly.

"Oh, my God." Her knees didn't feel quite steady under her. She reached for the granite counter reflexively. "This is what you intended all along. I'm nothing more than revenge on your ex-wife."

Regret stung Gabe hard. He'd mishandled things with Brianne, no question. He could see that now. He hadn't intended to hurt her, and yet he'd put her in the most awkward position imaginable with the media. The caption made her sound like she'd been domestic help for Theresa, when Brianne had been employed solely by his company.

Worse, he was responsible for that devastated expression on her face right now. And the dawning sense of betrayal in her eyes.

"No." Shaking his head, he needed to explain himself. Fast. "I didn't marry you for any kind of revenge. Far from it."

But his new wife was already pacing the kitchen, anger and distrust evident in the quick churning of her feet, the impatient sweep of hair from her eyes.

"Yet this photograph was taken by a maid personally employed by your half brother's outrageously wealthy wife. Am I to believe she sold out the McNeills for the sake of a few hundred bucks from a tabloid?" She shook her head. "The McNeills are notoriously private and they pay their servants well to protect their interests."

"Please, Brianne." He set aside the phone and took a step after her. "Listen."

"I should know, right?" She swung around to face him, holding her hands above her head in disbelief. "As one of your employees—your *gardener*—I signed confidentiality agreements, too."

He needed to end this line of argument before she got any more wound up. It was time to set the record straight. "I compensated the maid to distribute the photo to the press."

Brianne's mouth dropped open for a moment before she snapped it shut again. "Without mentioning it to me. Why would you do that if not to get under Theresa's skin?"

"I wanted the nuptials to be a matter of public record as quickly as possible." He ground his teeth. He wasn't accustomed to justifying himself or his actions to anyone.

But in a marriage, he understood he needed to make a better effort at that. When he and Theresa had been together, their lives had run on parallel tracks; they hadn't really connected. If he wanted a better relationship with Brianne, he would have to work on communication.

And, damn it, he did want a better relationship. He'd thought they were already on their way to having one.

"It's a legal union and very much part of the public record even without paparazzi coverage," she reminded him, folding her arms across her chest.

In her spa robe with tousled dark hair spilling down her shoulders, she looked more vulnerable than in her day-to-day cargo pants and T-shirts with her hair scraped back in a ponytail. He doubly regretted not discussing this before their wedding night. He couldn't stand the thought of her believing the worst about him after the incredible things they'd just shared.

"What I meant to say is that I wanted to make Theresa's publicity team and attorneys aware of our connection as soon as possible and I knew this would be the fastest approach." He ventured another step closer. "Can we sit down to talk about this?"

"I'm not sure what there is to discuss." Brianne didn't budge. She simply stared at him from the far end of the formal dining table for twelve cut from a raw hardwood slab. "You used our privately contracted union as a way to get on your ex-wife's radar. Either you want her attention, or you want to make her regret her loss. I can't imagine any other reason you'd do this, especially when you purposely didn't mention the plan to the bride."

Right. The only positive about the situation was that the more Brianne talked, the more Gabe understood why his actions hurt her to this degree. Of course, understanding didn't do anything to erase what he'd done. But seeing the way this affected her—knowing that he'd upset her this much—pained him. When he'd hidden the full intent of his agenda, he never guessed she'd view his omission in this light.

"I can see now why you might think that." He took another step closer, hoping he could salvage this night. He wanted to touch her. Hold her. "But I only used the leak as a way to fast-track the news so that everyone in Theresa's camp knows that Jason is in a stable, two-parent home."

Brianne pursed her lips and tilted her head to one side. "I don't understand why that's relevant. You've assured me, numerous times, that you want to encourage Jason's mom to be a part of his life."

"I do." He wished, more than anything, that his son would know the unconditional love of both his parents. "But despite my best efforts to facilitate visits between Jason and Theresa, she has resisted every overture." He'd never been comfortable sharing the deepest disappointments of his life, but he'd have to offer Brianne a whole lot more than he had before. "Until last week, when she phoned to say she wanted to get together with Jason for a Valentine's Day photo shoot for an online feature about her new album."

Brianne frowned. "She doesn't visit for Jason's sake, but when she needs an adorable baby in her pictures she's ready for a meeting?"

Gabe hated the way that made Theresa sound. But he'd certainly thought as much himself. Truth just stunk sometimes. Especially when it came to his ex.

"I'm hoping that this is a product of immaturity and being excited about all the new career opportunities." He had to hope for the best. "But if she's truly not going to be a meaningful part of his life, I can't afford to have her show up whenever she wants to jet our son around the globe because he's a useful accessory for her public image."

Brianne let out a low whistle between her teeth. "And you think that letting her know about our marriage will make her less likely to do that?"

"Not in the slightest. But if she ever gets the idea to sue for custody and renegotiate the terms we've agreed to, I think her attorneys will tell her she doesn't have a shot of winning Jason back permanently." Gabe needed to protect his son at all costs. And if Theresa refused to put the boy's best interests first, Gabe would be Jason's advocate and protector. "I want the people around her to know what they'd be up against before they try coming after the child Theresa abandoned."

Finally, Brianne nodded. Her arms fell back to her sides even if her expression was still guarded. "I can understand that, Gabe. You want to protect Jason's best interests, and that's honorable. But I wish you'd just let me know your plan to disseminate our wedding photo to the media."

He reached for her, wrapping a hand around her wrist beneath the heavy robe sleeve. "I'm still coming to terms with how I failed Jason when I couldn't make Theresa stay." He rubbed his thumb along the soft skin on the inside of her wrist. "It hurts to admit to myself, let alone share it with you. But I should have."

Slowly, she nodded. "And that's your biggest reason for entering this union to start with, isn't it? It wasn't so much about Malcolm's will as making sure Jason was safe?"

"I can guarantee Jason has an inheritance no matter what Malcolm decides." Gabe would work his ass off his whole life to ensure Jason had security. "But I can't protect my son if a judge decides Theresa deserves another chance to abandon him. Or to break the boy's heart when he's old enough to be hurt by her inconsistency."

Brianne nibbled her lip, her gaze shifting away from him to stare out the floor-to-ceiling windows at the spinning snow squall blowing at the glass.

"And what about a year from now, when our contracted time together ends?" she asked finally, her voice a barely there scrape of sound as she returned her gaze to his. "How will you protect him then?"

Gabe had already been thinking about that, of course. Not that he'd planned on sharing the idea with her. But he'd just learned that keeping his agenda private wasn't a good way to proceed with Brianne. Perhaps he'd be better served confiding the possibility that had been teasing the corner of his mind ever since he got the idea for the marriage.

Gently, he swept her hair behind her shoulder, smoothing his hand over the dark waves still a little curly from their dip in the hot tub.

"That agreement we signed is just to be sure you have everything you need if we sever our union." He'd read it carefully. Double-checked the wording. "There's nothing in there that says we *ever* have to end this marriage."

Eleven

Stay married?

The next day, the shock from Gabe's proposition still circled around in Brianne's mind as she sat alone in the master suite, the clear, bright Wyoming sun streaking in through the windows lining one wall.

She had been too exhausted and stunned the night before to press him about what he meant. She'd avoided responding altogether, redirecting the conversation toward their next meal. And then after her late dinner, she went to sleep. Or pretended to sleep.

Between the travel, the worries about her grandmother and all the directions Brianne's emotions had been tugged in, she simply didn't have the resources to quiz Gabe about his radical implication that they could remain married.

He'd probably been as tired as her and not thinking clearly anyhow. She'd pleaded for a time-out on the discussion and hoped that things would make more sense in the light of a new day. Her mind in turmoil, she'd finally fallen asleep in Gabe's arms and barely moved this morning when he told her he was going to make some preparations for the meeting with Malcolm and Quinn today.

Now, three hours later, he still hadn't returned, but he'd texted her that she should dress casually for dinner tonight since they were taking a snowmobile over to the main ranch house.

A snowmobile.

She was kind of excited about that, even though she worried that casual attire wouldn't be right for meeting Gabe's superwealthy grandfather, who probably traveled with a whole fleet of servants. Not to mention the McNeill cousins that Malcolm had so far won over in his efforts to connect with Donovan's family. Brianne decided to dress in her nicest jeans and a butter-colored cashmere sweater she'd discovered in the closet. Gabe had requested plenty of wardrobe choices for her, his thoughtfulness all the more welcome since she didn't own a winter wardrobe.

But even hours after she'd rolled out of bed, she was just as confused as ever about her conversation with Gabe last night. Would he really sacrifice his chance at true love to give his son stability? Or had he been implying that he could envision his feelings for her growing into something more?

Butterflies flitted through her stomach at the thought of him falling for her. How many times had she secretly dreamed about him?

But she didn't dare to let herself hope. Not when there was a chance he might be thinking of a purely practical arrangement. Already she knew that sleeping with him had been a mistake, sure to hurt her in the long run. He hadn't been honest with her about his reasons for marrying her in the first place, quietly using their wedding photo to solidify his custody arrangement without letting her know. What else might he be keeping from her?

Desperate to divert her thoughts while she waited for Gabe to return, Brianne curled into one of the matching recliners in the master suite and opened her laptop to check the photos emailed by the security company that had packed up Nana's apartment. There were so many images, including a video of the entire operation, but she could easily sort through the items by room, including the findings in the broom closet.

Not that she deluded herself Nana had hidden away anything terribly valuable. But she was curious to know what her grandmother had deemed most important to keep out of Wendy's hands. After fast-forwarding the video through to the broom closet and the removal of the very clever false wall, Brianne set the video footage at regular speed and watched.

The guys in charge of the packing were systematic, holding up item after item for the camera and cataloging what went into their boxes. Sometimes they narrated what they were doing, sometimes not, but everything was numbered and itemized.

"Autographed copy of the Beatles' *A Hard Day's Night*," the first packer said in a monotone for the camera.

"Autographed?" the other packer asked, his hand reaching forward into the picture. "By who?"

"It says it's 'To Rose.' Looks like all the Beatles signed it." Packer Number One—a muscular man in a tight-fitted T-shirt only visible from the back—pointed to the writing on the record sleeve. "Here's John Lennon's signature. And the other three are here."

Brianne couldn't believe her ears.

He passed the record into a box, while, off camera,

the other packer let out a string of soft curses. "Are you kidding?"

She hit the pause button on the video, thinking. Brianne knew that her grandmother had met a lot of famous people during the years she'd worked as a singer. But the Beatles? And were records like that worth anything if they weren't in great condition? Nana's treasures had been packed away for a long time.

When she tuned back into the video, the guys were hauling out a lot more music memorabilia from Rose Hanson's brief career. She'd married her piano player, but the union had been tumultuous and Nana had kicked her cheating husband to the curb within a year; they'd been married just long enough for her to give birth to Brianne's father. And, of course, that cut short her time on stage.

Now those years of Nana's life were returning in full color as the two strangers pulled treasure after treasure out of that broom closet. There were what appeared to be mint-condition posters from performances Rose had given that had been headlined by groups like the Platters and Bill Haley and the Comets. Other posters advertised Rose as the main act and featured photos of her that Brianne had never seen. One showed Rose dancing on stage while shaking maracas, dressed in a gorgeous costume. Rose had given up everything she'd worked for to raise a son who hadn't been good to her. Brianne had her own reasons for resenting her father, but now she saw his selfishness through fresh eyes. And it made her more determined than ever to be true to herself.

True to her heart and her own dreams.

Brianne wasn't certain how much time had passed when Gabe appeared in the master suite. But seeing him in the doorway, his arms full of shopping bags, made her realize that the sun had almost set. Out the windows, twilight cast purple shadows in the room.

"Is everything all right?" Gabe set down the purchases on the floor, then crossed the room to join her, his blue eyes unswerving from her face.

He was undeniably handsome. He had a few snowflakes in his dark hair, and his coat and scarf were open, revealing a jacket and tie with dark jeans—his answer to Cheyenne casual, apparently.

"I'm fine." Self-conscious, Brianne swiped at a tear that she hadn't realized was trickling down her cheek. "I'm just looking over the memorabilia from Nana's music career that she had hidden away."

"Music career?" Gabe frowned, and it wasn't until that moment that Brianne made the connection between Rose and Gabe's first wife, Theresa.

And the very different choice Nana had made as a mother. Then again, maybe that was simply a product of the times. If she had it to do all over again, would Nana still leave her singing career to be a full-time mother?

One thing was certain: if she'd chosen to keep singing, she would have found a way to balance motherhood and work. Abandoning an innocent child would have never occurred to Nana.

"Yes." Brianne turned the laptop around so he could see the still images she'd been reviewing—all the concert posters, photos of Nana with famous people, signed records and matchbook covers. There were a few costumes and pairs of shoes. "Nana gave up her career when she married and had my father, but she kept some of the things from her days as a singer."

Just like Gabe was giving up everything for his son. The work that he liked best. The chance at real love to be with a woman he trusted to care for Jason. Suddenly, his proposal that they stay married made more sense. And yes, Brianne had been foolish to think for a minute he could be falling for her.

Cold from the outdoors still hovered on Gabe's coat. It didn't keep her from wanting to get closer to him. Memories of the night before had been blindsiding her all day long. Vivid, sensual thoughts about the way he had made her feel kept twisting up with the sense of betrayal that had come afterward. The frustration of knowing he would hold on to their marriage for the sake of his child. She understood, but it still hurt to be used that way.

"Wow." Gabe used the touch screen to scan through the photos and pull up one of Nana on stage. "I can sure see the resemblance to you in this."

"Really?" Brianne tipped her head to see the screen better, more than willing to be distracted from the painful direction of her thoughts. "Do you think so?"

"For sure." He sketched a touch along the screen. "Through the eyes and mouth. A great beauty, just like her granddaughter." Turning Brianne's chin toward him, he kissed her lips.

Slowly. Thoroughly.

Her laptop would have fallen if he didn't catch it when it started sliding. Setting it aside, Gabe pressed closer. She lost herself in the kiss. The touches. Gabe had been the man she dreamed about for so long, and the reality of his arms around her was so much better than she'd ever imagined.

And maybe a part of her needed this moment with him to reassure herself last night hadn't been a fluke. That the chemistry between them was every bit as amazing as she'd thought.

"Put your arms around me." Gabe's whispered command told her he wanted the same thing she did.

Wordlessly, she gripped him, her defenses melting away like they'd never existed.

"Hold on tight," he told her, right before he lifted her from the chair.

And deposited her on the nearby bed.

The need for him was a physical ache this time. She pulled impatiently at her own clothes while he shed his. His efforts were more effective, however, his hands steadier as he ditched his shirt, pants and everything else. Her fingers were shaky from how much she wanted this. Him.

When he joined her on the bed, he made quick work of the rest of her clothes, kissing her all the while. Closing her eyes, she allowed herself to simply feel.

He lingered over her breasts, igniting an answering heat between her thighs. She clutched his shoulders harder, needing the completion he could bring. Restless and hungry for more, she arched into him. His groan was gratifying, a rough acknowledgment of how much he wanted her, too. By the time he entered her, she was beyond ready for him. The feeling transported her, taking her higher with every movement of his hips. Every skilled kiss.

She tossed her head against the pillow, seeking the bliss he had shown her the night before, a surprise gift that she hoped to feel again.

"Brianne." Her name on his lips was as tempting as his touches, especially when his eyes locked on hers.

She wanted to lose herself in this feeling. To stay here with him until they understood one another. Until this heat between them made sense and she could give him everything. Not just her body, but her heart.

The realization rolled through her at the same moment Gabe shifted the pace, thrusting harder.

The tension inside her went taut for an instant. Then her release came, hard, fast spasms that made her shudder over and over. Maybe it was the way she moved against Gabe that made him find his own peak right afterward. Their shouts mingled, leaving her breathless and spent.

Leaving her certain she'd never experienced a more perfect moment. Though as he shifted to lie beside her, she had to acknowledge that it would have been even more perfect if Gabe trusted her enough to be honest with her.

If he loved her the way she'd loved him.

Wrenching her eyes open, she knew it was futile to deny it. Her heart had been Gabe's since long before this marriage. But now he possessed the power to hurt her more deeply. How unwise she would be to allow that to happen again and muddle her thoughts.

"We should head over to your grandfather's." She untwined her legs from his and levered up on one elbow, her body still humming pleasantly from Gabe's lovemaking. Except it couldn't really be lovemaking, could it? Not when Gabe didn't return her feelings.

"What's wrong?" He studied her face, no doubt sensing her retreat. His hand covered her hip.

Even now, with her emotions raw and her body sated, she felt herself sway toward him.

Wanting him again.

"This is all happening too fast for me." That was true enough even though there were more complicated reasons for why she wanted to keep her distance. She needed to be true to herself and follow her dreams instead of swooning over a man who would never love her. "I will execute our agreement, Gabe, but I think we'd be wise to keep physical intimacy out of the arrangement."

* * *

Gabe gave the throttle more gas, pushing the snow-mobile faster as he sped the few miles between the guest cabin and the main ranch house.

Riding behind Gabe, Brianne wrapped her arms around his waist and tucked her head against his back, her warmth welcome even though he knew the contact wouldn't be happening if not for the excuse of the snow-mobile ride.

He'd screwed up with her and didn't know how to fix it. His heart wasn't in this meeting with Malcolm, but maybe spending the evening with outsiders would give Gabe a better handle on how to approach Brianne.

Clearly she hadn't forgiven him for not being more forthright about his reasons for marriage. And he understood. But didn't their connection override that? He'd thought, after she'd let her guard down with him again, that she was willing to move forward, but that hadn't been the case. He'd been stunned when she'd pulled away after sex.

He regretted hurting her. More than he could say. But at least he'd been honest about taking a more mercenary approach to matrimony.

Who wouldn't after what he'd gone through with Theresa?

Snow swirled in his face as he turned the sled down a well-marked path. The terrain was firmer here, the snow hard-packed, and the machine picked up speed. He could feel Brianne tip her head back, experimentally extending a hand into the rooster tail of snow that kicked up as he turned.

"Careful," he warned, needing to keep her safe.

"It's so beautiful out here," she shouted over the roar of the motor as her hand slid around his waist again.

He ground his teeth together against the seductive feel of her touch. A touch she wouldn't be sharing with him anytime soon unless he could figure out a way to fix things between them.

He had bought early Valentine's Day gifts for her this afternoon, hoping to entice her to stay in Cheyenne for the next week. After seeing the acres of pristine forests for himself, he wanted to share it with his son. He'd made arrangements for Nadine and Jason to travel tomorrow so they could all be together in this winter wonderland.

But it wouldn't be as fun if Brianne didn't want to be a part of it.

As the main ranch house came into sight, lights blazing in every window of the three-story Craftsman facade, Gabe slowed the snowmobile. Similar in style and construction to the guest cottage where he and Brianne were staying, the main house was bigger with more rooflines and additions. For a moment, Gabe felt the itch to run a hand over the rough, unfinished beams providing support to the building, his carpenter's eye seeing more possibilities in the wood.

But he wasn't a carpenter anymore, he reminded himself as he helped Brianne off the seat. For his son's sake, he was going to form a relationship with Malcolm McNeill and become a part of the man's formidable empire. He ground his teeth, remembering Brianne's words to him just a few days ago.

What if you teach your son that success can be found in things that make you happy?

She had a point, of course. But for now, success came in the form of McNeill Resorts. Until Jason had a stake in the company, the one that he was legally entitled to as an heir, Gabe's personal pursuits would have to wait.

Beside him, Brianne tugged off her shiny metallic helmet and set it on the seat of the snowmobile.

"I hope you let me drive home." She combed her fingers through the dark hair she'd swept into a high ponytail. She was flustered and he knew that had to do with the awareness between them. "That looked like fun."

He knew she was confused about their relationship and he regretted that.

"There's not much I wouldn't give to make you happy, Brianne." He wondered if she had any idea how important she'd become to him.

Not just since the wedding, either.

He was beginning to see that she was one of the most honest voices in his life, and her opinions were something he could count on. That had been true since long before the wedding vows.

Her smile faltered for a moment before she recovered. She was putting a wall up between them, so thin he could see right through. "If you mean it, then please don't let me make a fool of myself in front of your family tonight."

At first, he found it hard to believe she was serious. But then he recalled the insecurity her stepmother had instilled in her at a young age.

"They'll be fortunate to know you." He wanted to fold her in his arms. Kiss her until she bloomed with self-confidence and sensual fulfillment. But he would honor her request about physical intimacy until he could—he hoped—change her mind. "Come on."

He took her hand and led her toward the front door. He'd touched her that way when they were just friends, so he wasn't going to stop now.

"I did some reading on Quinn." Her breath formed a visible cloud in the cold air. "He has his own hedge fund.

I think that makes him wealthy enough to buy and sell small countries."

Gabe paused in front of the wide steps leading to the front door. "Someone once told me that success isn't about making a buck. Remember?"

She worried her lower lip, her uncertainty visible in her eyes as they stood under the bright porch lights. "Does anyone in the McNeill family believe that, though?"

"As long as you believe it, that's all that matters." He didn't like the idea of Brianne being intimidated by anyone in his family. He was already regretting the way their wedding photo had circulated with the caption referring to her as his anonymous gardener.

Why hadn't they simply used her name? She was so much more than her job.

"I do believe that." Nodding, she tucked her free hand into the pocket of her red parka. "Thank you for the reminder."

They headed up the stairs toward the eight-foot-tall double doors with matching sidelights. The design was impressive but his carpenter eye couldn't help but reimagine the space. He rang the bell, then heard the latch turning and the right door swung wide.

"Welcome, brother." The tall guy who extended his hand had the look of the McNeills: the blue eyes, dark hair and same sharp jaw that Gabe saw in the mirror every day.

But even in a relaxed pair of chinos and a dark button-down shirt, Quinn was a shade more refined than the others. Certainly more so than Gabe, Damon and Jager. Quinn's hair looked like it saw a barber often, for one thing. For another, Gabe could spot the difference between his own custom-made shirts and the kind of threads Quinn sported. The personal tailoring took high-end to the next level.

"Brianne, this is my oldest brother, Quinn. Quinn, I'd like you to meet my new wife, Brianne McNeill. Formerly Hanson." He presented her quickly, hoping she wouldn't be nervous.

Her grin looked relaxed enough now. "Nice to meet you, Quinn. And excuse me for gawking, but the family resemblance is uncanny."

If anyone was gawking, it was Gabe. At her. She was so beautiful. So charming and unpretentious with her warm smile. His chest ached at the thought of disappointing her somehow. He's been her husband for a day and he was already screwing up his marriage.

Quinn smiled warmly at her as he took their coats and hung them in a nearby closet. "I understand completely since I still do a double take when I see Cameron with Damon. Welcome to the rapidly expanding McNeill family. Come on in. Gramps can't wait to meet you."

Gabe took in the relaxed decor of the ranch house. The rooms were sprawling and emphasized space over furnishings, although perhaps that was because the place had been on the market.

"Rapidly expanding?" Brianne seized on Quinn's words as they strode deeper into the house, past a main-floor guest room, formal dining room and a bar area, every room well lit.

The scent of a meal hung in the air. There were savory spices and a lemony sweetness, too.

"Sorry." Quinn paused by a series of cowboy paintings in the wide corridor. "I didn't mean that to be as crass as it sounded. I've just been going a few rounds with Gramps, trying to ascertain the full extent of the family history before he springs any more relatives on us."

"You can't blame Malcolm for my brothers and me," Gabe reminded him. He'd come to terms with the fact that he had a useless father years ago, so he was hardly going to apologize for it. Quinn surely knew how it felt to have the man check out on him. "That was all Liam's doing."

"And from what we both know of our father's global adventures, I wouldn't be surprised if he reveals other offspring one day." Quinn shrugged before he continued down the hall. "My frustration today is that Malcolm erased all traces of his older son from our world—no photos, no shared memories, no nothing. And then, twenty-seven years after his feud with the guy, he wants a reunion even though our uncle is clearly still hostile about the split."

"That's a long time to hold a grudge," Brianne said, lowering her voice as they stepped down into a sunken family room with leather couches and a huge, two-sided stone fireplace.

Gabe spotted his grandfather already seated in a chair-and-a-half, a highball glass and folded copy of a New York newspaper on the cocktail table beside him.

"Gramps, our guests are here," Quinn called into the room.

Automatically, Gabe slid an arm around Brianne's waist. Was it a protective instinct? Or simply a chance to touch her when he craved being close to her? He breathed deep, hoping for a hint of her fragrance.

"It's a good thing." Malcolm lifted a mahogany cane in a kind of salute toward them, but did not get to his feet. Silver-haired and blue-eyed, he wore an honest-to-God smoking jacket over his suit. The red-and-gold satin coat was belted at the waist. "Some of my grandsons are getting weary of my company, it seems. I need new relatives to bother."

Gabe drew Brianne over to his grandfather's chair while Quinn followed behind them and said, "Gramps, you're not a bother."

Malcolm winked at Gabe and extended his hand. "It's an old man's prerogative to be a pest to his family. Good to meet you, Gabe. It means a lot that you traveled all this way to see me."

Gabe ignored the extended hand and went in for the hug, giving his grandfather a squeeze around his shoulders. "Truth be told, I was glad to learn my father had quality people in his family. It gave me some hope for me." He was only partly joking. He turned to Brianne. "Granddad, this is my wife, Brianne Hanson McNeill."

"Brianne." Malcolm enveloped Brianne's hand in both of his. "Welcome to the family, my dear."

"Thank you, sir." She leaned closer and kissed the man's cheek. "I don't have much family of my own. I've been looking forward to meeting Gabe's."

Malcolm fairly cackled at that. "You see, Quinn?" He turned in his chair toward his other grandson. "Not everyone is getting tired of having relatives."

"I like relatives just fine, Gramps. It's secrets that I'm not so crazy about." Quinn lifted his drink in a silent toast behind his grandfather's head. "Gabe, there's a wet bar against the far wall if you or Brianne would like a drink. I'm going to check on dinner."

Excusing himself, Quinn stepped away, leaving Gabe alone with Brianne and Malcolm.

"Brianne, can I get you anything?" Gabe moved toward a granite-topped cart with a handful of decanted drinks.

"Club soda or water would be great." She took the seat closest to his grandfather, setting her beaded yellow clutch on the hearth nearby.

While Gabe poured two drinks, he heard Malcolm settling back in his chair.

"So how was your trip, my dear?" Malcolm asked her. "I know it was difficult to coordinate flights from opposite coasts."

Brianne paused a moment, as did Gabe. He glanced over his shoulder toward his grandfather, wondering if the older man's health issues led to confusion sometimes.

"Gabe and I flew together from New York, actually." Brianne answered after a beat. "We thought a trip to Wyoming sounded like a fun honeymoon."

A drink in each hand, Gabe moved to rejoin them.

Malcolm laughed as he retrieved his drink from the cocktail table. "A belated honeymoon, considering you have a son. How old is the boy again?"

"Grandad, you must be confusing Brianne with my former wife." Gabe passed her a glass and settled into the leather love seat next to her. "Brianne and I just got married yesterday."

Frowning, Malcolm picked at the belt on his smoking jacket. "You're not the singer?" he asked finally, peering up at Brianne. "Flying in from LA?"

Gabe tensed, knowing his ex-wife was the last topic Brianne would wish to discuss, especially given their disagreement the night before.

"I'm a landscape designer," Brianne said politely to clarify, though Gabe could see the stiff set to her shoulders. "Gabe's ex-wife is a singer."

Malcolm's frown deepened.

"I fear I have been talking to the wrong person online." Malcolm reached over to the cocktail table by his chair, knocking his newspaper off as he patted around for his cell phone. Turning on the screen, he thumbed through applications. "I got a direct message on Twitter after I announced a visit from Gabe and his wife."

A knot fisted in Gabe's chest. Rising, he went to the older man's side. Gabe glanced over at Brianne, but she stared into the flames snapping and popping in the huge fireplace. Her jaw was set.

"Here it is." Malcolm held up the phone so Gabe could see. "Theresa someone?"

"Bauder." Gabe tilted the screen so he could read without a glare. See you soon, Gramps. Where are you staying this week?

Brianne's head whipped around. "Does she have this address?"

Malcolm shook his head. "I'm so sorry, Brianne. I thought I was talking to—"

"Gabe's wife," she said, finishing for him, her polite smile tight. "It's an understandable mistake."

Anger simmered that Gabe's ex-wife would pull a stunt like this. He thumbed through the exchange, which included directions to the Cheyenne ranch, small talk about Jason—which was rich considering she hadn't seen her son in months—and an assurance she would arrive "soon" for a visit.

"But I would have never invited her if I had realized..." Malcolm trailed off, clearly flustered. "Maybe Quinn will have an idea how we can fix this. Or I could message her—"

"No need." Brianne rose from her seat and laid a comforting hand on his arm. "Please don't worry on my account. It's fine. And considering how little notice Theresa had about this marriage, I don't blame her for the confusion, either." She lifted her dark gaze to Gabe. "I think a family meeting is overdue."

Twelve

Every time the doorbell rang at the ranch house, Brianne held her breath, convinced that Gabe's ex-wife would come waltzing into the living room with her music-industry entourage and couture clothes. Although Brianne had never had much direct interaction with the woman when Theresa had resided at the Birdsong, Brianne sure remembered the emotional wreckage after her defection. Gabe had poured everything into convincing her to return home. How would he feel to see her again? Of course, as protective as Brianne might be about him, those emotions were a double-edged sword since any pain Gabe might experience could also indicate his feelings for Theresa still lingered.

By comparison, meeting Gabe's Wyoming cousins tonight suddenly seemed far less intimidating.

During the cocktail hour before dinner, Brianne received an education on Donovan McNeill's offspring, half of whom had agreed to give their grandfather a chance and shown up at the evening gathering. At least trying to keep the McNeill relatives straight helped Brianne take her mind off Theresa Bauder's possible appearance—and what that might mean to Gabe.

Malcolm had chosen to rent out this particular ranch house because it sat between a handful of properties northwest of Cheyenne owned by Donovan McNeill's family members, making it easy for them to travel here. Donovan had three sons with his first wife, ranch heiress Kara Calderon. Their oldest two boys were twins, Cody and Carson. The youngest, Brock, was the only one of Donovan's sons slated to show up this evening, though he hadn't arrived yet.

When Donovan's first wife died just a few years after Brock was born, Donovan had married local bartender Page Samara, with whom he had three girls, Madeline, Maisie and Scarlett. Maisie had arrived first tonight—on horseback in the dark, which apparently wasn't as dangerous as it sounded if you knew the terrain as well as she did. Dressed in jeans and red leather boots, Maisie's white blouse and long, angora sweater vest had a Western vibe without being too kitschy. No more than twenty-five, Maisie sat in a corner of the living room drinking Chivas with her grandfather and relating the story of an accident in the lambing pen—whatever that was.

Her dark hair was chin-length and blunt-cut, her blue eyes paler than those of the McNeill men Brianne had met so far. Maisie was beautiful, utterly self-possessed and had a dry sense of humor. So, with that being Brianne's first introduction to Gabe's cousins, she was unprepared for Scarlett, the youngest of the siblings, who breezed in wearing an ice-blue lace dress, white go-go boots and dark hair with bangs, curls and crystal barrettes.

"Greetings, family!" She hailed Brianne and Gabe

from the doorway, waving both arms as she spotted them on the other side of the living room.

Quinn was still trying to take her coat—a shearling jacket as long as her dress—yet Scarlett didn't stand still long enough, and came rushing down into the sunken living room with her arms wide.

Luckily, Gabe set down his drink before she reached him so that when she flung her arms around him, he didn't spill anything.

"It's great to meet you!" she trilled before edging back to study him more closely. "A McNeill who doesn't wear boots. I love it." She hugged him again before turning her bright blue gaze to Brianne. "Hi." She smiled crookedly. "You're totally gorgeous, but not who I was expecting. Gramps said—"

"Looks like your ticket to Los Angeles didn't pan out," Maisie said from her spot on the couch, patting the seat next to her. "Sit by me and I'll catch you up to speed on how Granddad mixed up our cousin's wives."

"Oh." Scarlett managed to appear both sympathetic to Brianne and disappointed at the same time. "Awkward but forgivable." She bent to kiss Malcolm's cheek. "I can barely keep track of my siblings, so I give you credit for keeping as many people straight as you do, Gramps."

Quinn dropped onto the sofa beside Brianne while Gabe's new cousins drew him into conversation about his plans in Cheyenne.

"Are you sure you don't want to upgrade that club soda to something stronger?" Quinn asked Brianne with a knowing look in his blue eyes.

"Actually, considering the evening I'm having, I'd better not drink anything that might loosen my tongue." She sipped her drink, feeling utterly out of place in this room full of McNeills.

She wasn't really one of them. And right now, she felt foolish for even making an appearance here tonight. She already understood that Gabe didn't have the same kind of feelings for her that she had for him. Why torment herself more at a gathering that was for family?

Quinn lowered his voice further while the volume in the rest of the room increased. "For what it's worth, I can tell you that my grandfather is mortified about his mistake."

Nearby in the kitchen, Brianne heard one of the catering staff exclaim in French. How funny that the language made her feel nostalgic for Martinique. The Caribbean island wasn't her native land, but it was more home than anywhere else, and right now she felt like an interloper in Wyoming. She wondered how long she would have to remain by Gabe's side before she could return to the Birdsong with Rose and finish her landscape design work there.

As much as it would hurt not to see Gabe for weeks or months on end while he worked with Malcolm, Brianne knew it would be for the best if they resumed their lives separately. They could honor a contract marriage without living in the same home. She didn't want to ruin their friendship, the bond they'd spent a year building, although part of her feared they already had.

"I certainly don't blame your grandfather," Brianne assured Quinn, grateful for his kindness on a day when she felt so deeply alone. "Gabe and I just wed yesterday. Most people wouldn't know about the marriage anyway."

"But he takes pride in the family and knowing as much about each new member as possible." Quinn watched his grandfather for a moment before turning his gaze back to Brianne. "When he first came up with this idea that he wanted to change his will and require his heirs to be married, my brothers and I argued with him for weeks about it. He never wavered for a moment, insisting he wanted more family."

Tempted to tell him that the marriage requirement only fostered fake relationships, Brianne bit her tongue. It wasn't her place, and it wasn't her family. Still, she could weigh in diplomatically, couldn't she?

"He might be glad to surround himself with more family for now, but what if the influx of McNeills results in a spike in divorces because they rushed to the altar?" Maybe she hadn't bitten her tongue as well as she'd planned.

Quinn didn't appear alarmed by the idea, however. "Time will tell. I worried about that, too, at first. But now? I wonder if he knows what he's doing after all."

The doorbell rang again. Brianne's heart stuttered. Would Theresa's arrival be the end of her own tentative relationship with Gabe?

Gabe's gaze landed on her, but she refused to meet it, afraid of how much it might reveal about her feelings for him.

Grinding her teeth, she moved closer to Scarlett in the hope of drafting her into conversation while Quinn got the door.

"Brianne." Gabe's voice in her ear set her nerves on edge. "I'm sorry about this. We can leave if you want."

She shook her head in silence, straining to hear some hint of an exchange at the front door.

"My grandfather will understand," Gabe continued, his hand a warm presence on her shoulder.

"No. Thank you." She couldn't help the bite in her tone. The tension in the room was sharp enough to hurt.

Maisie leaned forward in her seat. "That's not Brock at the door," she announced. "It's a woman."

Brianne's stomach dropped. Still, she appreciated the warning because a moment later Theresa Bauder strode into the room. All six feet of her, rail-thin and lovely. Brianne was tempted to glance at Gabe to gauge his reaction, but she was afraid of what she might see.

Old feelings. Deeper feelings than he had toward her.

"I hope I'm not too late for the McNeill reunion." Theresa seemed to strike a pose on the step above the sunken living room. She wore a head-to-toe red pantsuit, and her brown leather bucket purse contained a tiny white papillon dog with fluffy, butterfly-shaped ears.

Behind her trailed two more tall and spindly companions—a wheat blonde and a glossy brunette—each dressed in what looked like the runway's answer to Western wear. One had a leather vest complete with silver bolo tie, but she wore it with a plaid, floor-length skirt.

"Theresa, this is a family meal," Gabe informed her wearily.

For a moment, Brianne empathized. She understood his disappointment in a woman who had abandoned their son for purely selfish pursuits. Truly, she did. But unleashing yesterday's wedding photo online hadn't done anything to ease a difficult situation with a woman he already knew to be immature. And for that reason, Brianne made no move to help him.

"But as Jason's mother, I will *always* be family, Gabriel," his ex reminded him, motioning her cohorts forward as she started down the steps toward the group congregated around the stone fireplace. "I'm so excited for our Valentine's Day mother-son photo shoot next week in New York to publicize my new album. Have you told Jason about it?"

Brianne could feel the tension and resentment radiating off Gabe from all the way across the room. And yes, she couldn't deny an empathetic ache for him.

"Jason might be a little young to understand the photo shoot," Gabe finally said. "But he will be there."

Scarlett leaned closer to Brianne, curls brushing against her shoulder, and whispered, "Don't worry. Watch me dive on the land mine."

"Theresa Bauder!" Scarlett exclaimed at full volume, hurrying over to fuss over the newcomer's clothes, friends and dog, thoroughly distracting and welcoming Theresa at the same time.

While Scarlett made a noisy production of finding an appropriate water dish for the papillon, Brianne took a deep breath and plotted how to get through the meal. She'd endured her stepmother for years as a kid, so she could definitely handle one pampered singer for the course of a dinner. Thankfully, just then the caterer called them to the table, moving the evening along. Apparently they weren't going to wait any longer for Brock, Maisie and Scarlett's half brother, who had planned to join them.

"You will sit near me." Malcolm's voice rumbled in Brianne's ear. He walked beside her, leaning lightly on Quinn as the group moved toward the formal dining room.

The antler chandeliers were on a low setting, and candles flickered down the length of the table decorated with pink roses in heart-shaped red bowls in a Valentine's Day theme. The place settings were white china, but each woven mat had a smattering of red rose petals. Simple but pretty.

"Thank you," she told Malcolm, "but I can hold my own. You should enjoy your meal."

"I will enjoy it most learning more about you." He steered her toward the chair at his right as they approached the table. "I insist."

"I'll take the flank," Maisie announced, grabbing the seat on Brianne's other side. The woman's dark hair fell forward as she tucked her chair into place. "Since husbands and wives can't sit together anyhow. Scarlett might provide good interference, but honey, I'm the *wall* when it comes to annoying women."

Maisie reached for the bottle of red wine on the table and poured herself a glass. Brianne couldn't resist a smile. She didn't believe in girl bashing on principle, but exceptions could be made for ex-wives who chose to stir trouble. It upset Brianne to think that Theresa's idea of visitation with her child was a photo shoot to promote an album. The defensiveness Brianne felt for the boy made her glad that Gabe was protecting his custodial rights. No child should be subjected to the whims of a parent who couldn't be bothered to make real time for them.

"Thank you." Brianne's gaze went to Gabe briefly. He and Quinn were attempting to work out a seating arrangement for the rest of the table while Scarlett and Theresa were coaxing the dog—apparently named Roxy—to her travel bed in a corner of the dining room.

"I'm guessing she only bothered showing because Malcolm McNeill is... Malcolm McNeill." Maisie sipped her wine, peering over the assembly with a cool, assessing gaze. "Everyone sees dollar signs when his name is mentioned."

"You think so?" It provided a small comfort to Brianne to think Gabe's grandfather was more of a target than Gabe himself.

Because no matter how much she told herself she wasn't falling for Gabe, it was happening. And fast.

It hurt to imagine the mother of his child returning to the picture and wooing him away from Brianne, even though a better woman than her might root for that exact scenario. Ideally, Jason would then know the love of his mother.

"She abandons her kid two weeks after his birth but suddenly wants to be at a McNeill gathering in Nowhere, Wyoming?" Maisie's dark eyebrow lifted before she rolled her eyes. "Trust me, money motivated this visit. Uh-oh." She nudged Brianne's arm and pointed to the corner of the dining room. "Look."

Gabe had engaged Theresa in conversation, and it was turning animated. Her girl squad had their phones at the ready, pretending to be texting but more likely taking photos or video.

Brianne didn't want to be a part of the drama. Nowhere in her contract with Gabe did it say she needed to be involved in a public standoff with his ex. Especially when their marriage was a facade put into place for very specific reasons.

To protect Jason. To help Nana.

It was Brianne's fault for seeing more in the relationship than that. But she didn't need to keep making the same mistakes with Gabe, perceiving more in his actions and attention than what was really there. Gabe didn't need to make a fool of her. She'd managed as much just fine on her own.

Not anymore.

"Excuse me," Brianne murmured to her table companions, who were already engrossed in the developing drama. "I really need to get home."

She wasn't sure that anyone even noticed her slip out the door.

Gabe could not abide his ex-wife insinuating herself at his grandfather's dinner table—after she'd been completely absent from their son's life since mere weeks after his birth—on a night he had planned to make special for Brianne. He wanted Brianne to consider making this marriage permanent. He knew he could make her happy if she gave him the chance.

But he sure as hell wasn't off to a good start if he allowed Theresa and her friends to simply bluster their way into a family meal. Now, as he tried to reason with her quietly, she raised her voice.

"Why would I leave?" She threw her hands up in the air as if the answer was obvious. "I have every right to know my son's family. It's only fair that I know the people he spends his time with while I'm busy pursuing my own career."

"Our son is not here," he reminded her, aware of all the eyes on them. Especially Brianne's. He hadn't wanted to hurt her like this. "And you haven't shown any interest in Jason since he was born, rejecting every single attempt I've made to help you spend time with him. I think it's important he has some sense of family around him, especially since his mother has been absent from his life."

"News flash, Gabe, you should be introducing our son to Malcolm McNeill instead of our *gardener*. Jason should be here, benefiting from that connection." Theresa pointed a red talon at his chest.

Tension turned to anger. He could not allow her to disrespect a woman with a heart as kind and tender as Brianne's, a woman who had always put the needs of the people she loved ahead of her own. A woman he was falling in love with, he realized.

The knowledge of his feelings was a wake-up call, an alarm that sounded louder than any of the smoke-screen arguments that Theresa made. Love for Brianne suddenly made everything else go quiet inside him. His feelings for her had been growing deeper every day for a year.

The emotions had sneaked up on him because he'd seen it as friendship, and a father's appreciation for her kindness and warmth toward his child.

But it was so much more than that. He loved Brianne with a fierceness that wasn't going to go away in a year or an eternity.

"Brianne is my *wife*." The word meant everything to him. It had never meant much to Theresa, he knew, but Brianne devoted more to a fake marriage than Theresa had ever committed to a real one.

That alone spoke volumes about their respective characters. And, sadly, it said something about his that he'd given his heart to a woman who wasn't worthy of it, while he'd given a legal document to another who deserved the world at her feet.

"She is a domestic who stole you out from under me!" Theresa's voice hit a screechy note, and the theatrics of the performance made him aware of her friends trying to capture the scene on their camera phones.

Turning on his heel, Gabe had no more to say to her, or time for her piece of performance art. But as he looked back at the dinner table full of relatives he'd only just met, he realized the one person he needed to see most wasn't there.

The woman he loved.

Heart sinking along with his hopes of salvaging his marriage, Gabe sprinted for the door without saying good-night.

Thirteen

Outside the ranch house, the snow was falling again. Near the front steps, Gabe saw the snowmobile still parked with two helmets sitting on top. So Brianne hadn't taken it back to the guest cottage. While he felt a moment's relief that she wasn't driving alone on unfamiliar back roads in the dark, he wondered where she'd gone. He withdrew his phone from his pocket to call her and noticed she had messaged him.

Your cousin Brock arrived for dinner just as I was leaving. He gave me a ride. Please take your time and work things out with your family. I'm going to pick up Nana and bring her back to Martinique with me.

Not if Gabe had anything to say about it. Pocketing his phone, he strapped on a helmet and fired up the snowmobile, determined to reach her in time to change her mind. What if she'd convinced Brock to take her all the way to the airport? But he couldn't text her back now that he was speeding through the dark void of ranch acreage with only the half-moon overhead for light to guide him.

Brianne had been right. He'd made a tactical error in releasing the wedding photo the way he had, unwittingly antagonizing Theresa when he needed her goodwill and cooperation. He'd thought the strategy would ensure he spoke to Theresa less, but his ex-wife had also been right about one thing tonight—she would always be a part of his family and he could not afford to alienate Jason's mother. The situation with her would always require careful handling in order to give Jason the best possible experience with his mother, without flipping his world around anymore than it already had been, and likely would be again, given her temperament.

Branches scraped Gabe's face as he pushed the snowmobile as fast as it would go. He didn't want to give Brianne enough time to pack and leave, but he knew any truck could speed through the terrain faster than his vehicle.

A few minutes later, though, he reached the guest cottage and found the lights still on. There was no movement outside, but through the huge floor-to-ceiling windows, he caught a glimpse of Brianne moving from room to room.

Relief coursed through him even though he knew the tougher job lay ahead of him. How would he convince her to stay? To take a chance on him again when he hadn't valued her or her opinions enough the first time?

She brought a sense of peace to his life he'd never known before. Well, peace and passion. His chest ached at the thought of losing her.

After killing the engine, he rushed to the front door and charged up the main staircase to her bedroom—

the guest suite where she'd put her things even though they'd shared his bed the night before. He couldn't bear for it to be the last time. Not after what they'd shared. Not after the way she'd captured his heart so completely. This wasn't some friends-with-benefits situation. And it wasn't a marriage of convenience for him—not anymore. This was the real deal, and he couldn't accept that he might lose her.

"Brianne." Gabe knocked lightly on the door frame even though the door wasn't shut. He was unwilling to invade her space when she had every right to be angry with him.

Her suite was smaller than the master bedroom, but similarly decorated. There was a simple white duvet on the king-sized bed. The natural wood furnishings had yellow and red accents. A painting of the Grand Tetons sat on the mantel among a handful of antler accessories. Brianne had her suitcase on the bed, with several items already folded inside.

"I messaged you," she said, moving quickly as she brought a toiletry bag from the bathroom toward the suitcase. "I'm going back to New York to get Nana."

"I saw your text." He wanted to touch her. Intercept her. But he could see the tangle of emotions in her eyes and worried about doing the wrong thing at a time when he could not afford a misstep. "Can we talk first, because—"

"I'm flying commercial. There's a flight in two hours. I really need to be on it." She thunked the bag into her suitcase and headed back toward the closet. "A car will be here to pick me up in—" she checked her phone screen "—ten minutes."

That left him no time. He stalked closer. "Let me drive you instead. Or we can fly back to New York together in the morning."

"I think it's better I do this on my own." Her dark eyes flipped up to meet his. No hesitation. No doubts.

She sidled past him and kept packing, her gaze refocused on her work.

Fear of losing her touched off a new fire in him. "I know I made a mistake when I released that photo to the media. But seeing Theresa again only made me realize how much of an idiot I would be to lose you, Brianne."

"You don't need to say that. You're not losing me. We have a year on our contract, and I plan to honor that. I'll hold you to your end of the bargain, too. But we can't live under the same roof. Not when—" She hesitated. Bit her lip. "Not when the boundaries get all mixed up."

He saw an opening. A chink in her plan and a flicker of hope for them. "So let's get rid of the boundaries. I love you, Brianne. I don't want any more walls between us."

He could tell by her expression that he'd caught her off guard. She hadn't expected him to fall in love with her, but he had. Her lips moved soundlessly for a moment, but then she shook her head. Straightened.

"Perhaps you do love me," she acknowledged. "But what you feel for me is friendship. A camaraderie and trust that's important to both of us and that we don't want to sacrifice for the sake of a contract marriage." She tossed a couple of shirts into the suitcase without folding them, leaving behind all the shopping bags full of winter clothes he'd bought for her. "But that's not enough for the long haul, Gabe."

"I love you." He said it again, all the more certain of it. And certain that she was wrong to tell him how he felt. "And that's not enough?"

"You haven't even had time to grieve for your first marriage. I don't want to be the rebound romance only to have my heart shattered in a million pieces two years from now." She stuffed her arms in the sleeves of the red parka and shoved her phone in her pocket.

He was offering her everything and she was rejecting him? The fear inside him grew colder. "That wouldn't happen. I can promise you that family means everything to me."

"I know." She swiped a hand across her eyes. "For Jason's sake, you're willing to construct the facade of a family. But he deserves the real thing."

"This *is* the real thing," he insisted, knowing that he'd just seen the difference with his own eyes back at his grandfather's house. "I have no illusions about my ex-wife, Brianne. She never cared about me or our son."

"And I do." She sounded so certain of herself. "I always will. But my grandmother sacrificed everything to remove me from a dysfunctional family. I won't dishonor that by sliding right back into another situation where I have to fight for scraps of affection." She pursed her lips. "I love you, too, Gabe, but I deserve more."

He was so stunned, he didn't even move to carry her suitcase for her as she headed toward the door. She couldn't possibly turn her back on him. On the promise they'd made to each other.

"Brianne. Wait," he called out, belatedly rushing after her to try again to convince her of the truth.

To convince her that he understood about real love, damn it.

But she was already gone. He saw the taillights of an SUV glowing red in the Wyoming darkness as she rode away, taking his heart with her.

The next morning, Brianne awoke to the sound of a Count Basie recording playing a few rooms away.

Blinking against the bright sun streaming in, it took her a moment to remember where she was. She'd traveled more this week than she had in the whole rest of her life combined. New York. Cheyenne. New York again.

Resisting the urge to burrow deeper under the high-thread-count sheets, Brianne forced her eyelids all the way open while "Kid from Red Bank" reminded her of her grandmother's love for big-band music. Because who else besides Nana would be playing Count Basie? Nadine and Jason were still in the apartment, but she'd never heard Jason's nanny blasting horns and trumpets. Rose had lived and breathed swing and big-band music, though.

The nostalgia for visiting Nana's apartment as a kid was a small bright spot on a day when Brianne's heart threatened to shatter in a million pieces if she moved too quickly. Gabe had given her almost everything she could have ever wanted last night, even saying he loved her.

But how could she believe that when he'd had his heart torn out by the worst possible marriage experience less than a year ago? According to Gabe, Theresa had served him divorce papers as soon as she found out she was pregnant. He'd refused to sign them until after Jason was born, meaning his divorce was less than a year old.

Who could get married so fast after something like that and have the relationship be anything meaningful? No. Gabe had married her for a very specific reason, and he'd chosen her because she was his best friend.

She'd honor that friendship if it killed her. And judging by the way her heart felt today, it very well might. But she wasn't going to allow her friend to be hurt again. Not by her or anyone else. She could do that much for him.

As for her?

Her heart was toast already. That was no one's fault but her own. She'd allowed herself to sleep with him when she'd had a mad crush on him for over a year. Of course, that would turn out to be a disaster of epic proportions.

Forcing herself out of bed as "Kid from Red Bank" shifted into "One O'Clock Jump," Brianne told herself she still had her family. Having Nana back in her life was more than she'd expected to have at this point, so she should be celebrating that instead of crying over Gabe. Or celebrating that she'd stood up for herself, refusing to settle for less than true love.

But it was better to focus on Nana, since the refusing-to-settle part didn't feel like a victory when it left her so thoroughly hollow inside.

She washed her face and brushed her teeth, then dressed slowly. It was late again—almost noon. Her schedule had been out of whack between the travel and the late nights—first in the ER and then on her honeymoon.

She felt another pang remembering the tenderness in Gabe's touch. Cursing her weakness, she went back to the bathroom to splash cold water on her face and cool the burn of tears behind her eyes.

Heading out into the kitchen, she found Nana, her nurse and Nadine dancing around. Nana, with one arm in a cast and sling, wore a baby carrier strapped to her front, with a fascinated Jason tucked inside. The child stared up at her as if she was the most fascinating person on earth, which Brianne could appreciate, even as she hoped her grandmother was truly strong enough to bear the extra weight of the baby.

"Woo-hoo, Brianne!" Nana called to her. "Look at me! I have a little one to love on. Isn't he the sweetest?"

Nadine stopped dancing, looking worried. "We tried to talk her out of it, Miss Brianne, I swear we tried."

"I've been keeping track of her vitals," Adella said quickly. "She's been doing so well."

"I've got a nurse on one side and a nanny on the other," Rose said, slowing down her moves as the music came to a stop. "I told them I've never been safer. And besides, this baby, he loves to dance." She rubbed noses with Jason, making him laugh.

Brianne's heart melted. She'd missed Jason so much. Her first thought was that she wished Gabe was here to see all the love lavished on his child. And damn if her eyes didn't start burning all over again. She wanted to be a family with him. With Jason.

"Honey, what's wrong?" Rose must have noticed Brianne's expression, because her own clouded over. "You're not worried about me, I hope."

"Here, Rose, let's get you back in a chair," Adella urged her. "I can show your granddaughter those vitals of yours that are better than most people half your age."

Working as a team, Nadine lifted Jason from the baby carrier while Adella unfastened the straps, freeing Rose from the cloth contraption. In the kitchen, Brianne belatedly noticed the homey Valentine's Day preparations. The romantic holiday was just a few days away. Heart-shaped sugar cookies cooled on a wire rack on the sleek gray granite countertop, and the whole kitchen was scented with vanilla and a hint of almond. A glass bowl of pink icing sat nearby, along with a half-dozen jars of candy decorations.

Nearby, at the table in the breakfast nook, there were paper hearts in a long chain, with multiple sets of scissors littered around the table. No doubt the group of women had been working on the heart chain when they got inspired to dance. A few toys were scattered on the spotless kitchen floor along with a plastic bowl and wooden spoon.

Rose had a seat at the breakfast nook while Nadine took the baby to the fridge to look over his lunch options. Adella retrieved a blood-pressure cuff and wrapped it around Rose's good arm.

"Honey, come sit with me." Rose gestured to the seat on the opposite side of the table. "Enjoy this beautiful day in the most beautiful apartment I've ever seen." Rose tipped her head toward the weak winter sun streaming in through the windows, where Central Park was visible. "Tell me about your honeymoon and how married life is treating you."

And that's all it took.

Brianne was mortified as she burst into tears.

An hour later, she'd shared the whole tale.

From her ill-fated crush on her boss-turned-best-friend, to the day she got Nana's letter and Gabe's suggestion they marry, to the basic details of the marriage contract.

"You shouldn't have run out during that dinner," Nana said finally, cutting out a few more paper hearts from the stack of pink, red and white construction paper. Despite her cast, she used both hands well enough. Apparently Adella had brought the paper with her to make decorations and valentines for the retirement home where she worked on the weekends.

Brianne was decorating the cookies, taking comfort from lavishing frosting and pretty candies on the sweets so that *someone*—namely, Adella's patients—would enjoy their Valentine's Day. She hated to think of how poor Jason would be spending the day: getting hauled to a photo studio for a promotional shoot with a woman he barely knew.

"I didn't run out," Brianne argued, digging in her heels on that point. "I wanted to give Gabe the time and space to work things out with his ex-wife."

Rose made a skeptical sound. "Sure sounds like you ran out to me. And his whole family was so nice to you."

"They were nice." From Brock giving her a ride, to Maisie and Malcolm insisting on sitting beside her, and Scarlett doing her best to divert Gabe's ex. "But don't you think Gabe needs to work things out with Theresa so they have a reasonable coparenting relationship?" Brianne asked. But a part of her so desperately wanted someone to give her a rock-solid reason why she was wrong to be afraid.

"She gave up her child—that beautiful, beautiful boy—before she ever laid eyes on him. Doesn't matter that she spent a couple of weeks with him after he was born. She told your Gabe that she wasn't ready to be a mother long before that, and that's okay. Not every woman dreams of having a baby to complete her and make her happy." Nana set down her scissors. "Maybe she's a better person for acknowledging that up front than someone like your own mama or stepmama, who were—excuse my saying so—sorry excuses for parents."

"Maybe so," Brianne admitted. "But it's Gabe who needs to work things out with her. Not me."

"There's bound to be a lot of hurt in that relationship, Brianne. You agreed to be his wife for at least a year. I would say that means you'll fight in his corner, or at the very least, be by his side during the awkward dinner parties." She met Brianne's gaze over her pink paper. "Marriage hasn't changed that much since back in my day."

Worry niggled at Brianne. "You think I chickened out?"

"I think you love this man like a house afire." Rose pointed at Brianne with the safety scissors. "And you're running away from the chance to make a real marriage with him. Call it what you will."

Ouch. Regret stung her hard.

"I was trying to do the right thing, Nana." Had she screwed up? Should she have stayed in Cheyenne and tried to work things out with Gabe? "I just can't bear the thought of him settling for me, you know? Like second prize at the fair."

She'd been selfish. Just like his horrible ex.

Nana put down her paper and scissors and shoved them aside. "Brianne, that man is a McNeill. Women in this city would form a nice neat line around the block for a chance to date him, let alone marry him. He chose *you* because he already trusted you and he liked you. You've been his closest friend. And now, he thinks he loves you? Call me crazy, but I don't know why you wouldn't believe him."

Because she was scared. It had taken her a lifetime to work up the courage to have sex after her first time was such a disappointing embarrassment. Maybe she needed to start taking more chances. To risk embarrassment or getting her heart broken.

"You're right." She finished decorating the last of the cookies and set the knife on top of the frosting bowl. "I need to call him. Or go back there. Or...what do you think I should do?"

Rose pursed her lips. "I've actually got some inside information about this."

"What do you mean?" Brianne heard Nadine singing a song to Jason a few rooms away.

"I've been texting with Malcolm."

Stunned, Brianne could only stare at her grandmother. "Malcolm? As in Malcolm McNeill?"

"He sent out a tweet about the wedding, you know." She retrieved her phone. "I have you to thank for my fancy new unlimited data plan. Because I've had a blast texting with him. Do you know he saw me perform at the Stork Club? I can't believe he remembers, that was so long ago." Nana patted her hair and laughed.

Suddenly, the dancing and the party in the kitchen made all the more sense. Nana had been raving about the lovely day, and she was as happy as Brianne could ever recall seeing her.

"Nana. You've been flirting with my grandfather-in-law."

"Maybe I have." Rose shrugged a shoulder. "At my age, I've learned to wrap my arms around the happy moments and hold tight. Tomorrow, I could be back on Bushwick Avenue. But today, look at me in a Central Park hotel apartment like I'm queen of Manhattan."

"Good for you, Nana. He seems like a nice man. And he's very handsome." Brianne could picture that nice, gentlemanly Malcolm McNeill flirting with her grandmother. And how adorable was it that they had a social-media relationship? "But you said you had inside information about what was happening between Gabe and me. What did you mean? Did Gabe's grandfather share anything about what's happening in Cheyenne?"

She couldn't help the hopefulness in her voice. She ached for a chance to make things right with Gabe, if he would still listen to her after the way she'd walked out on him.

"He did." Nana leaned across the table. "He told me—"

A commotion erupted from the living room. A

door opened and closed, and exclamations went up all around—Jason, Nadine and a deeper, masculine voice that was so familiar it hurt.

Brianne felt hope and fear tangle in a fierce knot inside her belly.

Nana straightened in her seat. "Well, the cat's out of the bag now. Sounds like your husband is home, Brianne."

Fourteen

Brianne's old crush on her boss might have died a swift and brutal death when he'd walked down the aisle with another woman. But as she faced Gabe McNeill again in the living room of the luxuriously appointed apartment— no doubt with eavesdroppers posted at every doorway— she knew that the death of the crush had only made her real feelings for him deepen.

He would always be staggeringly handsome, charming and wealthier than any man had a right to be. Yet none of those reasons accounted for why she loved him. She just hoped she could make him understand how she felt and why she'd walked away despite his love for her.

Because Nana was right. She'd been too scared to take a risk. But not anymore.

Now, with Nadine whisking away Jason to give them at least the illusion of privacy, Brianne and Gabe were alone in the living room. She took in the dark suit he had worn for the flight and the aviator sunglasses propped in his hair. As he set a leather duffel bag on the floor at his feet, she studied him more closely, noticing the weary lines around his eyes from traveling. Or was some of that exhaustion more of an emotional variety, like hers? The need to wrap him in her arms was so strong she had to shove her hands in the pockets of her olive-colored cargo pants. She searched for the right words.

"Gabe—"

"Brianne—"

They began at the exact same time, but were out of synch with one another in every way possible.

"A gentleman would let you speak first," Gabe continued after a pause, plucking the sunglasses off his head and setting them on a sofa table. "But I've thought so damn hard about what I would say to you if you gave me the chance." He shook his head. "I don't want to lose my place."

Surprised that a man like Gabe would ever be at a loss for words, she simply nodded. But even as she agreed to listen first, she half feared she'd made a mistake. What if he pulled the plug on them before she had a chance to take her risk with him?

He waved her toward a pair of high-backed chairs positioned side by side looking out onto Central Park. She took a seat blindly, worry twisting her stomach.

Gabe lowered himself to the seat next to her. "Brianne, I know you saw what it was like for me when Theresa left," he began.

The ache in her gut only deepened as she nodded.

"I fought for her to stay, but not because I was so madly in love with her. I know that makes me a bad husband, but I was furious with myself for falling for a woman so fickle that she rejected our child like that."

The haunted look that passed through Gabe's eyes might always be there, she realized.

Maybe this was something that would always be a part of him. Something he'd never "get over."

Empathy had her reaching for him. She laid her hand on his forearm and squeezed. "I know that was awful for you."

"It's awful for Jason," he responded, correcting her, his gaze holding a sense of purpose and an absolute clarity about the situation. "My feelings for her died, but I would have been right there beside her forever, doing everything I could to be a good family man if she had shown any interest in raising Jason together."

"I know that." Brianne nodded, picking through all the things she'd come to understand and love about Gabe. "It's one of the reasons that I was scared to believe you when you said you loved me. I know you have that tenacity to protect your child at all costs, and to do anything to make his life better."

Gabe shook his head. "Brianne, I fought for you—and I'm going to keep fighting for you—because I love *you*. I love who you are, and that doesn't have anything to do with Jason."

Surprise had her wishing she could rewind his words and listen to them again. Had he really just said that he wanted to keep fighting for her?

"But you married me for Jason's sake," she said, even though that wasn't at all what she meant to say. She needed to tell him she'd love him forever.

"Because I knew I could trust him with you. You'd never hurt him—and I don't think you'd hurt me, either, if you could help it." He took her hand that she had let linger on his arm and flipped it over. Tracing soft touches along her palm, he stared into her eyes. "That's one of many things that I love about you. You're so good with Jason. So warmhearted and easy to be around. I was falling for you long before I should have. But I didn't marry you for Jason's sake, no matter what I spouted at that time."

"You didn't?" Her words were barely there, just a hint of sound, as fragile as the hope that curled all around them.

"Absolutely not. It was easier to tell myself that I wanted you in my life for practical purposes because then I didn't have to face how much I already cared about you."

Brianne thought she heard a feminine whisper from behind the open archway that led into the kitchen, but it might have just been the voice in her head that sounded a lot like Nana, urging her to speak up.

"I was scared to let myself love you." She announced it without finesse or segue, awkward to the bitter end around this man she loved so very much. "I knew you'd lost so much faith in love and marriage—and who could blame you—so I worried you'd always carry some of that bitterness with you. That you wouldn't allow yourself to ever truly love again."

The blue of Gabe's eyes shifted somehow as he looked at her. There was something different in his expression that was special. Just for her. She could feel it, and it wrapped around her heart and squeezed tight.

"Don't be scared." He stroked a knuckle along her cheek like she was the most precious thing on earth. "I'd do anything to protect you, Brianne. I'd never, ever hurt you."

A watery smile trembled on her lips. "I love you, Gabriel McNeill. And if you'll have me back in your life as your wife, I promise I'll never run out on you again."

He captured her mouth for a kiss, inhaling the last of her words and soothing all that fractious, fearful hope, turning it into simple, delicious pleasure. When he broke the kiss, he gazed into her eyes like he had all the time in the world for her.

"And I promise you there won't be any more awkward dinner parties with my ex."

"There will be, though. She's going to waltz into Jason's first violin recital and his kindergarten graduation and expect us all to be very impressed with her." Brianne would find a way to deal with her, to keep the peace while promoting healthy boundaries. "But that's okay. She was right about one thing. She'll always be family. Together, we'll figure out times that she can be a part of Jason's life in a happy way."

"You're amazing," Gabe told her with a soft reverence that made her heart do a little tap dance. "And I might not deserve you, but I'm so glad you're going to give me a chance to be the best husband you could have ever imagined."

"You already are." She flung her arms around his neck, needing to hold him tight so she could feel the reality of him. Of this magical, delectable love. "You gave me Nana."

This time, there was no denying the feminine chortle of satisfaction Brianne heard from the eavesdropper on the other side of the wall. But it didn't matter. It would save her from having to recount the whole story.

Gabe's eyes darted toward the archway as he grinned. "Is it just me, or are we not alone in celebrating this love?"

From behind the archway there was a scuffle before Nana entered the room, holding up her phone and pointing the lens of the camera toward them. "Well, shoot, if my cover is blown, I'd like to at least have a nice photo to send to your granddaddy, young man. He's as invested as I am in finding out how the story turns out."

Brianne leaned in to Gabe and smiled for the picture while Nana's camera flashed. Adella took a tentative step into the room behind her. She was followed by Nadine holding Jason, who had probably only been quiet for this long because he was eating a Valentine cookie. Red frosting decorated both his cheeks. His dark curls bounced as he bopped to the tune he seemed to hear in his head.

"Gah!" he announced between bites.

Brianne's heart was so full she feared she would burst into tears for the second time that morning. Instead, she swallowed back that swell of emotion and cupped Gabe's face with her hands, knowing that all her dreams would come true with this man at her side.

"I love you so much, Gabe." She kissed his lips, but it was a teeth-knocking kiss since they were both grinning. "We're going to have the best time being married and loving each other for the rest of our lives."

"I'm never going to let you forget that you're the only woman to have my heart, Brianne." His words felt so right, honest and true. "Forever."

Epilogue

Seven months later

"Y ou must feel like you won the lottery living here every day," Scarlett McNeill observed between sips of a fruity umbrella drink. She jabbed at a lemon wedge with her straw, jiggling ice as she lay on a beach lounger beside Brianne.

Gabe's youngest cousin had come for a vacation to escape the ranch life in Cheyenne. But her official pretext for the visit had been to help Brianne get the nursery ready for the daughter she was expecting three months from now.

Already, her pregnant belly made a mound she had to stare over when she looked out at the crystalline blue water of the Caribbean Sea. Not that she minded. She still wore a bikini to admire the miracle of a life growing inside her.

So what if she hadn't made much headway on the nursery since Scarlett's arrival? Gabe's cousin made an excellent sunbathing companion. For the first time in Brianne's life, she was taking a real, honest-to-goodness vacation, having abandoned all her landscape-design chores at the Birdsong. Gabe had been hiding her pruning shears on a regular basis anyhow, insisting she rest and focus on baby-brewing.

And with Scarlett around, she had a partner in crime to accompany her to the beach every day. When they weren't reading juicy romance novels or trading opinions on the growing relationship between Rose and Malcolm McNeill, they spent time playing in the kitchen, blending tasty fruity drinks—without alcohol for Brianne and with alcohol for Scarlett.

"That's exactly how I feel," Brianne observed, stirring her mango-passion fruit concoction while she flipped through a magazine full of nursery décor ideas. "Every day is like a lottery win with Gabe."

She had moved into his cottage on the property while he added on a huge addition to accommodate their growing family. She didn't want anything too big, and she hadn't wanted to build off-site since she had so many happy memories right here on the Birdsong property. They'd fallen in love while she gardened and he built things, so as far as Brianne was concerned, they could spend every day that same way for the rest of their lives.

Gabe had indulged her, but he was sparing no expense on the addition to the Key West-style "bungalow" with enough square footage to house most of the McNeills whenever they wanted to visit.

"'With Gabe.'" Scarlett mimicked Brianne and rolled her eyes, swiping her dark curls into a high ponytail with a pink elastic band she'd been using for a bracelet. "You're such a newlywed. I'm sure life with my cute cousin is wonderful, but when I mentioned the lottery win, I was thinking more along the lines of this view. This weather. The exotic flowers everywhere. It's paradise."

Listening to the waves roll onto the shore with their calming music, she had to agree.

"It is just about perfect. But I'm bringing the kids to Cheyenne next winter so we can play in the snow." And at the rate Malcolm was going, flying Rose to New York and Cheyenne for frequent visits, Brianne would need to go there to see her grandmother anyhow.

At least Nana had promised to be in Martinique for the birth of the baby.

"Snow. Ugh." Scarlett tipped her face into the breeze. "Maybe I'll house-sit for you when you're up there."

"House-sit?" A shadow fell over Brianne as her husband entered the conversation. "I'm wondering if you'll consider babysitting, since I'd like to steal my beautiful wife for a few minutes."

Brianne's whole world lit up as she glimpsed Gabe trying to hold Jason's hand before the little sprite sprinted into the surf. At almost a year and a half, the boy ran everywhere, his legs churning nonstop all day long until he fell into an exhausted sleep at eight o'clock every night.

"Mama!" Jason patted Brianne's belly gently, slowing down long enough to very careful with her.

A McNeill already.

Scarlett came to her feet. "You mean I get to play with this cutie?" She scooped Jason up for a kiss before putting him back down so he could run toward the shoreline. "I like that trade."

The two of them squealed and splashed on the beach, dancing along the waves.

"I quite like that trade, too." Gabe kissed Brianne's forehead and then her cheek. Then her lips. And that kiss lingered. "How are my girls today? Do you want to go for a walk with me?"

She squinted up at him in the sunlight, loving the way a light sheen of sawdust still covered his upper arms. He must have been working on the addition.

"I'll go most anywhere with you, Gabe." She started to get up, but before she was off her chair, he was tucking an arm under her elbow and guiding her to her feet. "And both of your girls are happy as can be."

"Good." His smile was possessive and all-male as his gaze raked over her. "Have I mentioned how much I love the bathing suit?"

"You might have worked that into conversation a few times." She grinned at him, giving his side a light pinch. "Especially since all I've done is laze around on the beach since Scarlett arrived."

"I couldn't have come up with a better way to distract you myself. I'm a whole lot happier seeing you in a bikini than battling vines and roots with the gardening shears."

Brianne tipped her forehead against his shoulder, inhaling the light scent of sweat and sawdust that was a serious turn-on.

"Doesn't it feel like every day we've won the lottery?" she asked, thinking Scarlett had really nailed it with that observation.

Gabe slowed his step and stopped, turning to look in her eyes. "Every. Single. Day."

* * * * *

RAGS TO RICHES BABY

ANDREA LAURENCE

To Dr. Shelley—

Thanks for dusting off your MoMA catalog and helping me navigate the modern art references for this book. I never would've found those pieces on my own. I also never expected to find myself watching a YouTube video of naked women in blue paint pressing against a canvas while a string quartet played. Your suggestions were perfect for the book! Thank you!

One

"And to Lucy Campbell, my assistant and companion, I bequeath the remainder of my estate, including the balances of my accounts and financial holdings and the whole of my personal effects, which entails my art collection and my apartment on Fifth Avenue."

When the attorney stopped reading the will of Alice Drake aloud, the room was suddenly so quiet Lucy wondered if the rest of the Drake family had dropped dead as well at the unexpected news. She kept waiting for the lawyer to crack a smile and tell the crowd of people around the conference room table that he was just kidding. It seemed highly inappropriate to do to a grieving family, though.

Surely, he had to be kidding. Lucy was no real estate expert, but Alice's apartment alone had to be worth over twenty million dollars. It overlooked the Metropolitan Museum of Art. It had four bedrooms and a gallery with a dozen important works, including an original Monet, hanging in it. Lucy couldn't afford the monthly association fees for the co-op, much less own an apartment like that in Manhattan.

"Are you serious?" a sharp voice cut through the silence at last.

Finally, someone was asking the question that was on the tip of her own tongue. Lucy turned toward the voice and realized it was her best friend Harper Drake's brother, Oliver. Harper had helped Lucy get this job working for her great-aunt, but she'd never met Harper's brother before today. Which was odd, considering she'd cared for their aunt for over five years.

It was a shame. He was one of the most handsome men she'd ever seen in real life and since he was across the conference table from her, she had a great view. Harper was a pretty woman, but the same aristocratic features on Oliver were striking in a different way. They both had the same wavy brown hair, sharp cheekbones and pointed chins, but he had the blue-gray eyes and permanently furrowed brow of their father. His lips were thinner than Harper's, but she wasn't sure if they were always like that or if they were just pressed together in irritation at the moment.

His gaze flicked over Lucy, and she felt an unexpected surge of desire run down her spine. The tingle it left in its wake made a flush rise to her cheeks and she squirmed uncomfortably in her seat. She didn't know if it was the surprising news or his heavy appraisal of her, but it was suddenly warm in the small conference room. Lucy reached for the button at the collar of her blouse and undid it as quickly as she could, drawing in a deep breath.

Unfortunately, that breath was scented with the sharp cologne of the man across from her. It teased at her nose, making the heat in her belly worsen.

It was painfully apparent that she'd spent far too many years in the company of a ninety-plus-year-old woman. One handsome man looked at her, and she got all flustered. Lucy needed to pull herself together. This was not the time to get distracted, especially when the man in question was anything but an ally. She closed her eyes for a moment and was relieved to find when she'd reopened them that Oliver had returned his focus to the attorney.

Yes, Lucy definitely would've remembered if he'd stopped by to visit. Actually, she hadn't met any of these people before Alice died and they all started showing up to the apartment. She recognized a few of them from pictures on the mantel, but they hadn't visited Alice when she was alive that Lucy was aware of. And Alice certainly hadn't gone to see them. She was ninety-three when she died and still an eccentric free spirit despite confining herself to her apartment for decades. Lucy had been drawn to her radically different beat, but not everyone would be. She'd thought perhaps Alice's family just didn't "get" her.

Judging by the stunned and angry looks on their faces, they all seemed to think they were much closer to Aunt Alice than they truly were.

"Really, Phillip. Is this some sort of a joke?" This time it was Thomas Drake, Harper and Oliver's father and Alice's nephew, who spoke. He was an older version of Oliver, with gray streaks in his hair and a distinguished-looking beard. It didn't hide his frown, however.

Phillip Glass, Alice's attorney and executor of her estate, shook his head with a grim expression on his face. He didn't look like the joking kind. "I'm sorry, but I'm very serious. I discussed this with Alice at length when she decided to make the change to her will earlier this year. I had hoped she spoke with all of you about her wishes, but apparently, that is not the case. All of you were to receive a monetary gift of fifty thousand dollars each, but she was very clear that everything else was to go to Lucy."

"She must've been suffering from dementia," a sour-looking woman Lucy didn't recognize said from the far end of the table.

"She was not!" Lucy retorted, suddenly feeling defensive where Alice was concerned. She'd had a bad heart and a fondness for good wines and cheeses, but she wasn't at all impaired mentally. Actually, for her age, she was in amazing shape up until her death.

"Of course *you* would say that!" the woman retorted with a red flush to her face. "She was obviously losing her senses when she made these changes."

"And how would you know?" Lucy snapped. "Not a one of you set foot in her apartment for the five years I've cared for her. You have no idea how she was doing. You only came sniffing around when it was time to claim your part of her estate."

The older woman clutched her pearls, apparently aghast that Lucy would speak to her that way. Lucy didn't care. She wouldn't have these people besmirching Alice after her death when they didn't know anything about how wonderful she was.

Harper reached out and gripped Lucy's forearm. "It's okay, Lucy. They're just surprised and upset at the news. They'll get over it."

"I will not get over it!" the woman continued. "I can't believe you're taking the help's side in this, Harper. She's basically stealing your inheritance right out from under you!"

"The *help*?" Harper's voice shot up an octave before Lucy could respond. The time for calm had instantly passed. "Wanda, you need to apologize right now. I will not have you speaking about my friend that way. Aunt Alice obviously felt Lucy was more than just an employee as well, so you should treat her with the same respect."

Lucy started to shut down as Alice's relatives fought amongst themselves. The last few days of her life had been hard. Finding Alice's body, dealing with the funeral and having her life upended all at once had been too much on its own. That was the risk of being a live-in employee. Losing her client meant losing her friend, her job and her home.

And now she found herself in the middle of the Drake family money battle. Lucy wasn't one for conflict to begin with, and this was the last thing she'd anticipated when she'd been asked to come today. At best, she thought perhaps Alice had left her a little money as a severance package until she could find a new job and a place to live. She had no real idea how much Alice was worth, but from the reactions of the family, she'd been left more than a little money. Like millions.

For a girl who'd grown up poor and gone to college on a scholarship and a prayer, it was all too much to take in at once. Especially when Oliver's steely blue eyes returned to watching her from across the table. He seemed to look right through her skin and into her soul. She felt the prickle of goose bumps rise across her flesh at the thought of being so exposed to him, but she immediately tried to shelve the sense of self-awareness he brought out in her. If he was studying her, it was only to seek out a weakness to exploit or an angle to work. He might be Harper's brother, but he was obviously no friend to Lucy.

The spell was finally broken as he casually turned away to look at his sister. "I know she's your friend, Harper, but you have to admit there's something fishy about this whole thing." Oliver's rich baritone voice drew Lucy back into the conversation.

"Fishy, how?" Lucy asked.

"I wouldn't blame you for influencing her to leave you something. You're alone with her day after day. It would be easy to drop hints and convince her it was her idea to leave you everything." Oliver's blue eyes narrowed at her again, nearly pinning Lucy to the back of her leather chair with his casual accusation.

"Are you serious?" She repeated his earlier question. "I had no idea about any of this. We never discussed her will or her money. Not once in five years. I didn't even know why Phillip called me in here today. I'm just as surprised as you are."

"I highly doubt that," Wanda muttered.

"Please, folks," Phillip interjected. "I realize this is a shock to all of you. I wish I could say something to make things better, but the bottom line is that this is what Alice wanted. Feel free to retain a lawyer if you're interested in challenging the will in court, but as it stands, Lucy gets everything."

Wanda pushed up from her seat and slung her Hermès purse dramatically over her arm. "You bet I'm calling my attorney," she said as she headed for the door. "What a waste of a fortune!"

The rest of the family shuffled out behind her until it was only Harper, Lucy and Phillip sitting at the table.

"I'm sorry about all that, Lucy," the attorney said. "Alice should've prepared the family so this wasn't such a shock to them. She probably avoided it because they'd have pressured her to change it back. With this crowd, I'd anticipate a fight. That means you won't be able to sell the apartment and most of the accounts will likely be frozen until it's resolved in court. Alice put a stipulation into the will that authorizes me to maintain all the expenses for the apartment and continue paying you and the housekeeper in the event the will is contested, so you won't have to worry about any of that. I'll do my best to get some cash available for you before her family files, but don't go spending a bunch of it right away."

Lucy couldn't imagine that was possible. She'd made a lot of wealthy friends while at Yale, but she'd always been the thrifty one in the group by necessity. Thankfully, her sorority sisters Violet, Emma and Harper had never treated her any differently.

Having her penniless circumstances change so suddenly seemed impossible. Nearly every dime she made from working for Alice went into savings for her to finish school. She wouldn't even know what she'd do with money in her accounts that wasn't earmarked for something else.

"Wanda is full of hot air," Harper said. "She'll complain but she won't lay out a penny of her own money to contest the will. More than likely, they'll all sit back and let Oliver handle it."

Lucy frowned. "Your brother seemed really angry. Is he going to take it out on you?"

Harper snorted. "No. He knows better. Oliver will leave the battle to the courtroom. But don't be surprised if he shows up at the apartment ready to give you the third degree. He's a seasoned businessman, so he'll be on the hunt for any loophole he can exploit."

Lucy's first thought was that she wouldn't mind Harper's brother visiting, but his handsome face wouldn't make up for his ill intentions. He intended to overturn Alice's wishes and was probably going to be successful. Lucy didn't have the means to fight him. She could blow every penny she'd saved on attorneys and still wouldn't have enough to beat a man with his means. It was a waste of money anyway. Things like this just didn't happen to women like her. The rich got richer, after all.

That did beg the question she was afraid to ask while the others were still around. "Phillip, Alice and I never really discussed her finances. How much money are we talking about here?"

Phillip flipped through a few papers and swallowed hard. "Well, it looks like between the apartment, her investments, cash accounts and personal property, you're set to inherit about five hundred million dollars, Lucy."

Lucy frowned and leaned toward the attorney in confusion. "I—I'm sorry, I think I heard you wrong, Phillip. Could you repeat that?"

Harper took Lucy's hand and squeezed it tight. "You heard him correctly, Lucy. Aunt Alice was worth half a billion dollars and she's left most of it to you. I know it's hard for you to believe, but congratulations. It couldn't happen to a better person."

Lucy's breath caught in her throat, the words stolen from her lips. That wasn't possible. It just wasn't possible. It was like her numbers were just called in the lotto. The odds were stacked against a woman like her—someone who came from nothing and was expected to achieve even less. Half a *billion*? No wonder Alice's family was upset.

The help had just become a multimillionaire.

So that was the infamous Lucy Campbell.

Oliver had heard plenty about her over the years from his sister and in emails from his aunt. For some reason, he'd expected her to be more attractive. Instead, her hair was a dark, mousy shade of dishwater blond, her nails were in need of a manicure and her eyes were too big for her face. He was pretty sure she was wearing a hand-me-down suit of Harper's.

All in all, she seemed incredibly ordinary for someone with her reputation. Aunt Alice was notoriously difficult to impress and she'd written at length about her fondness for Lucy. He'd almost been intrigued enough to pay a visit and learn more about her. Maybe then he wouldn't have been as disappointed.

She had freckles. Actual *freckles*. He'd never known anyone with freckles before. He'd only remained calm in the lawyer's office by trying to count the sprinkle of them across her nose and cheeks. He wondered how many more there were. Were they only on her face, or did they continue across her shoulders and chest?

He'd lost count at thirty-two.

After that, he'd decided to focus on the conversation. He'd found himself responding to her in a way he hadn't anticipated when he first laid eyes on her. The harder he looked, the more he saw. But then she turned her gaze back on him and he found the reciprocal scrutiny uncomfortable. Those large, doe eyes seemed so innocent and looked at him with a pleading expression he didn't care for. It made him feel things that would muddy the situation.

Instead, Oliver decided he was paying far too much attention to her and she didn't deserve it. She was a sneaky, greedy liar just like his stepmother and he had no doubt of it. Harper didn't see it and maybe Alice didn't either, but Oliver had his eyes wide open. Just like when his father had fallen for Candace with her pouty lips and fake breasts, Oliver could see through the pretty facade.

Okay, so maybe Lucy was pretty. But that was it. Just pretty. Nothing spectacular. Certainly nothing like the elegant, graceful women that usually hung on his arm at society events around Manhattan. She was more like the cute barista at the corner coffee shop that he tipped extra just because she always remembered he liked extra foam.

Yeah, that. Lucy was pretty like that.

He couldn't imagine her rubbing elbows with the wealthy and esteemed elite of New York City. There was new money, and then there was the kind of person who never should've had it. Like a lottery winner. That was a fluke of luck and mathematics, but it didn't change who the person really was or where they belonged. He had a hard time thinking Manhattan high society would accept Lucy even with millions at her disposal.

His stepmother, Candace, had been different. She was young and beautiful, graceful with a dancer's build. She could hold her own with the rich crowd as though she'd always belonged there. Her smile lit up the room and despite the fact that she was more than twenty years younger, Oliver's father had been drawn to her like a fly to honey.

Oliver looked up and noticed his driver had arrived back at his offices. It was bad enough he had to leave in the middle of the day to deal with his aunt's estate. Returning with fifty thousand in his pocket was hardly worth the time he'd lost.

"Thank you, Harrison." Oliver got out of the black sedan and stepped onto the curb outside of Orion headquarters. He looked at the brass plaque on the wall declaring the name of the company his father had started in the eighties. Tom Drake had been at the forefront of the home computer boom. By the turn of the new millennium, one out of every five home computers purchased was an Orion.

Then Candace happened and it all fell apart.

Oliver pushed through the revolving doors and headed to his private elevator in the far corner of the marble-and-brass-filled lobby. Orion's corporate offices occupied the three top floors of the forty-floor high-rise he'd purchased six years earlier. As he slipped his badge into the slot, it started rocketing him past the other thirty-nine floors to take him directly to the area outside the Orion executive offices.

Production and shipping took place in a facility about fifteen miles away in New Jersey. There, the latest and greatest laptops, tablets and smartphones produced by his company were assembled and shipped to stores around the country.

Everyone had told Oliver that producing their products in the US instead of Asia or Mexico was crazy. That they'd improve their stock prices by going overseas and increase their profit margins. They said he should move their call centers to India like his competitors.

He hadn't listened to any of them, and thankfully, he'd had a board that backed his crazy ideas. It was succeed or go home by the time his father handed over the reins of the company. He'd rebuilt his father's business through ingenuity, hard work and more than a little luck.

When the elevator doors opened, Oliver made his way to the corner suite he took over six years ago. That was when Candace disappeared and his father decided to retire from Orion to care for their two-year-old son she'd left behind.

Oliver hated to see his father's heart broken, and he didn't dare say that he'd told him so the minute Candace showed up. But Oliver had known what she was about from the beginning.

Lucy was obviously made from the same cloth, although instead of romancing an older widower, she'd befriended an elderly shut-in without any direct heirs.

His aunt Alice had always been different and he'd appreciated that about her, even as a child. After she decided to lock herself away in her fancy apartment, Oliver gifted her with a state-of-the-art laptop and set her up with an email address so they could stay in touch. He'd opted to respect her need to be alone.

Now he regretted it. He'd let his sister's endorsement

of Lucy cloud his judgment. Maybe if he'd stopped by, maybe if he'd seen Lucy and Alice interact, he could've stopped this before it went too far.

Oliver threw open the door to his office in irritation, startling his assistant.

"Are you okay, Mr. Drake?" Monica asked with wide eyes.

Oliver frowned. He didn't need to lose his cool at work. Letting emotions affect him would be his father's mistake, and look what that had done. "I am. I'm sorry, Monica."

"I'm sorry about your aunt. I saw an article about her in the paper that said she'd locked herself in her apartment for almost twenty years. Was that true?"

Oliver sighed. His aunt had drawn plenty of interest alive and dead. "No. Only seventeen years," he said with a smile.

Monica seemed stunned by the very idea. "I can't imagine not leaving my apartment for that long."

"Well," Oliver pointed out, "she had a very nice apartment. She wasn't exactly suffering there."

"Will you inherit her place? I know you two were close and the article said she didn't have any children."

The possibility had been out there until this afternoon when everything changed. Aunt Alice had never married or had children of her own. A lot of people assumed that he and Harper would be the ones to inherit the bulk of her estate. Oliver didn't need his aunt's money or her apartment; it wasn't really his style. But he resented a woman wiggling her way into the family and stealing it out from under them.

Especially a woman with wide eyes and irritatingly

fascinating freckles that had haunted his thoughts for
the last hour.

"I doubt it, but you never know. Hold my calls, will
you, Monica?"

She nodded as he slipped into his office and shut the
door. He was in no mood to talk to anyone. He'd cleared
his calendar for the afternoon, figuring he would be
in discussions with his family about Alice's estate for
some time. Instead, everyone had rushed out in a panic
and he'd followed them.

It was best that he left when he did. The longer he
found himself in the company of the alluring Miss
Campbell, the more intrigued he became. It was ridiculous, really. She was the kind of woman he wouldn't
give a second glance to on the street. But seated across
from him at that conference room table, looking at him
like her fate was in his hands…he needed some breathing room before he did something stupid.

He pulled his phone out of his pocket and glanced at
the screen before tossing it onto his desk. Harper had
called him twice in the last half hour, but he'd turned
the ringer off. His sister was likely on a mission to
convince him to let the whole issue with the will drop.
They'd have to agree to disagree where Lucy and her
inheritance was concerned.

Oliver settled into his executive chair with a shake
of his head and turned to look out the wall of windows
to his view of the city. His office faced the west on
one side and north on the other. In an hour or so, he'd
have a great view of the sun setting over the Hudson.
He rarely looked at it. His face was always buried in
spreadsheets or he was doodling madly on the marker
board. Something always needed his attention and he

liked it that way. If he was busy, that meant the company was successful.

Free time…he didn't have much of it, and when he did, he hardly knew what to do with it. He kept a garden, but that was just a stress reliever. He dated from time to time, usually at Harper's prodding, but never anything very serious.

He couldn't help but see shades of Candace in every woman that gave a coy smile and batted her thick lashes at him. He knew that wasn't the right attitude to have—there were plenty of women with money of their own who were interested in him for more than just his fortune and prestige. He just wasn't certain how to tell them apart.

One thing he did notice today was that Lucy Campbell neither smiled or batted her lashes at him. At first, her big brown eyes had looked him over with a touch of disgust wrinkling her pert, freckled nose. A woman had never grazed over him with her eyes the way she had. It was almost as though he smelled like something other than the expensive cologne he'd splashed on that morning.

He'd been amused by her reaction to him initially. At least until they started reading the will. Once he realized who she was and what she'd done, it wasn't funny any longer.

Harper believed one hundred percent in Lucy's innocence. They'd been friends since college. She probably knew Lucy better than anyone else and normally, he would take his sister's opinion as gospel. But was she too close? Harper could be blinded to the truth by her friendship, just as their father had been blinded to the truth by his love for Candace. In both instances, hundreds of millions were at stake.

Even the most honest, honorable person could be tempted to get a tiny piece of that pie. Alice had been ninety-three. Perhaps Lucy looked at her with those big, sad eyes and told Alice a sob story about needing the money. Perhaps she'd charmed his aunt into thinking of her as the child she never had. Maybe Lucy only expected a couple million and her scheme worked out even better than she planned.

Either way, it didn't matter how it came about. The bottom line was that Lucy had manipulated his aunt and he wasn't going to sit by and let her profit from it. This was a half-billion-dollar estate—they weren't quibbling over their grandmother's Chippendale dresser or Wedgwood China. He couldn't—wouldn't—let this go without a fight. His aunt deserved that much.

With a sigh, he reached for his phone and dialed his attorney. Freckles be damned, Lucy Campbell and her charms would be no match for Oliver and his team of bloodthirsty lawyers.

TWO

Lucy awoke the next morning with the same odd sense of pressure on her chest. It had been like that since the day she'd discovered Alice had died in her sleep and her world had turned upside down. Discovering she could potentially be a millionaire and Alice's entire family hated her had done little to ease that pressure. It may actually be worse since they met with Phillip.

Someone would undoubtedly contest the will, which would put Alice's estate in limbo until it was resolved. When she asked Phillip how long that would take, he said it could be weeks to months. The family's attorneys would search for any way they could to nullify the latest will. That meant dragging their "dear aunt's" reputation through the mud along with Lucy's. Either Alice wasn't in her right mind—and many would argue she never had been—or Lucy had manipulated her.

It made Lucy wonder if she could decline the inheritance. Was that an option? While the idea of all that money and stuff seemed nice, she didn't want to be ripped to shreds to get it. She hadn't manipulated Alice, and Alice hadn't been crazy. She'd obviously just decided that her family either didn't deserve or need the money. Since she never discussed it with anyone but Phillip and hadn't been forthcoming about her reasoning even to him, they would never know.

Alice had been quirky that way. She never left her apartment, but she had plenty of stories from her youth about how she enjoyed going against the flow, especially where her family was involved. If it was possible for her to listen in on her will reading from heaven, Lucy was pretty sure she was cracking up. Alice would've found the look on Wanda's face in particular to be priceless.

While the decision was being made, Lucy found herself at a loss. What, exactly, was she supposed to be doing with her time? Her client was dead, but she was still receiving her salary, room and board. After the funeral, Lucy had started putting together plans to pick up her life where she'd been forced to drop it. She had a year left in her art history program at Yale. Her scholarship hadn't covered all four years and without it, there was no way she had been able to continue.

Working and living with Alice had allowed her to save almost all of her salary and she had a tidy little nest egg now that she could use to move back to Connecticut and finish school. Then, hopefully, she could use the connections she'd established the last few years in the art world to land a job at a prestigious museum.

Alice and Lucy had bonded over art. Honestly,

Lucy'd had no experience as a home health nurse or caregiver of any kind, but that wasn't really what Alice needed. She needed a companion, a helper around the apartment. She also needed someone who would go out into the world for her. Part of that had included attending gallery openings and art auctions in Alice's place. Lucy had met quite a few people there and with Alice Drake's reputation behind her, hopefully those connections would carry forward once she entered the art community herself.

Today, Lucy found herself sitting in the library staring at the computer screen and her readmission forms for Yale, but she couldn't focus on them. Her gaze kept drifting around the apartment to all the things she'd never imagined would be hers. Certainly not the apartment itself, with its prewar moldings, handcrafted built-ins and polished, inlaid hardwood floors. Not the gallery of art pieces that looked like a wing of the Met or MoMA. It was all lovely, but nothing she would ever need to worry about personally.

Except now, she had to worry about it all, including the college forms. It was September. If this court hearing dragged through the fall, it would mess with her returning to school for the spring semester. Phillip had recommended she not move out, even if she didn't want to keep the apartment. He was worried members of the family would squat in it and make it difficult for her to take ownership or sell it even if the judge ruled in her favor. That meant the pile of boxes in the corner she'd started to fill up would stay put for now and Yale in January might not happen.

All because Alice decided Lucy should be a millionaire and everyone else disagreed.

The sound of the doorbell echoed through the apartment, distracting Lucy from her worries. She saved her work and shut the laptop before heading out to the front door. Whoever was here must be on the visitor list or the doorman wouldn't have let them up. She hoped it was Harper, but one glance out the peephole dashed those hopes.

It was Oliver Drake.

Lucy smoothed her hands over her hair and opened the door to greet her guest. He was wearing one of a hundred suits he likely owned, this one being navy instead of the black he'd worn to the lawyer's office the day before. Navy looked better on him. It brought out the blue in his eyes and for some reason, highlighted the gold strands in his brown, wavy hair.

She tore her gaze away from her inspection and instead focused on his mildly sour expression. Not a pleasure visit, she could tell, so she decided to set the tone before he could. "Oliver, so glad to see you were able to find the place. Do come in."

She took a step back and Oliver entered the apartment with his gaze never leaving hers. "I have been here before, you know. Dozens of times."

"But so much has changed since the nineties. Please, feel free to take a look around and reacquaint yourself with the apartment." Lucy closed the door and when she turned around, found that Oliver was still standing in the same spot, studying her.

"You know, I can't tell if you're always this cheeky or if you're doing it because you've got something to hide. Are you nervous, Lucy?" His voice was low and even, seemingly unbothered by her cutting quips.

Lucy crossed her arms over her chest and took a step

back from him, as though doing so would somehow shield her from the blue eyes that threatened to see too much. "I don't have anything to be nervous about."

He took two slow strides toward her, moving into her personal space and forcing her back until the door-knob pressed into her spine. He was over six foot, lurking over her and making Lucy feel extremely petite at her five-foot-four-inch height. He leaned down close, studying her face with such intensity she couldn't breathe.

Oliver paused at her lips for a moment, sending confusing signals to Lucy's brain. She didn't think Harper's arrogant older brother would kiss her, but stranger things had already happened this week. Instead, his gaze shifted to her eyes, pinning her against the door of the apartment without even touching her. By this point, Lucy's heart was pounding so loudly in her ears, it was nearly deafening her during his silent appraisal.

"We'll see about that," he said at last.

When he finally took a step back, Lucy felt like she could breathe again. There was something intense about Oliver that made her uncomfortable, especially when he looked at her that way.

As though nothing had just happened between them, Oliver stuffed his hands into his pockets and started strolling casually through the gallery and into the great room. Lucy followed him with a frown lining her face. She didn't understand what he wanted. Was this just some psychological game he was playing with her? Was he looking to see if she'd sold anything of Alice's? How could he even tell after all these years?

"So, I stopped by today to let you know that my attorney filed a dispute over the will this morning. I'm sure Phillip explained to you that all of Aunt Alice's assets would be frozen until the dispute is resolved."

Lucy stopped in the entry to the great room, her arms still crossed over her chest. Harper was right when she said that her brother would likely be the one to start trouble for her. "He did."

Oliver looked around at the art and expensive tapestries draping the windows before he turned and nodded at her. "Good, good. I wouldn't want there to be any awkward misunderstandings if you tried to sell something from the apartment. I'm fairly certain you've never inherited anything before and wouldn't know how it all worked."

"Yes, it's a shame. I was just itching to dump that gaudy Léger painting in the hallway. I always thought it clashed with the Cézanne beside it, but Alice would never listen to reason," she replied sarcastically. Calling a Léger gaudy would get her kicked out of the Yale art history program.

Oliver narrowed his gaze at her. "Which painting is the Léger?"

Lucy shelved a smirk. He thought he was so smart and superior to her, but art was obviously something he didn't know anything about. "It's the colorful cubist piece with the bicycles. But that aside, I was just kidding. Even if I win in court—and I doubt I will—I wouldn't sell any of Alice's art."

He glanced over her shoulder at the Léger and shrugged before moving to the collection of cream striped sofas. He sat down, manspreading across the loveseat in a cocky manner that she found both infuriating and oddly intriguing. He wore his confidence well, but he seemed too comfortable here, as though he were already planning on moving in to the place Lucy had called home for years.

"And why is that?" he asked. "I would think most people in your position would be itching to liquidate the millions in art she hoarded here."

She sighed, not really in the mood to explain herself to him, but finding she apparently had nothing better to do today. "Because it meant too much to her. You may have been too busy building your computer empire to know this, but these pieces were her lover and her children. She carefully selected each piece in her collection, gathering the paintings and sculptures that spoke to her because she couldn't go out to see them in the museums. She spent hours talking to me about them. If she saw it in her heart to leave them to me, selling them at any price would be a slap in the face."

"What would you do with them, then?"

Lucy leaned against the column that separated the living room from the gallery space. "I suppose that I would loan most of them out to museums. The Guggenheim had been after Alice for months to borrow her Richter piece. She always turned them down because she couldn't bear to look at the blank spot on the wall where it belonged."

"So you'd loan all of them out?" His heavy brow raised for the first time in genuine curiosity.

Lucy shook her head. "No, not all of them. I would keep the Monet."

"Which one is that?"

She swallowed her frustration and pointed through the doorway to the piece hanging in the library. *"Irises in Monet's Garden,"* she said. "You did go to college, didn't you? Didn't you take any kind of liberal studies classes? Maybe visit a museum in your life?"

At that, Oliver laughed, a low, throaty rumble that unnerved her even as it made her extremely aware of her whole body. Once again, her pulse sped up and her mouth went so dry she couldn't have managed another smart remark.

She'd never had a reaction to a man like that before. Certainly not in the last five years where she'd basically lived like her ninety-year-old client. Her body was in sore need of a man to remind her she was still in her twenties, but Oliver was *not* the one. She was happy to have distance between them and hoped to keep it that way.

"You'd be surprised," Oliver said, pushing himself up from the couch. He felt like he was a piece on display with her standing there, watching him from the doorway. "I've been to several museums in my years, and not just on those painful school field trips. Mostly with Aunt Alice, actually, in the days when she still left her gilded prison. I never really cared much about the art, but you're right, she really did love it. I liked listening to her talk about it."

He turned away from Lucy and strolled over to the doorway to the library. There, hanging directly in front of the desk so it could be admired, was a blurry painting, about two and a half feet by three feet. He took a few steps back from it and squinted, finally being able to make out the shapes of flowers from a distance. He supposed to some people it was a masterpiece, but to him it was just a big mess on a canvas that was only important to a small group of rich people.

Even then, he *did* know who Monet was. And Van Gogh and Picasso. There was even a Jackson Pollock hanging in the lobby of his corporate offices, but that was his father's purchase. Probably Aunt Alice's suggestion. He didn't recognize the others she'd mentioned, but he wasn't entirely without culture. Aunt Alice had taken him to the museums more times than he could count. It was just more fun to let Lucy think he didn't know what she was talking about.

When she blushed, the freckles seemed to fade away against the crimson marring her pale skin. And the more irritated she got, the edges of her ears and her chest would flush pink as well.

With her arms crossed so defensively over her chest, it drew her rosy cleavage to his attention. In that area, she had the cute barista beat. Lucy wasn't a particularly curvy woman—she was on the slim side. Almost boyish through the hips. But the way she was standing put the assets she did have on full display with her clingy V-neck sweater.

"Irises are my mother's favorite flower," Lucy said as she followed him into the library, oblivious to the direction of his thoughts.

Or perhaps not. She kept a few feet away from him, which made him smile. She was so easy to fluster. It made him want to seek out other ways to throw her off guard. He wondered how she would react when she was at the mercy of his hands and mouth on her body.

"I've always appreciated this piece for its sentimental value."

When Oliver turned to look at her, he found Lucy

was completely immersed in her admiration of the painting. He almost felt guilty for thinking about ravishing her while she spoke about her mother. Almost.

It wasn't like he would act on the compulsion, anyway. His lawyer would have a fit if he immediately seduced the woman he'd decided to sue the day before. He did want to get to know her better, though. Not because he was curious about her, but because he wanted to uncover her secrets. He knew what Harper and Aunt Alice had thought of her, but he was after the truth.

This sweet-looking woman with the blushing cheeks and deep appreciation of art was a scam artist and he was going to expose her, just like he should've exposed Candace before his father was left in ruins with a toddler. He was too late to protect Aunt Alice, but that didn't mean he couldn't put things right.

Turning to look at Lucy, he realized she was no longer admiring the painting, but looking at him with a curious expression on her face. "What?" he asked.

"I asked what you thought of it."

He turned back to the painting and shrugged. "It's a little sloppy. How much is it worth?"

"Your aunt bought it many years ago at a lower price, but if it went to auction today…probably as much as this apartment."

That caught his attention. Oliver turned back to the wall, looking for a reason why this little painting would be worth so much. "That's ridiculous." And he meant it. "No wonder my cousin Wanda was so upset about you getting all of Aunt Alice's personal belongings as well as the cash. She's got a fortune's worth of art in here."

Lucy didn't bother arguing with him. "It was her passion. And it was mine. That's why we got along so well. Perhaps why she decided to leave it to me. I would appreciate it instead of liquidating it all for the cash."

Oliver twisted his lips in thought. It sounded good, but it was one thing to leave a friend with common interests a token. A half-a-billion-dollar estate was something completely different. "Do you really think that's all it was?"

She turned to him with a frown. "What is that supposed to mean?"

"I mean, do you honestly expect everyone to believe that she just up and changed her will to leave her employee everything instead of her family, and you had nothing to do with it? You just had *common interests*?"

Lucy's dark eyes narrowed at him, and her expression hardened. "Yes, that's what I expect everyone to believe because that is what happened. I'm not sure why you're such a cynical person, but not everyone in the world is out there to manipulate someone else. I'm certainly not."

This time, Lucy's sharp barb hit close to home. Perhaps he was pessimistic and became that way because life had taught him to be, but that didn't mean he was wrong about her. "I'm not cynical, Lucy, I simply have my eyes open. I'm not blinded by whatever charms you've worked on my sister and my aunt. I see a woman with nothing walking away from this situation with half a billion dollars. You had to have done something. She didn't leave the housekeeper anything. You're telling me you're just that special?"

The hard expression on Lucy's face started to crumble at his harsh words, making him feel a pang of guilt for half a second. Of course, she could just be trying to manipulate him like she did everyone else.

"Not at all," she said with a sad shake of her head. "I don't think I'm special. I'm as ordinary as people come. I wish Alice had explained to me and everyone else why she was doing what she did, but she left that as a mystery for us all. There's nothing I can do about it. You can take me to court and try to overturn her last wishes. Maybe you will be successful. I can't control that. But know that no matter what the judge decides, I had nothing to do with it. Just because you don't believe it, doesn't make it any less true."

Boy, she was good. The more she talked, the more he wanted to believe her. There was a sincerity in her large doe eyes and unassuming presence. It was no wonder everyone seemed to fall prey to her charms. He'd thought at first she wasn't as skilled and cunning as Candace, but he was wrong. She'd simply chosen to target an older, vulnerable woman instead of a lonely, vulnerable man. A smarter choice, if you asked his opinion. She didn't have to pretend to be in love with a man twice her age.

"You're very good." He spoke his thoughts aloud and took a step closer to her. "When I first saw you at Phillip's office with your big eyes and your innocent and indignant expression, I thought perhaps you were an amateur that I could easily trip up, but now I see I'm going up against a professional con artist." He took another step, leaving only inches between them. "But that doesn't mean you're going to win."

Lucy didn't pull back this time; she held her ground. "The mistake you're making is thinking that I care, Oliver."

"You're honestly going to stand there and tell me that you don't care whether you get the apartment, the Monet and everything else?"

"I am," she said with a defiant lift of her chin. Her dark eyes focused on him, drawing him into their brown depths. "See, the difference between you and me is that I've never had anything worth losing. If I walk out this door with nothing more than I came in with, my life goes on as usual. And that's what I expect to happen. To be honest, I can't even imagine having that kind of money. This whole thing seems like a dream I'm going to wake up from and I'll go back to being Lucy, the broke friend that can never afford the girls trips and expensive clothes her friends wear. Things like this don't happen to people like me, and the people in the world with all the money and power— people like you—are happy to keep it that way."

"You're saying it's my fault if you don't get your way?"

"Not my way. Alice's way. And yes. You're the only one in the family that lawyered up."

That was because he was the only one in the family with nerve. "Someone had to."

"Well, then, you've made your choices, Oliver, and so have I. That said, I'm not sure there's much else for us to say to one another. I think it's time for you to go."

Oliver raked his gaze over her stern expression and smirked. He didn't have to leave. She had no more claim on the apartment than he did at this point. But it was too soon to push his luck. Besides, the more time he spent with her, the softer his resolve to crush her became. The closer he got, the more interested he was in breathing in the scent of her shampoo and touching her hand to see if her skin was as soft as it appeared. He would have to tread very carefully where Lucy was concerned or he'd get lured into her web just like the others.

"I think you're right," he said, pulling away from her before he got even closer and did something he might regret, like kiss her senseless so he could feel her body melt into his. He walked through the gallery to the foyer and opened the door that led to the elevator.

"Until we meet again, Lucy Campbell."

Three

"I don't know why you insisted on me wearing this dress, Harper. It's a baby shower, not a cocktail party."

As Lucy and Harper walked up the driveway of the sprawling Dempsey estate, she looked down at the white strapless frock her friend had practically pushed on her. It had taken nearly two hours to drive out to the property where Emma had grown up, and Lucy had doubted her clothing decision the whole way. Why they couldn't have the party at the Dempseys' apartment in Manhattan, she didn't know.

Harper shook her head and dismissed Lucy's concerns, as usual. "That J. Mendel dress is perfect for you. You look great. It's always a good time to look great."

"You need to print that on your business cards," Lucy quipped.

Even then, she felt incredibly overdressed for a baby

shower, but Harper insisted they dress up. It was a couples shower for their friend Emma and her new husband, Jonah. Since they were both single and the event was coed, Harper had got it in her head that they should look even cuter than usual, in case there were some single friends of Jonah's there as well. At least that was what she'd said.

"You need to remember you're not just the poor friend from Yale anymore, Lucy. You have to start acting like someone important because you are someone important. You were before the money, but now you have no excuse but to show the world how fabulous you are."

Lucy sighed and shifted the wrapped gift in her arms. "I'm still the poor friend from Yale and I refuse to believe otherwise until there's cash in my hand and in my bank accounts. Thanks to your brother, I may not get a dime."

"We'll see about that," Harper said with a smirk curling her peach lips.

Oliver had made that same face when he visited the apartment the other day. The brief encounter had left her rattled to her core. Thankfully, no one else had decided to drop in unannounced. But seeing that expression on her friend brought an anxious ache back to her stomach. She intended to get some cake in her belly as soon as possible to smother it.

"Who does a couples baby shower anyway?" Lucy asked. "Any guy I know would hate this kind of thing."

"Knowing Emma and her mother, this will be anything but the usual baby shower. It's more of an event."

Lucy paused at the steps leading up to the Dempsey

mansion and caught the distant sounds of string music playing. Live music for a baby shower? They'd passed dozens of cars parked along the drive up to the house from the gate. "I think you may be right."

They stepped inside the house together, taking the butler's directions through the ornately decorated house to the ballroom. Lucy bit her tongue at the mention of a ballroom. Who, other than the house in the board game *Clue*, had an actual ballroom?

Apparently, the Dempseys.

They rounded a corner and were bombarded by the sound of a huge party in progress. Lucy was instantly aware that this was not the punch-and-cake gathering with cheesy baby shower games she was expecting. A string quartet was stationed in the corner on a riser. Round tables were scattered throughout the room with sterling gray linens and centerpieces filled with flowers in various shades of pink.

A serpentine table of food curved around the far corner of the space, flanked by a silver, three-tiered punch fountain on one end and an even taller cake on the other end. A mountain of gifts were piled onto tables in the opposite corner. There were easily a hundred people in the room milling around, and thankfully, most of them were dressed as nicely as she and Harper were.

Lucy breathed a sigh of relief for Harper's fashion advice. At least for some of it. Harper had tried to get her to wear a piece of Alice's jewelry—a large diamond cocktail ring that would've matched her dress splendidly, she said—but Lucy had refused. It wasn't hers yet. She wasn't touching a thing of Alice's until the deal was done.

"I think Emma's mother went a little overboard for this, don't you?" Harper leaned in to whisper. "I guess since Emma and Jonah eloped in Hawaii, Pauline had to get her over-the-top party somehow."

Lucy could only nod absently as she took in the crowd. Being friends with Emma, Harper and Violet in college had been easy because they'd all lived in their sorority house and their economic differences were less pronounced. After their years at Yale, they all returned to New York, struggling to start their careers and make names for themselves. It leveled the playing field for the friends. This was one of the few times she'd been painfully reminded that she came from a very different world than them. She tried to avoid those scenarios, but this was one party she couldn't skip. Even with Alice's fortune, she'd still be a nobody from a small town in Ohio that no one had ever heard of.

"I see someone I need to talk to. Are you okay by yourself for a while?" Harper asked. She was always good, as were all the girls, about making sure Lucy was comfortable in new settings that were second nature to them.

"Absolutely, go," Lucy said with a smile.

As Harper melted into the crowd, Lucy decided to take her gift to the table flanked with security guards. There were apparently nicer gifts there than the pink onesies with matching hats she had picked out from the registry. One of them had a sterling silver Tiffany rattle tied to the package like a bow.

Without immediately spying anyone she knew, she decided to get a glass of punch. At least she would look like she was participating in the event.

"Lucy!" A woman's voice shouted at her as she finished filling up her crystal punch glass. She turned around to see a very pregnant Emma with a less-pregnant Violet.

"You two are a pair," Lucy said.

"I know," Emma agreed with a groan as she stroked her belly. "Four weeks to go."

"I wish I only had four weeks." Violet sighed. "Instead I have four months."

Just after Emma and Jonah announced their engagement and pregnancy to the world, Violet had piped up with a similar announcement. It had come as a surprise to everyone, including Violet, that she was expecting. She and her boyfriend had been on and off for a while, but finding out she was pregnant a few weeks after she'd been in a serious taxi accident had sealed the deal. Her boyfriend, Beau, insisted he wasn't losing her again and they got engaged. The difference was that Violet wanted to set a date after the baby was born. She, unlike Emma, wanted the big wedding with the fancy dress and wasn't about to do it with a less-than-perfect figure.

"Speaking of how far along you are," Lucy said, "how did the ultrasound go?"

Violet's cheeks blushed as she turned to Emma. "I'm not announcing anything because it's Emma and Jonah's night, but I'll tell you both, and Harper when I see her. We're having a boy."

"Oh!" Emma squealed and wrapped her arms around Violet. "Our kids are going to get married," she insisted.

Lucy suffered through a round of giggly hugs and baby talk. Since Violet discovered she was pregnant, it had been all the two of them could talk about. Lucy understood. It was a big deal for both of them. She just felt miserably behind the curve when it came to her friends, in more ways than one. She hadn't even dated since college. Marriage and children were a far-off fantasy she hardly had time to consider.

"Darling." An older woman with Emma's coloring interrupted their chat. It was her mother, Pauline Dempsey. "I want to introduce you to a couple business acquaintances of your father, and then I'd like you and Jonah to join us up front for a toast."

Emma smiled apologetically and let her mother drag her away. Violet turned to Lucy with a conspiratorial look on her face. "So... Harper said you have some news."

Lucy twisted her lips in concern. A part of her didn't want to talk about Alice's estate until she knew what was going to happen. She didn't want to get her hopes—or anyone else's—up for nothing. Then again, keeping a secret in her circle of friends was almost impossible. "It's not news," she insisted. "At least not yet."

"I don't know," Violet teased. "Harper said it was huge. Are you pregnant?"

Her eyes went wide. "No, of course I'm not pregnant. You have to have sex to get pregnant."

Violet shrugged. "Not necessarily. I mean, I don't remember getting pregnant. I assume sex was involved."

"Yes, well, you were in a car accident and forgot a week of your life. I'm pretty sure that missing week included you and Beau making that little boy." Lucy was suddenly desperate to change the subject. "Any names picked out yet?"

"Beau wants a more traditional Greek name, but I'm

not sold. I was thinking something a little more modern, like Lennox or Colton."

"Where is Beau, anyway?" Lucy asked. "This is a couples shower, right?"

"Yes, well, he's been working a lot lately. Finding out we were pregnant put him in a tailspin. He's been empire-building ever since. This isn't his cup of tea, anyway."

Lucy nodded, but didn't say anything. As a friend, she tried to be supportive, but she didn't like Beau. He and Violet argued too much and their relationship was so up and down. It was hard on Violet. He seemed to rededicate himself after her accident, and later, when he found out she was having a baby, but Lucy still worried about her friend. She wanted it to work out like the fairy tales claimed. But fortunately, with or without Beau, Violet would be fine. She was the sole heir to her family's Greek shipping fortune and could easily handle raising her son on her own if she had to.

"I'm going to sit down for a bit. My feet are swelling something fierce and I'm only halfway through this pregnancy," Violet complained. "Come find me in a bit. I still want to hear about this big news of yours."

Lucy waved Violet off and took a sip of her punch.

"Big news of yours?" A familiar baritone voice reached her ears just as her mouth filled with punch. "Do tell."

Lucy turned around and felt that anxiety from earlier hit her full force. She swallowed the gulp of punch before she could spit it everywhere and ruin her white dress. She wished it were spiked; it would help steel her nerves for round two of this fight.

Oliver Drake was standing right behind her with a ridiculously pleased grin on his face.

Oliver was willing to admit when he was wrong, and his prior opinions of Lucy's attractiveness were way off base.

Where had this version of Lucy been hiding? He had no doubt that Harper, his fashion-conscious sister, had gotten ahold of her tonight.

Lucy's dark blond hair was swirled up into a French twist with a rhinestone comb holding it in place. Her dress was white and cream—a color combination that on most women, brides included, made them look ill. For some reason, Lucy seemed to glow. It was off the shoulder, and with her hair up, it showcased her swan-like neck and the delicate line of her collarbones.

It was hard to focus on that with the expression on her face, however. The rosy shade of her lipstick highlighted the drop of her jaw as she looked at him in panic. She hadn't been expecting him here tonight and he quite liked that. Catching her off guard was proving to be the highlight of his week lately.

"This big news," he repeated. "I hope it's something exciting to help you get over the shock of inheriting, then losing, all that money."

At his smart words, her lips clamped shut and her dark brow knitted together. When she wrinkled her nose, he noticed that only a few of her more prominent freckles were visible with her makeup on. He found he quite missed them.

"You've got a lot of nerve, Oliver Drake! How dare you come to the party for one of my best friends, just so you can harass me! Is nothing sacred to you? Tonight is about Emma and Jonah, not about your ridiculous vendetta against me."

Oliver looked around at the dozen or so people who turned and took notice of her loud, sharp words. Apparently their banter was about to escalate to fighting tonight. He had no plans to cause a scene here, despite what she seemed to think. Reaching out, he snatched up her wrist and tugged her behind him. There were French doors not far from where they were standing, so he made a beeline through them and out onto the large balcony that overlooked the east grounds of the Dempsey estate.

"You let go of me!" Lucy squealed as he hauled her outside, the end of her tirade cut off from the guests inside by the slamming of the door. Thankfully, the weather was a touch too chilly for anyone to be out there to overhear the rest of their argument.

"Is nothing sacred to *you*?" He turned her question on her. "Stop causing a scene in front of my friends and colleagues."

"Me?" Lucy yanked her wrist from his clutch. "You started this. And they're *my* friends and colleagues, not yours."

Oliver noticed the palm of his hand tingled for a moment at the separation of his skin from hers. He ached to reach out and touch her again, but that was the last thing he needed to do. Especially right now when she was yelling at him. "Yes, you. And you don't get to lay claim on everyone inside just like you laid claim to my aunt's fortune. They're my friends, too."

"I didn't lay claim to your aunt's fortune. I would never presume to do that, even if I had the slightest reason to think I should get it. Despite what you seem to think, it was a gift, Oliver. It's a kind thing some people do, not that you would know what that's like."

"I am kind," he insisted. The collar of his shirt was suddenly feeling too tight. Oliver didn't understand why she was able to get under his skin so easily. He'd felt his blood pressure start to rise the moment he'd seen her in that little dress. And then, after he touched her... "You don't know anything about me."

"And you don't know anything about me!"

"I know that yelling is very unbecoming of a lady."

"And so is manhandling someone."

"You're correct," Oliver conceded and crossed his arms over his chest to bury his tingling hand. "I'm not a lady."

Lucy's pink lips scrunched together in irritation, although there was the slightest glimmer of amusement in her eyes. Could she actually have a sense of humor? "You're not a gentleman either. You're a pain in my a—"

"Hey, now!" Oliver interrupted. Ixnay that thought on the sense of humor. "I didn't come here to start a fight with you, Lucy."

She took a deep breath and looked him over in his favorite charcoal suit. He'd paired a pink tie with it tonight in a nod to Jonah's baby, but he doubted Lucy would be impressed by the gesture. At the moment, he wanted to tug it off and give himself some room to breathe, but he wouldn't give her the satisfaction of seeing him react to her, good or bad.

"So why are you here?" she asked.

"I'm here because I was invited. Jonah and I are friends from back in prep school. Did Harper not tell you that?"

"No, she didn't." Lucy looked through the window with a frown lining her face, then down at her dress. It was short, ending a few inches above her knee with a band of iridescent white beads that caught the light as she moved. "Although a lot of other things make sense now."

Oliver couldn't help the chuckle that burst out of him in the moment. "You actually thought I'd driven two hours out of my way just to come here and stalk you tonight?"

Lucy pouted her bottom lip at his laughter and turned toward the stone railing of the balcony. "Well... it's not like we've ever run into each other before this. You have to admit it seems suspicious that you keep showing up where I am."

He stifled the last of his snickering and stood beside her at the railing, their bodies almost touching. He could feel the heat of her bare skin less than an inch away. "Maybe you're right," he admitted.

Oliver turned to look down at her. She was wearing white and silver heels tonight, but even then, she was quite a bit shorter than he was. Outside, the flicker of the decorative candles stationed across the patio made the golden glow dance around her face, a game of shadow and light that flattered her features even more.

She met his gaze with her wide brown eyes, surprised by his sudden agreement with her. "I'm *right*? Did I actually hear you say that?"

"I said you *may* be right. Maybe I got all dressed up, dropped a ton of cash on a registry gift and came to this baby shower in the middle of nowhere just in the hopes I would see you here."

Lucy turned away and stared off into the distance. "I don't appreciate your sarcasm. I also don't appreciate you accosting me at a party. I'm missing one of my best friend's baby showers to be out here with you."

Oliver turned toward her and leaned one elbow onto the railing. "You're free to go at any time."

She turned to face him with disbelief narrowing her gaze. "Oh yeah, so you can start something else inside? Or throw me over your shoulder and carry me off next time? No. We're finishing this discussion right now. When I go back inside, I don't want to speak to or even lay eyes on you again."

He looked at her and noticed a slight tremble of her lips as she spoke. Was she on the verge of tears? He wasn't sure why, but the idea of that suddenly bothered him. "Are you okay?"

"Yes, why?"

"You're trembling. Are you really that upset with me?"

Lucy rolled her eyes and shook her head. "No, I'm shivering. It's freezing out here. I'm not dressed for an alfresco discussion this time of year."

Without hesitation, Oliver slipped off his suit coat and held it out to her. She looked at it with suspicion for a moment before turning her back and letting him drape it over her bare shoulders.

"Thank you," Lucy said as reluctantly as she could manage.

"I'm not all bad."

"That's good to know. I was starting to feel sorry for Harper having to grow up with you."

"Oh, you can still feel sorry for her. I was a horrible big brother. I made her life hell for years." Oliver laughed again, thinking of some of the wicked things he'd done to his sister. "One time, when she was about eight, I convinced her that my father's new Ming vase was made of Silly Putty and would bounce if she dropped it onto the floor. She got in so much trouble. Dad wouldn't believe her when she said I'd told her that. He grounded her for an extra week for lying."

Lucy covered her mouth with her hand to hide a reluctant smile. "Why are you being nice to me all of a sudden?" she asked. "You're not here to fight with me, and yet you're out here making small talk with me instead of inside with Jonah and your friends. What's your angle?"

That was a good question. He hadn't exactly planned any of this. He'd just wanted to get her away from the crowd before they made a scene. Once they stopped arguing, he was surprised to find he enjoyed talking with Lucy. There was an understated charm to her. The longer he spent with her, the more he wanted to spend. It was an intriguing and dangerous proposition, but one that explained his aunt's bold decision. If he felt swayed by her, his elderly aunt hadn't stood a chance.

"I don't have an angle, Lucy." Or if he did, he wasn't going to tell her so. "I guess I'm just trying to figure out what my aunt saw in you."

Lucy opened her mouth to argue, but he held up his hands to silence her. "I don't mean it like that, so don't get defensive. I've just been thinking that if my aunt really did want to leave you half a billion dollars, you had to be a pretty special person." Oliver leaned closer, unconsciously closing the gap between them. "I guess I'm curious to get to know you better and learn more about you."

Lucy's nose wrinkled, but for the first time, it didn't appear to be because she was annoyed with him. "What do you think so far?" she asked.

"So far..." He sought out the smart answer, but just decided to be honest. "...I like you. More than I should, given the circumstances. So far, you've proven to be an exciting, intelligent and beautiful adversary."

Lucy's lips parted softly at his words. "Did you say beautiful?"

Oliver nodded. Before he could respond aloud, Lucy launched herself into his arms. Her pink lips collided with his own just as her body pressed into him. He was stunned stiff for only a moment before he wrapped his arms around her waist and tugged her tighter against him.

Kissing Lucy wasn't at all what he expected. Nothing about her was what he expected. She didn't back down from what she'd started. She was bold, opening up to him and seeking his tongue out with her own. Oliver couldn't help but respond to her. She was more enthusiastic and demanding than any woman he may have ever kissed before.

This wasn't the smart thing. Or the proper thing. But he couldn't make himself pull away from her. She tasted like sweet, baby-shower punch, and she smelled like lavender. He wanted to draw her scent into his lungs and hold it there.

But then it was over.

As she pulled away, Oliver felt a surge of unwanted desire wash over him. It was the last thing he needed right now—with Lucy of all women—but he couldn't deny what he felt. It took everything he had not to reach for her and pull her back into his arms again. He was glad he didn't, though, as his need for her was stunted by a sudden blow to the face as Lucy punched him in the nose.

Four

"What the hell do you think you're doing?" Lucy asked with outrage in her voice as she backed away from him.

Oliver didn't immediately reply. First, he had to figure out what the hell had just happened. He was being kissed one second, hit the next and now he was being yelled at.

"Me?" He brought his hand up to his throbbing nose and winced. It wasn't broken, but there was blood running over his fingers. He'd never actually had a woman hit him before. One for the bucket list, he supposed. "*You're* the one that kissed *me*!"

"I did not," she insisted.

Oliver frowned and sighed, reaching into his coat for his pocket square to soak up the blood. Harper had never mentioned Lucy being impulsive, but he was learning new things about her all the time. It had been ten seconds since their lips had touched and it hadn't been his doing. Surely she recalled that. "Yeah, you did kiss me. I said you were beautiful and you threw yourself at me."

Lucy must have been caught up in the moment, because she seemed very much embarrassed by the truth of his blunt description. Her skin was suddenly crimson against her white dress and she wasn't even the one who got punched. "Yes…well…you kissed me back," she managed.

What was he supposed to do? Just stand there? Oliver was not a passive man, especially when the physical was involved. "My apologies, Miss Campbell. Next time a woman kisses me, I'll politely wait until she's finished with me and hit *her* instead."

Lucy took a cautious step back at his words, making him grin even though he shouldn't.

"I'm not going to hit you," Oliver said, dabbing at his nose one last time and stuffing the handkerchief into his pocket. "I've never hit a woman and I'm not going to start now. Although it would be nice if you would extend me the same courtesy. What ever happened to an old-fashioned slap of outrage? You straight-up punched me in the face. You hit hard, too."

She twisted her pink lips for a moment before nodding softly. "I take kickboxing classes twice a week. I'm sorry I hit you. It was almost a reflex. I was… startled."

"You were startled?" Oliver snorted in derision at her Pollyanna act and immediately regretted it as his nose throbbed with renewed irritation. "How could you be caught off guard when the whole thing was your doing?"

"Was it?" Lucy asked. "You weren't complimenting me and moving closer to me with that in mind?"

Oliver didn't remember doing that, but it was entirely possible. Lucy had a power over him that he hadn't quite come to terms with yet. Despite his best intentions, he found himself wanting to be nearer to her. To engage her in conversation, especially if it might fluster her and bring color to her pale cheeks. He'd wondered several times, in fact, how it would feel to have her lips against his and her body pressed into his own. Unfortunately, it had all happened so suddenly just now that he'd hardly been able to enjoy it.

He wasn't about to tell her that, though. She might be a pretty, nice-smelling con artist, but she was still a con artist. She'd worked her magic on his sister and his aunt. He'd had no doubt she would eventually turn her charms on him to get him to drop the contest of Aunt Alice's will, and she'd tried it at her first real opportunity. Letting her know she'd gotten to him would give her leverage. No. Let her stew instead, thinking her plan hadn't worked and she'd flung herself at a completely disinterested man. She'd have to find a different way to get what she wanted.

"I didn't come to this party to see you and I most certainly didn't come to this party to try and seduce you. I can't help it if I'm a charming man, Lucy, but that's all it is. I'm sorry if you confused that with me being attracted to you."

Her mouth dropped open for a moment before she clapped it shut and pressed her lips into a tight frown.

"That wasn't exactly the kiss of a man that wasn't interested," she pointed out.

Oliver could only shrug it off. "Well, I don't want to be rude, now, do I?"

Lucy balled her hands into fists and planted them on her narrow hips. "So you're saying you faked the whole thing just to be polite?"

"Yes. Of course." The arrogance of his response nearly made him cringe as the words slipped from his lips. Normally, he wouldn't speak to anyone this way, but Lucy was a special case. He wasn't handling her with kid gloves. She needed to know she wouldn't get her way where he was concerned.

Her brown gaze studied his face for a moment before she shook her head. "No. I don't believe you. I think you're just too arrogant to admit that you're attracted to me, of all people. That you could actually want the help. The trash that robbed you of your inheritance."

Oliver narrowed his gaze at her. She was good. Not only was she able to get under his skin, she was able to get into his head as well. That was disconcerting. He was the one who was supposed to be finding out all her secrets so he could expose her as a fraud, and there she was, calling him elitist in the hopes that his knee-jerk reaction would be to deny it and somehow fall prey to her charms to prove her wrong.

"We've established that we hardly know each other, Lucy. I'm not sure why you're so confident about who I am and what I do or don't think of you. But here… I'll prove to you that you're wrong."

He took two steps forward, closing the gap between them. Lucy stiffened as he got closer, but she held her ground. He had to admit, it impressed him that she didn't turn tail and run.

She wanted to, though. He could tell by her board-straight posture and tense jaw. "What are you doing?" She looked up at him with big brown eyes that were full of uncertainty.

She thought she could just call his bluff and he'd back down. No way. He was going all in and winning the hand even with losing cards.

Oliver eased forward until they were almost touching. He dipped his head down to her and cupped her face in his hands. Tilting her mouth up to him, he pressed his lips against hers. He wanted this kiss to be gentle, sweet and meaningless, so he could prove his point and move on with his night. He'd kissed a lot of women in his time. This would be like any other.

Or so he thought.

The second her lips touched his, it was immediately apparent that wasn't going to be the case. It was like a surge of electricity shot through his body when they touched. Every nerve lit up as his pulse started racing. The pounding of his heart in his ribcage urged him to move closer, to deepen the kiss, to taste her fully. In the moment, he couldn't deny himself what he wanted, even knowing his reaction played into her hands.

Lucy didn't deny him either. She melted into him, just as he'd expected. She wrapped her arms around his neck, her soft whimpers of need vibrating against his lips. Her mouth and her body were soft, molding to his hard angles. When she arched her back, pressing her belly against his rapidly hardening desire, she forced him to swallow a groan.

With her every breath, he could feel her breasts pushing against his chest, making him ache to touch them and hating himself for the mere thought. He wanted to press her back against the wall of the Dempseys' mansion and feel them beneath his hands. He was certain his father had felt the same way when he was swept up in Hurricane Candace.

This was getting *way* out of hand.

Oliver pulled away from Lucy at last, nearly pushing himself back although it was almost physically painful for him to do it. That simple kiss was supposed to prove to both of them that the other kiss had meant nothing. Instead, it had changed everything. Now he wasn't just curious about her as the woman who'd charmed his aunt out of a fortune. He wasn't just playing a cat-and-mouse seduction game. He wanted her. More than he'd wanted a woman in a very long time. His plan had clearly backfired in spectacular fashion, but he could still recover.

"See?" he said, taking another large step back to separate himself further and regain a semblance of control. He struggled to keep as neutral and unfazed an expression as he could, as though she hadn't just rocked his world in the midst of a stuffy baby shower.

"See what?" Lucy asked with a dreamy, flushed look on her face. She'd obviously enjoyed the kiss just as much as he had. On any other woman at any other time, that expression would've convinced him to swoop in again and push the kiss even further. Instead, he had to retreat before she caught him in her web for good.

"Do you see that you were wrong? That kiss was all an act, just like the first one. Honestly, it didn't do a thing for me." The truth was anything but, however he couldn't let her know that and think she had any chance of winning him over with feminine wiles.

Lucy's expression hardened as she came to realize that he was just messing with her and her plans had failed. Her jaw tightened and her hand curled into a fist again. Thankfully, he was out of her reach if she tried to take a swing at him a second time. "Are you kidding me?" she asked.

Oliver smiled wide and prayed his erection was hidden by his buttoned suit coat. "Not at all. I told you I wasn't attracted and then I proved it. That was skill, not attraction. Nothing more. Anyway, I'm glad we were able to clear that up. I wouldn't want there to be any other confused encounters between us. Now, if you'll excuse me, I'd like to get back in to the party. It appears as though they're about to do a toast for the new parents."

Lucy stood motionless as he nodded goodbye, brushed past her and headed back inside the ballroom.

What a pompous, arrogant jerk-face.

Lucy stood alone on the patio for a few minutes just to get her composure. The last twenty minutes of her life had thrown her for a loop and she just couldn't go back inside and act like nothing had happened.

First; she was too angry to return to the party. She knew she was flustered and red, and the minute one of the girls saw her like that, they would swarm her with questions she wasn't ready to answer. In addition, her hand was still aching from when she'd popped him in the face. She'd probably bruised her knuckles, but her only regret in hitting him was that it was premature.

He'd certainly earned a pop in the nose with the nasty things he'd said later.

Second, she wasn't ready to run into him again so soon. It was a big room filled with a lot of people, but she knew that fate would push them together repeatedly until one of them surrendered and went home. The alternative was another fight, this one more public, ruining the party. She didn't need that. It was bad enough that whispers would follow about them being alone on the balcony together for so long. Or if they came back inside together. Or came back in separately.

There was no winning in this scenario, really. Tongues would wag and there had already been enough tongue wagging on the patio tonight. At best, she could make sure she was presentable before she went back inside.

Reaching into her small purse, Lucy pulled out her compact. Her hair and makeup were fine, save for her lipstick that was long gone. She wasn't surprised. That kiss had blown her socks off. Oliver could yawn and say it was as much fun as getting an oil change, but she knew better. She could feel his reaction to it in the moment. Men lied. Words lied. Erections…those were a little more honest. And his had been hard to ignore.

What was his angle, anyway? Yes, she'd kissed him. It was possible she'd read the signs from him wrong, but she really didn't think so. He responded to her. He held her like a man who wanted to hold her. But then he'd turned around and laughed the whole thing off like it was nothing and made her feel stupid for thinking it was anything else.

She felt the heat in her cheeks again as her irritation grew. Why would he toy with her like that? Was it because he was determined to think she was some sort of crook? Why couldn't he just get to know her and make up his mind that way instead of jumping to hurtful conclusions? Didn't he trust Harper's judgment at all?

Lucy finished putting on her lipstick and returned it to her bag. She might as well go back inside. If she waited until she wasn't angry any longer, she'd sleep out on the patio. Instead, she took a deep breath, pasted on her best smile and headed back into the house.

Apparently, she'd missed the toast. The string quartet was playing music again and the crowd had returned to mingling. Her trio of girlfriends were together and looked her direction when she came in the door.

Lucy stopped short in front of them. "What?"

Emma arched a brow at her. "Seriously?"

"I'm sorry I missed the toast. I had to get some air," she said, making a lame excuse so she wouldn't hurt Emma's feelings.

"Air out of my brother's lungs," Harper quipped.

Lucy froze. "What? How did you—"

"That's a wall of windows, Lucy." Violet pointed over her shoulder. "Anyone who looked that direction could see the two of you playing tonsil hockey on the veranda."

Lucy turned and realized that she and Oliver had been far more visible on the patio than she'd anticipated. She'd thought for certain that the dim lights of the patio and the bright lights of the ballroom would've given them a little privacy. "Uh, we were having a discussion."

Emma snorted. "Quit it. Just tell us what's really going on."

"Yes, is this your big news? That you're dating Harper's brother?"

"Heavens, no!" Lucy blurted out. "That..." She gestured back to the patio. "What you guys saw was just..."

"Amazing?" Emma suggested.

"A CPR lesson?" Harper joked.

"A trial run?" Violet tossed out.

"A *mistake*," Lucy interjected into their rapid-fire suggestions. "And when I tell you the big news Harper alluded to, you'll understand why."

"Let's sit," Emma suggested. "I'm worn out and I want to hear every detail."

They selected a table in a far corner that wasn't quite so loud and gathered around it. The girls waited expectantly for Lucy to start her story as she tried to decide where to begin.

"Alice made me a beneficiary of her will."

"That's great," Emma said. "I mean, it makes sense. You two were so close."

"Yeah," Lucy agreed. "There's just one problem."

"How could an inheritance be a problem?" Violet asked.

"Because she left me damn near all of it. About half a billion dollars in cash, investments and property."

The words hung in the air for a few moments. Emma and Violet looked stunned. Harper sat with a smug smile on her face. She was confident that all of this would work out. Perhaps because that was the kind of life she led. Things were different for Lucy.

"You said billion. With a *b*?" Emma asked.

Lucy could only nod. What else did you say to something like that?

"And why aren't you more excited? You didn't even seem like you wanted to tell us." Violet's brow furrowed in confusion. "You'd think you'd be shouting it from the rooftops and lighting cigars with hundred dollar bills."

That would be a sight to see. "I'm not excited because I don't believe for one second that it's going to really happen the way Alice wanted."

"And why not?" Emma asked.

"Because of Oliver," Harper interjected. "He's all spun up about the whole thing. The family is convinced that Lucy is some kind of swindler that tricked Alice into giving her everything."

"I swear I didn't even know she did it," Lucy said.

"You don't have to defend yourself to us, honey." Violet shook her head. "We know you better than that. If Alice left you that money, it's because she thought you deserved it. Who are they to decide what she could and couldn't do with her own money?"

"I think they're trying to prove that she wasn't mentally competent to make the change. She only did it a few months ago. It doesn't look good for me, so that's why I didn't say anything. I didn't want to get anyone's hopes up and have it all fall through. Oliver has a team of fancy attorneys just ready to crush me. Honestly, I don't think I stand a chance."

"So why, exactly, were you kissing Oliver on the patio if he's the bad guy?" Emma asked, bringing the conversation back around to the part Lucy had wanted to avoid.

Once again, the other three women looked at her and she was at a loss for words. "When I saw him, I thought he'd followed me here. He showed up at the apartment the other day and we argued. When we started to argue again, he pulled me outside so we wouldn't cause a scene at the party. Somehow... I don't really know how...we kissed. Then he kissed me a second time to prove that kissing me was meaningless."

"What happened to his face?" Harper asked. "He was all red when he came back inside."

"It might have been because I punched him in the nose."

Violet covered her mouth to smother a giggle. Emma didn't bother, laughing loudly at Oliver's expense. It didn't take long before all four friends were laughing at the table together.

"You seriously punched him?"

Lucy nodded, wiping tears of laughter from her eyes. "I did. And he didn't deserve it. At least not yet."

"Oh, I'm sure he deserved it," Harper added. "He's done something to warrant a good pop, I assure you. Taking Alice's will to the judge is cause enough."

"Do you really think he'll get it overturned?" Emma asked. "He doesn't even need the money. Jonah says he's loaded."

"He is," Harper said. "He's done very well with Daddy's business the last few years. But it isn't about the money, I'm pretty sure."

"Then what is it about?" Lucy asked. "Because this has been the most confusing week of my life. I'm rich, but I'm not. I'm unemployed, but I may not need to work ever again. I'm homeless, and yet I may own a Fifth Avenue apartment. I'm applying to go back to Yale and finish school, but I may not even need to bother when I have an art gallery in my own living room. I've barely had time to grieve for Alice. Your whole family has a vendetta against me and I didn't do anything. I just woke up one day and my entire life was turned upside down."

Harper reached out and took Lucy's hand. "I know, and I'm sorry. If I'd thought for a moment that Aunt Alice was going to toss you into this viper pit, I would've warned you. But know it's not personal. They'd go after anyone. They all wanted their piece and they've been waiting decades for her to die so they can get their hands on it."

"What a warm family you have," Lucy noted. "I bet Thanksgiving was really special at your house."

"It's not as bad as I make it sound. Everyone had their own money, it's just that most of them were mentally decorating their new vacation homes and planning what they'd do with the money when the time came. Then nothing. In their minds, you yanked it out from under them, whether you meant to or not."

"Can't you talk some sense to Oliver?" Emma asked.

"I've tried. He's avoiding my calls. I think we just have to let the case run its course in court and hope the judge sees in Lucy what we all see. Once the judge rules in her favor, there's nothing any of them can do about it. But I didn't know he was bothering you, Lucy. If he shows up at the apartment again, you call me."

Lucy nodded. "I will." Looking around the crowded room, she was relieved not to see him loitering around the party. "But enough about all this. We're here to celebrate Emma and Jonah's baby, not to rehash all my drama. We can do that any day."

"I'm actually starving," Emma admitted. "Every time I think I should make a plate, someone starts talking to me or wants to rub my belly or something."

"Well, I'm pretty sure it's almost time for you to cut that beautiful cake. We can at least get you some of that to eat without interruption."

Lucy smiled as Emma's eyes lit up with excitement. "It's a vanilla pound cake with fresh berries and cream inside. At the tasting, Jonah had to take the plate from me so he could try a bite."

"Ooh…" Violet chimed in. "That sounds amazing. I've been nothing but hungry the last month. Beau keeps chastising me for eating too much. He says I'm going to overdo it, but I say pregnancy is my only chance to enjoy eating without feeling guilty. The baby and I are ready for some cake, too."

"Well, it's settled then," Lucy said. "Let's get these pregnant ladies some cake."

Five

"What are you doing here?"

Oliver could only grin at his sister's irritated expression as she opened the door to the apartment. A large portion of his life had been dedicated to goading that very face out of her. It was an unexpected bonus to the day. He hadn't actually been certain she was at Aunt Alice's apartment; he hadn't seen her since the baby shower the week before. But when he saw the Saks Fifth Avenue commuter van unloading downstairs, he knew that Harper was involved somehow. Where expensive clothes went, his sister was sure to follow.

"I saw the people from Saks unloading downstairs and I thought I would pop in to say hello. Personal shoppers coming to the house. It's as though someone has come into some money. Is that for you or for Lucy?" he asked, knowing full well that Harper was far too particular to let someone else shop for her.

"It's for Lucy."

Harper made no move to step back and let him into the apartment. Fortunately, the elevator chimed behind him and a well-dressed woman stepped out with a rack of plastic-wrapped clothing pushed by two gentlemen.

Harper's entire expression changed as she turned from her brother. "Hello, come in!" she said, moving aside to allow the crew in.

Oliver took advantage of the situation by going in after them. He happily took a seat on the sofa in the living room, waiting for what would likely be an interesting fashion show. After seeing what she'd worn the few times they were together, he knew Lucy needed a new wardrobe. Anything she wore that was remotely high quality was a hand-me-down from his sister. Honestly, he was surprised it took them this long to start shopping.

What would she buy first with her pilfered millions?

The two men from Saks left the apartment, leaving the rolling clothing hanger near the fireplace. He watched as the woman moved quickly to unwrap the clothes and present them to what she presumed was her wealthy client.

Lucy spied him the minute she entered the room, despite thousands of dollars' worth of clothes on display beside her. "What is he doing here?" she asked, echoing Harper's question.

Harper turned to where he was sitting and sighed. "I don't know, but it doesn't matter. We've got to find you an outfit for the gala. Perhaps a man's perspective will be helpful."

Lucy wrinkled her nose as she studied him and turned back to the clothing. "Harper," she complained,

"these outfits are all way, way out of my price range."
She picked up one sleeve and gasped. "Seriously. I
can just wear something I already have in the closet."

"Absolutely not. You're a millionaire now and you
have to look the part, especially at this gallery event.
You want to work in the art world, don't you? This
is your chance to make an entrance as Miss Lucille
Campbell, not as Lucy, the assistant sent by Alice
Drake. The invitation had your name on it this time,
Lucy. Not Alice's."

Oliver watched curiously as Lucy shook her head
and looked at the clothes. "How did they even know
to invite me? I haven't told anyone about the money."

"Things like that leak out whether you want them
to or not. I'm sure Wanda couldn't wait to share her
outrage with her circle of friends and it spreads from
there. The art world is small and people were probably eager to find out who would get Alice's estate.
Honestly, I don't know how you've managed to keep
it a secret."

Lucy pointed over to where Oliver was sitting on the
couch. "That's why. He's why. You act like I already
have this massive fortune, but I don't. All I have is what
I saved to go back to school. I'm willing to spend some
of that to get a dress for the gala, but not much. I have
no guarantee that I'm ever going to see a dime of that
money to replace what I spend."

"Will you at least try some of it on? You never know
what you might end up liking."

"Yes, fine."

The saleswoman pulled out what was probably the
most expensive designer dress on the rack. "Let's start
with this one. Where would you like to change?"

She and Lucy disappeared down the hallway and Harper started sorting through the clothing on the rack.

This was an unexpected development. He thought for certain that Lucy would jump at the chance to buy some expensive designer clothes and start flaunting herself around Manhattan. Yes, he was responsible for putting a hold on the flow of cash from his aunt's estate, but there were ways around that. He was certain she could probably get a loan from a bank to front her lifestyle until the money came in. At the very least, charge up a credit card or two.

But she didn't. It was curious. She didn't seem to enjoy the position she was in at all, much to Harper's supreme disappointment. That woman loved to shop. Of course, so had Candace. She was full speed ahead the moment she'd gotten her hands on one of his father's credit cards. Candace had insisted that she just wanted to look as beautiful as possible at all times for his father. It was amazing how much money it took to make that happen.

Perhaps Lucy had a different angle. Her wide-eyed innocent bit was pretty convincing. Perhaps not spending money was part of it. Or maybe he was overthinking all of this.

He'd run through that night on the patio in his head dozens of times in the last week. Was she sincere? Did it matter? His body certainly didn't care. It wanted Lucy regardless of her innocence or guilt. Of course, his father had proved that following the advice of one's arousal was not always the best course of action. His dad had followed his right into near bankruptcy.

Speaking of what his groin wanted...

Lucy stepped back into the room wearing a gown.

It was a sheer, tan fabric that looked almost as though she was wearing nothing at all but some floating tiers of beaded lace. It looped around her neck and when she turned to show Harper, it was completely backless.

"This one is Giorgio Armani," the saleswoman said proudly. "It looks lovely with your coloring."

The women talked amongst themselves for a moment before Harper turned to him. "What do you think, Oliver? If you're going to sit on the couch and gawk at her, you should at least make yourself useful."

It did look nice. He felt almost like a Peeping Tom, getting a look at her that he shouldn't have, but he'd rather see her in some color. "She looks naked. She could go naked for free. If she's going to pay that much money, she should at least look like she has an actual dress on."

Lucy laughed, clapping her hand over her mouth when she saw the saleswoman's horrified expression. Oliver was pleased that he'd gotten her to laugh, although he wasn't entirely sure why. She did have a beautiful smile. He hadn't really gotten to see it before. She spent all her time frowning at him, although he probably deserved that.

Harper just shook her head. "Okay, it's not my favorite either. Let's try this one," she said, pulling another gown from the rack.

"What are you dressing her up for?" he asked once Lucy disappeared again.

"The charity gala they're holding at the Museum of Modern Art Saturday night."

"Ah," Oliver said. "I got invited to that. Champagne, weird sculptures and people pressuring you to write checks. I bet the only reason they invited her was to get their hands on some of that money she's inheriting."

Harper put her hands on her hips. "And why did they invite you, hmm? The same reason. It's a charity event. That's the whole point. At least she knows what she's looking at when she walks around the museum."

Oliver shrugged off his sister's insult. It wasn't ignorance on his part when it came to art. He'd taken all the required art appreciation classes in college, as many class field trips as any well-educated child in New York, and followed Aunt Alice around museums on the occasional Saturday. He just didn't get it. Especially modern art. And if he didn't like it, why should he waste his brain cells remembering who this artist was or what that piece symbolized? He just didn't care. He could name maybe six famous painters off the top of his head, and four of them just happened to also be Teenage Mutant Ninja Turtles.

The saleswoman returned to the room looking very pleased with herself, but when Lucy came in behind her, she looked anything but. To be honest, this time Oliver had to hold in a chuckle. The dress was black with sheer fabric that highlighted the black structure of the dress like lingerie of some sort. On its own that would've been fine, but it also had red and pink cutouts all over it, looking like some kind of couture craft project.

"What on earth is that?" he asked.

"Christian Dior!" the saleswoman said with an insulted tone.

"No, just no," Lucy said, turning immediately to take it off. Apparently, she agreed with him.

"Is there anything on that rack that isn't a neutral

or see-through?" Oliver asked. "I don't know what's wrong with color these days. The women are always wearing black or gray. Lucy should stand out."

The saleswoman clucked her tongue at him before turning to the rack again. "So no black, nude or white…" She flipped until she got to the last dress on the rack. "I guess we'll try this one, although it's not my favorite. The designer is relatively new and not very well-known."

"Give it a try," Harper said encouragingly. "You're not really helping us," she said to Oliver when they were alone again.

"It's not my fault her personal shopper picked out ridiculous outfits. I mean, you saw that last one, right? I know it's for a modern art event, but she doesn't want to be confused for an exhibit."

Harper's lips pressed together as she tried to hide a smirk. "Yes, well, this one is nice and I like it. You'd better like it, too, or go home so we can do this without your help. Don't you have a business to run, anyway?"

Oliver shrugged. It was a well-oiled machine and at the moment, he was far more concerned with what was going on with Lucy. For multiple, confusing reasons.

When Lucy returned a moment later, Oliver struggled to catch his breath. The dress was a bright shade of red with cap sleeves and an oval neckline that dipped low enough to showcase her breasts. It fit Lucy beautifully, highlighting her figure and flattering her coloring with its bright hue. It had a sash that wrapped around Lucy's tiny waist, but other than that, wasn't particularly flashy. No beading. No lace. No sheer panels. No wonder the saleswoman hated it. If Lucy picked this gown, her commission would hardly be worth the trip.

"I really like this one," Lucy said. "Especially this part." She turned around and surprised everyone. The dress was completely open in the back, almost like a reversed robe that was held in place with the sash. It was paired with a pair of black satin capris.

Oliver wasn't even entirely sure if that qualified as a dress or a pantsuit, but he liked it. It was different and for some reason, he thought that suited Lucy. He liked the flash of skin along the whole length of her back. Any man who asked her to dance at the gala would get to run his palms over her smooth, bare skin. While he might enjoy that, he felt an unexpected surge of jealousy at the thought of her dancing with anyone else. Plus, the capri pants accented the high, round curve of her ass. He hadn't noticed before, but it was quite the sight.

When Lucy stopped preening, she sought out the price tag and sighed in relief. "This is the one," she said at last.

Oliver watched the women discuss the dress, tuning out the noise and noting nothing but the stunning vision in red. He hadn't intended on going to the museum gala on Saturday, but if Lucy would be there, in that dress, he might just have to amend his plans.

Lucy was fairly certain the woman from Saks Fifth Avenue was never coming back. There weren't nearly enough digits in the price of the dress she selected for the woman's taste. She just didn't see the point in spending thousands of dollars on a dress. A wedding dress, maybe, but not just some pretty outfit to wear to a party.

As it was, the price still seemed pretty steep—nearly a week's worth of her usual salary. But Harper was right; she needed to make a good impression on her first event out. Hopefully the inheritance would come through and she wouldn't have to worry about blowing that much on a single dress, but if not, she would be wearing that red outfit to every damn thing she could think of.

The apartment seemed to clear out all at once. The men returned and hauled the clothes out with a grumpy-looking saleswoman in their wake. Harper had an appointment and left soon after. That just left Oliver mysteriously perched on the couch when she went to change. She hoped by the time she got back, he would be gone, too.

Back in her own clothing—a nice pair of jeans and her favorite sweater—she returned to the room and found him sitting right where she'd left him.

"I still don't understand why you're here. Or still here, for that matter."

Oliver smiled and stood up. "I had some business on this side of town and when I saw the Saks truck, thought I'd pop in. Where Saks goes, Harper follows."

"And now she's gone," Lucy noted. "And you're still here. Want to ask me more questions? Hook me up to a lie detector this time?"

He strolled across the large Moroccan rug with his hands in his pockets. She tried not to notice how gracefully he moved or how he looked at her as he came closer. "Are you hungry?"

"What?" He'd completely ignored everything she

asked him. How was she supposed to have a conversation with him when he did that?

"It's lunchtime. I'm starving. I'd like to take you to lunch if you're hungry."

She stood awkwardly, considering his offer for far too long. "Okay," she blurted out at last. If his sole purpose of coming by here was to uncover her dark secrets, he wouldn't find much. She might as well let him buy her lunch in the meantime. "Let me just grab my coat."

They walked silently out of the building together and downstairs to the street. Although they didn't speak, touch or even make eye contact as they strolled down the street together, she found herself keenly aware of his physical presence. Her body had somehow become attuned to Oliver, and the closer they stood, the harder it was for her to ignore even the tiniest of his movements or gestures.

Lucy was almost relieved when they encountered a more congested area and she had to drop back and follow his lead through crowds of people. The distance helped her nerves, at least until Oliver noticed she'd fallen behind. Without hesitation, he reached out and took her hand, pulling her back to his side. The skin of her palm buzzed with the sensation of his touch, making her whole body hum with awareness as though he intended to do more than just keep from losing her in the crowd.

Lucy expected him to let go once she'd caught up to him, but his grip on her held tight as they walked a few more blocks to a restaurant she'd never been to before.

"Do you like Korean barbecue?" Oliver asked as he finally released her hand.

Lucy peered in the window and shrugged before self-consciously stuffing that hand into her pocket. "I don't know, but it sounds like an experience."

Oliver smiled and held open the door for them to head inside. They were taken to a quiet table in the back with a grill set into the center. The host turned on the table and handed them both menus. It didn't take her long to realize that Korean barbecue involved cooking the meat at their individual table. When the waiter arrived, they selected their drinks and meats. Oliver opted for a glass of red wine and Lucy decided to stick with a soda. After their last encounter at the baby shower, she wasn't sure what to expect when she was alone with Oliver. There was no need to add alcohol to that mix.

Especially with her hand still tingling. Beneath the table, she rubbed it over her jean-clad thigh and wished the feeling away. She needed to keep her wits about her when she was alone with Oliver. She couldn't let her guard down no matter how much she tingled or how he smiled at her. This might all be part of his plan to undermine her claim on Alice's estate. She didn't know how, exactly, but she refused to believe he just wanted to take her to lunch to be nice.

The waiter arrived with their drinks, then placed half a dozen bowls on the table. There were different vegetables, rice and a few foods she didn't recognize. One had tentacles.

"Can I ask you something?" Lucy said once the waiter disappeared from their table. Her bravery where food was concerned was starting to wane, so she opted for a distracting discussion instead.

"Sure." Oliver picked up his glass of wine and awaited her question.

"I lived in that apartment with Alice for over five years. Harper was the only family member I ever saw visit, and in part, she was there to see me. I don't understand it. Why didn't you ever visit your aunt?"

Oliver nodded and focused for a moment on the wood grain of their table. There was an intensity about his expression when he was thinking that Lucy found intriguing, even when he was antagonizing her. He had the same look on his face when he was studying her. She didn't know what he saw or what he expected to see when he looked at her so closely. It made her uncomfortable, especially after those kisses on the patio, but she still liked watching the wheels turn in his mind.

"Aunt Alice didn't like having guests. You wouldn't know it if you went by, she'd treat you like royalty, but inside, she hated it. I missed her, and I wanted to see her, but I knew that it made her anxious, just like leaving her apartment made her anxious. So I gave her a computer, got her all set up and we emailed every day."

Lucy perked up at the last part. "You spoke to her every day?" How could she not know that? And why didn't she realize company made Alice uncomfortable? She'd never said a word about it to her.

Oliver nodded. "Aunt Alice was a complicated woman, although few knew it. Since you asked me a question, I'll ask you one. How much do you really know about my aunt?"

Lucy opened her mouth to answer, but when she thought about it, she realized she didn't have that much to say. "We shared a common love of art. She liked

Chinese takeout from the place a few blocks away. She only drank hot tea with cream and one lump of sugar." There, she stopped. Most of the things she could think of were inconsequential, like being an early riser and watching *Jeopardy!* every weeknight.

"Now that I'm thinking of it, I guess she never really shared that much about herself. Not really. She never talked about her family or her childhood. I don't know if she ever worked or married or anything else. When I told you I didn't know anything about her will or how much money she had, it was true. We never talked about things like that."

"Aunt Alice never married," he began. "My father told me once, a long time ago, that she'd been in love with a young man in the forties. Unfortunately, he got shipped off to World War II right after they got engaged and never came home. She never dated anyone else, to my great-grandfather's dismay. He constantly thrust well-to-do men in front of her, hoping to secure business deals or strengthen ties, but you know her. She had none of it. I guess she never got over losing her first love."

Lucy sat back in her seat and frowned. "That's horrible. There's an old black-and-white photograph of a soldier in a frame beside her bed. That must be his picture."

Oliver nodded. "She got used to being alone, I think, and when everything else happened, she just decided it was better to be alone."

"What do you mean by 'when everything else happened'?"

"The terrorist attacks of September 11, 2001. It affected every New Yorker differently, but the whole thing really shook her up. She was supposed to go downtown to meet with a financial advisor later that morning. Then she turned on the news and realized what was happening. If her appointment had been an hour or two earlier, she would've been in the North Tower of the World Trade Center when the first plane hit. It scared the hell out of her. She never set foot out of her apartment again."

Lucy's jaw dropped as Oliver spoke. All this time, she'd been pointing fingers at him and his family for not visiting or even knowing Alice at all, when in truth, Lucy didn't know her either. Of course, she'd wondered why Alice never left the apartment, but it seemed rude to ask, so she never did. Some people developed agoraphobia without any particular incident at onset.

"What was she like before that?" she asked, suddenly curious about the friend and employer she knew so little about.

Oliver smiled, the sharp features of his face softening. "She was fun. After my mother died, sometimes my father would leave Harper and me with her for an afternoon while he worked. She would take us to the park or the zoo. The art museums, of course. She never worried about getting dirty or eating too much junk. As kids, we thought she was the greatest aunt in the world. It wasn't until we got older that we realized she was going out less and less. She was getting older, too, but I think she was feeling less comfortable out in the city. The attacks were the last nail in the coffin for her, I think. She decided it was safer to stay inside. And in time, she wanted less and less company, until she was almost completely closed off from the world."

"Why?"

"Fear, I guess. It's odd considering she seemed like the most fearless and exciting person I'd ever known. I sometimes wonder what she would've been like if her fiancé hadn't died. If she'd had a family. Would she still have closed herself off the way she did? I don't know. I hated it, though. I hated seeing that light in her extinguish."

The waiter appeared with their tray of meat and started to cook the first portion on the grill, effectively ending that line of conversation. Lucy was glad. Learning about Alice was enlightening, but also sad. There was a good reason why her employer hadn't talked about her past. She'd lost her chance at love and chosen to spend the rest of her life alone rather than be with someone else. Whether it was incredibly romantic or just sad, Lucy didn't know. But at the rate her love life was going, she might end up alone, too.

The server expertly flipped the meat, putting the finished pieces on their plates and explaining the different sides she'd been eyeing earlier. Once he was gone, they started eating and Oliver tossed a few raw pieces of Korean short ribs onto the grill to eat next.

Lucy watched him as he ate, thinking about their interactions since Alice died. She was a little ashamed of herself after everything she'd said and done. Yes, he was determined to prove she was a scam artist, but what did he know of her? Nothing. And she knew nothing of him. Or Alice, apparently. But she could tell that he had genuinely cared for his aunt. He couldn't fake the affection that reflected in his blue eyes when he spoke about her.

"Oliver, I want to apologize."

He paused, his food hanging midair on the end of his fork. "Apologize for what?"

"For judging you so harshly. For judging your whole family. All these years, I had this burning resentment for all of you. Sometimes I'd see Alice sitting in her chair looking at family photos and it ate me up inside that no one ever came to visit. She seemed so lonely and I felt like everyone had abandoned her for some reason."

Lucy shook her head and felt her cheeks start to flush with embarrassment. When she tilted her head up and looked him in the eye, the softness of his expression took away the last of her worries. She wasn't sure what she'd expected from Oliver, but it wasn't patience and understanding.

"That's why I lashed out at the reading of the will. When all these people showed up after her death, it felt like circling sharks drawn by chum in the water. Now I realize that it was how Alice wanted it. Or at least, how she needed it to be. So I'm sorry for anything ugly I said to you about all that."

Oliver held her gaze for a moment before smiling and popping a bite of food into his mouth. "It was an easy assumption to make," he said after swallowing. "I think we're all guilty of doing that to some extent, don't you?"

His gaze was fixed on her, with almost a pleading expression on his face. He wasn't going to apologize for the things he'd accused her of, but maybe this was his way of acknowledging that perhaps he'd judged her too harshly as well. It didn't mean he was going to call off his lawyers, but maybe he wouldn't show up at the apartment to give her the third degree any longer.

"A truce, then?" Lucy asked, lifting her soda and holding her breath. While she would be glad to put an end to the fighting, she worried what could happen between the two of them without it keeping them apart. It was a dangerous proposition, but a part of her was anxious for him to say yes.

Oliver smiled and lifted his wine to clink her glass. "A truce."

Six

"Welcome, Mr. Drake. So good of you to join us this evening."

Oliver strolled into the Museum of Modern Art and stopped as he was greeted by a table of committee members organizing the charity event. The older woman who stood to welcome him looked familiar, but he couldn't place her.

"I am so sorry to hear about your aunt," she said. "She was a valued patron to the museum and the art world as a whole."

He nodded politely. "Thank you." Turning to the table where a young male volunteer was checking off guests on the attendee list, he leaned in. "Can you tell me if Miss Campbell has already arrived?"

"She has." The young man beamed. Apparently he was a fan of her new outfit, too.

"Thank you."

They directed him up the short staircase to the second-floor atrium where the main portion of the event was taking place. At the top of the stairs, a waiter with a large silver tray offered him a flute of champagne, and he accepted. This type of event was not his idea of a good time, but at least there was alcohol involved. It helped to open people's pocketbooks, he was fairly certain.

The wide-open room with white walls that reached for the sky was dominated by a large pyramidal sculpture in the center. He was ashamed to admit he hadn't been to the museum since it had been redone years ago. A couple hundred or so people milled around the space, chatting and sipping their drinks. A band was playing in a corner of the room, but no one was dancing yet. The far wall was peppered with special pieces that his invitation said were being offered on silent auction to raise funds for the nearby LaGuardia High School of Music & Art and Performing Arts.

It didn't take long for Oliver to locate Lucy in the crowd. His eyes were immediately drawn to the crimson red of her dress that stood out amongst the sedate blacks, tans and whites of the people who accepted what the saleswoman pushed on them without question. The outfit looked equally stunning tonight, although now it was paired with elegantly styled hair, glittering jewelry and flawless makeup.

Altogether, it made for a woman he simply couldn't ignore. His body was drawn to her, urging him to cross the room and join her immediately. The only thing that held him in place was his desire to prolong the anticipation.

He enjoyed watching her chat with a couple about

the large Monet that dominated an entire wall of the museum. Oliver could tell she hadn't spied him at the gala yet. When she knew he was nearby, there was something about her that changed. A stiffness, almost as though she were holding her breath when he was around. He wasn't sure if she was just more guarded, he made her nervous or if the palpable attraction between them simply caused her to be uncomfortable in his presence.

At the moment, she was sipping her champagne, smiling and speaking animatedly with a couple he recognized from other events around town. He liked watching her with her guard down. It was a side of her he'd never gotten to see, not even in the past when they'd called a truce or shared a kiss. That was his own fault, he supposed, but it made him want to know more about this side of Lucy. Perhaps it was the last piece of the puzzle he was missing.

Oliver watched as the couple finally dismissed themselves to say hello to someone else, leaving Lucy standing awkwardly alone. She bit at her lip, the confident facade crumbling without the distraction of conversation. Now was his chance. He moved through the crowd of people to join her.

When their eyes met, Oliver felt a jolt of electricity run through him. Lucy smiled wide as he came closer, possibly relieved to see someone she knew. He could imagine that being in this situation and knowing almost no one must be quite intimidating. When she attended for Alice, she could fade into the background, but with that dress, she couldn't hide from anyone. A familiar face, even his, would be cause for excitement. Or maybe, just maybe, she was happy to see *him*.

"Good evening, Miss Campbell," he said with a wide smile of his own. Lately just the thought of her brought a grin to his face. As his gaze flicked over her beauty up close, he wished he hadn't waited so long to approach her. "You're looking lovely tonight."

Lucy blushed almost as red as her dress. "Thank you. I didn't expect to see you here this evening. I don't recall running into you at any of the events I attended for your aunt. I thought you weren't much of a fan of art."

Oliver shrugged. He wasn't about to say he'd only come because her might see her. "I'm always invited, but I usually have other engagements. Tonight was for a good cause and I had time, so I dusted off my tuxedo and came down."

Her gaze ran over his Armani tux for a moment with appreciation before she awkwardly turned away to glance at the art display across the room. "Have you looked at the pieces they have for sale tonight? There's some really lovely ones if you're looking to add to your personal collection."

"I haven't." The moment he'd seen her, the rest of the museum had faded into the background.

Oliver politely offered his arm and escorted Lucy to the other side of the atrium where maybe twenty-five paintings and sculptures were set up with silent auction sheets posted at each.

"Some of these were done by students at the school and others are donated by local artists. These kids show so much promise for their age. It's amazing."

He knew at this point he could let her arm go, but he didn't. He liked the feel of her against his side. A lot. "Did you ever have a desire to be an artist yourself?"

"Oh no," Lucy said with a nervous chuckle. "I love to look at it, to study it, but I can't draw a stick figure. I mean look at this one." She gestured toward a large painting of the Manhattan skyline with the Brooklyn Bridge stretching across the foreground. "This piece gets more amazing the longer you study it."

Oliver stepped closer to try to figure out what distinguished the piece from every other one they sold on street corners around the city. It was only when he got a foot or so away that he could see the image wasn't painted, but actually made up of millions of tiny hearts. Only from far away did the colored hearts make up the image of the city.

"The artist loves New York," Lucy continued. "The painting practically screams it. The color palette she chose, the light in the sky…it's a very well-balanced piece."

"It sounds like you really like this one. You should buy it," Oliver suggested. Part of him was waiting for her to start spending his aunt's money. Where was the joy in achieving one's goal when they couldn't enjoy it? He leaned in to look at the current bid. It was well within her means if the windfall went through. "It's only up to ten thousand dollars right now. If this artist is half as talented as you think she is at seventeen, this painting will be worth triple that one day. It's a great investment."

Lucy laughed off his suggestion and he realized how much he liked that sound. Arguing with her was fun, but he much preferred this version of his aunt's companion.

"You're just as bad as Harper," she said. "Counting chickens that may never hatch, no thanks to you. As far as I'm concerned, I have no money. Just some savings that have taken me the past five years to accumulate. I'm certainly not spending it on art when I may have no place to live in a few weeks' time."

Oliver felt a momentary pang of guilt. He'd taken the fun out of this moment for her. How different would it be tonight if he hadn't contested the will? Would he be the one there for her when she made her first big purchase? "But what if you did? What if you had all those millions at your disposal right now?"

Lucy's crimson-painted lips twisted in thought. "I haven't given it much thought. But in this case, since it was for charity, I would consider buying it. I would at least bid. But otherwise I would just feel too guilty spending that much money on something like that."

Oliver couldn't help a confused frown. He turned to look at her with a furrowed brow. "My aunt spent a hundred times that on a single piece. Why would you feel guilty doing the same? It's your money to spend however you want to."

Lucy pulled away from him and the painting and started toward the staircase that led up to other exhibits. Oliver caught up and took her arm again, in part to be a gentleman and in part because he liked the feel of her so near to him. The moment she moved from his side, it felt like a cold emptiness sidled up against him. He was eager to feel the warmth of her skin and smell the scent of her perfume again. It was a soft fragrance, like a garden after the rain, that made him want to draw it deep into his lungs.

"It's not my money," she said after quite a few steps. "It's Alice's money. And if by some stroke of luck it does become mine, I couldn't just blow it on whatever suits me. It was a gift and I need to cherish it. Do something good with it. Help people."

Curious. He'd never once spoken to someone who felt like money was a kind of burden of responsibility. Especially someone who'd schemed to get the money in the first place. "You could give it all to charity, I suppose. But Alice could've done that herself. She gave it to you for a reason. I wish I knew what that reason was."

Lucy stopped on the landing and turned to him with an understanding expression softening her features. "So do I. It would make things easier for everyone if she'd let us in on her little secret, don't you think?"

Her words rang true in Oliver's ears, making his stomach start to ache. Had he made the wrong call with her? He'd started spending time around Lucy with the intention of finding out what she was really about and all he'd uncovered was a woman who seemed kind, thoughtful, caring and intelligent. She was attractive as well, but didn't seem too concerned with that.

Either she was one of the greatest con artists he'd ever met or he was way off base with this whole thing.

"This is my favorite part of the museum," she said, letting their prior discussion drop.

They had stopped on the surrealism floor. They started wandering through bizarre sculptures and even more bizarre paintings. "Your favorite, eh? Myself, I just don't get it," Oliver said, gesturing to the large painting hanging on the wall just ahead of them. "This one, for example."

Lucy sighed and stepped beside him. She studied the painting, but all he could focus on was the intriguing scent of her perfume and the glittering rubies at her ears. The sparkle drew his gaze to the long line of her neck. It was hard for him not to ogle, knowing the bare skin traveled down to the small of her back, exposed by the red dress she'd chosen from the personal shopper.

"This looks like something a child would doodle with crayons," he said.

"This is a popular piece by Joan Miró."

"Never heard of her."

"Him," she corrected. "This is part of his *Constellation* series from the early 1940s, and one of my favorites, actually. It's called *The Beautiful Bird Revealing the Unknown to a Pair of Lovers*."

Oliver forced his attention back to the painting and searched for whatever Lucy saw in it. He could find no bird, beautiful or otherwise, nor a pair of lovers. There was just a bunch of black circles and triangles scattered around a brown background with a couple random eyeballs. He turned his head sideways but it didn't help. It didn't make any sense to him. "Okay, Miss Art Connoisseur, show off your expertise and explain this piece to me."

"Okay," Lucy said with a confident nod. "This painting is well-known for its simplified color palette and line work designed to simulate a constellation in the night sky. What I've always appreciated about the piece is the sense of joy despite the chaos, which is a reflection of the artist's life at the time, in war-torn Europe. He worked on the pieces during the Spanish Civil War and actually fled the German advance into France with little more than this collection of paintings. He said that working on this collection liberated him from focusing on the tragedy of war. They were a joyful escape and

I see that in his works. You have the calm of night, the jubilant dance of the stars…"

Lucy continued to talk about the work, but Oliver was far more interested in watching her. It was as though she was finally comfortable in her own skin, but it had nothing to do with him. She was no longer the fish out of water amongst the rich, mingling crowds of the charity event. She was the contemporary art expert, finally solid in her footing. Her dark eyes twinkled and her face lit up with excitement for the beauty of what she was looking at.

It was transformative. The dress was pretty, the makeup and the hair were well done, but it was this moment that Lucy truly became stunningly beautiful in his eyes. His breath caught in his throat as she gestured toward the painting and the overhead lights cast a shadow across the interesting angles and curves of her face. Her full, red lips moved quickly as she spoke, teasing him to come closer and capture them with his mouth.

"Oliver?"

His gaze darted from her lips to her eyes, which had a twinkle of amusement in them. "Yes?"

"You're not listening to a word I'm saying, are you? I've bored you to tears. You did ask me to tell you about it."

"Yes, I did. And I was listening," he lied. "I just got distracted by the beauty."

Lucy smirked and turned back toward the painting. "It is lovely, isn't it?"

"I was talking about you."

Lucy's head snapped to look in his direction as she gasped audibly. Her ruby lips parted softly as she looked at him without finding any words.

"You know, the last time I said you were beautiful, you kissed me. And hit me. But first, you kissed me."

Lucy's mouth closed into a smile. "Yes, well, I don't intend to do either of those things here, no matter what you say." She took a sip of her champagne and continued to stroll through the exhibit.

Oliver grinned and hurried to catch up with her. They'd just see about that.

"This section of the museum is dedicated to works of the sixties," Lucy said as they rounded the corner. She didn't want to keep talking about how beautiful he thought she looked tonight or about the kisses they'd shared at Emma's baby shower. Nothing good could come of the way he was looking at her, especially on the mostly deserted upper floors of the museum where anything could happen without witnesses.

She hadn't dated a lot, especially since she dropped out of Yale, so understanding men was not her strong suit. She got the feeling that even if it were, she would still be confused where Oliver was concerned. He didn't seem outwardly to like her, and yet he was always around. He was insulting her integrity one moment and complimenting her so-called beauty the next.

His mood swings were giving her whiplash. There was one thing she was certain of, however—those kisses on the Dempseys' patio had been passionate, tingle-inducing and toe-curling. Maybe the best kisses of her life. And yet his calm dismissal of the whole thing had left her uncertain of him and what he wanted from her.

Since Lucy couldn't be sure where she stood with Oliver, she knew her best course of action would be to keep her distance physically. Truce or no truce, it would only lead to trouble. She might not be able to avoid him when he seemed determined to seek her out, but she didn't need to encourage him. At least until the court case was decided either way, she needed to stay away from Oliver Drake.

She just didn't want to.

On the wall ahead of them was the famous collection of Yves Klein. She'd studied his work extensively in college as his artistic techniques were quite the scandalous production back then, and even now, although for somewhat different reasons. She was relieved to have art to talk about instead of focusing on the unmistakable connection between the two of them.

"I think you'll like this collection by Yves Klein. It's called *Anthropométrie de L'époque Bleue*."

Oliver stopped to study the first piece with a confused expression furrowing his brow. "I didn't understand the other one we discussed, but at least I could tell it was an actual painting that took skill of some kind. This is a giant white canvas with blue smears all over it."

Lucy smiled. "That's the final outcome, yes. But Klein was more of a performance artist in his day than just a painter. He created all these works with live audiences and an orchestra playing music in the background. He was quite famous for the events he put on. His most well-known piece, *Fire-Color FC 1*, sold at auction for over 36 million dollars in 2012."

His jaw dropped as he turned to look at her in disbelief. "I can't imagine why anyone would want to sit and watch a man paint for hours, much less pay that much for the sloppy outcome."

If that was all he'd done, it wouldn't have been interesting, that was true. She couldn't help leaning in and sharing the critical tidbit about Klein's methods into his ear. She pressed her palm on his shoulder and climbed to her toes to brush her lips against the outer shell. "He painted with nude women."

The lines in Oliver's brow deepened as he turned to her. "So he painted with nude women standing around? A little distracting and gimmicky, don't you think?"

"No. He didn't use paintbrushes. He didn't even touch the canvas, actually. He used what he called 'living brushes.' He literally used the bodies of beautiful nude women smeared in paint. Or he traced their naked bodies onto the canvas and burned the image into the fabric with a torch."

"Seriously?"

Lucy nodded. "I've watched video recordings of his exhibitions and they were quite the spectacle. Just imagine all these well-to-do art lovers coming to a museum, and when they get there, they're greeted by a man in a tuxedo and maybe six young, attractive and very naked women. They sat there and watched as the women smeared the paint all over their skin, then pressed their bodies into the canvas, just as the artist guided them. He was more of a director, really, coaching the women into creating the shapes and images he wanted to portray. With the music and the lighting... it was such a sensual experience. To capture that kind of feeling in a work of art is amazing, really."

He squinted at the canvas, but Lucy could tell he needed help envisioning it in the peculiar shapes left behind.

She stepped between him and the closest painting.

"So picture me naked," she said with a smile. "There's buckets of blue paint and plastic tarps all over the floor. Even some canvases on the floor. I rub the paint all over my skin, covering everything as Yves directs, then position my body just so and press into the canvas." Lucy stood in front of the painting and tried to situate her body to mimic the imprint. "Can you see it now?"

He didn't answer. Finally, she dropped her arms and turned back to where he was standing. He was looking at her, but the expression in his eyes was not one of a casual appreciation for art. It looked as though he'd taken her far too literally when she'd told him to imagine her naked. A desire blazed in his blue-gray eyes as he watched her. So much for a distraction.

"I see it now," Oliver said, but he still wasn't looking at the painting. Instead, he took a step closer to her, closing the gap between them.

Lucy was suddenly very aware of her body. Despite the pleasant temperature of the museum, a blanket of goose bumps settled across her skin and made the hairs prickle at the back of her neck. She could feel the heat of Oliver as he hovered ever nearer, yet not touching her. The scent of his cologne made her long to press against him and bury her nose in his throat. All that talk about Klein's work had been the last thing they'd needed.

His hand reached out and his fingertips brushed across hers, sending jolts of electricity through her whole body. A warm rush of desire settled in her belly, urging her not to pull away from him this time. They'd both danced around this moment and she found she was desperate to see what would come next if they let things just happen.

Oliver leaned in, his face close enough to kiss her if either of them turned just right. "Lucy...?" he whispered.

She might be on a long celibate streak, but she knew what it meant when a man said her name like that. She wanted to say yes and throw her arms around his neck, but she wouldn't. This simmering passion just beneath the surface was dangerous, and she knew it. Did she dare give in to it? Could she trust the man who had previously been determined to call her out as a manipulative crook?

He certainly didn't seem interested in talking about his aunt's estate right now.

"Yes?" she replied, her voice trembling as her body ached to reach for him.

"Would you mind if we left the party a little early?" His breath was hot against her skin, sending a shiver down her spine.

"It just started," Lucy argued half-heartedly. It was a charity event and neither of them had been very charitable so far. "What about the school?"

Oliver leaned back and pierced her with his blue-gray gaze. "How about we go back downstairs, I write a check to make everyone happy and then you and I go back to my place. To talk about art," he added.

"A big check," Lucy suggested. He could afford it, even if she couldn't.

"Of course. You'll learn that with me, it's go big or go home," he said with a sly grin and a wink that promised more big things to come.

Seven

"Nice place," Lucy said as they stepped into his penthouse apartment.

Oliver just shrugged off the compliment. "It works for me. It's not a Fifth Avenue apartment overlooking the park or anything."

"Most people don't have that. Just because your aunt did doesn't make your place any less fantastic. If I hadn't been living with her all these years, I'd be renting a place the size of your entryway."

Lucy looked around in curiosity, taking in every detail of the place he'd paid to have professionally decorated. Oliver didn't really care about things like that. This was just a place to sleep at night. He did what was expected of him in this case because his apartment needed furniture and things on the wall. Thanks to all the money he'd spent, he now had expensive glass bowls that appeared to serve no real purpose and tiny statues that gathered dust. Thankfully he also had a cleaning service that came in to deal with that.

Oliver slipped out of his suit coat and threw it over the arm of the leather sofa. In his pocket, he found the receipt for the painting he'd just purchased at the charity event. He folded it neatly and tucked it away before Lucy could see it. She thought he'd simply made a donation to the high school before they left, but he'd actually gone in and placed a ridiculously high bid on the student painting she'd admired earlier. It ensured he would win the auction. Once the piece was assessed by the art department for the senior's final grade, it would be delivered anonymously to Lucy's apartment.

He wasn't entirely sure why he'd done it. Oliver wasn't exactly known for making flashy donations to charities or giving extravagant gifts. Most of the people in his life didn't need anything, so he quietly supported a few causes. In this case, however, he just knew he wanted to do something nice and unexpected for Lucy. She would appreciate it in a way few women he knew would. He hoped he'd be there when it was delivered so he could see the smile on her face when she saw it. That was enough for him.

"I see now why it's so easy for you to show up at the apartment unannounced," she said, pulling him from his thoughts. "You're only a few blocks away."

He approached her from behind as she stood in his living room and reached up to help her slip out of her coat. The night had grown chilly, but his apartment was very warm. He sighed as his eyes took in one inch after the next of her exposed back as the coat slipped down her arms and into his. The movement brought the scent of her skin to his nose, urging him to lean in closer. He longed to run his fingertip along the curve of her spine and follow the path with his mouth. Every time he looked at that outfit, he liked it more.

With the coat in his arms, Lucy turned to look at him expectantly. What had she asked about? Where he lived. "Yes," he responded. Oliver took a deep breath to push aside the building desire for a little while longer. He had no intention of attacking Lucy the moment he got her alone, as much as he might like to. "It's convenient to my offices and such. It's nice to live close to my father and sister as well. Dropping in on you so easily was just a bonus." He laid her coat across his own on the sofa. "Would you like a drink?"

"I would," she said with a polite smile. "Do you have a patio or a balcony where we could step out and enjoy it?"

He hesitated for a moment, not sure if he wanted to share that part of his life with her. At least not yet. It was one thing to want to seduce Lucy, another entirely to open up his most private place. His apartment didn't have a traditional balcony; it had something much nicer that was very personal to him. He'd actually never showed it to a woman he was dating before, and he wasn't even sure he'd call this situation with Lucy *dating*. "Not exactly," he replied as he disappeared into the kitchen to stall his response.

"What does that mean?" Lucy asked as she turned the corner to join him.

He wasn't entirely sure why, but he'd always kept that part of his life very private. Maybe it was watching his father give over everything to Candace, only to have her ruin it. Maybe it was just keeping something for himself that he didn't have to explain to anyone else. Harper had only seen his garden once.

And yet, he wanted to show it off to Lucy.

He'd never felt that compulsion before, and it unnerved him that he wanted to show her, of all people. "I have a large rooftop patio," he explained. "It's more of a garden, really. That's where I go when I want to…get dirty and unplug." From life, from stress, from all the drama of his family. He found his center when he was up to his elbows in potting soil. It was hard to explain that to the other rich CEOs who preferred racquetball, cigars and fine scotch to unwind.

"That sounds wonderful," Lucy said. "I'd love to see it."

Oliver worked on opening a bottle of wine and pouring two healthy glasses of chardonnay. He tried not to appear nervous about taking Lucy to see his handiwork. Surely he could manage to show it to her without letting her know how significant it was to him. "Sure. There's some great views from up there."

He handed her a glass and she followed him to a door in the hallway that looked like a closet, but actually hid a staircase up to the roof. Oliver took a soothing breath as he stepped out onto the patio with Lucy in his wake. "This is my retreat from the concrete jungle," he said.

Lucy's reply didn't come right away. Instead, when he turned to see what was wrong, he found her slack-jawed and wide-eyed. She looked around his garden as though she'd never seen anything like it in her life. And maybe she hadn't. He knew immediately that there was no way to hide how important this place was to him. It was obvious just by looking at it.

"I don't know what I was expecting," Lucy said at last. "Maybe some clay pots with petunias in them or something. But nothing like this."

That's probably because there were few rooftop gardens like this in the city. He had trees and shrubs in huge planters along the edges of the roofline that made the garden feel private and secluded. There were twinkle lights wrapped through the branches and strung overhead, mixing with the stars. Pea-gravel pathways made a complicated pattern around raised flowerbeds where he was growing all manner of flowers and a few vegetables he donated to the food bank. Many of the plants would soon die back for the winter, but most were still showing off their foliage and brightly colored blooms.

"I had no idea you were a gardener. Harper never mentioned it. How did the CEO of a computer company get into something like this?"

"Few people know about it. Harper knows, she just doesn't mention it very often because she's afraid I'm going to make her come up and pull weeds or something." Oliver stuffed his free hand into his pants pocket and slowly strolled along the gravel path.

"It's funny you should ask how I got into it… When I was very young, my mother had a garden like this on their rooftop, and I helped her from time to time. I guess I got my green thumb from her. After she died, my father basically let her garden run wild. He didn't want anyone up there messing with her things. Years later as a teenager, I got the stupid idea to go up there and grow some weed. It was such a mess that I didn't figure anyone would notice, but my dad saw me sneaking out there once or twice and eventually busted me."

"As my punishment, I had to clean up my mother's garden and maintain it flawlessly for six months. By the time my sentence ended, I'd found I really enjoyed it. I chose this apartment in part because of the roof access. It's all mine and since it's taller than most of the nearby buildings, it's incredibly private despite being surrounded by millions of other people. The previous owners had just put some patio furniture out here, but I transformed it over the last few years into a place that I think my mother would've loved."

Oliver had no idea why he kept rambling on about the garden and his love for it. He'd never told this story to anyone, and yet Lucy's simple question had prompted a flow of words that even he hadn't expected. He didn't understand why she had this effect on him. There wasn't just an attraction between them, there was more. A real connection that he wanted to build and maintain beyond this nonsense about the will. That was the scariest part of all.

"Are there still places to sit up here?" Lucy asked as she leaned in to smell a large, dark red rose.

That was one of his favorites—the Mister Lincoln rose. It gave off an amazing perfume in addition to being a beautiful, classic, crimson rose. "Yes. If we follow the path around, we'll see the pergola where I've put up some furniture."

They walked along the trail lined with rosebushes, gardenias and zinnias, to the trumpet vine-wrapped pergola on the south side of the building. It framed the best view from the roof, showcasing the ever-changing colors of the top of the Empire State Building. Under the pergola was a double chaise lounge that was perfect for sunbathing, naps or working evenings on the laptop with a glass of wine or scotch and ice.

"Wow," Lucy said. With the giddy grin of a child, she kicked off her heels and lay against the raised back of the chaise. She tugged up her dress to expose the cropped pants underneath and wiggled her pink painted toes in their newfound freedom. "This is amazing. I would spend every minute I had out here if I could."

Oliver smiled and settled onto the seat beside her. She'd jumped into the chaise without giving a second thought to getting her designer dress dirty and he appreciated that. "I don't spend much time just sitting here, actually. Maintaining the garden takes up most of my free time since I do it all myself. If I'm out here, I'm pulling weeds and repotting plants. Trimming back bushes and watering. It's a lot of work but it helps me keep my mind off of my worries."

Lucy sighed and snuggled against his shoulder as she took a sip of her wine. Oliver felt the heat of her body sink through the fabric of his tuxedo shirt and warm his skin. The feel of her so close made his pulse speed up. Suddenly, he had the urge to rip off his bowtie and tug her into his lap. He wasn't going to rush things tonight, though. There was no need to not take their time and enjoy it.

"And to think," Lucy said, "I assumed you were just some heartless workaholic with nothing better to do with your limited free time than screw with me."

That made him laugh out loud, chasing away his heated thoughts for a moment. Lucy just said whatever came to her mind and he loved that about her. There wasn't anything practiced or polished about her words. It was authentic and refreshing, even when it was mildly insulting.

"Well, I am a heartless workaholic, but I have plenty of things I could do with my limited free time. I simply chose to spend the time screwing with you because I…" Oliver turned his head toward her with his lips nearly pressing against her temple. "I like you, Lucy. More than I ever thought I would. Probably more than I should, if I were smart. But I can't help it. And I can't help wanting you."

Lucy was stunned to silence. It was one thing to say that they'd called a truce on their war over Alice's estate. It was another thing entirely for him to declare he wanted her while they were alone on a romantic rooftop patio. That was serious. That was the kind of statement that led to action.

So action is the course she took.

She set her glass of wine and small beaded black clutch on the table beside them and shifted onto her side to face him. His expression was different as he looked down at her in the glow of the garden's lights. The hard edge of his jaw seemed softer, the sharp glare of his blue eyes warm instead. Welcoming. And not just with need, although she could sense the tension of desire in the press of his lips into one another. There was something about being here, in this place that was so special to him, that had changed him or at least shown her a side of him she didn't know existed. She liked that part of Oliver. Liked him enough to throw the last of her reservations out the window where he was concerned.

"Sometimes the things we want aren't the smartest choices," she said softly. "But they're the chances you're the most likely to regret not taking. I hate having regrets."

Lucy followed her words by leaning in and kissing him. This was no desperate assault like their first kiss on the Dempsey balcony, but a sultry warm-up to something more. She melted into him as she felt his hands seek out her waist and pull her closer. His mouth parted and his tongue slid past her own. The caress sent a surge down her spine, making her skin prickle with goose bumps and her core throb with need.

She never expected to be here, in a place like this, with a man like Oliver. Despite her desire to make more of herself one day, she never wanted it to be because she dated up on the social ladder. Even though being friends with women like Emma and Violet exposed her to plenty of sexy, successful men, she didn't think for a moment they would be interested in her.

But Oliver was definitely interested.

His hands moved over her body, exploring and caressing each curve and hollow like he was trying to commit it to memory. When his fingertips brushed over the bare curve of her back and waist, she shivered from the sizzling heat of his hand against her skin.

"Are you cold?" He whispered the question against her lips. "Your skin is freezing. We can go back inside."

"I'm not cold. You're just hot." *In more ways than one*, she thought silently. "And I like it."

"Oh really?" He smiled and gripped firmly at her hip. "Then I think you'll like this, too."

Lucy let out a soft squeal of surprise as Oliver pulled her into his lap with a firm tug, guiding her to straddle him on the chaise. The position was much more comfortable than lying side by side and allowed her free access to his body with her hands. She ran her palms over his chest with a naughty grin, feeling the hard muscles beneath the starched fabric of his shirt. "You're right. I like this as well. I'd like it better with some of this fabric out of the way."

She moved quickly to his tie and the buttons of his shirt. He didn't resist, he just closed his eyes and tensed his jaw as her hips slowly moved back and forth, teasing at his rock-hard arousal.

"Damn," he muttered under his breath.

His response to her made Lucy bolder. Once his shirt was unbuttoned, she pushed it open and ran her hands across the golden bronze ridges of his chest. He wasn't a soft, pale businessman who spent all his time indoors in front of a computer. Apparently gardening was hard work that he did without his shirt on and she appreciated that.

He lay mostly motionless with his eyes still closed as she admired the gift she'd just unwrapped. Her fingers traced the edges of his muscles, grazing over his sprinkle of dark chest hair and trailing the path it made down his belly to his belt. She could feel his stomach quiver beneath her touch as she moved lower.

Oliver could only tolerate that for so long, it seemed; as his eyes flew open, he reached out to cup Lucy's face and pulled her mouth to his own. There was an edge of frenzy when he kissed her this time, the slow, sensual kiss from earlier harder to maintain as the tension built between them. She didn't mind. She gave as good as she got, touching him and pressing into his caresses to intensify the pleasurable feelings that they sent through her body.

Lucy only felt a moment of nerves as Oliver's fingers unfastened the strip of red fabric that held on her dress. There was nothing beneath it but the black cropped pants that paired with the open-backed gown, so she would be fully exposed. She didn't want to act nervous, however. She didn't want Oliver to know how long it had been since she'd been with a man or how badly she didn't want to screw tonight up. So instead, she pasted on her most seductive expression—at least that was what she was going for—and let the gown slip down her arms to pool with the rest of it bunched up at his waist.

She bit at her lip as Oliver studied her bare chest with appreciation. She held her breath until he brought his hands up to cover her breasts and knead them gently. He groaned aloud with approval as she leaned into his touch.

Oliver let go of her only long enough to tug the fabric of her discarded dress into a ball and cast it to the vacant side of the chaise. That allowed them to get closer, and he took advantage of that by sitting up, wrapping his arms around her waist and capturing one of her hard, pink nipples in his mouth.

Lucy's head went back with a soft cry she couldn't hold in. For a moment, she looked around, expecting to feel exposed somehow, but the garden was incredibly private. She could shout, cry and remove every stitch of clothing she had on without anyone being the wiser. It was an unexpected turn-on, titillating the inner exhibitionist she didn't know she had.

She clutched the back of his head with her hands, burying her fingers in the thick waves of his chestnut hair and holding him close. She was so caught up in the moment, the feel of his lips on her skin, that she didn't realize she was moving backward until her skin made contact with the chaise.

Now Oliver was on top with Lucy's legs clamped around his narrow hips. He held himself up with his arms planted to each side of her as he looked down with a satisfied smirk. Pressing forward, he rubbed his firm desire between her thighs. The sensation shot through her like a fiery arrow despite the pesky pants they both still had on. Not for long.

Oliver placed a gentle kiss on her lips, then continued down her body. One on her chin, each collarbone, her sternum, each breast, her stomach…stopping when he reached her capris. Those were quickly unzipped and pulled down her hips along with the lace hipster panties she was wearing beneath them. For every few inches of skin he uncovered, he placed another kiss on her skin. Each hipbone, her lower belly, the tops and inside of her thighs, knees, calves, ankles.

And then she was naked. Totally and completely exposed, panting and trembling with the overwhelming sensations he was stirring inside of her. She ached for him to touch her center, to fill her with the hard heat he'd teased her with so far. But instead, he stopped moving altogether.

Lucy opened her eyes to see him kneeling between her legs with an almost painful expression lining his face. "What's wrong?" No woman wanted to finally take off all her clothes and have the guy freeze up like that.

"I don't have anything," he explained with a sheepish look. "Protection, I mean. To be honest, I wasn't expecting this to happen. Especially not up here. It's not an excuse not to wear anything. I wouldn't do that.

I don't know why I didn't think of this sooner. I was just wrapped up in you…and now you're naked and so beautiful and I…"

Lucy smiled and leaned over to reach for her purse sitting on the table. There, she pulled out the duo of condoms she carried for emergencies. She'd never had an emergency in all the years leading up to now, but she knew better than to not be prepared. That was when bad decisions happened. "Here," she said, holding up the foil packets and saving him from the torture he was leveraging on himself.

Oliver took them from her, clutched them in his fist and grinned. "You're amazing. Thank God."

He leaned down and kissed her with a renewed surge of energy. Oliver pulled away for a few moments and when he returned to her, the pants were gone, the latex was in place and he was poised between her thighs. "Now," he said with a grin as he looked down at her. "Where were we?"

Lucy reached between them and wrapped her fingers around his length. He groaned as she rubbed the tip of him against her moist flesh, teasing them both to the point of madness, then positioning him just at her opening. "Right about here is a good place to pick up, I think."

"You're right," he agreed before pushing forward into her warmth. He moved at an agonizingly slow pace, savoring every inch until he was buried deep inside of her.

Lucy gasped at the sensation of being so completely filled after all the years she'd gone without it. She suddenly wondered why she'd allowed herself to become so much like her agoraphobic older client while only in her twenties, but at the same time, she wouldn't have traded this moment for anything. If five years of celibacy earned her a payoff like this, it was worth it.

It was as though he was the perfect key for her lock. Everything from the way he touched her, to how he kissed her, the taste of his skin, to the scent of his cologne, couldn't have been more right. And when he started to move, the floodgates opened deep inside of her.

She clung to his back, gasping and crying out to the inky black sky overhead as Oliver thrust into her. They rocked together on the chaise, their movements more frantic and their muscles growing more tense as the pleasure started to build up between them.

"You feel so amazing," he growled into her ear. "I don't ever want this to end."

Lucy couldn't respond. She was past the point of rational thought with her climax barreling closer with every surge. All she could manage was a steady chorus of encouraging yeses. *Yes, keep doing that. Yes, I don't want it to end. Yes, this is what I've been waiting for. Yes, yes, yes.*

That's when it finally happened. Like a tightly wound coil inside her body giving way, her orgasm exploded through her. It pulsated through her core, radiating to every limb and making her head swim with pleasure. Her hips bucked against his, forcing him in deeper as her muscles tightened around him. The combination sent Oliver over the edge a moment later. He thrust hard, finishing with a low groan of satisfaction.

They lay together that way—weak muscles, throbbing parts and harsh, panting breaths—for what seemed like an hour, but it was only minutes. Too exhausted to move far but content in each other's arms, they finally untangled and righted themselves on the chaise to snuggle up together. Lucy nuzzled into the crook of his arm and molded to his side. Oliver tugged her voluminous red gown over them to shield their bare bodies from the night air and they fell asleep there under the ever-glowing Manhattan sky.

Eight

Making love to Lucy was amazing, but Oliver found he quite liked just talking to her as well. After a short nap on the rooftop, they got chilly, gathered their clothes and moved downstairs to his bed. There, he made love to her again, but instead of being sleepy, they were energized with conversation. They'd managed to lie in bed talking to the wee hours of the morning. He could tell she was getting tired, but like a stubborn toddler, not willing to give in to sleep quite yet.

"Harper and I are taking the train up to Connecticut next weekend," Lucy said.

"A fun girls trip?" Oliver asked.

"Something like that. Do you have any plans? Maybe we can do something when I get back."

Oliver picked up his phone from the nightstand to check his calendar. He would be lost without it. "Yep.

I'm taking Danny to Coney Island. He's finally tall enough to ride the roller coaster and he's been pestering me for weeks."

"Who's Danny?"

Oliver frowned. Not at Lucy, but at the fact that he hadn't mentioned his brother to her in all this time. He supposed the focus of their discussions hadn't really been on his family aside from Aunt Alice. "Hasn't Harper ever mentioned our little brother?"

"Oh," Lucy said, the pieces almost visibly coming together in her mind. "Yes, she has, she just never uses his real name. She calls him Noodle for some reason. I honestly had no idea his real name was Danny."

At that, Oliver had to laugh. "His name is Daniel Royce Drake after my grandfather and my stepmother's favorite car, respectively. Harper has called him Noodle almost since the day he was born but has never told me why. Do you know?"

Lucy shook her head. "She's never said, and I guess I didn't ask. She just mentions doing things with Noodle or posts pictures with him on Snapchat every now and then. I have to admit, that's quite a nickname to grow up with."

Oliver shrugged it off. "I'm sure he'll be in therapy for far more serious things than a cutesy nickname his older sister gave him."

"Why would you say something like that? That's awful." Lucy frowned at him, wrinkling her freckled nose.

"It's true." Oliver's brow furrowed as he studied Lucy. Was it possible she didn't know the strange and sad tale of Thomas and Candace Drake? Surely Harper had mentioned it. She had just started at Yale when their father began dating Candace. Or perhaps Alice said something. Just because she didn't leave her apartment didn't mean she didn't know exactly what was going on in the family at all times. Or maybe Alice didn't know. At least to the full extent. Their father may not have wanted to admit he'd squandered his fortune on a beautiful woman.

"What could a little rich boy possibly have go wrong in his life to necessitate counseling?"

Only people without money would think that life was easy if you had it. Yes, the necessities of life were no longer a worry, but it came with a whole new set of troubles. Women like Candace being one of them.

"Nothing, now," Oliver admitted. "He was so young. I mean, I'm sure he misses his mother as a concept, but at the same time, she left when he was still a toddler. He may not remember much about her, only what's told to him. But eventually he's going to get old enough to realize that his mother used him as a pawn to get her hands on my father's fortune, and then dumped him when he wasn't useful to her any longer. When that dawns on him, it's going to hurt. And it doesn't matter how much Dad loves him, or Harper and I love him. It's going to make him question why he wasn't good enough for his mother to want him."

Lucy's big, brown eyes widened in concern, getting larger the more he said. "What kind of woman would leave her baby behind like that? That's horrible."

Her response and disgust seemed genuine. "A woman like my stepmother. Does Harper just not talk about our family at all?" he asked.

She shook her head. "Not really. I always got the feeling that talking about herself made her uncomfortable. I don't know why. Violet and Emma grew up with wealth and privilege like she did. I'm the broke outsider in the group."

"Not even when the stuff came up with the will? She didn't mention Candace?"

"No, she didn't."

Oliver sighed. He wrapped his arm around her shoulder and she snuggled in against his chest. "Candace is Danny's mother. My father remained single for over ten years after our mother died of cervical cancer. Mom's illness was hard on everyone, and when it was all over, he wanted to focus on raising us and running his company. There just wasn't any room left for a relationship, even if he had been ready to date again. After Harper went off to college, he met Candace and got all wrapped up in her. It all happened so fast. The whole situation was a nightmare from start to finish."

"Why was it a nightmare?"

"Because, for a start, she was three years older than *me*. Dad didn't seem to care about cradle robbing. She was beautiful and she fawned over him like he was the most amazing man she'd ever met. I guess he needed that after all those years alone. It was obvious to everyone but him that she was just after his money. He was blinded by her beauty and was so desperate to find someone to love him that he fell right into her trap. They got married within a year and she got pregnant with Danny pretty quickly. Before his second birthday, Candace had spent all my father's liquid assets and charged up all his credit accounts into the millions. When he finally put his foot down over her spending, it was only because he had no choice. She had wiped him out. He cut her off financially and she split almost immediately, leaving Danny behind. I guess he wasn't worth taking just for the child support checks when she could do better on her own. Last I heard, she married another tech billionaire from Silicon Valley. One of our competitors, if you can believe her nerve."

Oliver didn't want to drone on and on about Candace, so he got to the point as quickly as he could and waited to see what Lucy had to say about it. Very little, it turned out. Instead, they sat together in an awkward silence that seemed to stretch on forever.

Finally, Lucy spoke in a small voice. "So that's why."

"What do you mean?"

"That's why you automatically presumed that I'm an awful person. Because of her."

Now that he'd gotten to know Lucy better, he was ashamed to tell her as much, but he knew it was true. That's what experience had taught him. "I'll admit it colored my opinion, yes."

Lucy pushed herself up in bed and tugged the sheets to her chest defensively. She had a pained expression lining her brow and the corners of her mouth were turned down just slightly. "Colored your opinion, my foot," she snapped. "You didn't know me from Adam and you lashed out at me as though you'd seen a sketch of my face on a Wanted poster or something. You thought I'd conned your aunt just like your stepmother conned your father. Admit it."

"It's not—"

"Admit it," Lucy pressed. "You thought I was such a horrible person that I was willing to steal all your aunt's belongings out from under you all. Do you think I killed her, too?"

"Of course not!" Oliver replied. "Don't be ridiculous. Do you think I'd be lying in bed with you if I thought you were capable of something like that?"

"Okay, so not a murderer, but certainly a swindler."

Oliver twisted his lips in thought for a moment before he turned away from Lucy's accusatory gaze and sighed. "Okay, I guess I did. But you have to understand that the situation with Candace left me suspicious of *everyone's* motives, not just yours. On a date, the moment a woman asked what business I was in or what area of town I lived in, I could feel this anxiety start to creep in."

"Those are pretty common first date questions."

"I know," he said, feeling foolish about the whole thing but unable to suppress it. "But it felt like women were just trying to figure out how much money I had. Or if they knew my family and showed an interest, I convinced myself that it couldn't be because they were genuinely interested in me. Watching Candace work my dad over was hard. Especially since we couldn't say a bad word about her to him. Trust me when I say we tried, but he wouldn't listen. In the end, he looked like a fool and I never wanted to make that same mistake."

"So a woman couldn't possibly be interested in you because you're smart or handsome? Well dressed? Did you ever think that maybe one of those women was just interested in seeing if you had a big…garden?"

"I do have a larger than average garden." Oliver started to laugh, and then he clapped his right hand over his eyes in dismay. "Oh, you're right. I know you're right. I erred on the side of caution."

"And what good did it do you?"

Oliver looked down at Lucy, her naked body warm and curved against him. "It got you here, for a start. If

I hadn't been so suspicious of you, I might not have followed you around and therefore, might not have fallen for your many charms."

Lucy smirked at him, unimpressed by his flattery. "And now that you've fallen for my charms…do you still think I conned your aunt?"

He knew this was a critical moment in the relationship he'd never expected to have with Lucy. After spending this time together, he should know, one way or another, if she was guilty of everything he'd accused her of. If he thought she was innocent, he'd say so right now without hesitation. And yet the seconds ticked by without his answer as he struggled with his prejudices.

Finally, he found the right combination of words. They might not be the ones she wanted to hear, but it was an honest response. "I really like you, Lucy. More than I ever expected to. I don't want to believe you could do something like that. I'm not sure if that makes me idealistic or just plain stupid."

Lucy watched his face for a moment. He could tell by the dimmed light in her eyes that he'd still hurt her even though she was trying to act as though he hadn't. "Thank you for answering that honestly," she said at last. She sat in deep thought for a few seconds before a yawn overtook her and he could tell she was losing the fight to sleep. "I don't know how to prove to you that I'm not like your stepmother, but I'm not going to figure that out tonight. I guess all I can do is keep trying. Good night, Oliver."

She leaned in to give him a kiss, then she lay back down, cuddling against him with another contagious yawn. After a few moments in the dark silence, he could tell she'd drifted off to sleep. He wished he could fall asleep that easily. But not tonight.

Tonight, he was left with questions he couldn't answer. Not with enough certainty to make him feel better. When Lucy called him out for putting his hang-ups over Candace on her and painting them with the same guilty brush, he felt foolish about the whole thing.

Oliver had decided Lucy was guilty without a stitch of evidence to prove it. And his big plan to uncover her secrets hadn't resulted in a single incriminating thing about her since that day at the lawyer's office. Honestly, he hadn't really tried. A background check hadn't revealed anything insidious. She was the only child of two blue-collar parents from central Ohio who split up when she was only a few years old. No criminal record, no negative remarks on her credit report...even her transcript from Yale proved her to be an above-average student.

By all accounts, she was delightful to be around, thoughtful, smart and sexy as hell. He couldn't imagine her being a crook like Candace was.

Even then, he had a hard time turning off his suspicious thoughts.

He'd like to think that if he truly suspected she was guilty of tricking Alice into changing her will, he wouldn't be in bed with her at the moment. That had to be worth something. And yet he hadn't called off his lawyers either. It was entirely possible that his aunt had simply left her estate to someone she thought deserved it.

As far as she knew, no one in the family was truly hurting for money. He was fine. Harper seemed to be getting along okay. And despite his father's claims of being broke, he was far from it. He still brought in more income in a single month from his investment portfolio than most people earned in a year. It didn't last as long in Manhattan as it would other places, but he wasn't about to be out on the street. He also had his retirement from the company. Real estate holdings. It just wasn't enough to maintain the lifestyle Candace wanted.

His father may have been blinded by love, but Aunt Alice was no one's fool. If she could see all the quibbling going on over her will, she'd come back from the grave and tell them all to quit it because she knew full well what she was doing when she changed it. Lucy would have to be a very skilled scam artist to pull one over on her.

He didn't see that level of cunning in her. So why didn't he drop the protest? He was the only one keeping Lucy from getting everything she was due.

Maybe he would.

Oliver sighed and closed his eyes to try to sleep.

Maybe he wouldn't.

Lucy woke up in Oliver's bed the next morning. She wasn't sure if it was nerves or regret about last night, but she found herself wide awake at dawn with her mind racing over the night before. She didn't want to disturb Oliver, so she put on her capris, stole a T-shirt from his dresser and slipped out of the room.

She made herself a cup of coffee using the Keurig on his Carrara marble countertop, doctored it with half-and-half from his refrigerator and settled at the kitchen table. There was no reason she would be awake at this hour after staying up half the night, but there was an anxiety swirling in her stomach and in her head. It demanded she wake up, so here she was. There would no doubt be a nap in her future once she was back at her apartment.

For the time being, Lucy sipped her coffee. It felt strange sitting idly in Oliver's kitchen, but she felt equally weird about doing anything else in his home while he was still asleep. That left her the option of leaving, and she knew that wasn't the right path to take. Last night, while unexpected, had been amazing and romantic. This morning might prove awkward, and they might never share a moment like that again, but it wouldn't be because she chickened out and ran before he woke up.

Taking another sip of her coffee, she felt her stomach start to rumble. Unlike her friend Violet, who could charge through the day on a steady diet of coffee and the occasional protein bar before she got pregnant, Lucy liked to eat, and she especially liked to eat breakfast. Eggs, pancakes, waffles, sugary cereal, oatmeal, toast, bacon…you name it. She was a fan of the meal in general. She wasn't the kind who could make it to lunch without eating anything.

How long could she last today? She looked at the clock in the hallway. It was just after six thirty. There was a deli up the block where she could get a bagel or order delivery, but she didn't need to be seen by the general public. Especially not wearing silk capris, a hole-ridden old T-shirt, no bra, last night's makeup and morning-after hair. Lucy didn't need a mirror to know that she'd announce "walk of shame" to anyone she passed.

Including Oliver.

On that note, Lucy pushed aside the idea of food for

a moment and sought out the hall powder room to see how bad it really was. She winced in the mirror when she switched on the light. It was a rough look.

The clothes were what they were unless she wanted to wear her gown around the house, but she could clean up the rest. She splashed warm water on her face and used a disposable towel to wipe away the remnants of last night's smoky eye. Then she finger-combed her hair into a messy knot on the top of her head. It was still a far cry from her polished look at the museum the night before, but it was a casual, carefree messy instead of a hot-mess messy. The best she could do on an unplanned overnight stay.

The apartment was still silent when she stepped back out into the hall. Silent enough for her loud tummy rumbling to nearly echo. She couldn't put off breakfast for too much longer.

Lucy started rummaging through his cabinets for an easy option but found nothing she could grab like a pastry or a granola bar. That left real food. Oliver didn't strike her as the kind of man who did a lot of cooking, but she hadn't thought he was a gardener either. While the selection wasn't outstanding, she did find just enough between the contents of the pantry and the refrigerator to cobble together a decent breakfast for the two of them.

It was actually a dish that Alice had taught her to make in the years she'd lived with her. She'd called it Trash Casserole, but it was basically a crustless quiche filled with an assortment of breakfast foods. The idea was to make it with whatever was on hand, hence the trash, but Alice always made it following a strict recipe, which Lucy appreciated.

Her mother was an excellent cook after working at the local diner for twenty years, but it never rubbed off on Lucy. She wasn't a natural at it the way her mom was. Her mother could never explain how or why she did certain things, she just cooked it until it looked right and never followed a recipe. Eventually, Lucy just got frustrated with trying to learn and gave up.

Alice had been a lot easier to follow. She kept all her recipes on neatly handwritten cards in a brass box that sat in the cupboard. Those cards were gospel as far as Alice was concerned and she never strayed. Lucy had thought she would copy them all down for herself so she could make those dishes in her own home one day. Now, she realized, those painstakingly scripted cards were hers, along with everything else.

Maybe.

Lucy doubted that Oliver would begrudge her some recipe cards if she really wanted them, but at the moment, they were tied up with about half a billion in other assets of the estate. She'd tried not to think about Oliver as her adversary, but his aunt's will was definitely the elephant in the room with them. Lucy didn't expect him to drop the protest just because they'd had sex, but a part of her hoped that maybe he knew her well enough now not to confuse her with his greedy stepmother. Or perhaps not. Sex somehow could change everything and yet nothing all at once.

"Something smells good."

Lucy looked up to see Oliver standing near the Keurig. He was looking deliciously messy himself, wearing nothing but a pair of jeans and some heavy stubble. The hard, tan stomach she'd explored the night before was on full display with his jeans hanging low on his hips. He ran his fingers through his hair and smiled sheepishly. The combination sent her pulse through the roof. It was nearly enough of a distraction to make her burn their breakfast if the timer hadn't gone off that very second.

"Good morning," she said, anxiously turning away from him and focusing on pulling the casserole out of the oven. "Are you hungry?"

"Mmm-hmm," he muttered as he came in closer and snuggled up behind her. He planted a kiss on her neck that sent a chill down her spine and a warmth of awareness across her skin. She turned to give him a proper good-morning kiss but realized his attention had shifted to what she was cooking.

"Is that Trash Casserole?" he asked with a look of astonishment on his face.

Lucy nodded. "It is. Have you had it before?"

"Have I had it before?" He took a step back and shook his head. "It's only the best thing Aunt Alice ever made. She cooked it every morning for Harper and me after we stayed the night with her."

She turned off the oven. "Well, good. She's the one that taught me how to make it, so hopefully it's at least half as good as hers."

Oliver eyeballed the dish with a wide grin. "It looks exactly like I remember it. I don't think I've eaten that in twenty years."

Lucy looked at him with a confused frown. "How is that possible? You had all the stuff to make it in the house. It's not a particularly complicated recipe. You mean you've never tried to do it yourself in all this time?"

He shook his head and took a step toward the coffee maker. "No. I don't cook. Not even a little. I pay a lady to come in twice a week to clean and stock the fridge with a few things I can eat. I found if I didn't do that, I'd just eat takeout until I needed bigger pants. Anything you found in the house, she left here, I can assure you."

Lucy wasn't surprised. "Well you'll have to apologize to her for me when she comes by again and finds I've used up her supplies."

Oliver chuckled as he popped a pod into the coffee machine and turned it on. "She won't mind. I'm sure Patty would be happy to come here and find evidence of cooking instead of candy wrappers and take-out containers in my trash can."

Lucy made them both plates and they settled together at the kitchen table. It was a nice moment to share, diffusing any of the morning-after awkwardness. They were nearly finished when Oliver's cell phone rang.

She sat silently as he answered, giving one-word replies and frowning at the table. "Okay. I'll be there shortly. I just got up."

He hit the button to hang up and looked at her with an apologetic expression on his face. "That was my dad. They're taking Danny to the hospital in an ambulance. He had an accident at his riding lesson this morning. I'm sorry to cut our breakfast short, but I need to go meet Dad in the emergency room."

Lucy's soft heart ached at the thought of his little brother at the hospital without his mother there to comfort him. She was hardly a suitable substitute—she'd never even met the little boy Harper called Noodle— but she couldn't go home in good conscience. She had to do something to help. "I'll go with you," she offered, getting up from the table with her dish in her hand.

He flinched at the suggestion, making her wonder if she was crossing a line by imposing on his family even after the night they'd shared. Was it too soon? Perhaps his father wouldn't want her there. He hadn't seemed any more pleased with her at the will reading than the rest of the family.

"You don't need to do that, Lucy. I'm sure he'll be fine."

She wasn't about to let him push her away that easily. "I know I don't need to do it, but I want to. If we can just stop by my place on the way, I'll do a quick change of clothes and I'll be happy to keep you company. It sounds like it's going to be a long day for everyone. I can fetch coffee or something. Let me help."

Oliver's thin lips twisted in thought for a moment, then he nodded with an expression of relief. "Okay." He stepped forward and pulled Lucy into his arms, dropping his forehead down to gently meet her own as he held her.

"Thank you."

Nine

Danny was a trooper. Oliver had to give him credit for that. He wasn't sure he'd have handled all of this as well when he was his age. He'd broken his wrist riding his scooter when he was nine and had been convinced at the time that no one had experienced his level of pain, ever.

Danny had four broken ribs, the doctor had said. X-rays showed the breaks were clean and would come together on their own. There was no risk for the bones puncturing the lungs. It sounded bad and it was quite painful, but it could've been much worse. During his riding lesson, the horse had gotten spooked by something. It bucked Danny out of the saddle, then stomped on his chest while he was lying on his back in the riding ring. He could've been killed in about four or five different ways, so some bruises and a few cracked ribs were a best-case scenario, really.

Dad had gone back to the apartment to get a few things. The doctors were going to keep Danny overnight. The first twenty-four hours were the most painful and where his breaks were located, he couldn't do much of anything for himself, even raise a juice box to his mouth.

That just left Oliver and Lucy with him for the time being, as Harper was out of town. Although Oliver had initially been thrown off by Lucy's request to come with him to the hospital, she'd been a lifesaver today. She'd brought them food from the cafeteria, magazines from the gift shop, and she even had a phone charger in her purse when their phones started to die from the constant calls and texts. Having her here had been nice. Nicer than he wanted to admit to himself.

Waking up with her, sharing breakfast together, even weathering a crisis together…every moment he spent with Lucy made him want to spend more and more. This was going to be a problem.

"Can I have a popsicle?" Danny asked. He was sitting up in his hospital bed with pillows propped up under his arms and a thin blanket thrown over his legs. He looked so small in that bed, even smaller than the seven-year-old usually looked.

Oliver got up from the chair, relieved to have a quest to occupy his mind. "I'll go see what I can do. Are you okay to stay with him?" he asked Lucy.

She nodded from her perch at the end of his bed. "We'll be fine."

Oliver went down the hallway in search of a popsicle. The pain medicine was making Danny queasy, so he wasn't much interested in the food they were bringing him. If his baby brother wanted a popsicle, Oliver would find him one. The nurses didn't have any, just pudding and gelatin cups, so he headed downstairs in the hopes of finding something in the cafeteria or gift shop that would make Danny smile. He'd hit a street cart if he had to.

He scored a Bomb Pop, finally, and carried it back upstairs after about twenty minutes of hunting. As he neared the doorway to Danny's hospital room, the sound of voices made him pause. Danny wasn't normally much of a talker, but the pain medications had him chatting up a storm. He and Lucy were talking and Oliver was curious about what the two of them would discuss without anyone else around.

"The nurses cut off my favorite shirt when we got to the hospital," Danny complained. "It hurt too much to pull it over my head."

"I bet your daddy can get you another shirt just like that one."

"Yeah, but it won't be the same. My mother sent me that shirt for my last birthday."

Oliver froze in place. He'd never heard Danny mention his mother. He hadn't even known she was in contact with her son until now. Dad hadn't said anything about it. For a moment, Oliver wasn't sure if he should be happy she was involved or mad for stringing his brother along.

"Did she?" Lucy asked in a polite voice that didn't betray what she knew about Danny's mother. "That was nice of her."

Oliver leaned forward until he could see around the corner of the door frame. Danny was still sitting up in bed. Lucy was sitting at the end of the bed, turned toward Danny with interest.

Danny shrugged on reflex and winced with the movement. "Not really. She sends a package on my birthday and at Christmas, but that's it. A *good* mom would do more than that. A good mom would've stayed around or taken me with her. Or at least visit every once in a while. That's what people say when they think I'm not listening."

He could see Lucy stiffen awkwardly in her seat. What did you say to something like that, knowing it was absolutely true but not being able to fix it?

"I'm sorry to hear that. Not having both parents around can be hard. You know, my daddy left when I was young, too."

Danny perked up. "Why did yours leave?"

Lucy sighed. "Well, I was small, so I don't know all the details, but my mom said he met someone else and started a new family. I never saw or heard from him again."

"Do you have more brothers or sisters?"

"Yes. Someone told me that I have two little sisters somewhere. I don't know their names."

Oliver couldn't believe how little he actually knew about Lucy's past and her family. What little he did know had come from the file on her the private investigator gave him. She never really talked about her life before she went to Yale and met his sister. Now he knew why. Being a single parent was hard. His father had enough money to get help when he needed it, never having to worry about bills or childcare, but the average mother on her own had no one to depend on but herself.

He imagined that drove Lucy to work even harder at everything she did. Getting into Yale was no easy feat, and getting a scholarship to cover most of the sky-high tuition was near impossible. He knew that having to drop out when she couldn't afford the tuition had to hurt. Being the companion of a wealthy old woman probably hadn't been her goal in life, but then again, that detour could very well make her richer than any Yale degree ever could.

"I just have Oliver and Harper," Danny said. "I've heard people say that's because my mom learned her lesson with me. I was a lot of work and I ruined her body, she said. She got her shoes tied after I was born."

"Do you mean she got her tubes tied?" Lucy asked, stifling a chuckle at the seven-year-old's interpretation of the story he'd heard.

"That's it. I think." Danny sat thoughtfully for a minute, gazing down at the IV in his hand. "I'm sorry about your dad, Lucy. I guess my mom could be a lot worse. At least she sends nice gifts. She can afford to though, since she's married to a super-rich guy in California. I heard the housekeeper say that the guy invented a thing that's in every smartphone in the world. She wasted all of Daddy's money in just a few years, but I think it will take her a lot longer to spend all of the new guy's money."

Oliver was surprised to listen to how much his brother knew about Candace. He was young, but perhaps he wasn't as sheltered as Oliver thought. It sounded as though the grown-ups around him had the habit of talking about Candace as though Danny were too young to understand what they were saying. The knowledge seemed to steal a touch of his innocence too soon, but perhaps the truth wouldn't be as crushing as if he'd learned it all later. He was a smart, savvy little boy. Much more than Oliver gave him credit for.

He was also amazed at how deftly Lucy handled Danny. She was such a caring person, so unlike Candace. In a moment, she'd shifted the discussion away from bad parents and had Danny chatting animatedly about his favorite video game. Any bad emotions roused by their talk faded away as he prattled on about trolls and secret passages. Danny loved playing on any kind of gadget and would happily sit and get lost in a game for hours on end. Considering his family owned one of the largest computer companies in the world, it was probably in his blood.

Dad had actually forced Danny to take the riding lessons to get him out of the house. That had backfired a little, considering it had landed him in the hospital, but at least it had given him something to do that didn't entail cheat codes and warlocks. The next week of his recovery would be spent playing his game the moment he could hold up his own controller.

Lucy listened to him speak as though it were the most interesting conversation she'd ever had. She had that ability, that way of making you feel like you were the only person in the room. The most important thing in her life. No wonder Alice had been so taken with her. And Harper. And now, Danny, too. She was like a planet swirling around in space and pulling everyone else into her orbit.

He realized he was tired of fighting to escape her pull. The conversation they'd had in the late hours the night before had been enlightening for him. Danny's accident had occupied his mind for most of the day, but when he had a quiet moment, his thoughts always returned to Lucy. He had judged her unfairly. If he set all his prejudgments aside, he had no reason not to let himself fall head over heels for this woman. It was a leap he'd never risked taking before and he wasn't sure he was ready to do it yet.

But he could feel it coming. Before too long, the solid ground beneath him would crumble and he would have no choice but to fall hard for Lucy Campbell.

Oliver was startled from his thoughts by the drip of the popsicle onto his hand through a hole in the wrapper. He couldn't stand out in the hallway forever. Instead, he rounded the corner as though he'd just returned and presented the prize to the grinning little boy waiting for it.

After closing out the weekend at the hospital, the following workweek seemed to fly by. Lucy spent almost every evening with Oliver, returning to the apartment on Fifth Avenue when he left for work in the morning. During the day, she looked at apartments near Yale online and plotted out an itinerary for the trip she and Harper were taking up there the following weekend.

In all the time Oliver and Lucy spent together, they existed in a protective bubble—neither of them mentioning the fact that Alice's will was still pending a decision from the judge. They simply didn't talk about it, like an elephant in the room that they kept their backs to.

At this point, Lucy thought for sure that he should trust her enough to know she had nothing to do with the change in the will. And yet she didn't ask him to withdraw the protest and he didn't offer. They just carried on with their relationship as though the explosive events that brought them together initially never happened.

It lingered in the back of Lucy's mind, but at the same time, she was happy to ignore that aspect of their association. Things were so much better without that topic creeping into their conversations. She also tended to ignore the fact that she was planning on leaving Manhattan after the New Year to finish school regardless of what the judge decided. She hadn't mentioned that to Oliver either, and she didn't know why. Perhaps it seemed too early in the relationship to worry about the future.

If they were still together when the holidays rolled around, then it would be an important discussion. Now it would just be like putting a ticking time bomb out ahead of them, ready to blow their fragile relationship apart at its mere mention.

But would there be a better time, she thought, looking through the layouts of another apartment complex. Maybe.

Maybe not.

About six that evening, the doorbell rang and Lucy found Oliver standing in the foyer with sacks of take-out in his hands.

"What are you doing here?" she asked. "I was just getting dressed to come over to your place."

"I thought we could use a change of scenery," he said, stepping past her into the apartment. "I've also always wanted to eat in the formal dining room."

Lucy followed him curiously. "That's fine by me. What's so great about the dining room?"

Oliver set the bags down on the table, revealing

some Italian dishes from a place close to his office. "When we were kids, we weren't allowed to eat in the formal dining room because we might spill on the priceless Moroccan rug. We had to eat in the kitchen where there was tile. When I was an adult, we didn't come over any longer, so I've never gotten to eat in here."

Lucy laughed. She'd honestly never eaten in this room either, but it was more out of convenience than anything else. When it was just Alice and her, it was easier to eat in the kitchen or to take a dish into her room and eat in bed by herself. "It's a first for us both then."

They settled at the table, eyeing the cream silk tablecloth, the infamous Moroccan rug and the large containers of pasta with red and white sauces sitting in front of them.

"Let's eat in the kitchen," they both said in unison, getting up and carrying everything out of the intimidating space as they laughed together.

When they were finished, Oliver grabbed the small container of tiramisu and two forks, and took Lucy's hand to lure her into the bedroom. "It's time for dessert," he said.

Lucy groaned as she followed him into her bedroom. She had eaten so much. She loved tiramisu, but she wasn't sure if she could stomach another bite of food. "I'm not sure I'm ready for dessert yet."

Oliver looked over his shoulder and gave her a coy wink. "That's okay. I think some physical activity first might make some room for more."

"Oh yeah? What do you have in mind?" she teased.

Oliver entered her room and set the container on

the nightstand. Lucy came up behind him and ran her hands over his broad shoulders. She loved seeing him in his suits every day after work. She loved the contrast of the soft, expensive fabrics draped over the hard steel of his body.

He shrugged out of the jacket, letting it fall into her hands. She draped it over the nearby chair and they continued their familiar dance of undressing. It had felt strange at first to expose herself so easily to someone, and now her fingers couldn't move fast enough for her bare skin to touch his.

Oliver flung back her comforter and they crawled into bed together. He immediately pulled her body against his and captured her mouth in a kiss. It was amazing how quickly this had become like coming home to Lucy. It didn't matter where they were, being in his arms was what was important. The rest of the world and its problems just melted away and all that mattered was the two of them.

"I think I might eat some of the tiramisu now," he murmured against her lips, "if you don't mind."

Lucy did mind. They were in the middle of something and he wanted to stop and eat. But she kept her mouth shut and was rewarded for her patience.

He grabbed the container from the bedside table and carried it with him as he positioned himself between her thighs. Oliver kissed the inside of each knee before opening the container and filling the room with the scent of chocolate and espresso. He swiped his index finger through the cream on top and painted each of her nipples with it. Swirling more across her belly, he stopped at the satin edge of her neatly trimmed curls.

Oliver set the box aside and smiled widely at her as he prepared to enjoy his dessert. He licked a leisurely trail across her belly, circling her navel and climbing higher. Lucy squirmed with a mix of need and impatience, clutching at the sheets as he teased her. Finally reaching her breasts, his tongue teased at one tight nipple and then the next, sucking in the mocha-dusted mascarpone and swirling it around her skin with his tongue.

Lucy had never been someone's dessert course before and she found she quite liked it. The only downside to this arrangement was that she didn't have any for herself. When he picked up the box for more, she caught his wrist to stop him. "I want some, too," she requested sweetly and reached for it.

"I thought you were full," Oliver teased, holding the box out of her grasp.

She stuck out her bottom lip in a pout. "I just want a little taste. Please?"

"Well, since you said please..." Oliver dipped his finger in the dessert and offered it to her. She grasped his hand with her own, holding it steady as she drew it into her mouth and sucked every bit from his skin. When it was long gone, she continued to suck at him in a suggestive way that made him groan her name aloud with a hint of desperation in his voice.

"Okay. That's enough tiramisu for now," she said, finally releasing her hold on him. "I'm ready for the rest of my dessert."

"Very well," he said, tossing the carton to the far side of the bed. He lay down beside her. "Come here."

Gripping her waist, he pulled Lucy into his lap. She straddled him, feeling unexpectedly powerful as he looked up at her with a light of appreciation in his eyes. Lucy had never thought of herself as particularly pretty or having a good body—average at best—but Oliver looked at her like she was his fantasy come to life. It made her feel like maybe that could be true.

He brought his hand up to her face. His fingertips traced the curve of her cheek, then trailed across her swollen bottom lip. "You are so beautiful. I never want to close my eyes when you're near me."

How did this amazing man come into her life? Things had been so surreal since Alice died. The estate, the future...that was hard enough to believe. But Oliver—being with a man like him was beyond her wildest imagination. He was handsome, smart and successful. He was everything she'd dreamt of but never believed she would have. And yet here she was, straddling his bare hips and feeling his desire for her pressing against her thigh.

She sheathed him with a nearby condom, and shifting her weight, Lucy captured Oliver's firm heat and eased him inside of her. She closed her eyes and bit her lip as her body expanded and enveloped him. His palms cupped her hips and held her still. They both took a moment to savor the sensation of their bodies joining. Then at last, she moved her hips forward and back again, settling into a slow, steady rhythm.

They'd come a long way since that first day at the attorney's offices. It was hard to believe it had only been a few weeks since they'd met for the first time. Now she could hardly imagine her life without him. Just the thought was enough to make her chest ache in a way she could hardly describe. She'd never felt anything like that before. Lucy had spent more than one night lying in bed beside him, wondering what it could mean.

But now as she looked down at Oliver, she knew the truth of it—she was in love with him.

Did that mean she was making love to him for the first time? The realization intensified the sensations already building inside of her. She'd had a few partners in her life, but nothing she would call serious. Nothing that created the kind of emotional bond to the other person the way this did. This knowledge changed everything and she could feel it down to her core.

The pleasure started rippling through her, radiating from deep inside. She could feel her muscles tighten around him as her body tensed and prepared for her much-needed release.

"Yes," Oliver coaxed, his fingertips pressing into the flesh of her hips. "Give in to it."

It was a demand she couldn't help but follow. Her orgasm exploded through her like a shockwave. She gasped and cried out to the ceiling as the sensations pulsated through her like never before. Even as the pleasure filled her, it was the warmth in her chest that truly gripped her. That feeling of peace and happiness being here with Oliver seemed to envelop her. She bit her lip and savored it, even as Oliver's hoarse groans began to mingle with her panting breaths.

She collapsed beside him in exhaustion and contentment. After a moment, Oliver gave her a soft kiss. "I'm going to go get a drink from the kitchen. Do you want anything?"

Lucy shook her head. She had everything she wanted in this moment. It couldn't be more perfect. As she watched Oliver and his perfectly round tush saunter out of the bedroom, all she could think of, all she could feel, was this overwhelming sense of love. She loved him. Really, truly.

She hoped that wasn't a huge mistake.

Ten

"I don't understand why we're back in Connecticut looking at apartments," Harper complained.

"I'm too old to live in a dorm or a sorority house," Lucy explained. "If I'm going back to school, I'm getting my own place near campus."

It was a cool, crisp day in New Haven. Summer had lingered longer than expected this year and the first signs of fall were finally arriving even though it was late September. Soon it would be time for changing leaves, oversize sweaters and boots. And when she started in the spring term this January, she would've moved on to heavy coats, hats, scarves and gloves.

"I really don't know why you're bothering with any of this. I mean, once the inheritance goes through, do you really need to worry about going back to school? You don't have to work another day in your life if you don't want to, much less move into a cheap off-campus apartment with loud jocks living upstairs."

Lucy could only shake her head and look at the map of nearby apartments she'd been given by the campus housing office. No, moving from a Fifth Avenue apartment to one of these places wasn't ideal, but it was reality. No one else seemed to be functioning in reality except her.

"This has got nothing to do with my inheritance. Whether I get it or not, I want to finish my art history degree. That's been my plan all along. When I dropped out, it was so disappointing. I've saved up all these years to pay for school, and with Alice gone, now is my chance. If that means an old apartment with shag carpeting and a run-down laundromat I have to share with a hundred other residents, so be it."

Harper halted her complaints as they approached the closest of the rental complexes near campus. "This doesn't look too bad," Lucy said. "Since it's so close, it's probably the most sought after and expensive place, too."

They found the front office and the manager walked them to an empty one-bedroom apartment they could tour.

"I've got a one-bedroom just like this one coming up after the fall term," the manager explained. "They're graduating and moving out before the holidays. I have a couple two-bedroom apartments coming up, too. Any chance you would be interested in one of those?"

"No thanks," Lucy replied. She'd basically lived in a bedroom the last five years and a shared sorority bedroom the years before that. Spreading out into her own apartment would be luxurious. "It's just me. I'm not interested in roommates."

"Okay. Go ahead and look around. I'll be here if you have any questions."

Lucy and Harper stepped inside and she breathed a sigh of relief. It wasn't that bad at all. To the left, there was a spacious living room with a patio. To the right, a dining room and the kitchen. Down a short hallway was the bedroom and bathroom. The fixtures weren't the newest and fanciest, but it looked clean and well maintained.

"I could make this work."

Harper wrinkled her nose. "Have you considered buying a condo or a townhouse instead?"

"With what money?" Lucy asked. "I swear you rich people can't quite come to terms with what it's like to be broke. After I pay for classes, books and fees, I'll have just enough for this apartment and food. That's it. I can't pull a down payment out of my rear end." She held up her finger to silence her friend. "And don't you dare bring up the inheritance again. I haven't heard two words from the attorney since Oliver filed a dispute. I can't plan my life around money that may never arrive."

Harper sighed and crossed her arms over her chest. "Okay, fine. What about Oliver then?"

Lucy frowned. "What about Oliver?"

"You two are…together. Dating? Whatever you want to call it. Things seem to be pretty good between the two of you. Are you really going to want to leave him behind in the city come January?"

That was something Lucy had tried to ignore. Not even her recent emotional revelation had changed that.

Her plan before Oliver was to go to school and her plan remained the same. "We're hardly in what you would call 'a relationship.' Certainly not a serious enough relationship for me to give up my dream in order to be with him."

"I don't know. It hasn't been long, but you two seem pretty serious. It might not be love yet, but at the very least you're twitterpated."

"Twitter-what?"

"Twitterpated," Harper explained. "It's from the movie *Bambi*. It means you're infatuated. Maybe not 'in love' yet, but excited and optimistic and definitely 'in like.'"

Lucy ignored her observation and turned to study the appliances in the kitchen.

"You could transfer to another school that's in the city. Columbia? NYU? You don't have to go back to Yale."

Lucy turned to Harper with her hands planted on her hips. "I worked hard to get accepted to Yale and I want that degree framed on my wall with Yale University emblazoned across the top of it."

Harper didn't seem convinced. "It's not as though the schools I mentioned are community colleges, you know."

"Yeah, I know. But before Oliver or money came into the picture, I made plans to come back here. I'm already registered for the spring. It's happening. So are you going to help me find a place to live or complain the whole time?"

She rolled her eyes and pasted on a smile. "I'm going to help you find an apartment in New Haven because I'm a supportive friend who loves you."

"Good. Let's go."

They walked out of the apartment together with a brochure from the manager and her card to call when Lucy made a decision. They toured two more apartment complexes before they went to Vito's Deli, one of their former college haunts, for lunch.

"I'm starving," Harper declared as they lined up at the counter to place their order.

Lucy had loved this shop when they were in school, but suddenly, the idea of it wasn't as exciting as it used to be. The smell of meat and pickles hit her like a blast of unwelcome air when they walked inside. She hadn't been feeling great the last couple of days, but she figured it was something she'd eaten. Now she wasn't so sure.

"Lucy, are you okay?"

She turned her head to her friend. "Why?"

Harper cocked her head to the side with concern lining her eyes. "You look a little green around the gills. Do we need to go somewhere else?"

Lucy hated to do it, but she really needed some air. "Maybe if we just step out a second. The smell of dill pickles is really getting to me for some reason."

They stepped out onto the street, where Lucy sucked in a big lungful of fresh air and felt a million times better. The queasiness was still there, but she didn't feel like she was about to make a mess in the deli during the lunch rush. "Thanks. I don't know what's gotten into me lately. I felt puny yesterday, too. I thought maybe it was the chicken sandwich I'd had for lunch, but I should be over that by now. I had a bagel and coffee for breakfast. Pickles have never bothered me before. I love pickles."

"My dad told me that when my mom was pregnant with Oliver, she couldn't abide the smell, taste or sight of pickles. I always thought that was funny, considering it's the stereotypical pregnancy thing. Oliver has always hated pickles, too. When she was pregnant with me, she couldn't get enough of them and I love pickles."

Lucy chuckled nervously at Harper's story. "Well, that's weird, but of course, I'm not pregnant."

"I'm not saying you are. It would be a funny coincidence if you were repelled by pickles, though, since it would be Oliver's baby." Harper paused for a moment, then turned and continued to eye her critically. "Lucy, are you pregnant with my brother's baby?"

Lucy lowered herself down onto a nearby bench as she mentally ran through her biological calendar. How many days had it been? It was before Alice died. She counted on her fingers and shook her head. "No," she declared at last. "I couldn't be. I mean, we used protection. I am certain that I am not pregnant."

Harper sat down on the bench beside her. "Well, what if we popped over to the drugstore and you took a pregnancy test just so we know for sure whether you need an antacid for a stomachache or a baby registry? You haven't been feeling well. I'm sure it's just the stress of everything going on, but if you take the test, then you'll know. If it's negative, then no worries, right?"

No worries? That wasn't exactly the state of mind Lucy was in at the moment. The truth was she'd lied just now. She was anything but certain. If her math was right, her period was over two weeks late. She was never late. Her uterus was made in Switzerland.

With everything else going on, she hadn't even thought about it. But she *was* late. And they *had* used protection. It was just her luck that she'd fall into the three percent failure rate.

She couldn't be pregnant. Pregnant! And with Oliver's baby. How was she going to tell him? How was she going to handle all of these changes? Just as she was about to go back to college and start her life new. This was a major complication. One she simply wasn't prepared to think through on a bench in downtown New Haven.

"Come on," Harper said. She reached out for Lucy's hand and tugged her up from her chair. "We're going to the pharmacy, you're taking that test, and then we're going someplace less smelly to eat and celebrate the fact that you aren't about to give birth to my niece or nephew."

Lucy stood up and followed Harper down the block, but in her heart, she already knew the answer. Like it or not, she was going to be Oliver Drake's baby mama.

Oliver was surprised to get a message from Lucy, asking if he would meet her for dinner. He thought she'd gone away for the weekend with Harper, but apparently they'd cut their trip short. That was fine by him. He didn't want to admit it, but he didn't like not seeing her, even if it was just for a day or two. Since she left, it seemed like she was constantly on his mind and he couldn't focus on anything else.

The place she'd chosen for dinner was busy and on the louder side. Not exactly what he would've selected for a romantic dinner for two, but he wouldn't complain about it. Traffic wasn't the greatest, so he arrived to the restaurant a few minutes later than planned and Lucy was already seated at their table.

He smiled when he came around the corner and spied her sitting there. He couldn't help it. It had only been a few weeks and yet just the sight of Lucy made his whole body respond. The smile on his face, the increase in his pulse, the bizarre feeling in his stomach when she looked at him…he'd never reacted to a woman like this before. Could it be that this was what all the poets and musicians wrote about?

Then she looked up at him. When her gaze met his, he instantly knew there was something wrong. She wasn't beaming at the sight of him the way he was at her. He tried not to frown and take it personally. It was possible she was tired. Or maybe something had happened. He didn't know much about her family, but perhaps an emergency had brought her back from her trip early.

"Hello, beautiful," he said as he leaned down to give her a soft, welcome kiss.

She smiled and kissed him back, but he could sense some hesitation there. "Thank you for coming tonight."

"Of course," Oliver said as he unbuttoned his suit coat and sat down. "I was surprised to hear from you. I didn't think you were coming back until tomorrow."

Lucy nodded, her expression unusually stoic. "We decided to cut the trip short. Something…uh…came up."

Oliver stiffened in his seat. He was right. He didn't like the sound of that. "Is everything okay?"

The waiter arrived with imperfect timing to get their drink orders. Oliver was forced to drop the subject for a moment and scanned the menu. "Would you be interested in sharing a bottle of cabernet with me?"

"No, thank you. I think I'm just going to have a Perrier, please."

Oliver opted for a single glass of wine instead and the waiter disappeared. "What happened? Is it something serious?"

"Everything is okay. I'm fine. Harper is fine. Serious? I would say so. Whether or not it's good or bad news depends on how you take it. I just…" her voice trailed off for a moment.

Oliver had never seen Lucy so distraught. Not even at Aunt Alice's funeral. She seemed to be tied in knots over something. "Whatever it is, you can tell me. Let me help."

"I'm sorry, Oliver. I'm just going to have to come out and say this because I don't know how to do it any other way. I spent the whole train ride back from Connecticut trying to find a good way, and there just isn't one." She took a deep breath and let it out. "I'm pregnant."

Oliver's breath froze in his lungs and his heart stuttered in his chest with shock. He sat for a moment, not breathing, not thinking, just stunned. This wasn't possible. The restaurant was loud; maybe he just hadn't heard her correctly. He grasped at that straw in desperation. "I don't think I heard you right. Could you say it again?" He leaned in this time, praying to hear anything other than Lucy telling him she was having his child.

Lucy winced slightly and move closer to him across the table as well. "You heard me just fine, Oliver. I'm pregnant. With your baby," she added, presumably to ensure he was clear on that part of the news.

He was crystal clear on that point. She wouldn't be telling him like this otherwise. The pit of his stomach wouldn't ache with dread. No, it was obvious she was having his baby. *His baby.* He didn't even know what to say to that. Formerly stunned, his brain finally kicked into overdrive with a million thoughts running through his mind all at once. He couldn't settle on one, couldn't say a word until he'd come to terms with what she'd just said.

"I don't know what happened," Lucy continued, apparently uncomfortable with his silence. "We used protection every time. It didn't even occur to me that it was the cause of why I wasn't feeling well until Harper brought it up. I bought a pregnancy test at a drugstore and took it in the bathroom thinking it would come up negative and I could stop worrying, but it was positive. I have a doctor's appointment on Wednesday, but I don't think it will change anything. The test was pretty clear. We came back early so I could tell you right away."

He tried to listen as she spoke, but it was hard to focus on anything but the punchline. When the wheel of emotions stopped spinning in his mind, it landed on anger and betrayal, which burst out of him all at once.

"Of course you wanted to tell me right away," he said in an unmistakably bitter tone. "Who wouldn't want to inform their rich boyfriend that they got knocked up the first time they had sex? It's exciting news. Worst case scenario, you've locked down eighteen years of child support payments. If you're going to get pregnant, you might as well make sure the daddy is a millionaire, right?"

"What?" She flinched as though he'd reached out and slapped her.

This obviously wasn't the reaction she was expecting. He didn't know why. Did she think he would be excited over the prospect of the potential scammer having his child? Believe that fate had intercepted and brought them together to be one big, happy family? No. Life didn't work that way without someone like her pulling all the strings. She'd been manipulating him from the very beginning—perhaps angling for this outcome since the day they met.

"You certainly didn't waste any time," he continued. "You must have sabotaged that first condom you handed me in the garden. Pretty bold. And to think I was relieved you had one ready to go. Of course you did. My stepmother at least married my father and moved into the penthouse before she locked him down with a child and spent all his money. I guess you're in a hurry, though."

"A hurry for what?" she asked.

"Well, I mean, the judge will rule on my aunt's will soon. This really was the best way for you to ensure that you'll get a chunk of cash from the Drake family, win or lose."

A shimmer of tears flooded Lucy's big, brown eyes. Crocodile tears, he had no doubt. "Is that what you think I've done? Do you really believe I'm capable of getting pregnant on purpose? Derailing my whole life just for money?"

"Not just money, Lucy. A shit-ton of money." The flood of angry words rushed from his mouth and he was incapable of stopping them. "I had you pegged as shady from that first day. That Pollyanna ignorance when the attorney announced you were getting everything... I knew you were playing us all. Playing my aunt. Even playing Harper, unless she's in on it for a cut. I thought that if I got to know you better, I could figure out your game, but I was wrong. You're better at this than I ever expected. I was on the verge of dropping my contest of the will, you had me so convinced. I mean, well played, Lucy. Cover all your bases."

He clapped slowly with a wide smile that probably looked more like a grimace. The bitter words were the only thing keeping him from being sick. "You've set yourself up for a win-win situation. You could walk away from this with my aunt's fortune, half of mine and then that kid will be set to inherit more from my family someday. I thought Candace was crafty and cunning going after my father, but you've got her beat, hands down. You didn't have to sleep with a lonely old man to get what you wanted."

The tears in her eyes never spilled over, but the longer he talked, the redder her face got and the tighter her jaw clenched. "Yeah," she agreed in the coldest voice he'd ever heard pass from her lips. "I just had to sleep with a lonely, bitter young man instead."

Oliver laughed at her cruel retort. "Maybe I am lonely and bitter, but I never had to screw anyone to make my way in the world."

"I thought you were a better man than this, Oliver." Lucy threw her napkin on the table and got up from her seat. "Don't point fingers at me and act so self-righteous. You may not do it now or tonight or even in a year, but one night, when you're lying alone in bed, you'll realize the mistake you've made and it will be too late." She picked up her purse and slung it over her shoulder.

"Leaving so soon?" he asked as casually as he could muster. Of course she would act upset and insulted.

That was part of the charade. He wouldn't let her words get to him even if every arrow painfully struck the bull's-eye in his chest. He would keep up the facade of the bored businessman unfazed by her until she was long gone. He wouldn't give her the satisfaction of knowing she'd gotten to him.

Lucy just shook her head with sadness pulling down at the corners of her mouth. "You know, I am just as surprised by this whole situation as you are. I'm actually terrified and knowing now that I'll be doing it on my own makes it that much scarier. The difference is it's going to uproot my entire life, destroy my body and take over the next twenty years of my life, and you're just going to sit back and cut a damn check. If you don't want to be a part of your child's life, then don't bother sending money. That's an insult to me and the baby. Let's just skip the paternity test game with the attorneys and pretend we never met, okay?"

"Sounds fine. At this point, I wish we hadn't."

"Me, too. Goodbye, Oliver." Turning on her heel, Lucy barely missed a collision with the waiter as she nearly ran from the restaurant.

Oliver made a point of not watching her go. Instead, he calmly accepted his wine from the waiter and sipped it, ignoring the stares of the nearby restaurant patrons. After all that, he needed a glass of wine. Or some scotch. Anything he could get his hands on, really, to dull the pain in his chest and chase away the angry tears that were threatening to expose themselves in the restaurant.

The first large sip seemed to settle him. The blood stopped rushing in his ears and he was able to take his first deep breath since he arrived at the restaurant.

That was a start. Wine couldn't undo the mess he'd just found himself in, but it would get him through this painfully uncomfortable moment.

"Sir." The waiter hovered awkwardly nearby. "Will the lady be returning?"

Oliver shook his head. "She will not."

"Very well. Will you be staying to dine with us tonight?"

He might be known for being cool under pressure, but even Oliver couldn't sit here and eat as though his world hadn't just disintegrated in his hands. "No. I think I'll finish my drink and free up the table if you'd like to run the bill."

"Yes, sir." The waiter disappeared, as visibly uncomfortable on the outside as Oliver was on the inside.

Oliver went through the motions to wrap up, finished his cabernet and stuffed his wallet back in his suit pocket. Pushing up from the table, he made his way out of the restaurant and onto the noisy street. Once there, he felt his anger start to crumble into disappointment.

Why? Why had he let himself get involved with Lucy when he knew she was just playing him, and everyone else? Instead, he'd let himself get wrapped up in her smile and her freckles. He'd lost himself in the warmth of her body and the softness of her touch. And now she was going to have his child.

His child.

Oliver sighed and forced his feet down the sidewalk toward his building. It was a long walk, and he'd normally take a taxi, but he needed the time to think. It pained him to realize that as much grief and blame as he'd heaped on his father, he'd made the same mistake. He'd fallen for a woman and let himself be used. And he'd enjoyed it. Every single second. He supposed it was karma's way of teaching him that he wasn't any smarter than his father when it came to love.

Love? He didn't dare even think that word. It wasn't love. He didn't know what to call it, but it wasn't love.

One thing he did know, however, was that if Lucy was carrying his child, Oliver would be in his or her life whether Lucy liked it or not. It wasn't about money or child support or anything else but being a good father. Oliver knew what it was like to grow up without one of his parents. Cancer had stolen his mother away, greed had taken Danny's mother from his life, but Oliver had no excuse not to be there for his child.

So whether Lucy liked it or not, he would be.

Eleven

Sitting at Alice's desk, Lucy picked up the sonogram photo again, staring at the fuzzy black-and-gray image and wondering why the Fates got so much amusement by messing with her life. This tiny photo, these blurry little blobs, no bigger than a sesame seed, were about to change her life forever.

Twins, the doctor said. Not just pregnant. Pregnant with twins. She'd laughed hysterically as she looked at the two fat little circles side by side on the monitor. It was that or cry until she ran out of tears. Fraternal twins. Because a single baby wouldn't be enough of a challenge for her to raise on her own.

The doctor was concerned by her response, not entirely sure if she was happy or sad or freaking out. Honestly, it was a combination of all three spinning in her head so fast she could hardly keep up. It was early in the pregnancy, he'd warned. Things could change. One or both could fail. Both could last to term. Be in "wait and see" mode, he'd said. Perhaps wait until her twelve-week ultrasound to confirm the twins before announcing it to everyone.

That wouldn't be a problem. Lucy doubted she could say the words aloud. She'd hardly known what to say to him and the nurse anxiously watching her in the exam room. All she could do was lay there in her crinkly paper dress and watch her world start to crumble around her.

Putting the picture aside, Lucy focused on sorting through the apartment brochures she'd brought home from Yale. It was hard to believe how much her life had changed since she'd gotten on a train and toured that first apartment with Harper. Now, she was not just going back to college, she was doing it while pregnant. Hugely pregnant. She was having twins by herself. And even that was hard to focus on while she was also completely heartsick.

Somehow, the idea of Oliver thinking she was scamming his aunt hadn't hurt her that much. He didn't really know her, and given his past experience with his stepmother, she understood his suspicions. It was a lot of money to give someone who wasn't family. If she had been in his shoes, she might've had the same concerns, even if she didn't need a penny of Alice's money.

But when he accused her of getting pregnant on purpose—to hedge her bets, so to speak—that stung. She wasn't just some woman he hardly knew anymore. How many hours had they spent together over the last month? How many times had they made love and held each other? Enough to know she wouldn't do something like that.

And yet there wasn't a single moment, a flicker of expression across his face at that restaurant, where the news of her pregnancy stirred anything but anger in him. He'd probably think that her having twins would be karmic retribution for her scheming.

Lucy looked down at the apartment brochure for the place she'd liked the best. The price for the two-bedroom was pretty steep. Add tuition and books, furniture, baby *everything times two*…she wasn't even certain she could afford it all. Not on what she had saved, and that was all she could count on getting. Oliver certainly wasn't going to back down on his protest of the will. The news of her "deliberately trapping" him with a pregnancy would likely hurt her case, so odds were she wouldn't see a dime of Alice's estate.

In truth, that was fine by her. That was more money than she could fathom, much less handle properly. She was much better at barely getting by. Her mother had taught her well. But getting by with babies meant a job with medical insurance for all of them. Day care expenses times two. Diapers times two. Chaos times two. She'd always admired her mother's ability to make it work, but could she do the same?

She let the brochure fall from her fingers down to the desk as tears began to well in her eyes. Could she even do this? Was going back to school a pipe dream now? Was it smarter to put her savings into a place to live and things for the babies instead? Hell, maybe she needed to spend it on a plane ticket back home to Ohio. At least there, she would have her mother to help her with the twins. And she wouldn't run the risk of seeing Oliver again.

"Yes, this was absolutely deliberate, you ass," she said aloud to Alice's large, empty office. "I ruined all of my plans of going back to school and building my future so I could trap you with a child. Because that's the best way to keep a man you love in your life forever. But you get the last laugh, don't you? Twins!"

Lucy dropped her face into her hands and let the tears fall in earnest. She hadn't really let herself cry yet. It had been almost a week since the trip to New Haven and her breakup with Oliver, but she hadn't really let herself wallow in it. It seemed like a misuse of valuable time. Instead, she'd tried to keep herself busy with other things. After her earth-shattering doctor's appointment, she spent hours in different stores, studying everything from prenatal vitamins and stretch-panel jeans to onesies and twin strollers.

It was a tough realization to find she was completely unprepared for any of this. Before Oliver came around, she'd almost forgotten she had a uterus, much less spent time anticipating it to have not just one but two nine-month occupants. Kids were a far-off idea. One that came after love and marriage and the decision that it was time to start a family with someone she could count on.

At least she'd found the love part. Lucy did love Oliver. He didn't love or trust her one iota, but she had done her part and fallen for him. She knew now why they called it falling in love. It had been that easy, like tripping and smacking her face against the rough, hard sidewalk. Like a fall, she wasn't expecting it, but all of a sudden there she was, in love with Oliver. She could only hope that falling out of love with him was just as easy.

Easing back in the desk chair and resting her hand on her flat tummy, she knew that wouldn't be the case. Getting over him would be hard. Especially with two tiny, blue-eyed reminders of him staring at her from their cribs each morning.

It was easier than she expected to picture two wide-eyed toddlers standing in their crib in matching footie pajamas. Wild brown curls. Devious smiles. Pink cheeks. One sucking his thumb with a furrowed brow of concern while his sister clutched her favorite stuffed bunny and tried climbing over the side. In her mind, they looked like tiny clones of Oliver, although the boy had her freckles across his nose.

It was just a daydream, not a reality, but it made Lucy's heart ache. Life didn't always go to plan, but that didn't mean that she couldn't come up with a new plan. She needed to find a way to be happy about this, no matter what happened with Oliver or the will or with school. Things would work out and she had to keep that in mind. One of the pregnancy books she'd picked up had mentioned how her emotions could impact the babies. She didn't want that. No matter what happened, they would be just as loved and cared for as if they'd been planned.

A ring of the apartment's phone pulled her out of her thoughts. No one really called that line except for the doorman, so Lucy reached out and picked it up off the desk. "Hello?"

"Good morning, Miss Campbell. I have a large delivery for you."

Lucy frowned. A large delivery? She hadn't bought

anything. "Are you sure it's for me? Where is it from?" she asked.

"I'm sure. It's from the Museum of Modern Art. It's another painting for the collection, ma'am."

The staff at the building was used to priceless paintings and sculptures being delivered to Alice's apartment. Every few months, something would catch her eye on an auction website and a new piece would arrive. The difference this time being that Alice was deceased and Lucy hadn't bought any art. There had to be a mistake.

"Send them up," she said. She wouldn't know for sure until she saw what it was. Perhaps Alice had a piece on loan to MoMA that Lucy had forgotten about and was being returned.

About ten minutes later, two men came out of the freight elevator with a painting in a wooden crate. Lucy stood holding the service entrance door open as they brought it inside. "Where would you like it?" the older of the two men asked.

"The gallery," she said. That's where most of the paintings went, so it was a knee-jerk response. "I'd like to see what's inside before you leave, however. I didn't buy anything. This may be a mistake and if so, I'll want you to take it back with you."

After they set down the box, the second man pulled a sheet of paper out of his pocket. "You're Miss Lucille Campbell, right?"

"That's me," she replied, even more confused. If it was a piece on loan, it would've had Alice's name on it, not hers.

"Then this is for you."

The older man pulled out a crowbar to pry open the

side and expose the painting. They carefully pulled it out of the straw and paper bedding that protected it and held it up for Lucy to inspect.

She remembered the painting now. It was one of the items available at the silent auction. The painting of the New York skyline made entirely out of hearts. She'd loved it, but she hadn't bought it.

In an instant, that whole amazing night came flooding back to mind. Touring the museum with Oliver, leaving early after getting overheated, making love— and conceiving the twins—on the rooftop garden. There was only one painful answer to where this had come from—Oliver bought it for her that night before they left and it was just now arriving.

The timing was agonizing.

"You can leave it there," she said, indicating the wall where it was leaning.

The men nodded, gathered up the box and packing materials and made their way back out the door. Lucy watched them leave, then stood looking puzzled at the painting in front of her.

What was she supposed to do with it?

Part of her wanted to set it on fire, just to spite him. She didn't need a reminder of that night hanging on the wall, taunting her about everything she'd lost. But destroying it was an insult to the artist and the painting. It didn't have anything to do with the situation with Oliver, and she loved art too much to consider it for long. Besides, she wasn't sure how much he'd paid for it, but since she'd turned down child support in her anger, she might need to sell the piece to support the twins. Unlike everything else in the apartment, that belonged only to her. His romantic gesture come too late.

The thought made her knees quiver beneath her. Better safe than sorry, she lowered herself down to the cold, marble floor of the gallery. There, she had a better view of the painting. She really did love it. Under any other circumstances, she'd be thrilled to own it. It was just a painful reminder of Oliver that she didn't need.

Staring at it for a moment, she reached out and ran her finger along the edge of the painting. Lucy knew then that she would keep it. If nothing else, it might be the only thing the twins would have from their father.

With a sigh, she stood up and went in search of a place to hang it.

Oliver was miserable.

There just wasn't any other way to describe how he felt. He wasn't even entirely sure how long it had been since he spoke with Lucy and found out about the baby. The days had all started to blur together. He hadn't been in the office. Hadn't left his apartment. He hadn't even gone up to the roof to start trimming back for the fall because being up there reminded him too much of Lucy and the night they'd spent together there. Somehow, even his sanctuary was tainted by the situation.

He wouldn't go so far as to say Lucy had ruined it. He wasn't that ignorant. It had taken a few days for his temper to cool down so he could come to that conclusion, but he knew it was true. Start to finish, this was a mess of his own making. Nothing Lucy had done since the day he met her had warranted the horrible things he'd said to her at dinner that night. She had immediately come to him to do the right thing and tell him about the baby, and he'd thrown it in her face. And yet, after hours spent racking his brain for a way to undo the things he'd done, he'd come up with nothing.

Was that even possible?

Oliver Drake: CEO and savior of Orion Technology, eligible bachelor, millionaire and complete asshat.

He was stewing on his sofa when there was a knock at the door. That in itself was unusual since the doorman hadn't called. At the same time, it was concerning. He'd dodged calls from his family for days and they were the only ones who could get up here without his permission. He hoped Harper hadn't arrived to chew him out. He hadn't even bothered to listen to the fifteen voice-mail messages she'd left him.

With a frown, he turned off the television and crossed the room to the front door. Peering through the peephole, he was relieved to find his father and brother there instead of his sister. "Dad?" he asked as he opened the door.

Tom Drake looked at his son and shook his head. "You look like hell," he said, pushing past Oliver into the house with Danny in his wake.

His little brother had recovered remarkably well from his accident. You'd hardly even know he'd been in the hospital as he took off for the living room and changed the channel to pull up his favorite show. Oliver knew that when he was bored with that, he'd whip his latest gaming device out of his back pocket and play until Dad made him stop. Technology ran deep in the veins of this family.

With a sigh, Oliver shut the door behind his dad and followed him to the kitchen where he was making himself some coffee.

"I didn't think you drank coffee anymore, Dad."

Tom looked up at him with a dismayed frown. "It's not for me, it's for you."

"I don't need any coffee, Dad. I'm not hungover."

His father narrowed his eyes at Oliver, taking in the robe and pajama pants he had on, the week-old scruff that had grown on his face and his bedhead. "Even if you're not hungover, you're drinking this," he said at last. "You need something to wake you up."

"I'm not sleepy."

"I'm not saying you are. Sometimes in a man's life, he needs to wake up and take a look at what's going on around him. He gets too set in his ways, gets lost in a routine and doesn't notice things right in front of his face. I was like that once. I don't want you to end up like me."

Oliver scratched his head in confusion but accepted the coffee his father handed him.

"Sit down, son."

Oliver sat down at the kitchen table, trying not to think about the breakfast he'd shared here with Lucy. "I just needed a break, Dad."

Tom reached into the refrigerator and pulled out a bottle of water before sitting across from his son. "The hell you did. This is about that woman. Lucy."

Oliver hadn't said two words to his father about what had happened with Lucy, so his sister must've narc'd on him. "She's pregnant, Dad." It was the first time the words had passed his lips. Even days later, it felt alien on his tongue.

His father shrugged off his bombshell announcement. "It happens. What are you doing to do about it?"

"I don't know. I'm worried I'm going to make the same mistakes you did. I don't know that I can trust her. The whole family thinks she's some kind of crook."

"What do you think?"

"I…" Oliver stopped. He'd wrestled with this question since the day he'd met her. Now, he tried to answer honestly just as he knew her, not letting his fears answer for him. "I don't think she had anything to do with Aunt Alice changing her will. These last few weeks, I've found that Lucy is naturally charming. I think Alice would've wanted to help her out and do something nice for Lucy by leaving her the estate. At least that's my guess. But what if I'm wrong? What if she's just like Candace? How do I know the child isn't just another ploy to get her hands not only on Aunt Alice's money but mine, too?"

"You don't," his father said simply. With a sigh, Tom ran his hand through his mostly gray hair. "I think this is all my fault."

Oliver perked up in his chair. "What?"

"I thought you were old enough when all this happened with Candace, but I think I still managed to give you some trust issues. Listen, I was an idiot, Oliver. I got all wrapped up in your stepmother and made some choices that were pretty foolish in retrospect. But I was lonely so I took that chance. And now, years later, I would probably do everything exactly the same if I were given the chance to go back in time."

That surprised Oliver. He thought for sure that his father regretted what happened with his second wife. "Really?"

Tom chuckled at his son's surprise and sipped his water thoughtfully. "Yes. Despite our outward appearances, Candace and I really did have chemistry. She certainly put a dent in my finances, but it was a fine price to pay for a couple fun years and that little boy in the living room. If changing the past with Candace means that I wouldn't have Danny, then I want no part of it."

Both men turned toward the living room to watch Danny as he sat cross-legged on the floor and grinned at the television.

"Things don't always happen the way you plan, but that doesn't mean they didn't work out the way they were supposed to. If you believe Lucy didn't scheme her way into Alice's will, why would you think she's trying to trap you by getting pregnant? Maybe it was an honest mistake."

Oliver turned back to the table and studied the mug in his hands. The look on Lucy's face in the restaurant came to his mind. With a little time and perspective, he was able to see how scared she was to tell him. How hard she struggled to hide how nervous and confused she was over the pregnancy. She'd needed him in that moment and he'd failed her by turning on her and accusing her of such horrible things.

"Here's a better question," his father continued. "Does it really matter? Will it make you love your child any less?"

"No." That question was easier for Oliver to answer. If he'd figured anything out over the last few days, it was that he would love that child more than anyone on the planet had ever loved their child. The harder question was whether he was willing to love the mother just as much.

"And how did you feel about Lucy before you found out about the baby?"

"I thought that maybe I was falling in love. I guess that scared me. I've never felt that way about a woman before. It all happened so fast."

"It was that way with your mother, you know? We went from our first date to married in two months. It was intense and scary and wonderful all at once, but I couldn't stand the idea of being apart from her."

Oliver had never heard that about his parents before. He supposed that he hadn't asked, thinking it would be a sore spot for his father after his mother died. "Why did you decide to get married so quickly?"

Tom smiled and reached out to pat Oliver's shoulder. "You. Like I said before, it happens." He got up from the table and called out to Danny. "Daniel, we're getting ready to go." Then he turned back to Oliver and handed him a small box that had been stuffed into his coat pocket. "When you make up your mind, this might come in handy. It was your mother's. Talk to you later, son."

Before Oliver could really respond to everything his father had just said to him, his brother was gingerly giving him a hug and the two of them were out the door.

Alone in his apartment again, Oliver reached for the box on the table and opened the hinged lid. Inside, he found what could only be his mother's engagement ring. It was marquise-shaped with a single baguette on each side, set in platinum. It wasn't at all fashionable at the moment; it was more a throwback to another time. But it was simple, elegant and classic—the perfect ring for his mother, and he realized, perfect for Lucy as well. His mother had been one in a million and Lucy didn't fit into the mold either. It was just the ring he would choose for the mother of his child and his future wife.

If she would accept it.

In that moment, he wanted her to accept it more than he ever expected. Not just because of the baby, but because he was in love with her. Despite his suspicious nature and cautious approach, Lucy had slipped past all his defenses and reached a part of him that he'd managed to keep locked away from all the women before her. He didn't want to lock away that part of himself any longer. Like his garden, he wanted to share it with her. Share it with their child.

There was another knock at the door, startling him. Oliver got up, presuming Danny left something behind, but when he opened the door, he found a fuming Harper standing there instead. It was time to get the earful he'd avoided all week.

"You are a jerk! How could you possibly accuse Lucy of getting pregnant on purpose? That's absolutely absurd! She had plans, you know? That's why we were in Connecticut. She was planning on going back to college. How is she supposed to do that raising your baby on her own, huh? Especially with you holding all of Aunt Alice's money hostage for no good reason!"

With a sigh, Oliver stepped back to let his seething sister inside. He could tell she was just getting warmed up. Once she was done yelling at him, perhaps she could help him figure out how exactly he could clean up the mess he'd made with Lucy so everyone could be happy again.

Twelve

"Lucy, this is Phillip Glass. How are you?"

Lucy nervously clutched the phone. She hadn't heard from Alice's estate attorney in quite a while. Had the judge made a ruling yet? "Good," she answered and held her breath.

"Excellent. Well, I'm calling because I have some good news for you. Amazing news, actually. Mr. Drake has dropped his dispute over Alice's will."

Lucy slumped down into a nearby chair as her knees gave out from under her. Surely she hadn't heard him correctly. "What?"

"It's all yours now, Lucy. The money, the apartment, the art, all of it. Congratulations."

She knew she should say something, but she didn't have any words. This was not the call she was expecting to get. She'd prepared herself for the consoling discussion about how the judge felt Alice's state of mind may have been compromised at her age and given the change was so close to her death… Instead, she found she really truly had the winning lotto ticket in her hand.

An initial wave of relief washed over her. Not excitement, but relief. She'd been twisting her stomach into knots the last few days trying to figure out how she was going to support the twins on her own. Now, that question was answered and it didn't require her to go crawling to the twins' father. Although it did raise a curious question.

"Did Mr. Drake say why he dropped the protest?"

"He didn't. Honestly, I wish I knew what changed his mind, as well. Listen, I'm going to work on getting everything transitioned over to you and I'll be in touch in a week or two. There's some paperwork and hoops still to jump through, a huge chunk of estate taxes to pull out, but you can finally celebrate, Lucy."

"Thanks, Phillip."

Lucy hung up the phone and found herself still too stunned to move from her seat. She was more surprised by Oliver changing his mind than anything else. There had always been the possibility that the judge would rule in her favor, but she never thought he would back down, even when they'd gotten so close. That seemed too much like mixing business and pleasure where he was concerned.

What had changed?

Oliver had been so angry with her that night. He told her he didn't even want anything to do with his child and now, he was just handing over his aunt's estate after weeks of fighting over it? Was this his roundabout way of providing child support without paying a dime of his own money? She didn't dare to dream that it was an olive branch or first step on their way to reconciliation. Two miracles wouldn't happen in one day.

Lucy wasn't quite sure what to do. She felt like she should tell someone, and yet she was hesitant to even now. It didn't feel real. It never had. Just like looking at that sonogram.

An hour before, she'd been wondering if she could fit a bed and two cribs in the one-bedroom apartment near campus and now she could buy a house and a car, hire a full-time nanny and not have to work. Her life was undergoing a major upheaval every couple of days and she wasn't sure how many more big changes she could take.

She knew she should be excited. She was an instant millionaire hundreds of times over. Rich beyond her wildest dreams. Her children would never want for anything the way she had. Their college was paid for. Her college was paid for. Life should be easier, at least on that front. While she felt a bit of the pressure lifting from her shoulders, she still wouldn't call herself excited.

How could she be excited or happy with the way things ended with Oliver? It was impossible. All the money in the world wouldn't bring the man she loved and the father of her children back into her life. Honestly, she'd trade every penny in a heartbeat if he would knock on the door right now and tell her that he was sorry—that he loved her and their babies more than anything else. But that wouldn't happen. Not after all the horrible things he'd said. Oliver wouldn't change his mind and Lucy couldn't forget it.

The doorbell rang the moment after the thought crossed her mind, startling her from the sad path her thoughts had taken. She stood up from her seat, the phone still clutched in her hand from Phillip's call. Could it be?

Her heart started pounding in her chest, even as she tried to convince herself that it was probably the cleaning lady or Harper checking on her. Lucy stood at the door a moment, willing herself not to be disappointed if she opened it and found someone else.

Taking a deep breath, she opened it. And there, against all odds, was Oliver.

He was standing in the marble-tiled foyer looking like a tall glass of water to a woman lost in the desert. He was wearing her favorite gray suit with a blue shirt that made his eyes an even brighter shade than usual. His lips were pressed together anxiously, even as he clutched a bouquet of bright pink roses and blue delphinium in his hands.

"Hi," he said after a few long seconds of staring silently at one another.

Lucy wasn't quite sure what to think. She'd hardly recovered from the shock of her call with Phillip. "Hello." That was a start.

She took a step back to let him into the apartment. She was curious about what he had to say, but wouldn't allow herself to mentally leap ahead. Just because he was here didn't mean he was begging for her back. She didn't know what he wanted, or if she was even willing to give it to him if he did. She loved him, but she loved herself and her babies, too, and she knew she had to be smart about this. He'd been unnecessarily cruel to her and it would take more than a "sorry" and some flowers for her to forget the things he'd said.

"These are for you," he said, holding out the flowers

and smiling sheepishly at her. "I picked out the pink
and blue flowers for the baby."

"Thank you." Lucy accepted the flowers and turned
her back on Oliver to put them in water. She needed a
moment without his soulful eyes staring into her own.

When she returned from the kitchen, he was still
standing in the same spot in the gallery, only now he
was looking at the painting he'd bought her. She'd finally hung it on the wall.

"Thank you for the painting," she said, stopping
alongside him to admire the piece. "You didn't have
to do that."

"I know I didn't. That was the point of the gift."

Lucy set the vase of flowers onto the table in the
entryway and turned to him. "You also didn't have to
drop your contest of Alice's will. We could've seen it
through to the judge and let him rule on it."

Oliver turned to her and shook his head. "No, we
couldn't. I couldn't risk the judge's ruling. I dropped
the suit because I changed my mind."

Lucy crossed her arms defensively over her chest.
Standing this close to Oliver again after these horrible
few days, she felt like she needed the buffer to protect
herself. From herself.

"You changed your mind about what?" she snapped.
"That I was a seasoned con artist that manipulated
your elderly, agoraphobic aunt into leaving me all her
money? Or that I deliberately got pregnant to trap you
into financially supporting me and your child for life?"

Oliver swallowed hard, the muscles in his throat
moving with strain and difficulty. She'd never seen
him so tense. Not in the lawyer's office that first day,
not even in the restaurant when she saw him last. He

appeared outwardly calm, but she was keenly aware of how tightly strung he seemed.

"I'm sorry, Lucy," he said at last. "I'm sorry for all of that. I never should've given a voice to the doubts in my head, because that's all they were—my own demons twisting reality. You never did anything to deserve the way I treated you. You're nothing like my stepmother and I knew that, I was just afraid because I had feelings for you that I didn't know how to handle. I was scared to make a mistake like my father and instead, I made an even bigger mess by ruining the best thing I had in my life. I can only hope that one day you can see it in your heart to forgive me for that. I intend to try every day for the next fifty years until you do."

Lucy stood quietly listening to his words. They seemed painfully sincere, making her heart ache in her chest for him. But he wasn't the only one who was scared. She was scared of trusting him again too soon and having her heart trampled on. "Thank you," she said. "I know it wasn't easy for you to say all of that."

"I'll admit when I'm wrong, Lucy, and I have been in the wrong since the day we met. I wish we could start all over again, but I can't change what I've done. Can you forgive me, Lucy?" he pressed with hopeful eyes gazing into hers.

She could feel the pain and regret in every word he spoke. She'd never heard a sincerer apology. "I do forgive you for the things you said and did." She sensed that wasn't quite enough for him, but she wasn't betraying her heart too quickly.

Oliver reached out and wrapped his fingers around her hand. "Thank you. I'm so happy to hear you say that because to be honest, I'm head over heels in love with you and I thought I might never get the chance to tell you." He stopped, looking at her with an obvious question on his mind. "Do you think you might be able to love me someday?"

The warmth of his skin against hers made it hard for her to focus on his words. She could feel her body start to betray her. It longed to lean in and press against the hard muscle of his chest. She wanted to breathe in the warm scent of his cologne at his throat and feel his arms wrapped around her. She fought the urge, knowing this conversation was too important. It needed to happen and it couldn't if she started rubbing against him like a contented kitten.

She forced herself to look up at him. His eyes were pleading with her. But she had to tell the truth about how she felt.

"No," she said.

Oliver did his best not to react. He knew there was a risk in coming here—that she couldn't forgive him for how he'd treated her. He'd told himself that no matter what her answer, he would accept it, even supporting his child without being in its mother's life if that's the way Lucy wanted it. And sadly, it appeared that was how she wanted it.

"Okay," he said, dropping her hand even though it was the last thing he wanted to do.

"I can't love you *someday*, Oliver. That would mean I didn't love you now. And I do." She placed a gentle hand against his cheek and smiled warmly. "Even when I was angry and hurt, I still loved you. Of course I do."

Relief washed over him all at once and he scooped her up into his arms for a huge hug. "Oh, thank good-

ness!" he breathed into her ear. "I haven't blown it."
Pushing back to put some distance between them
again, he looked her in the eyes. "So you're telling
me I haven't ruined everything for us? For our new
family?"

A sheen of tears appeared in Lucy's dark brown
eyes. "We're going to be a family?" she asked.

"If you'll have me." Oliver scooped her hands into
his and dropped down onto his knee. He'd practiced
this speech twenty times since his father had given him
that ring, and in the moment, with adrenaline pump-
ing through his veins, he couldn't remember a word of
it. All he could do was speak from his heart and hope
that it was romantic and wonderful enough for her to
accept him.

"Lucy, I have spent the last few years of my life
living under a cloud of pessimism. I never believed
that a woman would love me just for who I am. I saw
what happened to my father and let it color my outlook of the world. A part of me had given up on the
kind of love others seemed to find. And then I met
you. And you challenged me at every step. You made
me question everything and I'm so thankful that you
did. It forced me to realize that I was hiding from my
life. And it forced me to realize that I am very much
in love with you.

"Unfortunately," he continued with a sheepish grin,
"I didn't know how much I loved you until I'd nearly
ruined everything for us. It was there, alone and miserable in my apartment, that I decided that I was willing to do anything to make it up to you, if I even could.
First, I had my lawyer withdraw the protest because
I wanted you to know that I believed you. Aunt Alice

wanted you to have that money, and I want you to have it, too, whether or not you wanted me in your life again. There's no strings attached."

"You really, truly believe me? You have no reservations at all about the will or the baby?"

He'd failed to answer this question properly the first time because he was plagued with doubts even as she lay in his arms. Now, he was confident in his decision. "You don't have a malicious bone in your body, Lucy. I can't believe I ever thought otherwise. And if I did, I wouldn't have taken this to the jeweler to be cleaned and sized just for you."

Oliver reached into his pocket and pulled out the jewelry box his father had brought him a few days before. He opened the lid to show her the ring inside. "This ring belonged to my mother," he said as she gasped audibly. "My father gave it to me in the hopes that I would stop moping around my place and start living my life with you in it. And not just you, but with our child, too."

Lucy looked at the ring expectantly, but she didn't say anything. At first, he thought that maybe she was just dazzled by the sight of it, but Oliver quickly realized that he was so nervous, he forgot to ask the critical question.

"Lucille Campbell, will you please do me the honor of being my wife, accepting all the love I have to give and standing by my side for the rest of our lives?"

At that, Lucy smiled through her tears. "Yes," she said. "There's nothing more I want than to be your lover and partner in life."

Oliver's hands were shaking as he pulled the ring from its velvet bed and slipped it onto her finger. "It's a little large on you right now, but the jeweler suggested sizing up so you could wear it well into your second and third trimesters."

"It's perfect," she said as she admired it on her hand. "I'm honored to wear the ring your mother once wore. I know she was important to you."

He clutched her hands in his as he stood up. With his eyes pinned on hers, he leaned in and planted a kiss on the ridge of her knuckles—one hand, then the other—before seeking out her lips. When his mouth pressed to hers, it was like a promise was made between them. The engagement was official—sealed with a kiss.

He wrapped his arms around her and pulled her close. Oliver didn't want to let go. Not after almost losing her for good. She felt so right here, how could he ever have said or done something to drive her away? He was a fool once, but never again. She would be his—and he, hers—forever.

When their lips finally parted, he leaned his forehead against hers. "I want us to be a real family. Like my parents had. These last few days thinking about you raising our child without me... I couldn't bear the thought of it despite what I said that night at the restaurant. I was upset and confused about the news. It may not have been planned, but this child will always know that he or she was wanted. I'll do everything in my power to see to that. But most of all I want to make you happy, Lucy. Anything you want, we can make it happen."

"I don't know what I could possibly ask for, Oliver. Today alone, you've proposed with your mother's engagement ring and given me a half a billion dollar estate. It seems greedy to ask for anything else."

"Harper told me that you were trying to go back to school. You never mentioned it to me before."

"Yes," Lucy hesitated. "That was my plan, but…"

"No buts. If you want to go back to Yale, you absolutely should do it."

"It's so far away, Oliver. From you and your job. I don't want to be alone in Connecticut while you're here running your computer company."

Oliver just shrugged off her concerns. "If you want to be in Manhattan every night, I'll have you flown to class and back on Orion's private jet each day. If you want to stay there during the week, we'll buy a nice place and I'll come spend every weekend I can with you until you graduate."

"I don't know," Lucy said. "That seems like it would make things far more complicated than they need to be. If I was moving up there by myself as I'd planned originally, that's one thing, but I'm not leaving you behind. Maybe I can look at some of the local programs. I'm sure Columbia or NYU has something that will allow me to stay in the city. And when the babies— er, *baby*—comes," she stuttered, "we'll all be together. That's the most important thing."

Oliver grinned. Of course, he preferred having her as close as possible, but that was completely up to her. "Are you sure? Like I said, whatever makes you happy, Lucy."

"Being with you makes me happy." Leaning in, she rested her head on his shoulder and sighed in contentment. "After everything that has happened, I may even defer school for another year or two. I'm not sure I can manage a wedding, a pregnancy and caring for an infant on top of the senior-level classes I need to graduate. The art will always be there when I'm ready. I want to focus on remembering every moment of these early months with you."

"If that's what you want." Oliver smiled. They certainly did have a lot coming up in their lives over the next year. "And don't forget, we have to decide where we want to live. We have two amazing Manhattan apartments to choose from."

"I want to move to your place," Lucy said without hesitation. "For one thing, I couldn't ask you to leave your beautiful garden. And for another, Alice's place is stunning, but way too formal and stuffy for children running around all wild."

Oliver smiled at her decision. "Children, huh? Are we already planning on having more than one?"

A curious expression came across Lucy's face. She wrinkled her nose and bit at her lip. "There's something I need to tell you," Lucy admitted.

"Yes? Anything, love."

"The doctor says we're having twins."

Twins? The room began to spin and close in on him.

Oliver was about to experience a lot of new firsts. His first time in love, his first time to be engaged, his first children were on the way... And this was the first time he'd ever fainted.

He was out cold before he hit the floor.

Epilogue

Lucy eyeballed the three paint swatches on the walls of what would soon be the twins' nursery. Three months later, they were both growing and thriving, pressing Lucy's belly out to a larger bulge than she anticipated this far along. She and Oliver had decided not to find out the sex of the twins, so she was comparing different shades of gray paints for the neutral design they had planned.

With her hands planted on her hips, she frowned at the wall and continued to after Oliver came up behind her. "The one in the middle," he said without hesitation. "And Emma is on the phone for you."

Emma's baby girl, Georgette, had been born right after Lucy announced her pregnancy. Little Georgie, named after her maternal grandfather, George Dempsey, had occupied most of Emma's time the last three months. Lucy accepted the phone from Oliver, curious as to what prompted the call from her friend.

"Hey, Emma," Lucy said. "I'm trying to pick out a color for the nursery. What's going on with you?"

"It's not me I'm calling about, it's Violet."

Lucy didn't like the way her friend said that. "What's wrong? Are she and the baby okay?" Violet was due any day now.

"They're both fine. She delivered a healthy baby boy this morning."

"That's wonderful!" Lucy gushed. "I'm glad you called, I hadn't heard anything yet. Stupid Beau. He was supposed to let us know when she went into labor."

"Yeah, well…" Emma said. "There's a reason he didn't call."

The feeling of anxiety returned to Lucy's stomach. "What's that?"

"It turns out the baby isn't his."

Lucy's jaw dropped. "What? How do they know that? Did he demand a paternity test so soon after she delivered?"

"No," Emma replied. "They didn't need one. Beau and Violet are both dark haired, dark skinned and dark eyed. Mediterranean lineage through and through."

"And the baby?"

"The baby is a fair-skinned, blue-eyed redhead."

A redhead? Violet had never once mentioned anything about a dating a ginger. She'd been on again, off again with Beau for the last few years, but even then, Violet hadn't dated anyone else. At least that Lucy knew about. "Then who *is* the father?"

"That's just it. No one knows. Not even Violet. Apparently she conceived the baby just before her car accident. When she hit her head and got amnesia, she lost the whole week, including any memories of being with someone else. She doesn't remember who her baby's father is!"

* * * * *

LET'S TALK
Romance

For exclusive extracts, competitions
and special offers, find us online:

f facebook.com/millsandboon

⊙ @millsandboonuk

𝕏 @millsandboon

Or get in touch on 0844 844 1351*

For all the latest titles coming soon, visit
millsandboon.co.uk/nextmonth